French Lessons

One Woman's Tale of Sex, Wine and House Renovation in la Belle France

ROBERTA SAMUELS

RedPenguin
BOOKS

Contents

Haystacks and Pigeon Cotes in Brousses-les-Antibels

CHAPTER 1

Buying My French House

I was very excited to become the owner of an 18th century farmhouse deep in the French countryside. It was the spring of 2003 and I had signed *le sous seing privé*, the final sales document that would make the house mine.

The house had a name, 'Pech Menal,' which meant 'little hill' in the old language, a language whose origins were lost in the mists of time. It was one of those ancient place names, *les lieux dits,* which dotted the French countryside.

Pech Menal was built in 1776. I could tell because the date of the house's completion was chiseled in the stone lintel above the front door. 1776! Imagine, Washington, Jefferson and Franklin were revolting against the British crown at the same time that the original owners built this house I was buying.

A smaller door off the entryway landing was marked in stone with a different, and more recent date, 2002, the year Monsieur de Paris, the seller, had finished the very extensive renovations to the property. Monsieur de Paris and I were meeting today at the *notaire's* office in town to finalize the sale. A *notaire* is a sort of French real estate attorney.

As if buying the house wasn't exciting enough, I was all a flutter to finally meet Monsieur de Paris. I hoped he was handsome and charming. I had heard that he was an eligible bachelor, a doctor with an adopted Asian son.

Here I was starting a new life's chapter in a new house, in a new country. *Could this man, Michel de Paris, with the last name of my new country's capital city, be a potential romantic interest for me? And an aristocrat to boot!*

That little particle *de* in his name indicated a member of the old landowning aristocracy from before the French revolution.

A nobleman for a boyfriend! A descendant of the houses of Orleans and Valois! Now that would show them all back home and bolster my flagging ego as well!

My self-esteem had taken a blow the previous year when my longtime marriage imploded. I was born Barbara Waldheim. But for nearly three decades, I was Barbara Newman, wife of successful attorney Alex Newman, and mother to our two wonderful sons. But last March, with the stroke of a pen, I suddenly became divorcée Barbara Newman, single mother Barbara Newman, taken for granted and overlooked Barbara Newman.

I felt like a failure. I never expected that *I* would get divorced; that was something that happened to other people. I was so disappointed in myself, and I was so angry with my ex. I was also intimidated by him. He had hurt me, and now he held all the cards. He was a lawyer and handled all of our finances, and he was upset that our marriage was ending, that I had finally mustered up the courage to leave him.

I was just 20 years old when we married at the Hilton Hotel in my hometown of Pittsburgh, Pennsylvania. I was in my senior year at Northwestern University, about to receive my BA in French and Art History. I had lived and studied abroad in French Switzerland and at the Sorbonne in Paris. I spoke fluent French, and I had just accepted a job as a French translator at the United Nations in New York. But all that changed when I married Alex.

My new husband preferred that I stay closer to home so I turned down the UN job and taught French enrichment classes from our home. Over time, Barbara Waldheim disappeared and became domesticated Mrs. Alex Newman. With the divorce, I had to resurrect who I was. Could I rediscover the independent young woman full of moxie from long ago? I could either curl up and retreat from life or take on a challenge that would completely change my horizons. No halfway measures. I decided to move ahead full throttle. The first thing I did was to go back to my maiden name, Barbara Waldheim. It felt almost like a rebirth. In an effort to reclaim my former self and forge a new path forward, I would escape to France, buy a house, and maybe find *Monsieur* Right in the process.

The house I was buying from Monsieur de Paris consisted of a main house, a barn and a stable set on two *hectares* or about four-and-a-half acres of property. Both the barn and the stable were even bigger than the house. A monumental staircase of giant lime-stone blocks led up to the small covered landing and the front door from which one had a lovely view of the surrounding coun-tryside and over to a nearby hill town.

Adjoining the house was a small, low building that contained the enormous bread oven. Once, this sort of pizza-style oven would have produced giant, round loaves of crusty French bread, enough for the whole farming community. It was now home to a family of mice. It was very decorative to look at and useful in the sense that the old chimney area behind it hid the modern hot water heater. This annex to the main house served as a kitchen with rudimentary, but usable cooking and washing up facilities: a sink, a hot plate and a microwave oven.

Across the front landing, there was a shower room. I wasn't sure how practical it would be to go outside the front door and cross the landing for a shower or to use the toilet in the cold of winter or the dark of night, but I supposed that I would learn to do it.

Monsieur de Paris had beautifully redone the house and outbuildings with new roofs and massive roof trusses. There were custom made golden oak windows and doors all round—a Dutch door that opened in two sections, a tall door, a stooped door, a more stooped door—as there is no standard size in France. The workmanship was exquisite. No expense had been spared. All the mechanical systems of the house were *aux normes,* meaning that the electrical, plumbing and sewer systems had been completely updated, a rarity in rural France.

Only the main front door had purposely been left *en état* to act as contrast to the beauty of the new renovations. It was a rustic affair with very worn, ill fitting boards painted in what must have once been red. This old-fashioned door was beautiful too, in its way, as only the passage of time and the touch of many hands could mellow materials in such a way. It closed with an iron bar bolting mechanism activated by a giant old key, a key that would soon be mine.

At 2 p.m., *14h* French time, I was ushered to my seat in the *notaire's* office for the document signing. Monsieur de Paris arrived soon afterwards. As he entered the office, I was so excited to meet him in person for the first time. My heart sank when I saw him. He was very ordinary; a small, slight man with a shock of dark hair and regular features. He was wearing a beige trench coat that he did not remove. His manner was gracious and respectful. He deferred politely to me and the *notaire.*

The seller's voice was so soft that the *notaire* and I rather strained to hear him. His accent was not the same as the local farmers and townspeople of the southwest of France. It was standard French, educated, but not pretentiously elegant.

To my surprise, the bill of sale specified my ex-husband, Alex Newman by name. As I said already, I had changed my last name back to 'Waldheim,' my maiden name, after the divorce. Monsieur de Paris' former spouse was named in full as well—a Vietnamese or Cambodian name, I noted. I asked the *notaire* why our ex-spouses names would be specified. He explained that in this manner dating back to the Napoleonic code, the French state gives notice that former spouses have no interest or claim on the property being transferred.

I had a short list of concerns to discuss with Monsieur de Paris before we went our separate ways. Would he remove an enormous dining table from the main room of the house? Yes, of course, he would. I also wondered if he would see to the removal of the left-over construction debris I had found in the double-story, open-sided barn. Yes, he would see to it.

Monsieur de Paris could not have been more cooperative—nor more distant. The reality of his presence didn't match up with my fantasy of him. He wasn't at all the image of a French love interest I had imagined. He was rather unprepossessing looking. He hadn't paid any special attention to me. I had hoped to be swept off my feet by a dashing Prince Charming.

My mind wandered as the *notaire* read the lengthy verbiage of the sales contract aloud as required. My memories crowded in, blocking out the *notaire's* office as the lawyer's voice droned on. I thought back longingly to my recent love affair with another Frenchman, handsome, naughty Luc Martin.

Now Luc had set my heart racing. He was a textbook French lothario, a bit like actor Alain Delon's dramatis persona, a good-looking rogue. Was it already more than a year ago that we had been together?

The *notaire's* voice calling my name jerked me back to reality.

"Madame Waldheim, Madame Waldheim," he repeated. "*Félicitations*. Congratulations." The signatures were recorded. The 18th century farmhouse was officially mine! I felt exuberant. We all stood up. Monsieur de Paris and I left the notarial office. He set off down the street with barely a cursory nod in my direction. My dream of a fairytale romance departed with him.

Ah, well. So much for girlish fantasies.

I found a telephone booth on the main square. I wanted to share the exciting news about the house purchase with my mother back home. I knew how to telephone to the United States from the phone booth with my prepaid *Orange* calling card. I had to enter many long sets of numbers. No matter. I knew the drill. I dialed my mother's number.

I hoped she would be supportive of me the way she had been two years ago when I had told her that I was getting divorced. Now that had been a difficult announcement to make! I had expected her to condemn me for leaving my long term marriage but much to my surprise she seemed to take the news in stride. She only asked why I had waited so long. She felt I was too old to start over again at 55 years of age.

"Mom, it's me, Barbara," I said when she picked up.

"Barbara! It's nice to hear from you," my mother said, sounding pleased that I had called. "How are you? Where are you calling from?"

"Mom, I did it! I bought the old farmhouse, Pech Menal. The closing just happened at the *notaire's*. I am so happy. I'm in Caussade, the town where the lawyer's office is. It's about 20 minutes away from my new house. I'm going over there right after I get off the phone with you. As soon as I get a mattress, I can sleep there and start to get settled."

The mood darkened quickly. My mother started to cry. Through her tears, she said, "I hope you know what you're doing, Barbara. Who do you know in France? I don't understand why you want to live there."

"What do you mean, mom?" I responded, getting upset that she was upset. She knew about my plans. I had expected her to be happy for me.

"I'll meet people, mom. I can live some months of the year in France and some months in Florida. You and I will still see one another. It's a big adventure for me. Can't you wish me well?"

"Of course, I wish you well, Barbara," my mother said hesitatingly. "But I would never choose this for you. I never thought you'd go through with it. I don't see the point. I don't like the French. They're unfriendly."

"Ok, mom," I replied, biting back tears myself. "I get it. Nice to talk to you. We'll stay in touch. I'll send you my telephone number when I get one. Love you." I hung up the receiver.

That was a bath of cold water! Well, what did I expect? Of course, she wouldn't understand. She would never have done something like I was doing. It would never have been part of her experience or possibilities. She seemed threatened and fearful about my departure from what she considered to be normal for a person in my situation. But I had to live my own life, didn't I? I wanted to spread my wings and offer myself this French adventure.

I left the phone booth and continued down the sidewalk toward *le café des Arcades* to have a celebratory glass of wine. I found the café and sat down at a little table. The young waitress approached and I ordered a glass of rosé. I shook off my mother's phone call and relaxed in the dappled sunshine sipping my drink, idly watching the play of light on the gazebo under the tall trees of the Caussade town square, *la place.*

Legal proceedings were always a bit stressful but they were behind me now. My old paramour, Luc Martin, popped into my mind again. Luc and I met when I was leading a small group of tourists visiting *la France profonde*, France off the beaten track. He was the driver of our minibus. He drove us around the country. He drove me wild with desire.

I could still see his long arms and big hands washing and rubbing every inch of the minibus with sudsy water just outside my hotel room window early one morning on the tour. The water from the hose sloshed and sloshed as Luc rinsed the soap away, splashing onto the pavement. It was nice that he was keeping the bus so clean but I'm sure he knew he was waking me up. *Had he seen me peeking out of the curtains in my nightie?*

It was just after my divorce. I was the tour organizer for a little company called 'Pepitours,' named for my business partner, Pepita. I had been faithfully and dutifully married for 30 years. I was ripe for a fling when I met Luc.

I remembered how our group was under the spell of our last visit for the day, the magnificent church of Vézelay, set high up on the hillside from which King Richard the Lionhearted and the King of France had launched a crusade in 1190.

Tour visit finished, we piled back into the minivan. Luc drove us a short way out of town to Monsieur and Madame Bellay's charming country inn. I distributed the keys and saw everyone happily settled into their pretty rooms until we met up again at dinnertime. Luc delivered everyone's luggage. By this time in the trip, there were no mix-ups. Luc knew whose suitcases were whose, without looking at the name tags.

Luc was staying in the same hotel as the rest of us. Taking a break, the two of us were sitting together in his room on a divan near the sliding door to the patio. It was pleasantly cool and the light was dim. All the rooms at the Bellay's *auberge* had a view of Vézalay set high on its hill in the distance. Sometimes clouds formed below the church and it appeared to be floating in the sky as we looked out. It was a beautiful setting as the sun declined towards the horizon. We were chatting amiably about the day's activities and a job well done when Luc leaned over to kiss me. It felt very natural and unforced.

His lips were soft and warm on mine and my mouth yielded under their touch. His tongue was probing. I returned his kiss as a delicious warmth suffused my whole body. I wanted him. Wordlessly we looked languorously into each other's eyes. Our mutual attraction had been building up to this moment for a long time.

Luc lifted me up off the low sofa and laid me down on the bed. He unbuttoned my blouse and caressed the top of my breasts, showering them with kisses.

"Wait a minute," I said huskily. "I'll take off my bra."

"No," said Luc. "Let me do it. For me, taking off a woman's lacy lingerie is like unwrapping a piece of candy."

His words made me swoon. Thankfully I was wearing the pretty new French lingerie I bought recently in Albi. There were more lingerie stores in a medium size French city than I could have ever imagined.

Suddenly I felt shy. It had been a long time since I had felt so desired and full of desire. Yet the thought of being penetrated by Luc was too intimate. It was all happening too fast. Somehow I couldn't allow myself to relinquish control and be totally swept away by the passion of the moment.

I rolled out from under him and reversed our positions so that I was kneeling over him, facing him on the bed. Smiling down at his handsome, tanned face, I began to undo his belt. He closed his eyes. His flat stomach was bare and brown. He groaned with pleasurable anticipation as I unzipped his pants. Given his state of arousal, it didn't take long to satisfy him.

In the afterglow, we cuddled together on the bed, my head nestled in the crook of his arm. He offered to gratify me in return but I explained that I was quite satisfied. And I was satisfied by the pleasure I had given him.

Was I becoming selfless or what? Next stop, sainthood? Was it the influence of the recent church visit?

Time passed by. We lay there in a reverie, each thinking our own thoughts.

"I'm going back to my room now to freshen up for dinner," I told him as I propped myself up on one arm. Luc nodded. *"À tout à l'heure,"* I said, putting on my clothes as I moved to the door. "See you at dinner. *20h,* 8 p.m."

Right on time, at eight o'clock, our hungry group was all seated around a big circular table in the restaurant section of the inn. Mme Bellay was the hostess and her husband manned the gourmet kitchen. Those of us who wished were having an apéritif while tuning up our appetites for the tasty dinner to follow shortly. Luc and I were right next to each other at the table. We both ordered a *whiskey,* what I called a scotch at home.

"Pas de glaçons, s'il vous plaît, Madame Bellay. No ice, please," I said as she bent down to serve me.

Luc took a long sip of his drink. He cleared his throat and announced boastfully in French "As good as this *whiskey* is, it's not as special as the elixir you just swallowed in my bedroom, Barbara." He smirked.

What! I thought. *Had I understood him correctly? Had Mme Bellay overheard him?!*

"Luc!" I protested, blushing to the roots of my hair. I shot him a warning look.

What a devil he was! To talk like that to your boss, I thought indignantly. *And in front of the others!* I gave a furtive glance at the unsuspecting tourists. Luckily the Pepitours clients didn't speak much French.

But Madame Bellay did. She chuckled throatily and flashed me a wink. "What may I serve you?" she asked as she continued around the table. *"Je vous sers quelque chose?"*

"Je vous sers quelque chose, Madame?" the waitress of the café asked me. "Another glass of wine? *Encore du vin?"* she said. I came back to the present with a start, a bit disoriented. The mist of my memories dissipated and I realized that I was at *café des Arcades* in Caussade.

"Non, non, merci," I declined. *L'addition, s'il vous plaît."* I paid the tab and set off to retrieve my car and drive to my new house.

Here I was at last, on my own, starting a new life in France, owner of my own French house. It was so exciting! There were so many details to take care of setting up housekeeping in a new country. I had my work cut out for me. At the same time, I was determined to have some fun finding a new love interest or two, if not the love of my life. *Why not a handsome Frenchman?* I asked myself. *Why not, indeed?* I was willing to kiss quite a few frogs to find one who might turn into a prince.

A Café Terrace in Caussade on a Hot Summer Day

CHAPTER 2

A Revelation about Monsieur de Paris

One day not long after the real estate closing at the notaire's office, I decided to take a break from getting my new house in order. I had been cleaning and straightening up non stop. Things weren't going quite as I planned at Pech Menal. I had underestimated the scope of the task at hand. It turned out that I had bought a very old house that had been redone and modernized in some ways—and then totally neglected.

On the positive side, everything was plumb. The corners and angles of the walls and ceilings were perfect. No cracks anywhere. The wood ceiling beams, window frames, doors and staircase to the lower level were new and radiated quality. But the bad news was all the unfinished projects, covered everywhere with thick dust and cobwebs.

One big problem was the bathroom. The only bathroom was outside across the landing and it was unfinished. The new plumbing had only been roughed in and the shower was just a pan on the floor and a hose sticking out of the wall. There was a basic sink and toilet. The walls and floor were bare, unpainted concrete. It was rudimentary. I could wash in there, but it was not a pleasant place to linger.

That was just one example of projects left half completed. There was no real kitchen. The floor of the bedroom level was unfinished. There was an opening in the roof to evacuate the smoke from a wood stove, but no stove. The property was barren. The trees and shrubs had been razed during the renovations.

The realization sunk in that I would have a lot of work to do to make Pech Menal comfortable and homelike. The present space was empty and soulless. I tried to keep my spirits up. The house had been left in suspended animation waiting for someone to use their time, money, and imagination to make it liveable and usable.

I seemed to have elected myself for the job.

For a change of scenery, I decided to do a little sightseeing around my new area. The beautiful village of Montpezat de Quercy was not far from the hamlet of Cayrièch where Pech Menal was located.

The church in the village of Montpezat boasted an outstanding set of original 16th century tapestries. I drove over there to see what the guidebook was raving about. As I was sitting at the village café drinking a *Perrier citron* before visiting the church, who should I run into but Madame Evelyne Lemoine, my real estate agent. She had handled my purchase of Pech Menal.

"Barbara!" Mme Lemoine called out to me. "*Comment ça va?* How are you?" We exchanged kisses on the cheek, *la bise*.

"*Mme Lemoine, quel plaisir*! How nice to see you. Please sit down," I said. "Let me buy you a coffee or something."

Mme Lemoine sat down at my table on the café *terrasse*. She had been instrumental in my purchase of Pech Menal. It was one of '*Quercy Immobilier*,' her real estate agency, *coup de coeurs*.

A *coup de coeur* was a listing that was one of her personal favorites from among all those house offerings that came across her desk. It literally meant a blow to the heart. There were lots of *coup* expressions: the political *coup d'état*, the off with your head or the final straw, *le coup de grâce*, the *coup de balai* or the *coup de torchon*, to give a touch up with a broom or a dust cloth, sometimes meaning a clean slate, the *coup de peigne*, to run a comb through your hair, the *coup de foudre*, love at first sight or a lightning strike and so on.

Mme Lemoine had a beautiful house in the market town of Caussade where the notaire's office was located. Well, almost every town was a market town. But Caussade's market was one of the biggest ones in the region. She felt that her house was American style and it did have a big double door refrigerator in the very modern fitted kitchen. A 'fitted' kitchen had the appliances built in. Traditionally, Europeans did not build in their kitchen appliances. Instead it was customary to take your stove, refrigerator and dishwasher, if you had one, with you when you moved to another house.

Mme Lemoine's husband, Sylvain, was a very successful *plombier/électricien*, the head of his own *entreprise*. The bathrooms at their house were also very modern since he had access to all the latest fixtures and the know-how to install them.

As we were sipping our drinks, I asked Mme Lemoine, "What brings you to Montpezat today? A real estate property?"

"No, no, Barbara," she replied. "I grew up on a farm near Montpezat. I was visiting my parents just now. They still live here."

So that explained it. Imagine. Elegant Mme Lemoine had been raised on a farm. As we were catching up, I mentioned that I had already found a yoga class to attend in my new area. I was taking classes with Amina Khan, Monsieur de Paris' girlfriend.

By a stroke of small town coincidence, I had recently gone to a yoga class in Caussade and it turned out that the instructor, Amina, knew all about Pech Menal. She used to live there with Michel de Paris.

"Barbara," Mme Lemoine whispered conspiratorially, leaning closer, "I must explain some things to you about M. de Paris, but this information must stay between us. Do you understand?"

"Of course," I agreed, thinking to myself, *who would I tell anyway? I hardly knew anybody.*

"Well," Mme Lemoine led with her headline, "Monsieur de Paris is actually Madame de Paris. He was until recently a woman. Michel is really Michèle, with an 'e' at the end."

She paused while I digested this startling information.

"She, I mean, he comes from a very aristocratic family in the Île de France, the area around Paris. His family disapproves of him and he moved here to the Midi-Pyrénées to get away from them."

"Really," I sputtered, getting a mental picture of the slight, soft-spoken figure in the beige raincoat from the lawyer's office.

"But his girlfriend, the yoga teacher," I said thinking aloud, trying to wrap my mind around the idea, no pun intended.

"Oh, that's over," Madame Lemoine informed me. "He's helping her to find a place in Toulouse and she will be moving to the big city soon."

"Is that why he sold Pech Menal?" I queried. "He put so much work into the property just to turn around and sell it."

Madame Lemoine leaned in closer over the table. "No, not at all," she said. "You see, Monsieur de Paris suffered some financial losses recently. His château outside of Paris was burgled. It was not insured. Many valuable objects were stolen."

"Oh my," was all I could muster, impressed by the mention of châteaux and nobility.

I always wondered about that last name of his—de Paris, with the particle.

Madame Lemoine continued confidingly. "He told me that the burglars even took a set of porcelain dishes which were a gift from Prince Rainier and the house of Monaco. M. de Paris used to get them out whenever Princess Stéphanie came to dinner."

Wow! That Princess Stephanie, I thought, *Grace Kelly's daughter?*

"But Evelyne, I mean Madame Lemoine, where does the little orphan he adopted in Cambodia fit into this story?"

I knew that Monsieur de Paris had a ward, a young Asian boy who had lived with him at Pech Menal, when my new house was his.

"The little boy is not adopted at all. That was just the story they told for public consumption. The little boy is Monsieur de Paris' biological son, to whom he gave birth when he was living as a married woman in Southeast Asia. M. de Paris is really the mother of the little guy."

Aha! Now I remembered the foreign name of Monsieur de Paris' ex-spouse from the sale document. *It must have been his husband's name, not his wife's. But since I couldn't interpret the gender from the Cambodian name, I had just assumed his former spouse was female, not male.* My head was spinning.

"It's a shame he had to sell Pech Menal, Barbara," Madame Lemoine said feelingly. "He and his son liked to play around in the rowboat on the little artificial lake behind the house. They had a big telescope for stargazing set up out there in Cayrièch away from the ambient light from any town. But it turned out well for you, my dear," Mme Lemoine concluded. "You made an excellent purchase."

"What will Monsieur de Paris do now?" I asked.

"*Eh bien*, he and his son are living in Caussade. Monsieur de Paris has a medical degree. He has a thriving practice with an emphasis on Ayurvedic and alternative medicine. Probably something he studied during his time in Asia. I hear he is much appreciated for his very gentle manner," she assured me.

Boy, I had forgotten all about the famous church tapestries I had come to see in Montpezat with this bombshell. As I thought it over, it all fell into place – Monsieur de Paris' fancy name, his diffidence, his unprepossessing physique, the beautiful house restoration – suddenly interrupted.

Mme Lemoine signaled to the waiter and paid for our drinks even though I had invited her. She was an energetic person who never stayed too long in one spot. We kissed cheeks goodbye. Then she stepped down from the café terrace into the street where her car was parked and opened the driver side door.

Glancing at her watch, she said, *"Mince!"* pronounced

'manse'. *Mince* was a polite substitute for *merde,* shit or damn it in English.

"Darn, Barbara. Look at the time! *Au revoir.* Stay cool," she advised. "It's a *canicule,* a real *canicule,*" she said with a delighted grin at the idea of the summer heatwave we were experiencing. And she was gone with a wave to me out of her car window.

As it happened I didn't completely keep the secret about Monsieur de Paris' change of gender.

Back at Pech Menal, I had hired some tile layers to redo the floor of my 'summer kitchen,' which was at present my only kitchen.

A 'summer kitchen' is a covered outdoor cooking area, which keeps the heat out of the main house in the warm weather, and is convenient for cooking and serving meals out of doors, right near the patio, terrace or garden where the French liked to eat, weather permitting. In the *Tarn-et-Garonne*, the weather mostly favored eating out of doors for half of the year or more.

My 'summer kitchen' was a charming stone building containing a giant bread oven. It was attached to the main house by a short covered walkway. It was fine for doing my cooking and washing up until I had an official, year round kitchen installed in the main house one day.

I had a basic sink with a drainboard and a microwave oven and hot plate in the 'summer kitchen'. They were serviceable enough for simple cooking but the floor was more suitable for the pigs that had once been kept there. The floor consisted of very rough slabs of stone with dirt in between them. I had to pay attention not to trip on the rough, uneven stone pieces. Besides, the dirt in between the stones left a coating of fine dust over everything in the kitchen.

I wanted to rectify the situation but I learned that it was hard to find artisans in the area to do home improvement jobs.

Everyone was *débordé*, overloaded with requests. To hire a workman with a good reputation, a homeowner had to wait years. Literally. And who would risk using an unknown?

I would. My little American self didn't have the necessary patience to wait that long. Nor the engrained, cautious French approach. After all, there were a lot of good people out there in the big, wide world, *n'est-ce pas?* So, when I saw a flyer tacked up in town advertising the services of two tile guys, I took a gamble and called them. I showed them the tile I had selected and quickly came to an arrangement with them to start on the job the next week.

The two big guys, Arnaud and Raphaël, got right down to work jack hammering the stones out of the old floor to be able to pour *une chape,* a smooth cement surface on which to set the new tiles I had chosen.

At noon they knocked off for lunch. They had put in a good morning's work. And at noon every Frenchman's stomach has a built-in alarm which reminds him that it is mealtime. Out from the same big truck where they got the jackhammer appeared an electric grill. Onto the grill, they popped a package of sausages, *saucisses tolosaines,* the sweet ones named for the big city of Toulouse about an hour away. They smelled delicious as they started to turn golden brown.

Raphaël and Arnaud invited me to join them, and I was happy to accept since I was hungry too. As we ate, Arnaud asked me about the house. I explained that it was a typical 18th century farmhouse of this region, *le Quercy,* in southwest France. The house was built out of the local white limestone, and it had the typical side stone staircase leading up to the second floor, or *le premier étage* as the French say, meaning the first floor above the ground floor, *le rez de chaussée.* What Americans call the second floor is the first floor in French. The French refer to the first floor as the street level, *le rez de chaussée.* That makes their first floor, *le premier étage,* what we call the second floor and so on and so forth. Clear?

Raphaël volunteered that he and Arnaud were not from around the area, but he didn't say where they did hail from.

So, I continued talking about my new house, as it was quite interesting to me. I extolled the beautiful workmanship of the huge beehive shaped bread oven in the 'summer kitchen'. I explained about the stone slab sink upstairs, which emptied out through a hole in the wall into the courtyard. Water had to be provided from a bucket. I was going to get it attached to the water supply and make it a wet bar. A sophisticated modern use of this original feature from olden times.

I also bragged about my *meurtrière* window, another ancient original feature. It was a narrow slit built in the stone wall on the ground level of the main house. This design allowed a defender to stay protected from incoming projectiles while shooting out at invaders. My *meurtrière,* or 'killing window,' faced north, as it seemed the attackers usually used to come from that direction, for example, the Norsemen.

The long extension cord of the grill wound its way along the sandy *castiné* drive to an outlet in the 'summer kitchen.' Sitting on plastic chairs in the sunny courtyard, we munched happily away on our grilled sausages with mustard, washed down with a bottle of red wine I had contributed. It goes without saying that we also shared a loaf of *baguette.*

"*Putain!* Damn, this hits the spot," exclaimed hairy Raphaël, the taller of the two guys.

"*Et comment*, you said it, Rapha," agreed muscle-bound Arnaud, playfully punching his friend on the arm.

We made an unusual trio. *What was this attractive, youngish, foreign woman doing here in this teeny French hamlet with many more cows than people?*

The conversation lagged. I searched around in my mind for a subject of conversation. I took up the slack by telling them about the house's former owner, Monsieur de Paris, and his sex change. I expected them to break out in big guffaws and make some ribald comments. Not at all. They listened sympathetically to the tale and their reaction was blasé. *How sophisticated and worldly-wise,* I thought. I was impressed. And I was impressed with their tile work too. They finished up the new floor tile in a few days and made a good job of it.

They drove off in their big, rattling truck and I never saw them again.

Sale Days at Cécile's Boutique in Caussade

CHAPTER 3

Le Tout Élec,' the Appliance Store Story

T he weather continued very hot and dry as Mme Lemoine had predicted the day I ran into her. Despite the heatwave, I had made progress getting things in shape at a Pech Menal. The new 'summer kitchen' floor that Arnaud and Raphaël had installed was working out great.

I needed a plumber and I would have liked to hire Sylvain Lemoine, my pretty real estate agent's husband. He was a plumber-electrician but he was completely *débordé,* one of those artisans whose waiting list was years long.

Jean-Claude Delpech, however, was available right away. Delpech had been Monsieur de Paris's plumber. I got his name from the receipts which the former owner had left for me.

Monsieur Delpech came and installed a small shower and toilet on the lower level of the main house near my bedroom so I wouldn't have to make the trip outside across the front door landing every time nature called.

He also installed a real bathtub and new toilet in my bathroom across the landing from the front door with the great view over the fields.

I found a box of old-fashioned blue and white tiles at a *brocante* flea market to intersperse with the plain blue ones which

I put on the wall behind the new tub. I was very proud of one of them with an image of a little boy playing with a hoop, rolling it with a stick. A real find! I put that one in the middle of my tile wall. I also found a tall, thin armoire with a pretty carved door at the used furniture dealer's, *le brocanteur,* where I checked in from time to time. *Brocante* is old stuff, not the same as *antiquités,* but the categories overlap.

Benoît Beynac was the *brocante* dealer's name. He was very tall for a Frenchman, like his tall piece of furniture, He had beautiful haircuts with sharply delineated sideburns. We got to know each other a bit over the course of my many visits to the old Quonset hut that housed his wares. The metal structure was cold in the winter and really hot in the summer but we were both undeterred, united by my desire to find, and his to sell, a treasure in those pre-internet days.

Benoît explained to me that the name for the tall 19th century armoire I was buying was a *bonnetière,* a cabinet to store hats. It had six widely spaced shelves on which you once arranged your bonnets. Or, as Benoît obligingly continued, you could remove the shelves which would leave just enough space for a man standing upright to hide in case your husband came home unexpectedly. For this reason, this kind of armoire was generally known as *un homme debout.* They thought of everything back then.

I was going to use my *homme debout-bonnetière* to hold the electric drill, the paint rollers and tray, the tools, hardware and assorted cleaning and fixing items that were fast accumulating all around at Pech Menal. It would just fit in the outside bathroom beneath the very high ceiling.

Prices at Benoît Beynac's place were not hard and firm. His metal shed was full to overflowing with a mixture of everything, trash and treasure. Items spilled out into the parking area as well. There was certainly no computerized listing of the merchandise.

One day, I found a not very old wrought iron table base which was a bit askew. It weighed a ton.

"How much, Benoît, for a good client like me?" I asked. To my surprise, he answered, *"cadeau,* it's a gift".

It made a great coffee table once fitted out with a beveled glass top. I put it in front of the new sofa I had purchased in Toulouse. I now had a place to sit in comfort.

I bought a TV and TV stand at a small electrical appliance store in nearby Caussade, *Le Tout'Élec.* I considered going to the big box stores off the *autoroute* called *la rocade* in Montauban, a bigger city. But I decided to stay local. So I went to *Le Tout'Élec,* 'Everything Electrical,' in Caussade.

At *Le Tout'Elec,* I bought a washing machine, a fancy steam iron and a television and an antenna with roof installation. Next I purchased an expensive German-engineered vacuum cleaner. I went a little overboard, but sooner or later, I needed all these items. Once I got the television working and the washing machine hooked up, Pech Menal would start to join the 20th century.

The day after I returned home with my electrical appliance booty, I decided that the TV stand didn't suit me. It was better to perch the television on an old suitcase from the *brocante* store. Very 'design,' *dee-zine,* as the French said, like a photo in a fancy shelter magazine.

I put the TV stand back into my newly-acquired and used station wagon, the Citroën *break* pronounced *Breck* like the shampoo, and headed back to *Le Tout'Élec* to return it to the store.

The owner was most perturbed to learn that I wanted to return the TV stand. *La patronne* was a short, red haired woman of middle age. Her hair was dyed that purple red or aubergine color which was popular among French women *d'un certain âge.*

"Madame," she complained to me after we had greeted one another and I had explained my mission, "How is it possible that you want to return the TV stand? Didn't you look at it here in the store yesterday when you bought it?"

"Why, yes, certainly I looked at it here. But once I got it back home, I saw that the style didn't please me. And then I found another place to put the television where I don't need any stand at all."

La patronne came out from behind the high counter in a hurry. "*Ce n'est pas normal, Madame,*" she remonstrated with me. "You cannot simply return something because it doesn't suit you."

"But *Madame,*" I retorted, getting annoyed with her inflexibility. "Just yesterday I spent several thousand francs in your store. I have the receipt right here. Please take a look. *Regardez-le, s'il vous plaît.*" *La patronne* studied the receipt.

"You are telling me that you will not take back the TV stand costing 600 francs? I find that hard to accept. I kept it at my house all of one day before hurrying to bring it back to you."

I calculated that the price of the TV stand represented about ninety of the two thousand American dollars I had spent at *Le Tout'Élec* the day before.

"We are a small store and we cannot accept returns," *la patronne* said huffily, retreating behind the counter again. "*Ce n'est pas normal.* It isn't normal."

"*Normal!*" I blew my stack. "I could have spent the money at the big box stores, '*Le But Géant, Leclerc* or *Le Bricomarché* in the *centre commercial* in Montauban, but I wanted to give a local merchant my business. I thought we would build a relationship and that the next time I needed a fan or a toaster, I would come to *Le Tout'Élec.*

Normal, Normal! You bet this isn't normal, not where I come from!"

I had worked myself up to a real fury. I was ready to fly out the door with smoke coming off my heels.

In fact, it was not general practice in France to be able to return purchases. Their old-fashioned idea was that a person only went shopping when they really needed something. Trying things out was not an option. This practice tended to depress one's shopping impulses severely. Even for clothes, if you bought the dress, it was yours forever once you left the store. There was no changing your mind, which made a person very cautious about buying something.

When entering a store, it was very bad manners not to say "*bonjour, Madame* or *Monsieur*" to the owner. He or she then asked you what you wished, "*Vous désirez, Madame?*"

In the United States it might be common to say, "I'm just looking, thank you." *Just looking?!* In France there was no just looking. You should have something in mind and the shop owner or a salesperson would help you to find it. The service was more personalized from one point of view, but more intrusive on the other hand.

A customer in France might be able to make an exchange by following the usually lengthy process which yielded an *avoir* or credit at the end of the wait. But getting your money refunded was not an option at all. "*Quel dommage! Désolé!* What a shame! So sorry!"

The French business owners didn't see that making returns and exchanges easier was actually good for their bottom line. In fact, each time clients entered a store for any reason, there was another chance that they might buy something.

The *patronne* of *Le Tout'Élec* hastened after me as I was heading out the door.

"*Eh bien, Madame,* perhaps we can come to some little arrangement. After all, this case is not *normal,* it is *exceptionnel.* I will credit you. As you point out, you are a very good client."

"Hmmph," I sniffed, "that's more like it."

"And please accept a little coffee while I do the necessary paperwork."

We drank an espresso together, she behind the counter and I standing in front. I tried to have good grace about it. After all, I had gotten my way. At least I had a credit to use at another time.

Driving back to Pech Menal from the appliance store, I slowly decompressed. I remembered another contretemps with a French store owner from a long time ago during my days as a French exchange student.

It was during my junior year in college. I spent the academic year of 1968-1969 at the Sorbonne in Paris. I was living with a family near the tony Place de la Concorde, not far from the hotel Ritz and the jewelry stores of the Place Vendôme. I was just acquiring my ability to to speak French in 1968, so I was more tongue-tied back then when I was confronted with the sexist behavior of a storekeeper near my landlady's house on the rue Saint Honoré.

As I said, my neighborhood was just down from la Place Vendôme with its fabulous jewelry stores and the fabled Hôtel Ritz. But I didn't spend time there. I was just a young student. This was my route to the laundromat, *la laverie automatique,* where I had to go from time to time to wash my clothes.

One day, I walked along with my laundry in tow wearing my black patent leather heels with shiny buckles. I also had on lacy black knee socks. As sometimes happened, I was followed by some young male admirers. The group of guys called out to me,

"*Belles chaussettes! Belles chaussettes!* Bell eh, sho-set-tuh." It came out like a lilting song.

'Pretty socks,' they dubbed me, teasing me to get my attention. It wasn't threatening, just a gallant reflex on their part.

I had learned over my months in France that the best way of discouraging this kind of behavior was to completely ignore it. All of us young women from my American university program in Paris were occasionally followed by young men earnestly beseeching us to have a drink with them.

"*Voulez-vous prendre un verre avec moi, Mademoiselle?*" was their plaintive refrain.

It was a kind of Gallic tribute to the opposite sex. If you responded at all, even with 'non,' you were lost. The only strategy was to act as if they didn't exist. If you acknowledged them, that led them on.

When my 'pretty socks' pursuers didn't quit, for once I broke my rule and turned around to face them on the sidewalk. As I confronted them, I pointed with big gestures of my right hand to the ring finger on my left, showing them my engagement ring. It was 1968. I was nineteen and I had just gotten engaged to my boyfriend, Alex, from back home in Chicago.

"*Je suis fiancée!*" I told them, my eyes flashing with somewhat exaggerated indignation.

"*O, désolés, Mademoiselle!* Sorry, sorry!" They were immediately so penitent.

"We didn't know," they said as they melted away. I had found another good way to shake pursuers–appeal to their sense of male solidarity. I was '*taken.*' That was men for you.

But back to my *louche* experience along my laundry route. It was sordid, yet kind of exciting.

On the rue St Honoré there was a jewelry store window displaying much more affordable wares than they showed on the Place Vendôme. A long necklace of semi-precious stones, mostly agates, caught my eye. After passing it by several times on my laundromat route, I stopped in to the store for a closer look at it.

As I remembered, the proprietor of the boutique was very friendly and we got to talking. He dared to touch the leatherette jumper I was wearing. As his hand brushed the material between my shoulder and my breast, I wondered if he was curious about the ersatz leather fabric which might have been new to him. I was nineteen years old and so naïve.

I recoiled slightly, but I was intent on studying the agate necklace from the window which he held in his hand. I wanted to buy myself a souvenir of my year in Paris before my time at the Sorbonne was over. The price was *abordable.* It was not completely outside of my budget, but the necklace was very heavy when I put it on my neck. It was more like three necklaces, if I wound the long string of beads around my neck two times.

As I was considering it, the jeweler insisted on showing me some other items. Before I could stop him, he pulled a statuette out from a safe in back of his desk. I peeked closer to see it and blushed bright red. It was a young boy copulating with a sheep.

"Beautiful workmanship, *n'est-ce pas, Mademoiselle?* It is Roman, genuine 2nd century."

I was shocked into silence.

"And do you see this automaton?" he continued, mistaking my immobility for interest. "It's a mechanical device which imitates human movement. Very cleverly done. Very lifelike," he opined.

He pressed a button and the figures of two beautifully attired dolls sitting on the edge of a little 18th century bed sprang into action, bumping and grinding their laps together.

What den of iniquity had I wandered into? I was dumbstruck. *Quel pervert!* He was old too, at least 40. Middle aged.

The old pervert wasn't quite finished with me. He extended me an invitation:

"Mademoiselle, I have a cabin cruiser on the Seine. Would you care to come out on the river with me some afternoon?"

In answer, I flew out of the shop and back into the safety of the street.

What a disgusting experience! 'Déguelasse!' Too bad about the necklace. 'Tant pis!' It was too long and heavy for me anyway. And the statuette of the boy and the sheep! An 'objet d'art'? Were there really collectors of that sort of thing?

Some Flower Pots by a Door in Montpezat de Quercy

From Kir Suze to Champagne: Flashback to My Voyage Aboard the Ocean Liner, France

Back in the present, at Pech Menal, I found my 50 year old self surrounded by real cows, not Roman statuettes of sheep. Cayrièch, the hamlet where my house, Pech Menal, was located had many fields of grazing cows–*les Salers,* the mahogany brown ones from a little further north, *les Aquitaines,* the creamy white ones, and an occasional black and white cow, a Holstein.

The white cows, *les Aquitaines,* were the most numerous around Cayrièch. *L'Aquitaine* was the old name for the part of France where my house was. The modern name for the old province was *le Midi-Pyrénées* region.

The breeds of cows were an illustration of the French concept of *terroir.* Over many generations, the *Aquitaine* breed had evolved to be best suited to the conditions that prevailed around Pech Menal in the former *Aquitaine.* Conversely, the type of grass and the climate of the region combined to make the *Aquitaines* thrive most easily there, yielding the most milk and the best quality of meat.

The French feel there exists a symbiotic relationship in which a certain kind of soil, an amount and type of rainfall or the lack of it, the angle of the sun, the exposure to wind, etc. develop a specific flavor or characteristic which is not able to be duplicated by growing conditions elsewhere. This gives rise to products perfectly suited to their environment. And it creates a tremendous diversity of varieties.

A shopping excursion to a French open air market makes an excellent case for the tastiness and variety of these home-grown products. The embarrassment of choice and freshness of the food sold in a French open air market showcase the success of this system which every Frenchman considers his birthright.

In addition, there is no comparison between the taste of an apricot picked off the tree an hour before you buy it and the apricot picked unripe and trucked or shipped to a far away store shelf.

The concept of *terroir* held true for wine, fruits and vegetables as well. The varieties of vegetables grown in the big vegetable garden across the dirt road from my house were the tastiest and best adapted to the growing conditions around Pech Menal. Certain varieties were successful there as nowhere else.

This *potager* garden was tended by my neighbors, an older, middle aged couple called Pierre and Clothilde Belon. Pierre was retired because he was no longer *valide,* i.e. he had some heart problems. He was still a tall, powerful looking man, although somewhat stooped over. His blue eyes snapped with good humor and intelligence. He had a ruddy complexion and a shiny bald head. He was often shod in those plaid slippers you could buy at the market.

Clothilde was nothing like the medieval damsel from the songs of the troubadours that I imagined from her name. She was a solidly built brunette. Her physique was well-adapted for hard work and her approach was no nonsense. She had been a full partner in the farm while raising three sons.

The Belons became my mainstay advisors as I navigated my way in my new environment. They never talked down to me, but they knew everything about Pech Menal and Cayrièch and I was pretty ignorant.

Where to buy wood for the Godin wood stove? "Call Monsieur Andurand."

Where to plant grape vines? "Noooo. Not there where you've chosen. They'll never survive there in the wind.

Over here, where it's sheltered. And here's the powder treatment you need to use on them."

Don't like the view of the new houses in the new housing development going up in the lotissement?

"Plant a screen of tall evergreens. No wait. We'll plant it for you."

The Belons introduced me to two very important facets of French country life: the *apéritif* hour and the village festival, *la fête du village.*

The *apéro* hour is an institution all over France. In private houses or on café *terrasses*, at around 6 p.m. or *18 heures* French time, people gather for a cocktail hour before dinner. Please note that one hour or one and a half hours is the *apéro* time limit. Then everyone repairs home for dinner, appetites sharpened.

Pretty much every day at 6 o'clock in the evening, *les Belon* and I would gather at their house or mine for a glass of *kir Suze.* Red wine and *Suze.* No *cassis.* It was their favorite cocktail.

Ordinarily, *kir* is red or white wine mixed with some *crème de cassis,* black currant liqueur. It is a very popular apéritif. There is no addition of *Suze* involved.

Suze is a herbal beverage made of gentian and other medicinal herbs which grow wild on the famous *garrigue,* the dry, scrubland in the mountains behind the Mediterranean coast in Provence. The liqueur is a bright greenish-yellow color and has a rather bitter taste that grows on you the more you sip. The sweet flavor of the red wine cuts the bitterness of the *Suze* a touch. *Suze* doesn't cost too much compared to *Lillet* or *Ricard,* other apéritif beverages, which is another advantage.

For a change of pace or for special occasions, my neighbors sometimes served me an *apéro* of *blanquette de Limoux,* which sparkled like champagne but was a pale substitute for the real thing.

I drank the *blanquette* but it was champagne I preferred. I liked its bright taste, its tiny bubbles and the idea it represented to me of a celebration or commemoration. I fondly remembered the first time I was sent a bottle of champagne by an admirer which happened when I was on my way to France to spend my junior year in college at the Sorbonne in Paris. My fellow college students and I were passengers on the ocean liner, *France*. She was the grand flagship of the French Line.

While my neighbors, the Belons, prepared to open a bottle of *blanquette* for *apéritif* hour, I was listening to their conversation with only one ear. A part of my mind was back on *le paquebot France* and I was 19 years old again. I was swept away by my memories.

"Fräulein Waldheim, Fräulein Waldheim!" the steward called out as he wandered in and around the tables in the ship's dining room. "Fräulein Waldheim, Fräulein Waldheim," he shouted. He had a bottle of wine resting on a white napkin under his arm as he went.

Oh my goodness, I realized with a start. That's me! "I think he's looking for me," I said to my tablemates. They were recent acquaintances. We were all from different American universities and colleges. We had met a few days ago when we boarded *le France*, the flagship of the French Line, in New York harbor headed for Le Havre and the start of our junior college year in France.

"It must be you," said my cabin mate, Mary, sitting next to me. "They're so international on this ship. They turned you into a German *mädchen* because of your last name."

I signaled to catch the steward's attention and he came over to our table. I blushed with excitement.

"Je m'appelle Mademoiselle Barbara Waldheim," I told him. "I am Miss Barbara Waldheim. Are you looking for me?"

"I have a bottle of champagne here for you, *Mademoiselle. Préférez-vous du champagne brut ou doux, s'il vous plaît?"*

I was momentarily at a loss. *Did I prefer my champagne dry or sweet? Hmmm, I hadn't really developed a preference one way or another.*

Rising to the occasion, I answered with authority, "Dry, please." I had heard somewhere that *brut* was more sophisticated than sweet.

"Of course," the steward said, presenting me with the card which accompanied the bottle. "Shall I serve the table?"

"Yes, please, I said, as I read the card. It said: *"Bon Voyage, All my love, Alex."*

Oh, the darling man! You are too much! I miss you too, I thought fervently to myself.

"It's from my boyfriend, Alex, back in Chicago. He's sent champagne to wish me a good trip," I announced to the table, blinking hard to keep from tearing up.

"Well, let's drink to good old Alex, whoever he may be," said Keith Van Dorn, one of the guys in our group. *"Santé! A vos amours!"* We clinked glasses all around the table.

Our group enjoyed dinner and was generally enjoying our five-day Atlantic crossing on *le paquebot France.* She was a beautiful ship. There was a full-size movie theater, a swimming pool, a library, and writing room among many elegant bars and lounges.

Our group of students were occupying some of the least expensive cabins way down near the waterline. But we did have a little porthole and we were also catered to day and night by a staff that was at our beck and call. If we needed the slightest little thing, needle and thread, midnight snack, we had only to ring for a steward.

Some of our group took excellent advantage of this service, making friends with the stewards in the process and practicing French too. I, however, couldn't really think of anything I needed.

I spent a lot of time in Mary and my tiny stateroom gazing at the bouquet of roses, which Alex had arranged to be delivered to the ship just before we sailed.

"Mary," I asked my roommate, "would you snap a photo of me in front of these flowers? I've put on my black party dress and I want to send Alex a picture of me holding the champagne bottle standing in front of the flowers he sent."

"Sure," Mary agreed. She took a snapshot with my 'Instamatic' camera. "But hurry and get out of that lacy dress. We have to get to class soon."

Mary was right. We had French class every day in one of the saloons—ship's saloons, not the western movie kind with the cowboys and swinging doors. We also had a safety drill where everyone reported to their station and put on a life jacket while the captain spoke to us over the intercom.

I don't know if the evacuation drill made me feel safer or less safe. As I looked out from the decks where I sometimes sat with a blanket in a deck chair, I was uneasy contemplating the endless expanse of deep blue water.

One day, I spotted dolphins leaping and frolicking in the lee of the great ship. They were certainly in their element. I was not in mine. When there was a bit of turbulence, many of us students quartered down in the bowels of the ship headed up to the reading room a couple of decks above to write a letter. I, for one, didn't like staying around to watch the waves smash against the glass in my cabin's little porthole.

On the final night of the voyage, I was invited up to first class for dinner by some friends of my parents who were by coincidence on the same crossing to Europe. The invitation meant that I would be able to enjoy a little time on higher and more lavish decks above those reserved for second class passengers like me. My parents' friends were an elderly couple, very elderly by my nineteen-year-old standards, and newlyweds. It was a second marriage late in their lives for both of them as their respective spouses had died. They were British and made a very cute couple, just like the figures of bride and groom on top of a wedding cake, but with gray hair.

I was excited to see the upper levels of the great ship. Some of my fellow students had snuck up into first class from the nether regions of second class where we were supposed to stay put. I don't know how they pulled that off. Helpful stewards? Keith Van Dorn might have just been idly boasting.

Wearing my black party dress, I met my parents' friends, the Prashkers, by the elevators where they had come down to collect me for dinner. We pressed the buttons to ascend to the higher decks and immediately got all confused as to which button meant what deck. Laughing and giggling together like school kids at our ineptitude, we agreed that this must be the reason the classes should stay firmly in their assigned places.

We finally 'got sorted', as the British say. The Prashkers were a lot of fun. They certainly didn't act their age. They led me to a bar which looked out over the stern of the ship. As we sipped our drinks, we watched the wake of the ocean liner float lazily away toward the horizon as the sun was setting.

I chatted happily with the Prashkers. I knew one of their granddaughters. They told me about their honeymoon plans. I felt comfortable with them.

Mrs. Prashker broached what she took to be a difficult subject, "Barbara, you must be so very sad with your parents sending you away and all."

"But true love will triumph in the end, my dear. You will see. You must be brave," said Mr. Prashker.

"What!" I said, "I don't exactly understand, Mr. Prashker. Do you think that I'm unhappy? Or being sent to France under duress?"

"No, no, my dear," Mrs. Prashker chimed in. "We just thought that you might be testing your relationship with young Alex back in Chicago before you got engaged. And rightly so, my dear. There is no hurry. No hurry."

"Yes, the path of true love is never smooth, and all that," Mr. Prashker added gruffly.

Oh ho! I got it. The Prashkers thought that I was being shipped off to France for a year to forget my unsuitable lover. How Victorian! They were so cute!

I set them right immediately. "Mr. and Mrs. Prashker, Norbert, Rose, if I may call you that. I think you may have gotten the wrong impression. I am delighted to be going to spend my junior year in France. It was entirely my decision. I will miss Alex. I already miss him. But I want to go on this program. I couldn't possibly pass up this opportunity to live and study abroad for a year...and receive college credit for it. I am over the moon about the whole thing and very excited."

"Well, that's fine, just fine then," said the Prashkers almost in unison, smiling back at me.

"And on that note," said Norbert, "let's go and have some dinner. Aren't you hungry? I am."

We arrived at the first-class dining room and descended a long, curved staircase. It made for a grand entrance indeed. I had read that the artist Salvador Dali used to love descending this staircase to the dining room with everyone's eyes upon him. We were shown to our seats as we passed by a serving table surmounted by a mountain of black Beluga caviar. Well, maybe not exactly a mountain, but a big hill of caviar.

I was so lost in long ago memories that I could almost taste the salty delicacy when my Cayrièch neighbor, Clothilde Belon, pushed a bowl of potato *sheeps*, as she pronounced them, under my nose.

"Barbara, help yourself to some potato chips. It's better to eat a little something with your *apéro* or you'll get tipsy."

Two Cows Against the Fence in Cayrièch

CHAPTER 5

The Village Festival Committee and la Fête du Village

At one of our many *apéro* hours, Pierre Belon, Clothile's husband and my neighbor across the lane, announced that I must absolutely join the festival committee. He and his wife, Clothilde, were members. We would meet in the Cayrièch town hall, the *mairie* in the village, and plan the summer party to take place in two month's time in June, near the date of the summer solstice.

It was called the Feast of Saint Jean, as it had been since the church took over from the Druids probably. There would be an outdoor meal organized for the whole village and guests. Dancing would follow and a big bonfire would be set ablaze after the sun went down.

It sounded like a lot of work and it was. First we met to strategize the arrangements and the menu. As you can imagine, I listened and observed rather than contributing. The committee chairwoman was called Isabelle, an attractive young woman who ran an equipment rental company with her handsome husband. Everybody pretty much deferred to her as chairman. Her big innovation for this year was the outlay for a tent, *un chapiteau,* to cover the tables and dance floor.

A committee member called Karine was strong willed and not

always in accord with the general consensus. Karine was on her own raising a very young son, *le petit René,* who was often wandering around during the meetings. She worked in town at the *Bricomarché* hardware store where I often saw her when I shopped there to buy things I lacked at Pech Menal.

I also met Suzy and her husband, Patrick. He worked for the town of Cayrièch as gardener and groundskeeper. It was partly due to his hard work that Cayrièch was awarded first prize in the most beautiful European village contest, France division for 2003.

Suzy, his wife, a pretty, perky blonde, had a job delivering meals on wheels to the aged and infirm around the district. She drove many miles each week covering the *secteur.* It was a second marriage for both and clearly high-spirited Suzy was stolid Patrick's *raison d'être.* They loved to dance. Or at least Suzy did.

I also met many others on the committee, or rather they met me. It was pretty hard as a newcomer to keep everyone straight while they had all known one another for years. Everyone was quite welcoming. The committee strategized and planned over the coming months.

Before long, the big day of the *fête* dawned very hot and dry. About one hundred tickets had been sold at 100 *francs* (about U.S. $18) apiece, a great value for a four course meal served with unlimited wine. Before dinner, *kir* and beer would be available at the bar kiosk for a small fee. Many guests brought their own cutlery so as not to have to use plastic, and places at the big tables were staked out early so families and big groups could sit together.

There was a lot to prepare for on the day of the evening party. And so to work. In the morning, a group of us women prepared 100 paper plates each with their bit of *pâté,* three pieces of various cold cuts, *charcuterie,* a *cornichon* pickle and a wrapped butter pat.

The next big job was to prepare the Quercy melons, the official ones. No bogus melons from Spain, the other side of the border. The melons from Quercy are famous for their sweetness and their velvety texture. A true *melon du Quercy* comes with a sticker on it that guarantees its origin.

A *melon du Quercy* is a smaller, rounder cantaloupe and especially delicious, if you get a really good one. The selection of melons was a science and art form practiced at the many roadside fruit stands near Cayrièch on the way to tiny Belfort du Quercy, the melon growing capital.

Woe to the fruit seller who tried to pass off melons from Spain as *melons du Quercy!* Only the special conditions of climate and soil around, or more specifically in, the fields of Belfort, could create the necessary conditions for growing Quercy melons. Another example of *le terroir.*

We halved the melons and cleaned them out, ready to be filled with *Porto,* or sweet port wine, just before serving time. As our small distaff group labored away under the hot sun cutting the melons and chatting, other committee members were setting up the tables in the field under the canopy which Isabelle, the committee chairwoman, had ordered. The melons had to keep until 8 p.m., *20h,* and a refrigerated truck was at hand to cool our handiwork down until then. The truck's shadow provided some much needed shade in which we sheltered while we worked.

The village festival tickets were sold out. The main course was *poulet à la basquaise,* chicken Basque style. A specialist was brought in, a *traiteur,* who set up an enormous cauldron which simmered away during the afternoon before the party. Last year there was a *paëlla géante.* The main course offering changed every year. The villages competed with one another to attract diners. People studied the menu and the price to see if they wanted to attend. There was always a crowd.

Some towns hosted an *escargolade,* all the snails you could eat. Or there was the *mouclade,* non-stop mussels. A recent variation was called *les moules à la paille* where hundreds of raw mussel shells were laid out on long tables covered with straw. The straw was then set ablaze. The mussels cooked quickly. The fire was doused with water from a hose. *"Ta da!"* Mussels for a hundred diners were now ready to serve at the end of the fiery spectacle.

The whole enterprise was brought off seamlessly from prep,

to serving, to clean up. Of course the committees had had years of practice. And this was the same for all the surrounding villages because every single one hosted their own *fête,* or several *fêtes,* a year. All powered by volunteer effort and organization.

In the slightly larger towns, it was the merchants—baker, florist, hairdressers, dress shop and hardware store owners, *garagistes*—who were on the festival committee. They set up the *fête,* manned the bar, served and cleaned up, etc. This was deemed to be a kind of *thank you* from the shopkeepers to the townspeople for providing them with a livelihood.

After my stint with the melons and plates of *charcuterie,* I had time for a long *sieste* back at Pech Menal before the start of the festivities. Suzy, the cute, perky blonde, was going to come over to get me at 6 p.m., *apéro* time, so we could go to the party together.

She arrived at the farmhouse as arranged to walk together over to the field where the festival tent was standing. She brought me our official festival committee tee shirt which I somewhat reluctantly put over the pretty black linen dress I had bought in Toulouse for the occasion. The powder blue tee shirt was cute. It had a cartoon figure on it and a saying written below which said in French:

"You don't have to be stupid to work here, but it helps." *Comité des Fêtes de Cayrièch.*

We also put on our official straw boater hats decorated with a powder blue ribbon which said, 'Festival Committee.' Straw boater hats had been made in the nearby village of Septfonds since the 18th century, so they were emblematic of our locale.

It was a beautiful evening for the party—quite hot under the canopy, but it was summer after all. The bar did a brisk business. I met Patricia, a statuesque, light skinned, black neighbor, wife of a man she called *le père,* father of her adolescent son with mischievous eyes. There were also Christiane and her husband. They raised ducks. I had enjoyed eating one of their production recently at the Belons. Jacky Legrand was there. He owned the corn field that adjoined Pech Menal on one side. He was divorced or separated and looked flirtatiously around the company.

A sophisticated family group from Toulouse were also in attendance. They had a summer house down the road with a nice *pigeonnier*. A pigeon cote was very desirable, not any longer for the pigeon guano fertilizer it used to provide, but because it was so interesting to look at. *Pigeonniers* came in many shapes and sizes. Some were separate, angular buildings. Some were round and set up on pillars. Some were built into your attic. In olden times you had to receive permission to build one on your property. This meant you were more prosperous than some of your neighbors and probably had a nicer farmhouse.

The *poulet à la basquaise* and the whole meal were delicious. We started with the melons filled with sweet *Porto* wine. Next came the plates of *charcuterie*. The serving of the plates was efficiently done. There were piles of *baguette* slices on each table. Few Frenchmen can imagine a meal without a piece of bread beside their plate. Red and rosé wine bottles were spaced out at intervals on the paper tablecloths—the local *vin des Côteaux du Quercy* of course. The local wine now had achieved a special category because it had recently won a coveted *appellation* from the *société du Tastevin* bigwigs in Burgundy.

The drawing for the *tombola* was won by my neighbors, the Belons! It was a beautiful gift basket of local food specialities. Clothilde was very pleased although she tried not to gloat. "*Félicitations!* Congratulations," I called over to her at her table. The Belons were sitting with family members. I was at a table with other members of the festival committee.

I enjoyed the chicken stew, Basque style, with mushrooms and red peppers. Next came the cheese course, a small package of *Brie* for each individual. And finally dessert was handed around—apple tart. Nothing too fancy, but very tasty. Very tasty indeed. A feast.

And on to the dancing. There was a live band which played old standards of many eras, including my own. When the band played a Beach Boys tune, 'California Girls,' I felt really homesick and I wasn't even from California! I had *le cafard*, as they say in French, which also means cockroach.

Someone came over to my table. "Would you care to dance?" the man said. He was medium height, sun tanned and gave me a big smile. It was Jacky Legrand.

"Oh yes," I said. "I'd like to dance. I know you. I've seen you around."

"Probably on my tractor. I own the field right next to Pech Menal."

"That's right. That's what I heard," I replied as the music struck up a sort of foxtrot and I got up to dance with Jacky.

We moved around the wooden dance floor trying to get the hang of the rhythm. As we passed a table of Jacky Legrand's friends, they whistled and catcalled. I blushed and M. Legrand did an idiotic little caper.

We couldn't overcome the awkwardness of the situation. Jacky Legrand had been brave to ask the *américaine* to dance, but he was at a loss to know how to continue. What was a farmer from Cayrièch to talk about with this foreign woman? She didn't even know the dance steps of the line dances that were so popular locally.

The song mercifully ended. We clapped. I said, "Thank you for the dance." Jacky deposited me back at my place at the table.

Shortly afterwards, the traditional bonfire of Saint Jean was lit. It marked the end of the evening. I slipped off to Pech Menal, a short walk from the meadow where the party tent stood. I could see the glowing sparks from the bonfire flying up into the dark sky as I made my way home along the dirt road.

I was tired and reflective. It had been a long, busy day including all the serving and cleaning up. The heat had been enervating. I had allowed myself to overblow the importance of the party. After all, I wasn't really a part of this little farming community. It had been interesting to participate on the festival committee, but I didn't really fit in. Nor did I really wish to do so.

How did I see myself, as the wife or girlfriend of a country farmer like Jacky Legrand? He was no doubt a hardworking, upstanding man in his way, but his world was tightly circumscribed by this little backwater—beautiful though it was.

I put myself to bed wondering about my future.

What I was doing rehabbing and perfecting this old farmhouse of mine so far away from home?

It was an adventure, that was for sure, but what was my motivation?

Was I preparing Pech Menal to be the background setting of my new life while I figured out just what that might be?

At a safe remove from my accustomed routine and familiar entourage back home in the United States was I experimenting with new approaches to life?

Was the house a sort of make-work activity which was actually a self-improvement project?

Was this really an effort to rebuild my confidence and refurbish my depleted spirit?

I yawned. *Enough introspection for now. Tomorrow is another day,* I reflected, not unhappily, but pensively.

A Doorway and Plane Trees in Caussade

CHAPTER 6

The Stranger With an Ascot

One fine day I was outside watering the new plantings along the fence when a mysterious stranger sauntered along the dirt track by the side of Pech Menal. He was wearing a straw fedora tilted at a jaunty angle and a silk paisley ascot.

An ascot in Cayrièch!

He tipped his hat to me as he passed by. I barely acknowledged his salute since I was busy hauling on the hose in my grubby clothes while Momo, my new garden helper, was making holes in it with an ice pick tool. We were installing a homemade automatic sprinkling system around the property of Pech Menal. The scheme was Momo's brainchild.

The *canicule* was in full force. It was a heatwave, just as beautiful Mme Lemoine had predicted that already hot day when I ran into her at the café in Montpezat.

All my new plantings were in danger of expiring if I couldn't water them regularly. Up to now I had been hauling the hose around so much that I felt like '*Jean de la Florette.*'

You know that famous movie where Gérard Depardieu and fellow movie star, Daniel Auteuil, are fighting to the death over water rights in the wild backcountry of Provence?

I also loved those elemental Jean Giono novels and the movies made from them where a few drops of water can mean the difference between life and death. And a woman is an equally rare and precious commodity, not that you treat her as such.

However in real life, the struggle between me and nature to keep my new hedge or *haie* alive was not so picturesque.

The south of France was experiencing a tremendously hot summer. Old people were dying alone in their houses from dehydration. Those in nursing homes were at risk. Air conditioning was almost non-existent because it had never really been necessary in prior years. The leaves of the trees were falling prematurely. The local fruit crops were in danger. Water use was rationed.

Some days I was pinned down in Pech Menal by the extreme heat. I holed up in a corner on the lower level and tried not to move too much. The heat was that intense. It wore on me. It wore me out.

My morale hit a low point. To my dismay, all the landscape plantings I had installed by M. Clamens, the owner of the *pépinière,* the plant nursery, hardly changed the look of the grounds. I had a bunch of baby plantings which would need to fill in over time.

Monsieur Clamens stressed one very important principle to me—watering. I would have to keep the plants well watered to get them established. Otherwise all this trouble and expense would come to nothing. My new olive tree, the flowering hedge, *la haie,* the parasol pine, the mulberry tree, the Italian cypress, the lavenders, the wisteria, *la glycine,* the bower of *charmilles* –they were all at risk.

I listened to the *météo* report for a forecast of rain. Nothing. I attached a length of hose I had bought to the tap at the bottom of Pech Menal's stone staircase and got some buckets. I went to work. I felt very, very alone in the wilderness of densely populated, intensively cultivated *douce France.*

Where was the sweet, soft, green countryside of the popular

songs? I felt like throwing in the towel or at least the watering can. I felt crushed by the weight of my responsibilities.

And then Momo offered to help me out. I had first met him through Mme Lemoine, the real estate agent. I needed to reupholster some of my *brocante* furniture finds. Mme Lemoine had a neighbor down the road in Caussade who did reupholstering in his spare time. Her neighbor was Momo.

Like most of the Moroccans I encountered in France, he was the warmest, most hospitable guy I ever met. His whole family adopted me. It was embarrassing. I really never knew how to reciprocate all the kindness they sent my way over endless glasses of mint tea poured out by Momo's wife on the recently completed patio at their house in Caussade.

Momo worked for a company down the highway that made airplane seats, which is how he knew the way to upholster club chairs, armchairs, sofas, you name it.

True, my redone club chairs were incredibly bouncy when he finished with them, but it made a nice contrast to how you used to fall into them like a sinking ship. True, a friend of his refinished away the valuable and irreplaceable patina of the *Louis XV d'époque* armchair which I had finally pried away from M. Lebars, the antique dealer in Montauban.

Momo had meant well. He preferred the new looking finish and he was sure I would too. In a couple hundred years, the patina of age would return.

Momo had a brother, Nasser, back in Morocco, who was coming to visit. Nasser was a teacher. It was his summer vacation. Nasser was an integral part of our plan to create a watering system for me, the *goûte à goûte*. *Goûte à goûte* literally meant drop by drop and everybody coveted such an automatic watering system that hot, dry summer.

Momo's plan for installing a homemade watering system at Pech Menal would save me hours of back breaking work.

Why didn't I just buy one and get it professionally installed like Jerry and Barbara, the Canadians, or like my friends, Charles and Eloise in St. Antonin, another town?

One reason was the expense. I had already spent so much money on the plantings. And then, I was caught up in Momo's enthusiasm. Once events got rolling, they were out of my control. Momo was like that.

First we had to clean the well and Nasser was willing to take on this dirty, dangerous job no Frenchman wanted to do. If we could get water flowing into the old well in sufficient quantities, I wouldn't be dependent on the municipal water supply.

There would be big monetary savings since as my neighbor, Pierre Belon said, "water from the town costs as much as the eyes out of your head. *L'eau de la ville coûte les yeux de la tête.* Imagine," Pierre pointed out, "you can get the well water tested and if it is potable, you'll never have to pay for city water again!"

I had never been particularly economical, but I was carried away by this reasoning. *Maybe this was a new, more fiscally sound 'me'.*

The first step was to pump out the water remaining at the well bottom. We borrowed a pump from the Belons for this purpose. Then Nasser went down the well with Momo supervising from the top. The descent was dangerous. We held our collective breath as Nasser descended to the bottom.

He reported that there were five little streamlets coming into the well. This seemed like an excellent sign. Five little water sources should provide some good water flow. A pick ax was handed down to him by Yuniz, a nephew, who was also helping with the project. Nasser used the ax to try to loosen the stones and increase the water flow from the little rivulets. Then came the dicey process of hauling him up out from the depths of the well.

When Momo pulled Nasser up over the edge and he stood on the stone edge again, we were all four exultant. He did it! It was a *Rocky Balboa* moment. Nasser posed arms raised in triumph like a winning boxer up on the well rim with a bright sun in the background. I snapped a photo.

The next step in Momo's plan for the irrigation system was to hook up lengths of plastic pipes to the water in the well and make holes all along the pipe with an ice pick. As we were working on that again the next day, the elegantly turned out gentleman came by the fence again. He was taking his morning constitutional. This time he leaned over the fence posts and inspected our efforts.

He said, "I do that kind of thing myself with the natives back in *la Guyane Française* where I live."

I gave him a tight smile. I wasn't exactly sure what he meant, but it didn't sound very complimentary to any of us.

"*Au revoir. Bonne journée.* Good bye. Have a nice day," and he continued on his way.

That evening, showered and dressed nicely after my yard work with Momo, I headed across the road for the *apéro* hour over at the Belons. As I rounded the corner of the big barn, I spied Pierre Belon and the stranger from this morning seated under the shade of the mulberry tree in the yard.

Clothilde was passing some glasses of *kir Suze* out the open top of the Dutch door of her kitchen. I loved how French houses had windows and doors that opened up directly to the out of doors without screens.

"*Ah, la voilà.* There she is," said Pierre. "Barbara, I'd like you to meet Jérôme Guchens, Clothilde's older brother."

"*Enchantée,*" I said and he responded, "*enchanté*" in return.

Clothilde joined us at the table underneath the tree. The siblings were quite different in looks and style. Clothilde was a nice enough looking woman, but a bit blowsy in her pinafore style flowered apron. She didn't take great pains with her appearance.

Her brother, Jérôme, on the other hand, struck me as somewhat of a dandy. He was thin and *soigné*. He wore a black eye patch over his left eye which, on him, reminded me more of the man in the 'Hathaway' shirt advertisement than of a pirate.

The *apéro* was pleasant as usual. I learned that Jérôme was on his annual visit to *la métropole*, mainland France, from his home in French Guiana where he was an engineer.

The Belons explained to me that they were going to take Jérôme on a little excursion up north of us to see the *Pont de Millau,* the new bridge on the *autoroute* which was being built over the formerly unbridgeable gorge up there. It was an engineering marvel which would soon open to highway traffic. The bridge was designed by the famous British architect, Norman Foster, and was somewhat of a tourist attraction. They invited me to join them on the outing and make it a foursome.

Why not, I thought. So I accepted the invitation.

On the weekend, we set off. Pierre drove. Clothilde was the navigator. Jérôme and I sat in the back seat for the two hour trip, not counting our stops at the overlook in Villefranche de Rouergue to study the town from the high vantage point of a roadside pull-off or our visit to the caves at Roquefort to buy some cheese. They called my attention to the town of Rieupeyroux which we passed through. I tried to pronounce it but failed as we all laughed.

The *Pont de Millau* was interesting enough to look at from below where there was a viewing platform set up. To my eyes, it resembled the Tampa Bay Bridge in Florida. In other words, I didn't find it especially spectacular.

The four of us were hungry after a very busy morning. Pierre steered us to a restaurant he knew where we had delicious steaks which came from the *Salers* cattle native to the *Cantal* region where we were.

At lunch I got to talking with Jérôme. I had never met anyone from French Guiana or ever given it much thought aside from 'Papillon,' the hair-raising story of the convict who escapes from *le bagne,* the French prison camp where criminals used to be exiled as punishment. The book was made into a hit movie with Steve McQueen.

Jérôme filled me in. He lived in the capital of the country, Cayenne. Cayenne peppers had originated there, but were now grown in India and other places in the world. Guiana was still part of France. It had never become independent.

"Doesn't it seem kind of isolated there on the top of South America?" I asked Jérôme.

"Yes, it's a pretty simple life. Very tropical. Foreign goods are expensive. There is some native culture. My wife is from Guiana so my son is *métis,* mixed race. Cayenne is a modern city. The closest international city is Miami so we keep up with American movies and TV."

Jérôme turned out to be a good conversationalist and clever. Or at least he thought I was clever. I was a little tipsy from the wine at lunch and I made a joke, a *jeu de mots* in French. Pierre, Clothilde and Jérôme all found it quite amusing. Encouraged by their acceptance and warmed by the wine, I was quite the life of the luncheon party. Jérôme pronounced me *charmante,* charming, pretty—a very complimentary term.

On the drive home, together in the back seat, Jérôme dozed off. The Belons said that I did too, but I denied it.

Clothilde's brother was visiting France for a month. Before his departure, he would head to Paris to visit his son, an engineering student. Until then, in the coming days, I saw quite a lot of him. He invited me on an excursion to Villefranche de Rouergue, just the two of us. We toured the town where he and Clothilde had been born. He took me to visit the Chapel of the Black Penitents which had beautiful decorations inside for such an ascetic order of monks. When they weren't flagellating themselves, they enjoyed nice surroundings.

We had a lovely lunch under the arcades of the old town. It was fun being escorted by a gallant older man. Jérôme made me feel very feminine.

We walked back to the car, crossing an old bridge over the river. He told me that he could still envision his sister and brother-in-law, Clothilde and Pierre, standing on the old bridge posing for a photo on their wedding day.

"They were both as skinny as two sticks in those days," he reminisced, holding up a finger.

I asked about his eyepatch and Jérôme explained that his

eyesight was a grave concern. He was afflicted with an incurable condition and would soon be legally blind. That was why he had asked me to drive us to Villefranche and back and I had agreed to do so. We were in my car and I was at the wheel. For a special treat, he asked me if he could take over driving for a little while on the back roads up there around Villefranche. He said he knew them like the back of his hand from his youth. And indeed, he steered the car confidently along the little roads. The sun was shining. The verges of the road were covered with wildflowers. We were the only car on the road.

I took over the wheel again and we returned to Cayrièch via Caylus, a town built on an incredibly steep hill, which came before Septfonds and then home. I stopped my car at the Belon's gate to let Jerome off when he asked,

"Barbara, do you have a moment to stop in? I'd like to show you some things I keep here at my sister's. They're stored in the outbuilding, *la dépendance.*"

"Of course," I answered. "What kind of things?"

"Oh, you know, I keep some old bits and pieces here. Things I don't really need in Guiana, but don't want to throw away."

I parked in the Belons' drive and we went into the house. After a brief word with Pierre and Clothilde, we excused ourselves and I followed Jérôme around to a barn-like annex to the house. He opened the big door. The interior was very dark and very warm since the day had been a hot one as usual. I hesitated a moment trying to see inside. We went in.

"Let me show you," he said, as he opened up a big metal *armoire* that I could barely make out leaning against a wall. The sultry heat suffused me in the dusky darkness. I was aware of Jérôme watching me although I could barely make out his form. He squatted down to reach for something at the bottom of the chest. I squatted too. As I did so, I was embarrassed to note a ripe, female smell emanating from under my skirt. *Did Jérôme notice? Was I imagining it?*

The enclosed atmosphere was like a hothouse. It was very quiet. *Why didn't he turn on a light?*

Jérôme spoke and broke the intensity. "Here it is," he said, straightening up. In his hand was a white object that glowed in the penumbra.

"This shawl belonged to my mother. I'd like you to have it."

He put a crocheted, fringed triangle into my hands. It felt uncomfortably wooly to the touch in the heat.

"Oh, Jerome, that's nice, but I couldn't accept it."

"Please, he said, I'd really like you to have it." So after some going back and forth, at his urging, I took the shawl and we went back to the main house.

Why do I feel that I escaped a fall from a precipice in that barn? There was a sort of feral atmosphere. Was it a test of some kind?

Shortly before Jérôme's scheduled departure for Paris and then Cayenne, he invited me out to a valedictory dinner, just the two of us. Of course, due to his eye condition, I drove us to the restaurant, '*Les Couleurs du Mexique*,' a new place in the old *gare de Montpezat*.

The old train station used to serve Montpezat de Quercy and other nearby towns before train service had been drastically reduced after the war. It was now repurposed as a hotel-restaurant. The station was not located right in Montpezat but out in the countryside of small vineyards and sunflower fields about ten kilometers out of town.

It was a beautiful drive to get there. We passed the teeny little town of La Penche, home of the '*Petit Bal Perdu*' where somewhere out in the fields there was a dance which gathered hundreds of people on Saturday nights from spring into fall. Suzy and Patrick, the dancing couple from Cayrièch, were faithful attendees.

We drove up to higher ground passing over the *autoroute* toward the melon growing capital, Belfort du Quercy. We continued along the beautiful valley near the town of Puylaroque. One of the Belons' sons, Jerôme's nephew, worked at the winery there for their friends, *les Camma*, the Camma family. The vines ran up the hill toward the house. Here and there, a rose bush bloomed at the end of a row of vines. I commented to my companion about it:

"Isn't it pretty to have planted a rose bush like that in the grapevines?"

Jérôme smiled and said, "It is pretty and useful too. The farmer hopes the rose bush will attract the insects away from his vines. It's an old method which doesn't require insecticide."

"Very ecological," I said. *"Très écolo."*

We talked easily together as we rode on in the beautiful summer evening, the heat of the day abating a little as the evening advanced toward our 8pm dinner reservation.

At the *'Couleurs du Mexique'* Restaurant, there was a round wool tent set up in the yard. It was a yurt, typical housing on the plains of Uzbekistan. I'd never seen one and the restaurant owners said we could take a look at it before dinner.

Later on in my life, I stayed in one and had the best sleep ever. It was like being rolled in cotton wool. Sounds were muffled. The outside world seemed far away from the softness of the protective white walls all around. Aside from a couple of poles holding up the white dome roof not very high above your head, the space was open. You could orient yourself however you liked. There were no sharp corners which delineated the space. It was kind of like floating. On the vast tundra of Uzbekistan, the Uzbeks arranged a stove for cooking and heating in the middle of the space which vented out the top.

Practically speaking, you had to find the flap door and leave the yurt in case you needed to pee in the middle of the night. At the *'Couleurs du Mexique'* it cost extra to spend a night in the yurt rather than in a room inside the hotel.

The *'Couleurs du Mexique'* menu was nothing like any Mexican place back in the States. Or in Mexico for that matter. There were no chips and salsa. French bread accompanied the not very spicy food. In general the French don't like hot spices. Sangria was on offer in addition to wine. I ordered their version of *enchiladas suizas* from the chalkboard menu. Jérôme followed suit. They turned out to be a pale rendition of the real thing.

The place was cute. It still looked a bit like the train station waiting room it had once been, but the orange painted walls were hung with some serapes and sombreros.

I asked Jérôme about his son, the one in Paris. "He's a good student," he told me proudly. "His engineering program is challenging. I'm looking forward to visiting him. I know a good, economical hotel near the Gare St. Lazare. I'll give you the name."

"How did you end up living in French Guiana?"

"France Telecom transferred me there after my stints in Southeast Asia. I spent several years in Vietnam and Cambodia. I got married to a woman from Cayenne. I've been there ever since. In fact, I'm about to retire."

"That's right. Your wife is a native Guinean. Your sister, Clothilde, told me she can't be prejudiced because her nephew is half black."

Jérôme nodded. "Correct. There is some tension between the native population and the French. Some people feel that France does not do enough to develop the country. The government is only interested in the French space station, which is in the city of Kourou. The European Space Agency also uses this facility."

Back in the car after dinner, I slid behind the steering wheel of my Citroën station wagon. Jérôme got in on the passenger side.

Dinner hadn't been a big success. We had been the only customers at the restaurant. The cuisine was forgettable, neither here nor there.

"Merci, Jérôme," I said. "Thanks for dinner."

In answer, without warning, Jérôme lunged for me. Sliding over the bench seat toward me, he stuck his tongue in my mouth and put his hand up my skirt. I was thunderstruck. *Where did that come from?* I felt his hot hand on my nether parts. It wasn't completely unpleasant but I couldn't really respond to such a maladroit attack.

"Stop, Jérôme, what are you doing?" I cried as I pushed him away.

"*Ooh là, ma chérie,*" he leered. "I told Pierre and Clothilde not to expect me home tonight."

No way, Jose, I thought, keeping the Mexican theme going. I was flustered in spite of myself.

"Well Jérôme, you are mistaken if you planned on spending the night with me."

We drove back to Cayrièch in uncomfortable silence and I let him off at the Belons' gate.

'*Ouf, quel embarras!*' Luckily he would soon be off to Paris.

Passersby in the Street

CHAPTER 7

A Paris Getaway

Jérôme left for Paris and then home. I decided that I wanted a change of scene myself. I needed a hiatus from my country life and the rehabbing of Pech Menal so I too headed to Paris on the overnight train from Montauban to the Gare de Montparnasse. I had a good place to stay lined up with my friend, Micheline Dubosc.

Micheline ran a *chambre d'hôtes,* renting out the guest room in her Paris apartment and providing breakfast too, along with as much advice about what to see and do in the French capital as you could absorb. She would also provide dinner for a fee, given sufficient advance notice. These were the duties of a *chambre d'hôtes* proprietress and Micheline took them seriously. We had met on one of my former stays in Paris. I started out as a client and as time went on, we became friends.

Her apartment was on the top floor of a newer high rise building in the Belleville section of Paris, which is a *quartier populaire.* This doesn't mean popular, but rather "of the people" or not too fancy. Belleville had always been a melting pot *arrondissement* even back when Edith Piaf lived there.

Now many of the immigrants were newly arrived Africans or

Chinese. It was a bustling crossroads of crowded sidewalks and double parked cars. Colorfully garbed black African women sold roasted corn cobs at the metro entrance. Chinese merchants offloaded crates of vegetables, stacking them high on the crowded curbs in front of their shops. They often spit into the gutter, which offended Mme Dubosc's sensibility.

Micheline was fighting a personal campaign to correct this uncivil behavior. She would accost the miscreant pointing with her cane at the offending discharge.

"Monsieur, s'il vous plaît. C'est inadmissible! En France, nous ne crachons pas dans la rue. We don't spit in the street here."

The reaction was usually an uncomprehending stare.

Madame Dubosc lived in a gated complex in the midst of all this hubbub. It was named after Gabrielle d'Estrée who was a mistress and advisor of King Henri IV, a sixteenth century monarch and one of France's greatest kings. Although the street name lent a romantic gloss to the enclave, in reality, it was a pretty ordinary, though well-kept, apartment development.

My friend's apartment was on the top floor of the first building and had a big terrace with a great view over eastern Paris. The guest bedroom with its *en suite* bathroom was small but comfortable. When the mechanical and metal shutter on the window was lowered at night, I felt somewhere between cozy and entombed. Closing the shutters at night time was a custom all over France. The tightly closed shutters effectively shut out all the light and noise from the street. They also kept in the heat and acted as a security system.

Micheline Dubosc herself was an older woman with a fringe of frizzled bangs on her high forehead that gave her an old-fashioned air. Her choice of tailored clothes, her very upright posture, the cane she carried, plus her no-nonsense demeanor, all lent her an air of dignity and authority. Micheline had worked in an administrative position at *Radio-France* for many years before marrying her husband, Paul, late in life.

Upon her retirement, she and Paul had moved from Paris to Draguignan in the beautiful Maures mountains area of Provence, in the south of France. There she had opened her first bed and breakfast under the auspices of an organization called *'les Fleurs du Soleil'* in which she was still very active as a director. Although her bed and breakfast was no longer housed in a provençal *mas* or old farmhouse, but rather in an apartment building in the northern city of Paris, she was still a part of the 'Sunflowers' group. In fact, that is how I had originally found her. I saw a brochure for *les Fleurs du Soleil* and I was intrigued to find one blooming in Paris.

Micheline had no children. Paul had two grown children from his first marriage which had ended in divorce. Micheline had such a strong personality that she overshadowed Paul completely. Her husband was a very gentle presence, always in the background. Micheline thrived on action. Her activity as a *chambre d'hôtes* hostess kept her busy with housekeeping and paperwork chores. It also enabled her to expand her acquaintanceship and share her extensive knowledge of local points of interest. In other words, she had plenty of people to talk to, to advise, and to boss around.

It did not surprise me to learn that she had gotten bored with the laid back lifestyle in the sunny climate of Provence. After giving it a try, Micheline and Paul had moved back home, north to Paris, where Micheline had the constant stimulation of concerts, theater and museum blockbuster shows. Paul probably would have been happy enough anywhere.

Once ensconced as usual at the Dubosc's, I wandered around Paris going to museums and window shopping. I knew the city rather well from my time there as a student. I revisited favorite haunts like my old school, Reid Hall, center of the American college programs in Paris.

I got to know places new to me like the Musée Guimet and its wonderful collection of objects from France's former colonies in southeast Asia. There were so many places of interest to discover. Sometimes I was excited to visit the recent renovation of an old gem, brought up to date, *le dernier cri.* The city was always renewing itself.

From time to time, Micheline, my *chambre d'hôtes* hostess, and I went to an art exhibition or a musical performance together. She kept up with restaurants and exhibitions worth a visit. I enjoyed her company occasionally, but I also enjoyed being on my own.

Although busy during the day, most evenings, I had no plans at all. I could watch 'Secrets of History' on television with Micheline and Paul. This was one of our favorite shows. Stéphane Bern, an unlikely looking, string bean of a host with a reedy voice, would take his TV audience to a European locale steeped in history. The camera showed the viewers wonderful footage of the setting for a little known or 'secret' historical event while Stéphane Bern explained all about it. His cameras often had access to places not usually open to the public.

No Stéphane Bern. Not tonight, I thought to myself, on the third day of my visit. *I'll go out somewhere. I'll make my own secret story.*

The next morning, I bought the little booklet, '*La Semaine de Paris*', at a corner kiosk. '*La Semaine de Paris*' gave a comprehensive rundown of everything going on in the city each week from Wednesday to Wednesday. I found a listing for a play taking place that evening at a little theater just off the Champs Elysées. I didn't know the theater, but the play sounded light-hearted and it wasn't too expensive. I decided to go. I called ahead and reserved a ticket for myself. Micheline could stay home alone with our favorite television host for once.

I spent the afternoon before the play in one of my favorite Parisian pursuits, browsing for bargain clothes on the shelves and racks of the '*Monoprix,*' the cut rate department store near Micheline's apartment. The clothes from the *Monoprix* had that unmistakable French flair without the corresponding high price tag. I never found such creative fabrics and feminine cuts back home in Florida. It was fun to play dress up *à la française* without breaking the bank.

In the evening, arrayed in one of my new outfits, a celery green boiled wool skirt and matching jacket, I took the métro to the Franklin Roosevelt stop on the Rond Point of the Champs Elysées and walked to the theater. The theater was a little jewel box on the second floor of a *pierre de taille* building, constructed of well-chiseled blocks of white stone. The performance was quite enjoyable. It was several one act plays loosely strung together. There were about forty people in the audience. Most of the seats were occupied. At intermission, I noticed a man across the aisle from me. We smiled at one another. The performance ended. The actors took their bows and we applauded warmly. I gathered up my new jacket and my purse.

As I was making my way out of the theater, the man from across the aisle caught up with me. He said *"bonsoir"* and asked me in French how I had liked the show.

"Oh, I enjoyed it," I said truthfully. "What did you think? *Qu'est-ce que vous en avez pensé?"*

One thing led to another. He introduced himself.

"Je me présente. Je m'appelle Avi."

"Enchantée," I responded. *"Et moi, Barbara."*

"Barbara, I am visiting Paris alone. Would you care to accompany me tomorrow to the city hall, *l'Hôtel de Ville*? There's a special exhibition there about the actor and singer, Yves Montand."

"Avec plaisir," I accepted his invitation. We arranged to meet the next day at the entrance to *l'Hôtel de Ville* at 11 a.m.

Amazed as always at how one chance encounter could lift one's spirits and dissipate the loneliness of the big city, I floated back to the *Allées de Gabrielle d'Estrée* in a happy, anticipatory mood.

I was also a little taken aback at my temerity. I had agreed to meet a stranger on the basis of the fact that we had both enjoyed the same play! Well, that was Paris' reputation—city of romance and naughty assignations—*le cancan, les cocottes* courtesans, the naughty night clubs, le Moulin Rouge and le Lido de Paris. And I had no real commitment to Avi. If I changed my mind in the light of morning, I simply wouldn't go to meet him.

At 11 a.m., I was at *l'Hôtel de Ville*, as agreed upon. Avi was already in line for tickets. The Yves Montand show was a lot of fun. It was set up like a cabaret, the sort of place where Montand had begun his career. There were café tables and bentwood chairs to sit on while Montand's life was explained with film clips and placards. From his younger days as a struggling Italian immigrant to his momentous meeting with Edith Piaf, whose friendship and collaboration helped his career to take off, his talent was evident. Montand was so handsome, so engaging, such a talented performer.

There were snippets of his films with his wife, Simone Signoret, who was as famous and talented as he. Their political activism was also highlighted. Then came an explanation of his Hollywood years and his infatuation with Marilyn Monroe. Or was it vice versa? All in all, it was a charming evocation of Yves Montand's life from his humble beginnings to the height of his fame.

My companion, Avi, was a lot of fun to share it with. As we chatted away, we soon discovered something about one and other which came as a shock to the both of us.

Avi learned that I was American, not French, and I learned that he was not French either. He was Israeli. This discovery gave us both pause. Our mutual imaginary image of a romance with an actual *parisien*, or in his case *parisienne*, was shattered. However, it meant that we could talk in English, which made things easier.

Soldiering on, we decided to go out for lunch. The meal was very pleasant. Avi insisted upon paying. I was equally adamant that I wanted to go 'Dutch treat.' I explained this expression to him. Rather put out, he said to the bartender,

"Have you ever heard of a woman who won't let herself be treated to lunch? It's positively un-French!"

The bartender agreed with him. But I wanted no entanglements, no sense of obligation that might lead Avi on. It was a brave gesture. However, when Avi invited me back to see his apartment in the trendy Oberkampf neighborhood, I went happily along with him.

He explained to me that although he was an Israeli citizen with a wife and family back in Tel Aviv, he had recently bought himself a bolt hole in Paris. Just a little place where he could get away. Life in Israel was so stressful that he simply had to occasionally escape the pressure cooker of bombings and kidnappings. It seemed to me that he also wanted to cheat on his wife from time to time, but I kept that to myself.

His apartment was not especially appealing. We didn't spend much time on preliminaries. The bedroom was dark and mostly occupied by a big bed. Avi was a mediocre lover. There was no foreplay and neither of us was particularly aroused. After a brief tussle on the bed, he was dissatisfied and voiced his dissatisfaction.

"You're too small," he told me.

I wasn't sure if he meant my height or something else, but it was no compliment. Rendered speechless by this unwelcome avowal, I cleared out of Avi's apartment as fast as my small self could go.

At first my mind was curiously numb on the way back to my room at Mme Dubosc's *chambre d'hôtes*. But then I got angry. *How dare he? What a pathetic loser! And to blame me! Quel culot! What a nerve!*

Luckily the avenue de Belleville where I was staying was not far from the Oberkampf métro stop. I let myself into the apartment with the key provided for Micheline's *chambre d'hôtes* clients. No one was about. All the better. I felt guilty at my misbehavior and exultant at the same time. I had allowed myself this illicit adventure and emerged unscathed with only a bit of injured vanity.

No, it had not turned out as expected. No romance had been kindled. It had been forgettable sexually speaking. When I reflected on it, the episode had its amusing side—Avi and I, two foreigners looking for sexual adventure in 'Gay Paree.' It was a stereotype. We had both been playing a role. The reality had not lived up to the image for either of us.

Le Café de la Halle in Saint-Antoin-Noble-Val

CHAPTER 8

How I Came to Buy Pech Menal or It All Began With Pepitours

Instead of telling you about the train ride back from Paris to the *Tarn-et-Garonne* and to my house, Pech Menal, let me explain about how I came to buy the house in Cayrièch.

Roll back the calendar to 1999. My junior year in France college studies were long behind me. I had been a student in Paris more than thirty years ago. I had kept up my French skills over the years by teaching and tutoring, reading French novels and seeing an occasional French film. My husband and I had also taken many trips to France during our married life.

Yes, I had stuck to the plan and married my college sweetheart, Alex, who had become a corporate lawyer. We had two almost grown up sons and lived just outside of New York City in suburban New Jersey.

At this point in our lives, I worked from my big, rambling house in New Jersey tutoring French and organizing after school enrichment French classes for children. I enjoyed this work and I was kept quite busy by all my students. But when a friend asked me to help out in her small-group tour business, I readily agreed.

My friend's little company was named Pepitours after herself, Pepita. Pepita would find photos of the places she was headed, cut and paste them onto a sheet of paper and add captions to illustrate the day by day itineraries. She made color copies on a copier machine and stapled the finished products together.

Armed with these homemade brochures, she would advertise the trips and their dates and prices in the 'ITN', the 'International Travel News', a monthly newsprint publication, inviting people to send in for a trip brochure. *Et voilà!* Pepita had found a niche market for those who loved to travel in a smaller group on a more personalized itinerary.

I was Pepita's gal Friday, keeping the home fires burning while she escorted the small groups of travelers to Argentina and Chile, where she was born, and to countries in Eastern Europe. My assignment wasn't a very hard job. Nor did it take up too much of my time. I checked in at the office, Pepita's suburban house, while she was away, collecting the mail, depositing checks at the bank and sending out the requested trip brochures.

When Pepita was at home, we both manned the phone lines, fielding questions. Pepita was very persuasive on the phone. One of her favorite adjectives was 'outstanding.' Lots of people probably ordered brochures for our 'outstanding' destinations and simply used the itinerary to take their own trip. But many others signed up to take one of our small group tours.

As time went by, Pepita got to know my abilities better and rely on me more. She was interested in expanding Pepitours tour offerings. As a Spanish speaker, she handled South America and she also had contacts in Eastern Europe through her church affiliation.

Since I had spent my junior year in Paris, spoke French and had traveled extensively all over the world with Alex, my experience could be an advantage for other destinations Pepitours could offer.

My husband, Alex, was also a Francophile and travel buff. It started with our first trip to Paris together when he came to collect me at the end of my college junior year in France program thirty years ago. We had done a lot of traveling together since then.

One day at Pepitours headquarters, the spare bedroom at

Pepita's house, my friend and boss surprised me by throwing out this idea, "Why don't you put together a French tour itinerary, Barbara? We can try to sell it in the 'ITN.'"

I needed no further urging. I designed a tour circuit brochure called '*La France Profonde*,' subtitled, 'A Trip Through France, Off the Beaten Path.' I included places I knew and loved and places that I had always wanted to see. It was the same sort of trip planning I had done many times for Alex and me, but with a slightly different slant.

Alex had nothing against the idea of us taking a little break from one another should the trip pan out. After 30 years of marriage, my husband and I were no longer as united as we once were. We were suffering the stresses and strains of a mid-life crisis. Relations between us were tense. We often kept a wary distance from one another, hoping that the tangled situation would improve. Some time apart might give both of us some breathing room.

As it turned out, Pepitours '*La France Profonde*' brochure attracted enough interested clients to run.

Next, I needed to find a van and driver to chauffeur our small group around from stop to stop on the tour. After a false start with a company in Alsace, I found a good fit for our needs with a smaller transport firm in *Poitou-Charente,* between Bordeaux and Paris. The driver assigned to us was called Luc Martin. The same alluring Luc Martin you've already heard something about in the first chapter. This is how I first met him.

Luc, our driver, was an integral part of the success of the Pepitours tour that first year. He was an ex-army man–tall, lean and rangy with an infectious grin. Midway through the fifteen day trip, we had an adventure that put us both to the test. When we arrived as scheduled in the little town of Saint-Antonin-Noble-Val in the southwest of France with our load of travelers, the owner of the hotel-restaurant, *le Lys Bleu,* the 'Blue Lily,' was very surprised to see us.

"*Madame,*" he exclaimed, as I approached the reception desk, the late afternoon sun behind me, "I was not really expecting you. I don't have any room for your group tonight."

My heart skipped a beat. I hadn't even introduced myself and there was a problem.

"Not expecting me!" I said, my eyes widening in astonishment. "But what about all these emails we've exchanged," I said, waving a sheaf of printouts under his nose. Email was rather new in 2000, but it had worked great communicating with this little hotel, or at least I thought it had.

Luc had quietly entered the hotel lobby and stood nearby. He said nothing but I felt that he had my back. I refused to get too upset. There must be some misunderstanding.

"Oui, Madame," explained *l'hôtelier,* "You see, several of my guests have not vacated their rooms *comme prévu,* as expected, and I cannot make them leave. It's the law."

"I don't understand, Monsieur. You guaranteed *en noir et blanc,* in writing, to provide one night's lodging, dinner and breakfast at your establishment for my group of travelers. The deposit was duly paid."

The hotel keeper shrugged, that Gallic gesture with the hands raised in the air and he looked perplexed, raising his eyebrows.

I gave a thought to the tour group waiting for me. For the time being, they were happily ensconced under the shade of an enormous tree at an outdoor café in the lovely town square.

And to think that I had been so pleased to light upon the *Lys Bleu Hôtel* and its gourmet restaurant as I searched the guide books for a place to stay in the area between Moissac and Conques. It was located in this beautiful small town, Saint Antonin, which had many attractions, not the least of which was its thriving Sunday market which we would visit the following morning. Assuming we would be staying in Saint Antonin after all.

What to do? What to do?

I stood at the reception desk of the *Lys Bleu* feeling pretty desperate. The minutes passed by. Despite my reserving ahead, the proprietor had no room for my group of eleven unsuspecting tourists sipping a drink nearby. Luc, the minibus driver, continued to lounge behind me against the lobby door awaiting the outcome of this kerfuffle. We seemed to have arrived at a Mexican standoff or rather a French *impasse.*

Saint Antonin was the perfect stopping point at this stage of the tour circuit. It possessed the oldest civic building in France with its pretty carvings, *la Maison des Consuls,* built in 1125. It had been restored in the nineteenth century by the famous Viollet le Duc, the architect who was responsible for saving many of the Gothic buildings in France from falling into ruin and demolition.

After the French Revolution, the Gothic style was considered to be irredeemably old-fashioned and downright ugly. Most people had no interest in preserving it. Cathedrals were put to use as arms depots and barracks. Their tumbled down stones were taken to repair walls. Squatters had built makeshift houses in the ruins. Even Notre Dame de Paris was almost destroyed at this period of the 19th century.

Then famous authors like Victor Hugo—after all the gothic cathedral of Notre Dame de Paris is the setting for his novel about the hunchback—Emile Zola and Alexandre Dumas helped to raise consciousness that it would be a shame to let France's medieval artistic heritage disappear into oblivion. They succeeded in raising public support for the rescue of France's patrimony from the Middle Ages, including towns like Saint Antonin and the walled city of Carcassonne to the east toward Montpellier.

All of a sudden, the hotel proprietor spoke up. He had come up with a creative solution for our lodging stalemate.

"Madame," he said, "I cannot displace the guests who are already occupying our hotel rooms, but I can house you in the apartments I own in a building down the street from the hotel. Would that be acceptable?

And since there is not enough space for all of you in my apartments," he continued, "for those clients for whom there is no room in the village itself, I will find rooms in the *chambres d'hôtes,* bed and breakfasts, owned by my acquaintances up and down the valley of the Bonnette river not far from Saint Antonin proper."

This plan would involve a lot of driving around by Luc, dropping clients off at their various bed and breakfasts and collecting them up again for dinner only to redeposit them back at their *chambres d'hôtes* for the night.

I gave Luc a searching look. He didn't hesitate a moment:

"*A tes ordres, commandante,*" he told me, removing the matchstick from between his teeth and snapping to mock attention with a wide grin.

"We accept your offer," I affirmed, shaking the hotel owner's outstretched hand.

Our minibus was equipped with a *gouverneur,* a device that recorded how many kilometers Luc drove each 24 hour period. The distance he was permitted to drive each day was limited by government regulation for the driver's protection and for our safety as passengers. Luc called this gadget *le disc.* I'm not sure how he handled the *disc* problem on such a busy driving day as the one we were experiencing. All I know is that he took care of it.

Luc drove everybody around and then rounded us up again for a delicious dinner at the 'Blue Lily' restaurant. Once we were all redelivered for the night, he himself went to stay overnight as arranged in Caussade, a less picturesque town nearby.

In the morning, he rounded us all up again for breakfast at *Le Lys Bleu.*

Mostly all of the tourists were in good spirits. The apartments down the street from the hotel were beautifully restored with all modern conveniences in a 15th century building. The *chambres d'hôtes* had turned out to be lovely too. The owner of the *Lys Bleu* was apologetic about the mixup. He offered to reduce the bill to make up for our trouble. I graciously accepted a little discount.

In the main, the tour members had enjoyed rolling with the punches. Everyone had been quite satisfied with their accommodations. As Harold, also known as Wolf on his passport, opined, "This is not your usual tour. I like it. It's exciting."

Wolf, aka Harold, was a German expat who lived in Bahia, Brazil. He had found Pepitours through his son who lived in Miami and saw our trip listed in the 'ITN'. With his courtly, old-world manner, Harold was enjoying probably the last of his many trips to France. He told me that in his younger days he had been a judge at the Carnival beauty pageant in Rio de Janeiro. *All those half naked beauties in feathers? Who was I to question him?*

At his advanced age, he was still a very dashing man with his white hair carefully combed *en brosse*, his cane in hand. He often waited for us at the entrance to a monument or a museum. While we visited on foot, he happily sat on a bench outside and made a friend of a passerby. I would find them deep in conversation when our visit ended and it was time to get back on the minibus. Language was no barrier for Harold.

Riding along in the bus, we covered a lot of territory and the passengers sometimes dozed off. Luc liked to say that they hadn't finished their night:

"Ils n'ont pas terminé leurs nuits."

During one of these quiet rides, Luc told me a bit about himself.

"I had no prospects as a young man. No higher education to speak of. No parental support. So I went into the army. It was a hard life but at least I could live decently," he explained in his tough, yet tender manner.

And then he recited a quotation from Racine or Corneille that he remembered from his school days. These 17th century classical French playwrights wrote in lines called *alexandrins*, a kind of declamatory poetry. They crafted some of the most beautiful language about love, honor and duty which exists.

As we drove along, Luc recited to me:

> *L'on peut me réduire à vivre sans bonheur,*
> *Mais non pas me résoudre à vivre sans honneur.*
> I can be forced to live without happiness
> But I will never consent to live without honor.

I studied his handsome profile as we drove along. He certainly was appealing.

For another week, the Pepitours tour group rolled over hill and dale along the beautiful secondary roads of *la belle France*, skillfully piloted by Luc, our driver. We enjoyed wonderful sights – some well-known and some less-frequented. We were favored with mostly sunny, mild May weather. By this time our congenial group gathered each evening for a delicious meal at that night's inn or small hotel. Each couple or tour member who liked wine took a turn buying bottles of a local vintage for those of us who wished to partake.

The tour finished up on a weekend in Paris, the highlight and culmination of our peregrination. Luc drove us around to the many attractions of the capital city. On Sunday, especially, there was little traffic which was lucky for us. The minibus followed us around on our visits to le Musée d'Orsay to see the Impressionists and to the Musée Marmottan in the Bois de Boulogne to see more Impressionists. We hopped from the Arc de Triomphe to the Palais de Chaillot to the Louvre.

It was wonderful to be chauffeured this way around the city. It saved a lot of time and maximized our ability to visit the most sights possible.

I had hired a tour guide, an elegant *grande dame parisienne,* to show us around the Île de la Cité, with Notre Dame de Paris, le Palais de Justice and la Sainte Chapelle. I never forgot that I was only the tour escort. For real tour guide expertise, I hired professionals from the tourist offices of the places we visited.

Our Parisian guide did a wonderful job of explaining the history of the Île de la Cité, the little island where a Gallic tribe called the *Parisi* had founded the wood palisade settlement which became Paris. We marveled with her at the *arcs boutants,* the flying buttresses supporting Notre Dame cathedral's apse, or rear side.

She spirited us past the security guards into the municipal court buildings where the jewel box chapel built for King, and later Saint, Louis was hidden on an upper floor.

I was pleased with my choice of guide. Our Paris hotel was a happy find as well. It was called '*Le Colbert*,' and was more restaurant than hotel. It was in a bustling, centrally located area near Les Invalides and Napoleon's tomb. We could walk from there to the Eiffel Tower in the evening after dinner and later take *bateaux mouches*, panoramic windowed tour boats, on the Seine from the nearby Pont de l'Alma.

The last evening in Paris, I organized a trip to Montmartre to the Moulin Rouge nightclub, the same place where Toulouse-Lautrec had spent many a happy evening with his much taller cousin, Dr. Gabriel Tapié de Céyleran. When we had visited Lautrec's birthplace, the city of Albi, earlier on the tour, our group had been guided around Lautrec's childhood chateau by de Céyleran's female descendant. The wizened old lady was not very tall herself. It ran in the family. I felt our group was kind of specializing in Henri de Toulouse-Lautrec and the Impressionists.

The old windmill exterior of le Moulin Rouge was still intact. The red velvet lined interior hadn't changed that much from Toulouse-Lautrec's time either. It was fun to see a spirited *cancan* performance and drink some bubbly champagne, toasting the end of the '*La France Profonde*' tour.

The departure day arrived. Luc picked us up with our luggage on the rue St. Dominique in front of *Le Colbert* and delivered us to Charles de Gaulle Airport. We separated into little clutches of couples and single travelers depending on our destination. As we said our goodbyes, I was surprised and delighted to receive some notes of appreciation from the tour members. More than a few envelopes contained some money, a thank you tip for my efforts. It was so generous! I was touched.

One nice lady from California, Edith, confided in me as she handed me my *pourboire*, literally some drinking money:

"I'm a little embarrassed, Barbara. It's quite a long flight back to California so I've reserved two seats for myself, side by side. I'm not as slender as I once was and I need some room to spread out over such a long trip. And even the purchase of two economy seats is much less expensive than one seat in first class."

I assured her that I thought she had acted wisely. I collected my luggage from beside the van and gave Luc a big goodbye hug, American style, along with his envelope. Then we did *la bise*, kisses on both cheeks, French style.

"I'll miss you, Luc. *Tu vas me manquer.* Take care of yourself."

"*Au revoir*, Barbara. We'll stay in touch."

"Say hello to your partner, Bernadette, for me." I had never met the woman Luc lived with, but he had told me about her. "I'm sure she's missed you." He nodded in agreement.

"*Au revoir!*"

"*Au revoir!*"

As I made my way into the terminal from the parking area, Luc's image receded into the distance and my thoughts turned towards home.

And what about my own partner, my husband, Alex, waiting for me at home?

Sooner or later I was going to have to face up to the deterioration of goodwill that once reigned supreme between us. After many years of married life, much of it happy, I now felt trapped, as if painted into a corner.

How was I going to get out? It seemed to be an insoluble problem. *Perhaps I just needed to step out the unpainted side of the corner? Could I do that? Could it be that simple?*

As I boarded my flight back to New Jersey, my mind was full of trepidation for the future. I wasn't sure that I had the courage to toss over the traces and start all over again.

View of Saint Antonin from Across the Aveyron River

Barbara's Divorce is Final and 'La France Profonde' Tour Rolls On for a Second Year

T he train back from Paris and I, along with it, arrived at Limoges. I had left Micheline Dubosc's *chambre d'hôtes* early that morning and I was now at the halfway point in my trip back to Pech Menal and the *Tarn-et-Garonne*.

Limoges had a museum of porcelaine and a few china factories were still active there making the famous dinnerware. Several passengers got off the train and others took their places. I had about two hours left before getting back to Pech Menal again. As the engine started to chug and we picked up speed, the refreshment cart reached my train carriage. I knew from experience that there was nothing good on offer, but I ordered a watery coffee anyway. I looked out the window at the passing countryside. We were in *le Limousin* province, named for the Gallic tribe that inhabited the area in Roman times. They had their own breed of cattle, *les Limousins*. In fact, that is where the word *limousine* comes from. *They must be especially big cows*, I thought. The ones I saw out of the window looked normal sized though.

The green hillsides flashed their reflections in the train window like frames on an old-fashioned reel of film. The train slowed down on a curve and I saw my face mirrored in the window pane. I studied my image and adjusted my hair. *Where had the time gone?* I drifted back to my memories of Luc and the Pepitours trips.

After the first Pepitours France tour ended, I was back in Florida at Alex and my house. I was trying to find the courage to confront our marital difficulties. We seemed to have reached a stalemate. The reserves of goodwill had dwindled and were now empty.

Alex, my husband of thirty years, and I had grown apart. It was a common enough story. The children were now adults and in college. Alex was semi-retired and we had moved from New Jersey to Sarasota, Florida where Alex felt we could make a new start on our relationship.

I had been willing to give it a try, but in the end, we didn't succeed in recovering the loving ties that had once bound us together.

And so we got divorced. It was difficult, terrifying even, to be entirely on my own again. However, it was also liberating to have faced up to the painful reality that my marriage had failed and envision moving on. By acknowledging the problem instead of continuing our charade, we were able to take action and start the slow and painful healing process.

Christmas time approached and I sent Luc Martin, the driver of the Pepitours van, a card in which I announced my divorce.

At New Year's, I was feeling pretty low, all alone in the house after Alex had moved out. I was surprised to receive a card from Luc and Bernadette, his significant other. When I opened up the envelope, a shower of confetti sprang into the air and landed all over the kitchen. I loved it! It brought a big smile to my face. It was as if a ray of sunlight had entered the kitchen along with the confetti. *Someone was thinking of me!* I was counting on Luc's participation in the following year's *'la France Profonde'* tour.

Luc and I kept in touch over the winter. He sent me a coffee table book called *'la France Insolite'* about unusual and out of the way places to visit in France. He certainly had my number. I wanted to send them some grapefruit in return, an example of

Florida's *terroir,* but grapefruit weighed too much to be a practical gift to send overseas.

The first year of the *'France Profonde'* tour had been a success. Pepita and I had even made a little money. Clients were lining up to join the second year's tour. Based on my experience, I set out to make the next trip better and run smoother. No more stopping overnight in Saint-Antonin-Noble-Val. I had learned my lesson there. Instead we would stay at Najac, a nearby hilltown with a picturesque ruined castle to visit at the end of a pretty walk along a dramatic ridgeline. The Mona Lisa, *la Joconde* as the French call it, had been hidden there briefly during World War II.

Pepita and I had no trouble coordinating arrangements for the second iteration of 'la France Profonde,' even though she was in New Jersey and I was in Florida. Luc was on board again as driver. At the last minute, Pepita herself decided to join the group this year. She wanted to experience it first hand. I was excited at the prospect of the new trip.

Since I was now divorced, I would be free to stay in France after the end of the tour and travel a bit on my own. I would have the whole summer ahead of me after the trip ended in June. Maybe I would stay for a while in Paris. As I was an amateur painter, maybe I could do a painting workshop in Saint Antonin like the one I had seen advertised last year. I had picked up a brochure in a gallery there and the *stage* looked intriguing. Or I could take up Luc's offer to spend a little time with him and Bernadette at their house near Parthenay in *Poitou-Charente.* I had lots of possibilities. I could even do all of them.

The second year's tour got off to a good start. I flew from Florida via Atlanta to Paris where Pepita and the New Jersey contingent would meet up with me and the rest of the group arriving from their various starting points.

I must admit that I had thought longingly of Luc many times over the winter while we had been apart. These thoughts never included Bernadette.

I even arranged for Luc and me to be alone together in my

room at the Ibis Charles de Gaulle Hotel after my plane arrived, but before the tour officially started. I thought he might be as excited to see me as I was him. I thought he might take the opportunity to ravish me or at least we could share a passionate embrace.

As I buzzed around the spartan bed where Luc was sitting watching me in the simply furnished hotel room, I tried to appear willing but not over anxious. Luc didn't pick up on my cues at all. Or if he did, he was indifferent. *Ah, well. Tant mieux.* All for the best, as they say in French. My amour-propre was hurt but it made things less complicated for the tour about to start.

Our group, including the California contingent, eventually assembled at the Ibis hotel at Paris airport on schedule. The Californians came a little later than we travelers from the East Coast. We all rendezvoused with Luc at the minibus and set off for Auxerre, a smallish city just west of Paris where I had engaged a guide to take us around.

Our first destination was the château of Fontainebleau and the Barbizon forest. My objective was to leave the expensive hotels and restaurants of Paris quickly behind. Our moderate tour price was based on spending less time at costly places—and as promised by the tour prospectus, more time at attractions off the beaten track. Paris was in reserve for the *grande finale* of the trip, just like last year.

One day, the group wanted to stop for lunch on the road at a French 'McDonald's,' we saw out the minibus window. 'McDonald's' is very popular in France where it is affectionately known as 'Mac Doh', its real name being hard to pronounce in French. Of course some Frenchmen detested the place as an example of 'le fast food' that was taking over French dining habits.

Our lunch turned out to be an interesting experience. I learned that 'Mac Doh' was more expensive than an American 'McDonald's' and better quality too. You could specify if you wanted your hamburger rare, medium or well-done, *saignant, à point ou bien cuit.* The desserts on offer were delicious dark choco-late pâtisseries and other such delights.

At the 'Mac Doh,' while I was having a cup of coffee, the espresso cup size, not the big American tub of coffee, I struck up a conversation with a broad shouldered Frenchman sitting there.

"Oh, you're American," he said to me as we got to talking. "Do you know the *montagnes rocheuses*?"

I didn't know what he meant. I didn't understand him so I backpedaled, "You like the mountains?"

"*Les montagnes rocheuses*," he repeated. "I've seen them in the movies, 'les westerns'."

Um, it took me a second to get his meaning. "You mean the Rocky Mountains?" I had never heard them referred to in French before.

Before we could talk further, Luc suddenly loomed up in my line of sight.

"Yes, she is American and with the accent to boot," he proudly and possessively told the stranger, effectively ending our exchange.

If I had doubted it before, I realized then that Luc had his eye on me after all. Perhaps he was just being protective of me as a newly single woman. It was time to go anyway. The group had finished their lunches and used the facilities.

Shortly later, we gathered together on a grassy area of the *autoroute* rest stop, *une aire,* to count heads before clambering back into the van.

"Let's make a circle and do some stretches before we continue our ride, I suggested. "I'll show you the sun salutation I learned recently in yoga class back in Sarasota. I can demonstrate and you can follow along or do your own thing."

The group watched attentively as I moved through the different positions of the *asana*. I got down on all fours for the posture called 'downward dog,' my backside wiggling in the air as required. I realized that everyone was watching me intently–Luc most of all. I straightened up, flushed from the exertion and from the thought of all the eyes trained on me. I laughed to break the tension. Luc looked away. Pepita applauded. Some of the group wanted to give it a try. After a while, reenergized, we piled back into the van to continue on our way.

At the hotel in Najac, we had a swimming pool. I love to swim. It was a beautiful late afternoon. I donned my bathing suit and headed for the pool. As I dove in the water, who did I spy out of the corner of my eye but Luc Martin, looking svelte in his tiny French style bathing suit made from that clingy, nylon material.

I started swimming my usual laps–crawl, backstroke, side-stroke and breaststroke. It occurred to me that I was showing off for Luc. *How silly of me!* I couldn't help myself. I was aware of him and he was aware that I was aware. As I hoisted myself, drip-ping, out of the pool, some more Pepitours group members came through the gate into the pool area.

I picked up my towel and moved off in the direction of their lounge chairs. I looked around for Luc. He had vamoosed.

As our group tour progressed, I couldn't help but observe Luc's behavior, on duty and in more relaxed moments. He was a study to me. For one thing, he had a kind of scientific, sociological interest in women.

To research this interest of his, he read women's magazines. He always had the latest issue of 'Femina,' hot off the newsstand. Returning from a tour visit, we would find him leaning against the minibus, reading the French equivalent of 'Cosmo' or 'Woman's Day.'

He took my situation as a recent divorcee to heart. Based on his reading of women's health advice columns and letters from the lovelorn, he tried to counsel me as best he could.

"Barbara," he asked me one day as we were driving along, "do you know what a *gode michet* is? Or *gode* for short ?"

"No idea," I told him.

Luc pointed to an illustration in one of his magazines lying open next to the driver's seat. It was a dildo.

Yikes! 'Gode michet' appeared to mean 'dildo' in French. This seemed like a shockingly inappropriate line of conversation.

"Do you have one, Barbara? Because if you don't, I think you should get one."

"Luc!" I squeaked. "No, I don't have a *gode michet*. What are you saying? You recommend that I get one?"

"Yes, I think it's important for a woman in your situation to stay sexually satisfied and yet be independent. You need to avoid potentially dangerous physical or psychological entanglements."

"Hmmm. Well, thanks, Luc. That's something to consider," I said with asperity.

I could see Luc meant well, but REALLY!

Luc chuckled to himself. He said, "You know, I don't speak hardly any English, but there is something funny I notice when you Americans talk together. You have an expression you use when you are happy, but also when things go wrong. 'You say, "Oh, my God!' When I hear you say 'God,' to me it sounds just like *'gode.'* In other words, it sounds just like you are saying 'dildo'."

This was interesting information. How funny! We shared a laugh at this crazy language coincidence and I relaxed.

"What is your romantic history, Luc?" I asked him. "Tell me about how you met Bernadette."

"How I met Bernadette? I met her at my local Leclerc shopping center."

E. Leclerc was a hugely successful, nationwide French grocery store chain. It was so omnipresent that it was almost considered to be a public utility. It was actually a fabulously successful private business with billions of dollars in sales. The Leclerc carried a panoply of fresh and off the shelf foods–a fish market, a bakery, butchershop, cheese store, fresh produce, canned goods, etc. It also sold clothing, electronics, small appliances, jewelry, you name it.

Luc continued, "Bernadette ran *le tabac* just inside the entrance to the *centre commercial*, the big shopping center anchored by the Leclerc near where I lived in Charente. You know, she sold the usual at *le tabac*: cigarettes, lottery tickets, and newsstand items. I bought my women's magazines there."

"Anyway," he explained, "whenever I passed by there, she was so overwhelmed by all the work, *débordée*. One day, I asked her if she wanted me to help her behind the counter for a minute and she accepted. It turned out that we made a good team, working together, handling the customers.

I became her official helper. One thing led to another. I had gotten divorced not that long ago. I had two kids, *deux gosses*, with my beautiful wife. But all of a sudden, my wife just stopped wanting me. She wouldn't sleep with me anymore."

At this point, Luc grimaced at the unfairness of it all. His expression was hurt and angry.

He picked up his narrative again:

"Bernadette was also divorced with a couple of kids, trying to make ends meet. Eventually, after a few years, we were able to sell the *tabac*. We bought an old farm property together. We've fixed up the house and barn as time has gone by. I'm handy like that. The kids are mostly grown and on their own now. We have chickens, a cow and a big *potager*, a vegetable garden.

You know, Barbara, I'm really a peasant at heart."

Un paysan, a peasant!? I thought with alarm. In French, it means a farmer, a man of the soil. In the U.S., 'peasant' is a rather derogatory term. I didn't like to hear Luc call himself that. But it was true that Luc did seem like a man who liked to keep things simple and uncomplicated. He certainly wasn't an aristocrat. Nor was he middle class, a bourgeois. What did you call a worker, *un ouvrier*, who lived in the countryside? The term *paysan* fit.

"Have you thought anymore about coming to visit us at the end of the tour this year, Barbara? You would be most welcome as I wrote to you. Bernadette said so too."

"That's such a nice invitation, Luc. Thanks again. Let me think it over and I'll let you know soon."

And then our relationship changed and Luc and I became lovers. I've already described how this came about. It was one of my favorite memories.

At the *Auberge Bellay* in Burgundy, Luc and I had sex overlooked by the *basilique* of Vézelay in the distance. It was bound to happen. The sexual tension between us had been building up for a long while. We had both danced around our mutual attraction on the first Pepitours trip. Now that I was divorced, I felt no more compunction to behave myself. I was flirting for real.

Luc and I pursued our naughty behavior, surreptitiously making eyes at one another during the day on the minibus, enflaming our desire as we waited for the nights. It was fun to play this game with the tourists as the unsuspecting audience.

One night, we were in Rocamadour, a beautiful city in Dordogne on the River Lot. Over dinner on a terrace, we watched the hot air balloons float lazily over the river lined with châteaux and ancient ruined fortresses. After dinner, everyone went back to the hotel which was at one end of the main street in town. Luc was staying just down the road in a slightly less pricey establishment.

I snuck out of the hotel room I was sharing with my boss, Pepita. She was snoring as soon as her head hit the pillow. She had removed her hearing aids and I knew that she was now quite deaf. I tiptoed out of the room, skulking in the elevator, worried about bumping into one of the Pepitours clients. Hopefully they were too tired out from the day's sightseeing to still be up and about.

I made it to Luc's hotel without blowing my cover. *Whew!* Now I had to brave the night receptionist at Luc's hotel.

What was Luc's room number? Was he in?

In front of the night receptionist, I put as good a face as possible on my late evening visit.

"Would you call up and announce me, please?" I asked the clerk. He said he would.

Luc opened the door at my knock.

He took me in his arms and kissed me deeply. It was a sexy move and made me glad that I had come to his hotel room to find him. As he pulled my compliant body down onto the bed with him, I told him, "I think they bought my story at the front desk."

Luc laughed. "Barbara, they know what you're here for. Don't fool yourself."

I had to admit that he was probably right. This guy, Luc, was enjoying my discomfiture and I was enjoying squirming.

Later, sneaking back to my hotel room on the darkened street, I felt pretty tawdry ... but it sure was exciting.

The next morning in the van, Luc got a photo out of his pocket to show me. It was a snapshot of a young airman in uniform standing near the cockpit of his airplane.

"That's me," he proudly announced.

"Really," I responded, a bit dubious, studying the black and white photo closely.

It did look very like Luc, handsome and tall in his flight suit. The close cropped hair looked perhaps more blond than Luc's hair appeared in person.

"Very nice," I said. "I didn't know you were in the Air Force."

"Ha, ha, ha," Luc teased. I fooled you. That's not me at all. That's my son. He's a jet fighter pilot. Right now he's stationed in Djibouti. The French *force de frappe* and the nearby Americans stationed in the Gulf play games of chicken to amuse one another and pass the time."

"He looks just like you. You must be very proud of him."

Luc beamed at me. "They were in Texas too, he and his family, for training."

"Oh, yes, and how did they like it in Texas?"

"They loved it," said Luc grinning. He gunned the engine of the minibus and we sped north from Dordogne towards Chartres.

The train conductor's announcement over the loudspeaker interrupted the flow of my memories. *Did he say 'Brive la Gaillarde'?* That was the station before Montauban, which was my stop.

I got up out of my seat and made my way to *les toilettes*, swaying with the motion of the train, ready to grab onto a passing seat back, should need be. The train toilets were usually pretty stinky and not too clean even though they were all made out of stainless steel. It was weird to see the tracks passing by through the bottom of the toilet, if you looked down there. However, in a five hour journey, at least one trip to the 'doubluh vay say,' the w.c., was unavoidable.

I walked back to my place, trying not to lurch too much. The train whistle blew. I settled myself back down in my seat and my mind immediately picked up the story of my reminiscing.

The cathedral of Chartres is easily recognizable from afar across the flat wheat fields of the Beauce region, the granary of France. The church has two high pointed steeples, one very plain pyramid shape from around 1160 and the other flamboyantly decorated all over from the 16th century. Chartres' stained glass windows possess an exquisite, intense blue color which has never been equaled. The secret recipe to make it was lost in the Middle Ages.

In our little hotel in the shadow of the cathedral, Luc and I pursued our affair by being more daring and experimental with each other than before.

There had never been any great tenderness in our lovemaking, nor was there much now. *He was a rogue!*

As I took an after dinner stroll along the riverbank with some of the tour members, I was privately replaying in my mind the scenes of our naughty behavior from a few hours before.

Luc and I were becoming incautious. So far as I knew, the tour members had not caught on to our affair. But surely, they had sensed our attraction to each other.

There was no need to put it into words, but Luc and I tacitly agreed to be very businesslike during the final days of the tour in Paris. We would wrap the trip up in fine style just the way we had done last year.

And we did finish out the trip in fine fashion. This year, before Paris, I included a stop in Giverny to see Monet's garden. I found a small hotel in Giverny itself where we could spend the night and have a meal. In this way, we had the opportunity to see the village, which is really just one main street, after all the busloads of other tourists had left for the day.

I discovered that the Terra Museum, a striking modern building with its own California style garden, was a fascinating counterpoint to the visit to Monet's house and garden proper. Daniel Terra, a wealthy Chicagoan with a fabulous collection of American Impressionist painters founded the museum in the 1990's.

I learned that many American artists came to Giverny in Monet's lifetime, to live and work near the master, Claude Monet. One of them, Theodore Butler, had even married Monet's stepdaughter and model. You just had to poke around in the gardens behind the houses and restaurants along Giverny's main street to find the *cabanes*, the outdoor huts where these painters had worked. If you looked closely, the restaurants still displayed their graffiti and some sketches on the walls.

There were many more connections between American and French Impressionist painters than I had been aware of. I was proud of the showcase that the beautiful Terra Museum presented to the world of tourists who came to Giverny. I was also moved to learn that it was American money that saved Monet's garden from falling into ruin, just as it was rich Americans who were the original saviors of Versailles and its gardens.

After a night in Giverny, we arrived in Paris at last. We visited all *les incontournables,* the unmissable sights we could see in a few busy days.

One day, as the minibus was stalled in traffic near la Place de la Concorde, I asked Luc to let me off on the crowded *rue St. Florentin* where I had lived in 1969 during my junior year in Paris program. I had spotted the big green doors leading to my old courtyard pavilion out the minibus window as we were stalled in traffic on my old street. I couldn't resist taking a quick peek inside for old time's sake.

I knew that Madame Beringer, my landlady, had died. Many years ago, my Christmas card addressed to her had been returned with a note from her naval officer husband. He wrote that *"notre pauvre Émeraude* had been stricken with Alzheimer's disease and was no longer with us."

Luc opened the minibus door for me and I quickly jumped down from the van onto the busy sidewalk. I ran to my old address, depressed the release button on the side wall and confidently pushed against the little green door cut into the big one. Nothing happened. It was immoveable. Perplexed, I took a closer look at the button. It now required a security code to open the door and gain entrance into the courtyard. I was stymied. I couldn't open the door anymore the way I used to back in the day.

The Pepitours minibus was blocking traffic by this time. Cars were honking. Passersby were looking at us in an accusatory way. Luc shouted out the window to the annoyed drivers and pedestrians as he reopened the door of the bus for me:

"Une américaine! Une américaine! She's American!" as if this explained everything.

I hopped back onto the minibus. "What were you looking for?" Luc asked me as our van moved along with the traffic flow again.

"I used to live right there back in 1969," I explained to him. "I just wanted to take a quick look, *'jeter un coup d'oeil,'* for old time's sake, but I couldn't get inside."

"Évidemment," Luc said, shaking his head in understanding.

I was not able to peek into my old courtyard. Like the title of Thomas Wolfe's novel, 'You Can't Go Home Again,' I couldn't go back in time either. And so, we continued forward with the finale of the Pepitours Paris visit for this second year.

Everything went off as planned. Luc and I delivered the tourists to the airport for their return flights without a hitch.

After their departure, Luc took me to pick up the rental car I had reserved from an agency at the airport. He waited with me while I got my assigned vehicle. We were going to meet up later at the house he shared with Bernadette, some 200 miles to the south; I planned to spend a few days with them. We couldn't drive together because Luc needed to drive the minibus back to his employer's company.

"Luc, how fast can I go without getting a speeding ticket?" I asked, consulting him.

"Just keep it around 130 kilometers per hour and you'll be fine," he advised me. "That's the speed limit on the *autoroute*. Don't go faster. See you in Parthenay in a few days. Bernadette and I are looking forward to it."

He waved to me as I set off out of the parking lot.

Luckily, I had learned how to drive a stick shift when I was married. Alex had a VW Beetle in the early days of our marriage and later we owned a little BMW 2002, which also had a manual transmission.

As I got rolling out on the highway, I was overwhelmed by a sensation of freedom so intense, it was like being high. It was thrilling to be on my own. I felt euphoric and I quickly revved the engine up to 130 *km* per hour, 80 m.p.h.

The Pepitours tour had been a resounding success. I was free to chart my own course for the summer months. I had just enough summer plans not to feel entirely at loose ends. My summer of solo adventures was underway. I turned the radio up high and sang along at the top of my voice:

"Baby, come ride with me. Whatever will be, will be. The future's not ours to see."

I wasn't unduly concerned about staying with Luc and Bernadette even though he and I had been intimate. If Luc could compartmentalize his life, I could too. Anyway, who knew what sort of understanding they had? It was possible that Bernadette chose to overlook Luc's less than faithful behavior when he was away from her.

My mind was untroubled and I was light-hearted. I had my own wheels at my disposal. I was an independent woman. I could treat my affair with Luc as just that, a passing fancy.

I stayed in France for a month after the end of the tour traveling on my own. When I got back to Florida, I gave Pepita a call in New Jersey so we could review the trip. She was highly satisfied with the experience, as was I. We agreed that she would look over my expense report and compute the amount of profit to be shared out. Then we moved on to more personal matters.

Pepita was not only my boss. She was a friend, even a sort of mother substitute. She knew my situation as a recently divorced woman with two grown sons. My divorce settlement had been generous. I had no connection to Florida except the house where my now ex-husband and I had briefly lived together. I was reluctant to move back to New Jersey where I had met Pepita and raised my kids. That seemed like a step backwards.

"You know, Barbara," Pepita told me during one of our telephone calls, "I think you should consider living in France for a while. I observed you during the 'France Profonde' trip and you seemed to be in your element."

"Really, Pepita," I said musingly. "That's funny because I did meet some foreigners living in France this summer during the painting workshop I took in Saint Antonin. There was a Canadian guy and his wife, also named Barbara. They had a house near St. Antonin in Cazals. They introduced me to their friends with a house up the hill from them, Charles, who's English and his American wife, Eloise. They're very nice.

They were encouraging me to buy something. They even pointed out a 'for sale' property with a swimming pool they thought might be just right for me. They didn't know that I had had enough of swimming pools in Florida."

"You see!" said Pepita. "Buying a house in France, especially in a place where you have already met some nice people, might be a good idea."

"It's a thought," I offered. "You have the apartment in Chile, at the beach, and that works out for you. But you were born in Chile. I'm not French."

"What about in *Charente* near Luc's house?" Pepita asked coyly. Pepita suspected that I had a 'thing' for Luc.

"*Poitou-Charente* where Luc and his partner, Bernadette, live is absolutely beautiful, Pepita," I told her. "You know, don't you, that I stayed with them for a few days after the tour ended?"

"Yes. You told me that was in your plans. How did it go?"

"They were absolutely adorable to me. They took me to a fascinating place called, *le Marais poitevin, a* kind of floating island area of old farms. Very unusual. Sort of like Venice, but rural. Luc poled me and Bernadette around on a flat bottomed boat like a gondolier.

They also insisted on taking me out to lunch in La Rochelle, a little Atlantic port which has a very picturesque harbor. We visited *la Corderie Royale* there. It's an enormously long building where the Navy used to manufacture by hand the miles of ropes needed for the King's sailing vessels.

We also saw some people who are building an exact replica of the *caravelle* that took the Marquis de La Fayette across the Atlantic to fight in the American War of Independence. Have you heard about that? When they're finished, they're going to sail the ship to America."

"No, I haven't heard about that," Pepita said. "That will be outstanding. But how did things go at Luc's house? I mean with Bernadette. What's their house like?"

"It's a very nice place," I answered. "It's a big house and barn and some other buildings. It's out in the country near a little town. The house is simple, but comfortable. They've fixed it up very nicely with a modern kitchen and a spacious family room. Luc laughed when I got my shoes muddy in the barn.

You know, he has this amazing dog, Duc, which Luc has trained to be in agility contests with him. Luc and Duc have won lots of trophies at agility meets. Luc has them on display."

"What's 'agility'?" Pepita asked.

"I didn't know either," I said. "The trained dog has to go through a series of jumps on a sort of obstacle course while his master gives him cues from the sidelines. Luc really likes having the dog obey him. He has got a practice course all set up there in a field."

"I never heard of that," said Pepita.

"Yeah, me neither. I think 'agility' is international, not just French."

"And Bernadette,?" inquired Pepita, "What's she like?"

"Oh, she's very nice," I replied. "She's a lovely person and lovely to look at too. She's a bit quiet, but friendly. I liked her."

"Sounds like the visit went well," Pepita said. "How long did you stay with them?"

"Well, actually, Pepita, I cut my visit short after a couple of days. I just really didn't feel comfortable after a while."

I didn't tell Pepita that one morning while I was trying to figure out how to open the aluminum drum of the French washing machine, Luc wasn't really being helpful. Instead he was studying my bare legs with a wolfish look in his eyes.

That did it! I decided to clear out of there as soon as I could. *Luc was such a philanderer! I couldn't do it anymore.* I felt disgusted with him and me.

To Pepita, I said, "Yeah, I felt like a third wheel. And anyway there wasn't long before I had to leave to drive down south to Saint Antonin for the painting workshop, *le stage.*"

Pepita and I said goodbye. But not before she floated the idea of my buying a house in France once again: "You wouldn't have to live there full time, Barbara. It could be a place to get away from Florida in the hot summers."

I said that I'd think about it. And I did let the idea percolate in the days and weeks to follow.

A month later, when I received a check from Pepitours for my part of the tour profits, Pepita also included a round trip air ticket to Toulouse, the big city closest to Saint Antonin. The accompanying note said: *"Go take a look for a house. My treat. Love, Pepita."*

And so the die was cast. I went to look for a French house and I found a wonderful place to buy, an 18th century farmhouse, no less. And the property was situated in an award winning flowering village, *'un village fleuri.'*

That was how, in a long, roundabout way, I came to own *Pech Menal* in little Cayrièch, France.

La Placette Across from the Café Battut in Montpezat

CHAPTER 10

Back Home in the Tarn-et-Garonne

I arrived back home from my getaway trip to Paris, picked up my car at the train station parking lot in Caussade and drove myself back to Cayrièch and my house. Micheline's apartment on the avenue Belleville and my big city adventures already seemed far distant in space and time from the *Tarn-et-Garonne*.

In fact, I knew many people from around Pech Menal who were quite happy and reassured by the idea that Paris was very far away from them and that they didn't need to pay much attention to what happened in their distant capital city.

There were plenty of local events and points of pride. For example, Caussade billed itself as 'the city of the hat.' Its sobriquet was '*la Cité du Chapeau*' because of its native hat making industry.

A resident of nearby Septfonds in the nineteenth century had started manufacturing hats by hand when the whole region was going through very hard times. At the time, the farmers were suffering from famine when a woman named Pétronille de Cantécor volunteered a possible solution. She suggested that they braid the straw left in the fields together into tresses as her Italian forebears had taught her how to do. The tresses, or flat braids of straw, could be wound around and sewn together to make hats.

Her neighbors were desperate and they decided to give this hat-making business a try. The timing was just right. Straw boater hats became all the rage and the local farmers and townspeople were saved from penury. The prosperous cottage industry grew and even today, hundreds of years later, there were several hat factories left in Septfonds and Caussade.

In Caussade, every Bastille Day on July 14, *le quatorze juillet,* the French National holiday, Caussade hosted an international hat competition and sale. Rows of white canvas pavilions were set up on the town square for hat designers, hat vendors and potential hat buyers who strolled among the stalls. The winning designers were awarded cash prizes at a gala hat fashion parade.

So Pétronille de Cantécor really started a tradition in Caussade. When you admire someone's actions, you say in French, *'Chapeau'* or *'Chapeau bas'* which is like the American expression, 'I take my hat off to you.' "*Chapeau* to you, Pétronille de Cantécor!"

Caussade had rather usurped Septfonds' glory over the hats, but little Septfonds had its own civic pride. Firstly, the village was known for the dolmens and menhirs which dotted its surrounding wooded area. These prehistoric burial places indicated that Septfonds had been inhabited since the Iron and Bronze ages. The big, ancient stones were objects of wonder.

Secondly, the village organized and produced the most creative festivals, the outdoor *fêtes de village,* of all the surrounding villages. Most towns had no theme for their festival or they kept to recreations of the Middle Ages. Septfonds dared to try to recreate *la Belle Époque* or the American Wild West in their town square on Bastille Day. People from all around the area would come to participate in the fun, particularly families with kids in tow.

I was impressed by the lovely costumes of *la Belle Époque* recreation in Septfonds but I felt that when the villagers dressed up as cowboys and Indians for the Wild West Days festival, they were having the most fun.

French people loved American westerns on TV and at the movies. Square dancing clubs where people went decked out in cowboy boots and fringed shirts were very popular. The idea of the huge spaces and vistas of the American southwest was mythic to Frenchmen as well as Americans. 'Grandiose' was the word which was always used to describe the American West and America in general. The United States was just so darn big.

America was very popular in spite of the politics of George Bush and Iran or Iraq. American pop culture was everywhere and winning over everyone. This homogeneity of ideas was a loss but globalization seemed unstoppable. And of course, the cowboys and cowgirls of Septfonds put their very French spin on the festival proceedings.

For two or three days, the precincts of the medieval *bastide* town were given over to the festivities. Where once townspeople in the Middle Ages defended against invaders at the sharp, right angled intersections of their village's maze of streets, festival goers now found lasso contests for the children as well as arrow shooting games. For the festival, there was a horse shoeing demonstration in the pretend livery stable. At intervals over the festival weekend, a mock shoot out was enacted by buckskin costumed villagers. Teepees were erected to represent a Sioux village. In the shade of the church, there was a lineup of vintage American cars to inspect: a Dodge Challenger muscle car, an old Cadillac with its big fins, a '56 Chevy convertible, among others. And all this fun was powered by volunteers from the village committees set up to make it all happen.

Plenty of food and drink was on sale at the various stands. *Des hamburgers* and *le ketchup* were available as well as cotton candy, *la barbe à papa*, cotton candy, fluffy like Dad's beard and of course, plenty of *coca, le Coca Cola,* to drink.

The locally made straw hats were, of course, for sale at a big booth. Craft sellers also offered painted roof tiles, embroidered baby bibs, decorated rock paperweights and all manner of creations at the little stands they tended around the village square.

The festivities ended with the typical communal, outdoor meal, in this instance, steaks, *des bifteks*. The grand finale was a fireworks display. This was very French, as well as part of the festival theme. The French had enjoyed fireworks' displays since Louis XIV's court at Versailles, if not longer.

On a more somber note, only one kilometer out of town, a monument and outdoor museum bore witness to a dark period in Septfonds' history. This was *'le Camp de Judes.'*

During the Spanish Civil War in 1939-40, sixteen thousand Spaniards were interned in this refugee camp. They were fleeing Franco and the Spanish Civil War just over the Pyrénées mountains. They were guarded by French Senegalese soldiers on duty to protect the general population from this *menace.*

From 1940 to 1942, the collaborationist Vichy regime, following the Franco-German armistice, interned 'suspicious' foreigners in *'le camp de Judes'* behind barbed wire enclosures. And from 1942 to 1944, Jews were held in the camp until their deportation to Auschwitz.

After the Liberation in 1945, the *'Camp de Judes'* was used to intern those who had collaborated with the Nazis.

The present day French Government had erected a stone marker flanked by French flags to commemorate this ill-omened place, which was now an open air museum.

What a creepy feeling it was to know that the parents and grandparents of my neighbors, the nice people in Caussade, Septfonds and Cayrièch had lived cheek by jowl with a wartime prison camp. And they had evidently condoned it, or at least accepted it.

As was so often the case in France and Spain too, some of the most beautiful and isolated landscapes had been the placement for wartime internment camps and prisons, as well as the setting for the atrocities endemic in those places.

Digging through the soil of Septfonds and its surroundings, you encountered layers of history from the prehistoric dolmens to the nineteenth century hat industry to the world wars. Some of the layers were quite unsavory. Not all were hidden gems like the truffles found by the trained dogs under the scrub oaks of the region.

My first months as a new homeowner of Pech Menal were proceeding nicely. I was making progress on getting the new house in shape. Sometimes, it was discouraging to look around and see all there was to do, but in the main, I was enjoying the challenges.

I had talked to Luc, the Pepitours bus driver back on his farm in Parthenay, a few times on the phone. I thought of asking him to come help with my remodeling projects since I knew he was very handy. However, I hesitated. I didn't want to stir things up all over again with him. It would be nice to have some romance in my life, but Luc was not the one for me. I could see that pursuing a relationship with him would lead nowhere.

My French was improving. I had always spoken well and understood most conversations, but practice really did make perfect. I would never be mistaken for a French person. A few people had trouble understanding me, but most French people admired my ability to speak their language. They would say how much they wished they could speak English as well as I did French.

It could be tiring living most of my life in a foreign language but as time went on, I built up my ability to stay concentrated until there came a point where I hardly noticed I had to make an effort. I was in a language bath, as they say. I watched French TV from documentaries and the news to silly variety and game shows. I saw many French movies in French. I read French books and magazines from high-toned classics and the high brow *le Monde* newspaper to pulp novels.

Occasionally I would pick up the little newsheet of classified ads, *'les Petites Annonces'* at the grocery store. There were lots of cars for sale. There were ads for sofas and ovens. You could peruse ads for stones from a demolished house. You might even find those old floor tiles called *tommettes,* which were so desirable but hard to come by and expensive.

The most interesting announcements were in the lonely hearts column. Most people were searching for a soulmate. I admired the honesty of those who forthrightly said they were just looking for an afternoon's delight.

The ads were organized by location.

Maybe I'll give one of these a try, I decided, throwing caution to the wind. I certainly wasn't meeting anyone interesting through the usual channels.. *Here's a man from Toulouse. I'd like to meet someone from a bigger city.*

Before I could lose my nerve, I called the contact number of '*les Petites Annonces*' as directed and left my telephone number, in case the man from Toulouse wished to get in touch with me.

A few days later, a deep-voiced stranger gave me a call. I went to meet him for a coffee in Toulouse at a hotel off the ring road, *la rocade.* That meeting went alright. The stranger was well educated and easy to look at. We agreed to see one another again, this time out near me in the Tarn and Garonne.

"We'll meet at the movie theater in Caussade. It's easy to find and there is a lot of parking. Then you'll get in my car and we'll take a drive to the *Château de Bonaguil,* a beautiful place in the *Lot departement* about an hour away. Have you been there yet, Barbara?"

No, I had not been. It sounded like a good plan. He seemed to know my area.

As it transpired, the excursion was not a success from my point of view. Although the drive was surpassingly lovely through gorgeous countryside, on little back roads, my companion never stopped talking. I thought I was proficient in *le français,* but my powers of concentration began to flag. I had trouble focusing on the great flood of French coming my way. There was hardly a question of my getting a word in edgewise.

As for the chateau of Bonaguil and its falcons, we didn't actually visit it. We sat in the courtyard of the town from which we could just make out the turrets. I was hungry but no offer of refreshment was forthcoming. I arrived back at the Caussade movie theater, tired and hungry. My mind was reeling with the torrents of French I had listened to. I felt a little shell shocked.

"When shall we see one another again?" my date asked.

"Um," I hesitated, "I don't know. Do we want to meet again?"

"I am ready to come to the 'States,'" my suitor said, puffing out his chest, as if surprised at his own bravery. The way he said the word 'States' made me cringe. Even I, a bonafide American citizen, rarely used that expression.

"But aren't you getting ahead of yourself," I said to my companion. "Why, we hardly know one another. We've never even kissed."

"Oh, that!" my date said dismissively. "*Le lit.* As for bed, I can already see there won't be any problem."

Hold it right there, I thought to myself. *Where am I in this equation? I've got to make it crystal clear that I can't accept this high-handed treatment. It was unbearable.*

Aloud, I said, "Monsieur, I never want to see you again. This is not an *au revoir.* This is *adieu,* a permanent goodbye."

My date was so dense and self-absorbed that he stared at me uncomprehendingly as I got out of his car and got back into my own. I headed home to Pech Menal to recuperate, checking in the rear view mirror to make sure I was alone on the road and he wasn't following me. Needless to say, I didn't want any further contact with the man from Toulouse. I was happy to know that he didn't know where I lived.

He did have my phone number, however, and for a while I was afraid that he might track me down. As time went by, I calmed down. As relentless as he had seemed, he disappeared from my life without a ripple.

I never heard from my overeager suitor again but the fastness of Pech Menal was invaded by a different sort of intruder.

One Sunday morning I sleepily opened my eyes and as I lifted my head off the pillow, the room came into focus.

"*Eek!*" I leapt out of bed with a start, hopping from one foot to the other. The new seagrass rug on the bedroom floor was littered with little insect bodies. Most of them lay inert on the carpet. A few brown exoskeletons in the corner were still twitching slightly.

What was going on here? I tiptoed and hopped my way gingerly from the bed to where my Miele vacuum cleaner was leaning against the stone wall. It was one of my purchases from *Le Tout'Élec*, the appliance store in Caussade. I loved that vacuum cleaner.

Mon Dieu! Bon sang! Merde! Putain de merde! Zut alors! Ô, la vache! Bordel! Bordel de merde! I waded through the bug bodies as I made my way to the vacuum to start vacuuming the insect corpses up.

Beurk! C'est dégoûtant! Dégueulasse! Disgusting! Had they jumped on me in the night? Where did they come from?

I plugged in the machine and delicately dipped the vacuum head attachment through the crunchy mass of carcasses, harvesting layer by layer until the carpet was visible again.

Are these grasshoppers? I got an envelope out of the desk and used a piece of paper to tip one of the little beasties inside it for safekeeping and further study. I wanted to understand what army had invaded Pech Menal overnight.

Getting dressed, I decided to take the envelope with its little cargo to the pharmacy in Puylaroque, not far away up the big hill. It was a Sunday and most everything was closed. The pharmacy in Puylaroque was open because it was the *pharmacie de garde* that day. The pharmacies in each area took turns being open on Sundays so that no sector was left entirely in the lurch in case of an emergency.

As I drove up the hill, I saw that the neon green cross of the pharmacy was blinking. It was indeed open. I went inside and approached the counter. The shelves behind were well stocked with common cold remedies, shampoos and hand creams. The pharmacist seemed rather harried, although the store was empty.

"*Bonjour, Monsieur,*" I said.

"*Bonjour, Madame,*" he acknowledged my presence. "How may I help you?"

"*Qu'est-ce que c'est que ça?*" I asked as I spilled open the envelope containing the insect corpse onto the counter in front of him.

The pharmacist was the most authoritative expert I could think to consult on a Sunday lunchtime in rural France. Almost everyone else was enjoying a big, four-hour-long family luncheon.

Glancing at the small, brittle object before him, the pharmacist rendered a quick verdict. He yawned.

"That's nothing. Nothing to be concerned about. *Ça, ça ne risque rien.*"

"But I have hundreds of these insects ankle deep on my ground floor. What are they?"

"Crickets," he said. "They're just crickets."

"Jiminy Cricket!" I exclaimed, in American, making a feeble joke to myself.

"It must be the heat," opined the pharmacist. "They came in from the outdoors, seeking a bit of coolness and they died.

Ah oui, Madame, la fraîcheur. We're all seeking a bit of coolness, *n'est-ce pas?*"

We were experiencing an historic *canicule.* The extended heat wave was making headlines. Air conditioning was uncommon in France since great heat was also uncommon. Also the French don't appreciate the same degree of interior coolness to which most Americans have become accustomed. They find it way too cold. They don't like ice in their drinks either. Which came first, lack of an icebox to make ice cubes or a dislike of very cold drinks? It's like the chicken and the egg.

Since most houses in southern France have very thick stone

walls and heavy wooden shutters, they are naturally insulated from extremes of heat and cold.

The typical French summer cooling system goes this way: Open all the windows and shutters in the house in the cool of the morning. Before the sun gets strong, then close everything up, leaving only a slit open for some air circulation. Or close everything up tight as a drum in extreme heat conditions.

In the evening, open all the windows and shutters up again, making sure to avoid the twilight mosquito hour. Remember there are no screens on the windows. The cooler air in the evening and overnight will cool the house down again.

Yes, this method makes the house rather dark during the day, but the idea is to trap the cool air inside the walls. Anyway most of life is spent outside the house in the shade.

Overnight the temperature usually cools off steeply, no matter how hot the day has been. The climate is Mediterranean—hot and dry during the day and much cooler after the sun sets.

However this unusual heat wave was *dérangeant*. It had disrupted the crickets as well as the humans. The trees were also losing their leaves ahead of schedule. The *nappe phréatique* was unusually low, as I had learned when Momo and Nasser tried to get more groundwater flowing into the well at Pech Menal. Even after all their valiant efforts, the well never filled up that summer.

Reassured and happy to put a name to my home invaders—*les sauterelles*—I drove back down the hill to the plateau and Pech Menal where I swept up the rest of the inert crickets with my trusty Miele vacuum cleaner.

I prepared myself a light lunch of pâté and *Brie de Méaux* cheese on some leftover *baguette* and a big, juicy *Tarn-et-Garonne* nectarine for dessert.

I took my meal downstairs to eat in the freshly vacuumed lower level of the house because it was cooler down there. This was another hot weather strategy for the non-air conditioned. Since the cooler air was heavier, it was more comfortable on the lower floors of a dwelling. But *ne vous en faîtes pas,* don't get overwrought. Summer should be hot and winter will be cold. There is a more accepting attitude and appreciation of this normal state of affairs in France.

The rest of the lazy day passed by uneventfully. All the stores were closed as they always were on Sundays. It was still too hot to bother with much of a dinner. I sat eating a yogurt looking out over the back forty, i.e. my two *hectares*, about four and a half acres. The sunsets were often beautiful facing that way. The red orb of the sun would sink slowly lower in a sky streaked purple, lavender and rose. As the setting sun disappeared below the horizon, the plum trees around the well would become silhouetted against the gloaming.

But it was too early for that effect this evening. In summertime, the sun set late in this latitude, at around 10 p.m. It wasn't yet nine o'clock.

I decided to go to a movie in Caussade. The movie theater was not air conditioned either, but as the building had been part of a 17th century convent, the old stones kept the temperature inside moderate.

I drove the 15 minutes it took to get into town and parked right near Marilyn Monroe. There was a big painting of her adorning one side of the movie house. Her skirt was blowing up over the air vent and just like in the famous photo, she was charmingly trying to push it back down over her legs in the painting.

The cinema in Caussade was never very crowded. In other words, it was mostly empty, as usual. The *mairie,* or town hall supported the cinema, which kept it going. I loved having it nearby. The old movie projector that sat in the lobby looked a bit like an alien monster or the mechanism they use at the planetarium to create the illusion of the night sky. There was an artificial starry sky made with little lights in the ceiling of the *salle,* where you sat on plush blue velveteen seats waiting for the lights to dim and the film to start.

When I approached the desk to buy my ticket, the acrid smell of the nearby toilets assailed my nostrils as usual. There was no food on sale. Popcorn was considered cattle feed, if it existed at all.

Patrick, the young man in charge, explained a change in the program.

"*Madame*, the film we advertised—an artsy adaptation of an English novel—did not arrive. Instead we are pleased to offer you Sylvester Stallone in *Rambo IV*."

These little *hics*, hiccoughs, were part and parcel of the excitement of moviegoing in Caussade. I decided to stay for Rambo. After all, I was already there.

Home again after the movie, I felt inspired by Rambo's exploits to take on the challenge of falling asleep back in the bedroom that had been inundated with bug bodies just that morning.

I went down the stairs, turned on the light and cautiously peeked around the room. I looked under the bed. All clear. "*Pas un seul petit morceau de mouche ou de vermisseau,*" as the poet La Fontaine said about his grasshopper in the 17th century fable. Not even one little part of a bug body to be found.

The insects were all gone. I gratefully crawled into bed. The brightness of a full moon shone through the three little windows that looked out across the courtyard to the fields beyond. I got up and closed the curtains. I went back to bed and drifted peacefully off to sleep.

Bonne nuit. Dors bien

Crash! Crunch! Strobe lights flashing. The beams were blinding even through the curtains. *It was the Invasion of the Body Snatchers! Where was I?*

Where was Rambo? Was it outer space? The jungle? What a huge noise!

I raced to the nearest window. The ground was trembling under my feet. *An earthquake?*

More crunching noises came from outside. I expected to see giant praying mantises, their mandibles snapping open and shut as they came for me. But what I saw instead was a harvesting machine methodically moving up and down the rows of corn in the field next door, sucking the stalks into its open maw and spitting the corn cobs up and out the chute into the waiting trailer.

Fully awake now, I went outside into the caressing air of a midsummer midnight. The driver of the harvester waved to me from across the field. It was Jacky Legrand, my dancing partner from the village *fête*. I waved back at him.

I understood now. It was too hot to harvest in the heat of the day, so why not harvest by the light of the full moon when it was cooler. Tonight the moon was beaming like an electric bulb in the night sky above us. It was almost as light as daytime except for the shadows.

Well, that was a shock, I said to myself as I crept back to bed. *I hope that doesn't happen too often.*

I had forgotten all about my problem with the *sauterelles*. My new environment was certainly full of surprises, not all of them unalloyed pleasures. It was keeping me on my toes.

"*Au moins, je ne m'ennuie pas.* At least, I can't say I'm bored," I said aloud to nobody. I yawned sleepily. And poof—*endormie* —I was sound asleep.

I met a great couple of *brocanteurs*, or antique dealers in Saint-Antonin-Noble-Val, the beautiful, prosperous town not too far from Cayrièch if you drove over a hill and dale on the *D* roads, the littlest tracks which crisscrossed the fields.

Saint Antonin had been very prosperous in the 16th century when the rich *pastel* merchants built their mansions there. *Pastel* was a crop from which you got a dye that turned cloth blue, quite a desirable color then as now. Fortunes were made in the Middle Ages by dealers in this commodity. *Pastel* is called *woad* in English.

Whereas Cayrièch was located up on the windy, dry plateau called *les causses,* Saint Antonin was down in the gorges cut by the

Aveyron River. It was very scenic topography and more green and lush than up around Pech Menal.

Saint Antonin had a wonderful market on Sundays, the same one I had first visited with the Pepitours tourists. It was so crowded that you could hardly snake your way through the stalls. The picturesque town had been adopted by the English who had bought second homes there in droves.

There was a rueful joke among the French—*we thought we had got rid of the English after the Hundred Years War. But they're back!*

The English had their own joke—*we love absolutely everything about France. If only the French didn't live there!*

I found René and Marielle's *brocante* shop in Saint Antonin by chance. It was just up the street from '*la Maison de l'Amour,*' a building with a carving of two lovers above the door, perhaps once a medieval brothel? It was across the street from the snack bar called *Le Carpharnaüm,* which also sold bits and pieces of bric a brac. What an esoteric name for a sandwich stand! It basically means 'a mess' in Latin. But the French didn't bat an eye. They had no trouble pronouncing the name either. The more vowels, the better.

I needed furniture for Pech Menal so the window of the *brocante* store caught my attention. I saw a sleigh bed, very *Louis Philippe,* i.e. circa 1840 and two art deco armchairs from the 1930's. I went inside to inquire about them. I was elated to find that the prices were reasonable.

As I told you, *la brocante* is more old stuff than antiques. *Antiquités* in France is a whole other more expensive category of objects and furniture which was mostly outside my price range.

René and Marielle not only sold *brocante* furniture, René refinished it in his home workshop, a barn up in the hills behind Saint Antonin. I know because they took me up there to see some other pieces, works in progress. René showed me an 18th century *buffet.* It was just a country piece, not fancy, but I loved its solid oak look and its simple rounded carvings. The chest was so commodious that I could store all my future crockery inside. I bought it along with a bedroom set from the 1940s, which included a big mirrored wardrobe and a *coiffeuse*, a vanity table with another mirror.

The furniture from the '40s was very inexpensive since that period was out of style. Any object from the 18th century, however, was quite desirable since the 1700's were the height of French design elegance and refined living.

As one antique dealer from Montauban told me in all serious-ness, *"Madame, you should have been here in the 18th century!"*

I learned that the 17th century means Louis XIV and equals furniture with straight lines. The 18th century means Louis XV and curved lines.

René and Marielle didn't just sell and refinish furniture. Delivery was part of the service. They had a young helper, Alain, the son of a widowed neighbor. It was René's hope that Alain, who showed real talent as a furniture restorer, would go to the prestigious furniture academy at Ravel near Carcassonne about two hours away and learn to become an expert in the field. However, Alain chose another path.

It is fortunate that he did so because the advancing tide of *IKEA* soon became a flood. Even René and Marielle succumbed. They gave up their store. I would see them at *brocante* fairs around the region, no longer selling furniture, just small bibelots and books. These small items were so much less arduous to tote around and more in tune with the changing tastes and budgets of young people.

When they delivered my furniture to Pech Menal, René and Marielle saw how much work there was to do on the property. We agreed that Alain, their young assistant, would help me out with the gardening for some small wages. He particularly helped me with the watering chores at Pech Menal. I had to keep my new plantings well watered so that they would become established despite the hot, dry weather.

Unfortunately for me, Alain was more interested in his

hobby, spelunking, than working at my odd jobs. There were lots of caverns to explore in the region. He told me that he wasn't afraid to get stuck in the little passages, which sometimes widened out into ballrooms of stalactites and stalagmites. A person might even find prehistoric wall paintings. That's how the famous Lascaux grotto cave paintings in nearby Dordogne were discovered.

I persisted in watering the hedge composed of a variety of bushes I had planted along the fence at Pech Menal to screen me from the road. Clothilde and Pierre didn't see why I would want to shield myself from the walking path by planting a hedge, *une haie*. There weren't many passersby anyway, but I wanted to feel more private. They were perplexed by some of my ideas.

For instance, Clothile had misgivings about the olive tree I had planted in the middle of the courtyard. Olive trees were more prevalent in Provence, the southeast of France, not in the southwest where we were. They grew very slowly and their twisted and gnarled trunks and branches were an acquired taste. I loved them and thought that the olive tree added a lot of interest to my property.

Clothilde, on the other hand, was less enthusiastic. She expressed concern about the tree's longevity even though I knew that olive trees could live for hundreds of years.

"Barbara," she warned me, "I don't think that *olivier* will thrive there in front of your barn."

"Why not?" I asked her. "Do you think it will be too cold in the wintertime?"

"No, not cold necessarily. There was an *olivier* in Septfonds for a while near the town hall and it caught fire."

"Oh, no," I said. "Due to extreme heat?"

"Not at all, *pas du tout,*" Clothilde replied. "A car ran into it. It caught fire and burned up."

Wait a second. Clothilde could be inscrutable.

I would take my chances with the olive tree. However, there

was a dead plum tree on the edge of the Belons' field that spoiled my view. I asked Pierre if he would consider cutting it down.

"*D'accord,*" he said. "I'll take care of it. *Je m'en occupe,*" although he himself didn't see any reason to bother about it. Plum trees were very common and popped up all over the place in our area. I told Clothilde how much I liked the jar of plum preserves she once gave me. She told me:

"This jam was made from the fruit of that half dead tree over there on the side of your house."

The implication was that this was the sort of tree I wanted to eliminate. Clothilde's point of view often diverged from mine. I told her one day how much I admired the wild poppies covering the field I could see from my landing as I went in and out of the house.

Her terse reply was, "*Quoi! Ces saletés?*"

"What! Those garbage plants!"

I asked her about a shop that I was curious about. It was never open when I went grocery shopping in Septfonds. This was unusual even allowing for the unpredictable opening and closing days of the *commerces* around town. I could never keep track of the days and hours of the post office, for example. In general, everything was closed from 12 p.m. to 2 p.m. for lunch. This was difficult for me since at home in Florida, I tended to really get into my stride around 11 a.m.

In every French town, as noontime approaches, there is a frenzy of activity as people make their final preparations for lunch. Then with a flurry of *bon appetit's,* doors slam shut and the streets empty out. Except for the terrace of the cafés and restaurants, the streets bask in somnolescent sunshine. Quiet reigns.

This is not a good time to call anyone on the telephone either. People are lunching.

"Clothilde," I queried, "what's the story about the shop called '*Le Fil de Fer*' in Septfonds? It looks interesting from the outside. Is it a hardware store or what?"

The name meant iron wire in French. Clothilde replied with her characteristic, no-frills sangfroid.

"Harumph! I've never set foot in there!"

What! She had spent all of her adult life eleven kilometers away from Septfonds and she had never even been inside one of the businesses there! I didn't know whether to despair of her lack of curiosity or admire the intensity of her focus on more important matters.

Talking with Clothile's husband, Pierre Belon, was more wide ranging. His perspective was broader. For instance, he was hopeful that the newly formed European Union would succeed. He felt that the European bloc would make a necessary and helpful counterpoint to U.S. world dominance. He didn't really understand how, even in jest, one of President George Bush's favorite songs could be *'Don't Worry, Be Happy'* by Bobby McFerrin. It seemed just too juvenile.

Since Pierre was retired, he and Clothilde had leased out some of their land to a certain M. Andrieu. M. Andrieu's nephew helped him out farming. The Andrieus were both unhealthily pale, frail men. Their brain development wasn't too extensive either. Talking with them was comical but also annoying. They didn't catch onto the train of the conversation, as if they were from another planet.

At *apéro* hour, from the sliding glass doors in the Belons' living room, we had a good view out over the field, which the Andrieus had planted with corn.

"Pierre," I asked my nice neighbor, "why are the furrows in that field so zigzagged? Is it very hard to plow straight out there?"

All the other fields around were kept as neat as a pin. Their checkerboard exactitude was a marvel to see. They were as beautiful as a Bruegel painting or an illumination from the 'Book of Hours of *le Duc de Berry.*'

Pierre answered laconically, "No, it's not hard to plow straight out there."

I concluded that the drunken furrow pattern was the

Andrieus' signature style, if you take my meaning. The Belons would never directly criticize their tenant or his drinking habits. It was all part of getting along in a small, tight knit community.

One day, the Andrieus' cows got out of another field they were renting from the Belons. There was a herd of about twenty of them. They followed the lead cow the short distance across the dirt lane over to Pech Menal, my house. They were shambling around the new olive tree and into the open sided barn, leaving big cowpats as they went. The Belons and I got them headed across the road and back into their gated meadow.

"What a mess!" I moaned. "*Quel bordel!*"

In just a few minutes the 'ladies' had deposited a load of steaming cow pies at my house that I would need to clean up.

"How can the Andrieus leave them unsupervised like that!" I complained huffily.

"I don't know," sympathized Pierre. "This isn't the first time they got out. One day they walked down into Cayrièch village proper and got into Madame Ballard's swimming pool. Now that was a problem! It took forever to round them up again."

"Is this the little string M. Andrieu uses to close the gate of the cow pasture?" I asked, pointing to a little wisp of white cord. "Why doesn't he use something more sturdy?"

Pierre shrugged, that famous Gallic shrug which says volumes. For all the canny peasant knowledge of the earth and the seasons I was encountering, there were sometimes I felt like I could be in Appalachia just as well as in the southwest of France.

Abandoned Buildings in Montpezat de Quercy

CHAPTER 11

My Painting Life

My life at Pech Menal had developed a pleasant rhythm. My weekly routine included outdoor painting sessions in Saint-Antonin-Noble-Val about 25 kilometers away from Pech Menal. These were the same painting classes, *les stages de peinture*, that I had discovered on my first visit to Saint Antonin with the Pepitours tourists.

Now I was a regular since I lived in the area, but other *stagiaires* came and went so there were always new people from around France to meet. And I continued to enjoy spending time with the small group of friends I had met last summer who lived in that direction, like Jerry and the other Barbara, his wife.

I liked Saint Antonin and the gorges of the Aveyron River. It was greener and leafier there in the river valley. There were little gems of towns to explore and investigate around that area as well as up on the *causse* near Cayrièch and Pech Menal. It seemed France had such a long and varied history that everywhere you went, there were interesting places to visit.

Of course, there were also plenty of times I was by myself. But I didn't mind. I had my house projects to occupy me and I enjoyed my own company. I discovered that I was rather self-sufficient. It was a good feeling.

On painting days, I stowed my canvases and paints in the back of the Citroën station wagon, *le break*, early in the cool morning and set off for class. True, it got hot and sunny painting out of doors, *en plein air*. The light changed very quickly so you had to work fast. It was challenging and hard work, but I thoroughly enjoyed it.

Driving the backway to Saint Antonin alongside fields dotted with sheep fenced in by crumbling stone walls, I passed through woods of scrub oak trees occasionally broken by tiny hamlets of only a few houses and barns. Then descending the steep decline into the Aveyron River valley, I would arrive in Saint Antonin in time to join the group of painters gathered there around the preeminent artist of the region, Éric Maurel. Or rather, I should say gathered round his girlfriend, Chantal Balitrand.

Éric, *le grand maître*, would occasionally breeze by, honoring us with his presence, while a group of us labored away trying to capture the purple shadows of the ruined tannery or the play of light on the giant rolls of hay which dotted the fields.

After painting all morning, it would start to get really hot outside about 12:30 p.m. So we would close up our paint tubes and fold away our portable easels. Tired and hungry, I would load my canvases and easel into the back of my green station wagon, trying to be careful not to smudge my work or get paint smears on the car seats. Once back home at Pech Menal, I would examine my morning's work in the cool of the 'summer kitchen,' perching my canvas on the lip of the stone bread oven. I would exalt in a painting which I found well done and kick myself over the failures.

I liked painting with Chantal, Éric Maurel's girlfriend. She took us to interesting, hard to find locations, like the ruined farm at *Bourdoncle,* a farm whose name made me think of a carbuncle. I would never have found *Bourdoncle* on my own. However, I found Chantal's ideas about painting rigid to the point of exasperation. It was interesting to contrast the French attitude of reverent, unquestioning adherence to Chantal's instruction to a more independent, North American approach to Chantal's established wisdom. Jerry, my Canadian friend, and I would dare to challenge Chantal:

"But Chantal, why do we have to work from light to dark colors?"

"But Chantal, this angle of the church steeple also seems interesting to me. Why can't I paint it from here?"

"But Chantal, why must we try to render the exact colors of the *Quercy blanc*? Why can't we use our imagination?"

Chantal was not used to us North American upstarts, but she basically took it in good part. After all, we had paid our tuition.

At first, I was awed and afraid of Éric Maurel himself. I would tense up when he came by to look at our progress. One day, as he stood behind me at my easel, I hurriedly painted over a very free gestural mark I had made. Éric said to my back,

"Too bad you erased that. It was *un beau geste.*

Why hadn't I trusted my own instincts!

I tried to recreate the mark. Not possible. There was a certain indescribable *je ne sais quoi* quality in the first gesture that I couldn't duplicate.

Éric turned out to be an *amour* beneath his gruff exterior and we became friends. I became friends with his wife, Nicole, as well. Yes, his wife. Eric lived with his wife, Nicole, and his much younger girlfriend, our instructor, Chantal. And they all took care of *maman,* Eric's invalid mother, when they weren't painting or framing or cooking. By which I mean Nicole and Chantal did, since Éric was clearly *le maître des lieux,* the master of the domain who did not himself perform the more mundane everyday tasks.

It seemed clear that this arrangement mostly benefited Éric, but they all seemed happy enough. I viewed it with a jaundiced eye from my North American perspective, but I tried not to be too disapprovingly provincial. This was *la vieille Europe* after all.

The artist was small in stature, but still an imposing figure with his piercing blue eyes and a leonine head, crowned with white hair which fell to his shoulders. He was quite an intelligent person and he did not suffer fools gladly. The first time I met him was in the *atelier* in Brousses at his house. It was raining or otherwise we would have been outside painting in a lavender field, or near a ruined pigeoncote on some farm. We *stagiaires* were clustered in the studio. Our task was to make a pencil drawing of a doll which had belonged to one of Éric's daughters.

Our teacher stalked around the room peering impatiently at our sketches. When he came to me he said in French to Chantal *sotto voce,* "Here's one who takes herself seriously."

"Shhh! *Chut,"* Chantal said in warning. *"Elle comprend bien le français.* She can understand you."

Well, yes, I did take myself seriously. *And who was this self important bigamist, safe in his little, self-curated cocoon to cast aspersions on me?*

I glowered at Éric. I hadn't left a 30-year-long marriage and ventured far away to experience life in a completely new setting in order to be shamed and disapproved of for thinking well of myself. My self esteem was on the ascendant. I was succeeding on my own terms and flexing my new found muscles, the muscles which allowed me to stand tall on my own two feet.

One of the things I liked best about the French was their acceptance of different behaviors. Although they could be quite conformist, like eating meals at the same time and appreciating the same traditional foods, they were quite tolerant of most of the vagaries of human behavior. If Éric Maurel lived happily in a *ménage à trois,* that was his look out. If the other Barbara, Jerry's wife, was a loner, that was their business. She freely acknowledged her preference for her own company. As she said proudly, *"Je suis sauvage.* I like to be alone. I acknowledge it. I own up to it. *J'assume!"*

I'd like to *assumer* a few things too.

Maurel, the artist, had his own distinctive painting style, somewhat impressionistic and very colorful. His aim was to capture the sights of the *Quercy blanc* region and portray the exact colors of the landscape, the shade of the light and the color of the sky and the fields.

Occasionally, he and Chantal would make a painting trip further southeast around Carcassonne to paint the *Aude* region where they would try to capture the *Aude* colors. Or they might venture up to Normandy for a complete change of painting scene to portray the harbors and the boats up there.

But their main subject was the stones and roof lines of the *Quercynois* houses and *pigeonniers*. Éric also painted the market stalls and their customers in Saint Antonin and Cahors, an ancient city just over the border in the Lot region which had a famous market. He also made many beautiful renditions of the white apple trees in blossom in the spring and the red fields of poppies of summer.

His paintings were very appreciated. His canvases, big and small, decorated the walls of the finer local restaurants. He kept a gallery in Saint Antonin on the main street where he displayed canvases showcasing his work. There was no one at the gallery. A little sign in the window invited interested parties to visit him up at his studio in Brousse-les-Antibels, where they would be most welcome.

No directions were given. You had to figure out the way. This was very French. Once up there, after a jaw-dropping ride on the precipitous Corniche Road overlooking the gorges of the Aveyron River below, visitors would be wined and dined. They could meet the artist himself. They could leisurely consider which of the many canvases stored in the racks of the studio to purchase. Or not.

Once I got to know Éric, I loved being invited up to his house. His wife, Nicole, was a great hostess. His girlfriend, Chantal, was decorative and served at table. Éric was a fascinating talker and stimulating host. He once explained to me his belief that he was a descendant of Louis XIV, the wrong side of the blanket, as they say. His aspirations to royal blood, albeit illegitimate, were at odds with his very liberal and progressive political views which he expounded upon at length. He was sometimes a blowhard and his ideas about race relations in the United States which had been formed during the upheaval of the Civil Rights movement, were out of date.

At that point in time, the French felt quite smug about their superior ability to handle the integration of their small immigrant population. Since the 1960's, however, American society had become more integrated, although not perfect, while French racism was on the rise.

On the other hand, Éric was an empathetic listener. He could be insightful too, when he wished to share his deepest thoughts and experiences.

The artist had moved to Saint Antonin and then to Brousse from Paris in the 1960s. He had found his little slice of paradise. He and his wife, Nicole, had two grown daughters who lived in Toulouse, the biggest city in the area and the home of *Airbus*. Portraits of the daughters' younger selves practicing the piano hung about the Maurel living room. It reminded me a bit of Renoir's portraits of his daughters except for a giant flat screen T.V. on the wall nearby.

The Maurels' relationship with their grown daughters didn't seem close. I had noticed that French people in general felt that adult children should be left alone to lead their lives as they saw fit. This was another of those refreshingly *laissez-faire* points of view of theirs which I appreciated.

Éric rarely left his domestic paradise except to go on painting expeditions with Chantal, the girlfriend. She too, was originally a Parisian, a former *stagiaire* or student who never returned home. The painter's wife, Nicole, had more wanderlust. She sometimes took trips on her own to Egypt or the Atlas Mountains of Morocco. I liked her very much. She was warm and friendly in her quiet way.

To get to the *atelier chez Maurel* in Brousse, you took the Corniche Road which wound its way from Saint Antonin higher and higher around many twists and hairpin turns yielding wonderful views of the old Aveyron River flowing lazily below you in the green valley. Coming through the little tunnel cut in the cliff face and into Brousse, you were met by the cleverest pair of scarecrows you ever saw sitting in a pretty garden.

Most people did a double take when they saw the handsome farmer and his adorable wife waving at them. Then a person realized that they weren't real, but skillfully done mockups.

Next, if you managed to see the discreet signboard announcing the Maurel workshop, you drove up the very steep drive and *voilà, enfin arrivé*. You had arrived. If you kept on the road past the entrance to Maurel's driveway, you arrived at the restaurant, *Les Papilles*, the 'Taste Buds', with its panoramic view over the gorges down to the river below.

Les Papilles was run by Serge Lepic, owner and chef. It was the finest restaurant in the area, or at least the one with the best view. Our group of painters had many a wonderful lunch there after class where Serge welcomed us cordially. He was a creative, if idiosyncratic cook. One never knew what would be on the menu. He let himself be guided by his mood and the market produce of the day.

It was a small place, a cozy house with a big stone patio for outdoor dining in the summer months. The changing list of dishes was written in chalk on the blackboard. Serge knew everybody and became fast friends with new clients like me. He had an effervescent personality which made it hard to complain when the kitchen ran out of menu selections mid-meal or the wait for the following course was extended, and then extended again. His was a one-man operation. He greeted you, seated you and took your order. Then he cooked and served you, his shock of red hair framing his freckled, smiling face.

Audrey, his wife, sometimes helped out, but she spent more and more time in Toulouse working at an office job which she clearly preferred over the barely controlled insanity of the restaurant.

Serge's marriage, like many romantic relationships I observed in France, was a more fluid construct than I was accustomed to back home in the U.S. There seemed to be a more widespread acknowledgement that two people lived their *histoire* together and then it might well be over and time to move on. No hard feelings. *C'est la vie.* This is an expression that the French seldom use themselves, but it does summarize a lot of their attitudes.

Although the French, like everyone, were always searching for *l'homme ou la femme de leur vie,* the one and only, the soulmate didn't always turn up. At least not permanently. I was attracted to this philosophy. Certainly in my own experience, although I had known a passionate and deep connection to my ex-husband, we had eventually outgrown our love story and were pulled in separate directions.

With an awareness that life was not eternal and time was passing by inexorably, I wanted to know what I had missed during those 30 years I had spent as a dutiful wife and mother. I supposed this was partly what I was doing in France.

Last summer after the end of my painting course, *le stage,* with Éric Maurel and Chantal, I had nowhere to stay for *une quinzaine de jours*, French for two weeks. Serge had offered me the use of one of the *gîtes* he owned across the road from *Les Papilles* restaurant in Brousses.

A *gîte* is a rural rental accommodation. There is a *gîte* rating system based on ears of corn, *des épis.* The fanciest *gîtes* are *trois épis,* three ears of corn and *de caractère,* meaning they are also built in the architectural style of the region where they are located.

Serge's *gîte* was not of that standard. It was maybe one ear of corn, just an ordinary place. It did have one of those charming, old-fashioned stone sinks with a hole out the wall for drainage. I learned from experience that this peasant system had a lot of drawbacks. You had to push any leftover bits of food from your dishwashing down the little stone hole where they fell out with the wastewater on the side of your house. It was especially hard to get rid of anything greasy.

The entrance to Serge's *gîte* was on ground level just off the road and the back of the building was built over a steep hill which dropped off precipitously.

One day I had a mishap. I got locked out of the *gîte*. I left my keys inside and closed the door about 10 o'clock in the morning.

Oops! Merde! Too late.

The key was inside and I was on the other side, the wrong side of the locked door.

Yep. The car keys were locked in the gîte as well. How could I be so careless! I castigated myself. *Dumb, dumb, dumb!*

There was no other word for my behavior. There was no one else to blame. No ex-husband, nobody. As my more experienced friend, Jennifer, had told me when I got divorced, now, I would have to take care of my own dead rats, kill my own spiders, take care of my own emergencies, etc.

Serge's wife had left much earlier for her job in Toulouse. Serge himself was nowhere to be found. I supposed he was busy with restaurant business matters. I sure didn't want to be locked out the whole day. I racked my brain for a solution.

I circumnavigated the gîte. Up high above me, I saw the double sided, casement style window out back which I had left open.

I thought so! It was very high up but it would be easy to climb in if I could just get to it. Thank heavens for no screens.

Necessity is the mother of invention, they say, or at least it emboldens.

Although normally rather shy, I decided to approach my neighbors with the cute scarecrow figures to ask for a ladder. When I walked over there, I saw that *Madame* was at home. Her husband was a *boulanger*, a baker by trade, she explained to me. He didn't have his own *boulangerie* but got up very early every morning to go to work making *le pain industriel* for a big company which supplied bread to the supermarket chains.

Yes, indeed, they had a big ladder. I was welcome to wait for her husband's return that evening so he could climb up and let me back into the *gîte*. After a minute considering the wait time, the height of the window and the length of the ladder, I decided to give it a go by myself.

Madame had no objection. She was somewhat distracted by a baby deer she was bottle feeding. It was very cute. She told me that it would soon be big enough to survive on its own. She had mixed emotions about setting her cute pet free. I made the proper sympathetic noises, but I was really thinking about my own problem being locked out.

I got the ladder *Madame* showed me from the barn. My neighbor went back inside her house. The ladder wasn't too heavy to carry. It was a nice aluminum extension ladder. I propped it against the back wall of my *gîte*. It must have been 10 or 15 feet up to the window. Taking a big gulp of air for courage, I gingerly mounted the rungs one at a time. I knew I was being foolhardy, but before I had time to retreat, I was up and in the window.

What a feeling! I had done it! There were the keys lying where I had left them on the table.

I was elated. *What a feat of derring do!* I was back inside the *gîte* safe and sound. I felt like pumping my fist like the tennis players do after a great shot. I turned on the radio and they were playing that catchy song about washing your car:

"All I want to do is have some fun. I've got a feeling I'm not the only one. All I want to do is have some fun, till the sun comes up over Santa Monica Boulevard."

I turned up the volume really loud and did a little victory dance.

On a big high of self reliance, I decided to take Daniel, the postman, up on his invitation to visit him. I had met him through Serge, the restaurant owner.

While I was living at the *gîte*, I spent some time with chef Serge at the restaurant in his off-hours. One day, I found him in the kitchen with a friend who was dressed all in navy blue. The friend was called Daniel, a tall, dark haired guy with a shy manner.

He was at the sink washing the dishes wearing his post office uniform, all dark blue with a vest with many little pockets.

After introductions were made, I said to Serge, "What's this? You've got your friend washing the dishes? He must be a good friend."

"Yes," Serge said. "We're old friends. He's lending me a hand because I don't have any help. The young English girl who was here for summer vacation has gone home now."

"I don't mean to be nosy, Serge, but why don't you hire someone to help you out with the restaurant. You are usually too busy to handle it all on your own."

Daniel spoke up from the sink, "Ah, but if Serge were to hire someone officially, not just an English summer girl, he would never be able to fire them when business gets slower in the winter."

"And I would have to pay the social security *cotisations* for them which would be too costly for a little business like mine," Serge chimed in.

This was a typical French problem for small businesses. It explained why almost every small businessman and artisan I knew in France worked on their own as a one man band. Helpers or employees were almost unknown. If you had a family member to pitch in, that was fortunate. Otherwise you accomplished the most prodigious feats of drilling through stone walls, hefting appliances into place, delivering furniture or running a restaurant all by yourself.

Serge and I sat at a little table while Daniel continued washing at the sink.

"Yes, Barbara, Daniel is a good helper. *Il sait faire la plonge.*"

"Really," I said. "He likes to high dive?"

They both burst out laughing.

"No, *faire la plonge* is slang for wash the dishes."

Was my face red! That's an expression I never learned in school. We all had a laugh together.

"You, 'Amur uh cans,'" Serge said, pronouncing Americans

with a pretend American accent, "don't know about the important stuff."

"Yes," said Daniel, "you guys are too focussed on oil, not water. Isn't that what this Kuwait war is all about?"

"Oil, oil," Serge chimed in. "The Americans have got to protect their oil supplies."

"Ha," I said, "you Frenchies are the ones to talk. Have you seen gas prices here? You are taxed through the nose for gasoline since you have almost no oil resources of your own."

We bantered back and forth about Saddam Hussein and George Bush. Political discussions in France were rare in my experience and usually conducted with a light touch.

Daniel had to go back to work at his post office. "Barbara," he said, pronouncing it the French way, Bar bar ah, with equal stress on each syllable, "I am *enchanté* to meet you. Maybe we could see one another again sometime?"

"Why not?" I replied with a smile. "*On se téléphone?*" And so it was agreed. We exchanged telephone numbers.

After Daniel left, I asked Serge for the scoop on Daniel.

"He's a nice guy. He's never had much luck. He lives on a big property left to him by his mother. You might like each other."

Okay, I thought. "Maybe I'll invite him over to the *gîte* one day when I've got dishes to do. He can help me *faire la plonge*."

"Ha ha," laughed Serge.

Feeling my oats after my exploit with the ladder, I gave Daniel a call. He was home. It was his day off. He would love me to come visit. I drove up to his place following the directions he provided on the phone. I took the road which followed the Bonette River away from Saint Antonin toward Albi. It was dark under the trees lining the river bank. I found the turn off up a steep road through the woods toward Daniel's house as he had indicated. It seemed very isolated.

The Eagles were blaring on my car tape player as I pulled into the drive. I sang along with them, "*I've got a peaceful, easy feeling, you won't let me down, cause I'm already standin' on the ground.*"

Daniel had heard my car coming up the road and was outside to meet me.

"I see you like *the Eagles*," he said, greeting me with *la bise,* kisses on each cheek.

"Bonjour, Daniel. Oui, I like them a lot. I've got a tape of their greatest hits for the car."

It was a good sign he liked one of my favorite groups.

Although this was a good start to the visit, things quickly went downhill from there. Daniel seemed depressed. The house and the property were down at the heel and lifeless. Somehow we ended up in bed together for lack of anything else to do rather than from any passionate impulse on either of our parts.

As I looked at my reflection in the mirror of the big mahogany armoire in Daniel's bedroom, I thought to myself, *what am I doing here?*

The whole lovemaking, if you can call it that, was dispiriting and disappointing. I extricated myself from Daniel's halfhearted embrace, got dressed, and drove back the way I had come.

Un échec. A failure. *"And another one bites the dust,"* to quote another one of my favorite bands.

I'd just have to keep looking.

Le Café des Arcades in Caussade

CHAPTER 12
I Made a Friend

I made a real friend while painting in a workshop with Éric Maurel and Chantal. She came out from Toulouse to do a painting *stage* in Saint Antonin. Her name was Yannick Duhamel. She was the daughter of a decorated French army colonel who had played an important role in WWII. In fact, he was awarded *la légion d'honneur*, France's highest military and civil honor, at the end of the war for his service. His code name in the Resistance movement was Durandal. At the end of the war, he led an effort to modernize the French army command by integrating proven Resistance fighters from non military backgrounds into the hide-bound, career professional army structure which dominated the institution.

Yannick came from a *famille nombreuse* and had six brothers and sisters. One of them was a Vietnamese orphan her father had adopted during his posting to South East Asia. Some of her childhood had been spent in Bénin, one of France's former African colonies during another posting.

Yannick was a pretty redhead. She attracted male attention wherever she went. And she told me that she considered me a flirt. ME! She had been married twice and had a child from each husband. Her son and daughter were grown up now and leading their own lives although neither of them had such an easy go of it. My new friend now worked in social services where she was a diligent, concerned counselor for the mentally challenged but basically she hated her job. She looked forward to retirement in a few years, although she was concerned about having enough money to live on comfortably.

After years of paying into the system, she told me, her retirement pension would be *dérisoire.* She was not the first person I had met who labeled their retirement income so small as to be 'derisory.' I loved how the French sprinkled big words like *dérisoire* into their conversation with ease. 'Derisory', for example. *Impeccable* was a typical way to say 'good,' to show approval of a plan, for example. My French cleaning lady talked in four syllable words which had long fallen into disuse for most Americans. Take the word *desuetude.* It means 'out of use.' The same word is out of usage in the U.S., but common coinage in French people's vocabulary except 'desuétude' has an accent in French. Otherwise, it is exactly the same.

When our two week painting *stage* in Saint Antonin ended, Yannick and I arranged to keep in touch. I think she glommed onto me, more than vice versa, but that was ok. She drove out to my house one day from her apartment near Toulouse to spend the afternoon with me in Cayrièch. I showed her around Pech Menal a bit and then she promptly fell asleep on the sofa. She was so tired out from her job and from stress in general. She slept a good three hours. She woke up quite embarrassed:

"I deserted you all afternoon, Barbara! Where are my manners? I came out to visit you and took a nap, *une sieste* instead. Will you ever forgive me?"

In actuality, I had really enjoyed a little down time by myself. I used it to work on the painting I was making of the new olive tree in my courtyard with the lavenders all around.

"Not at all, *ma belle,* " I told her. "I was enjoying myself, a little *solitude à deux.* "

I learned on further acquaintance with Yannick that she was a past master at taking a refreshing *sieste* to recover from a midday *coup de pompe*–running out of gas. I soon learned to follow her lead. I found that after a *petite sieste,* the mood was lighter and good humor reigned supreme for the rest of the day's activities and into the evening.

"Let's go out to dinner at a small bistro that has opened in Septfonds," I suggested, not anxious to cook for us. "It's new. It's called the *Saint Mamet*." Yannick agreed. "Yes," she replied, "That way we can talk and get to know each other better."

We set off in my car for the five kilometers down the road to *le St. Mamet.* The restaurant was in a small garden behind a warren of stone walls just off Main Street, *la rue principale* in Septfonds. The two owner-restaurateurs had been inspired by their Moroccan backgrounds to create a chic ambiance in the little stone alcoves of their restaurant. The menu was eclectic. The food was good. As soon as we entered, Yannick and I felt transported to a larger and more sophisticated metropolis than little Septfonds. *Le St. Mamet* was a real find, although its hours were idiosyncratic. It was only open when the two owner-chefs felt in the mood. Luckily, they were in the mood that night. As we ate and drank, Yannick expressed to me her complete and utter discouragement with men. She was finished with them, she told me in no uncertain terms.

"My first husband was a doctor," she explained. "We had a son together, Julien. When Jean, my young husband, committed suicide, I was left on my own with the baby. My husband overdosed. Too many drugs, too available, in the medical profession, the way I see it."

Yannick continued, "I married again and had a daughter, Lataëtia. My second husband, Étienne, turned out to be a complete rat. He never accepted my son from my first marriage. We were restoring a big house near Toulouse together, doing everything ourselves. We couldn't get along. The house was cold. It was dirty. The work on the house project was never ending. My husband was abusive to me and the children. I tried to stay in the marriage for their sake, but it just became too much for me. I eventually saw that they would be better off away from Étienne. I was literally afraid for their safety, especially for Julien, my son by my first husband. So I left Étienne. Then I had to figure out a way to support myself and the two kids. It has been somewhat of a struggle, let me tell you."

Whew! This was a lot to absorb. *Yannick surely had had her share of difficulties with men.*

My attention was drawn to a group of men seated at a table in the next alcove. Their area was lit with many shiny hanging lanterns. A pretty young woman was addressing them. Their eyes were all trained on her lovely face and form.

I overheard the words 'Bristol Myers Squibb.' I could hardly believe my ears. *What a coincidence! The very company where my ex-husband, Alex, had been head of the legal department. Small world!* It was evidently a business dinner of some kind. Perhaps it was one of those occasions where doctors are wined and dined by a pharmaceutical company hoping to introduce a new product to influential medical professionals. Even here in little Septfonds, the wheels of commerce, probably American commerce, were never entirely still.

Reminders of ex-husbands seemed to be the theme of the evening for Yannick and me. Yannick had decided to totally give up on the search to find a prince among all the frogs out there. I was not so disaffected. I felt luckier than she to have escaped with some good feelings for men left intact. Not for the first time, I realized that I had had a relatively easy divorce. I had been treated fairly. I wasn't cheated on or physically abused. I never feared for my children's safety.

"Let's get the check, Yannick," I suggested. "It's my treat."

This was the first of many meals, painting *stages* and excursions I shared with Yannick. She was an adventurous person and interested in having a foreign friend, someone outside of her usual circle of acquaintances. For my part, her friendship was an entrée into greater intimacy with a Frenchwoman of my own age and educational background, so to speak. Yannick had wider horizons than many of the people I met. Perhaps because of her far-flung upbringing, she didn't mind that I was different. In fact, she rather liked the *je ne sais quoi* air of foreignness that clung to me no matter how much I tried to fit in.

It was nice to have made a friend.

Boules Players in Sant-Antonin-Noble-Val

A Surprise Visit from My College Roommate Triggers a Flashback to our School Days in Paris and Biarritz

I got a telephone call from the United States out of the blue. It was Martha Galanz on the line. She was my roommate in Paris during the second half of our Junior Year in France program back in 1968-69. She had been a bridesmaid at my wedding to Alex later that same year. We had always stayed in touch over the years with Christmas cards and phone calls. Martha had been a brilliant student in economics at our university. We both attended the same school. Special allowance had been made for her, a non-French major, to spend a year studying in France. After graduation, she had pursued advanced studies in her field and her career had taken off after she received her doctorate from MIT. Presently, she was divorced and lived with her son in Washington, DC where she worked for an important government think tank.

"*Barbara, c'est moi, Martha!* It's me," she shouted exuberantly into the phone. "I'm going to a conference in Paris next week and I'd like to come down to Pech Menal and visit you and your new place for a couple of days."

"Why, Martha, that would be great! I'd love to see you. You won't mind sleeping on the sofa, I hope." I was a little embarrassed that I wasn't perfectly equipped for visitors. The house was big but there was no real guest area.

"Don't be a ninny," Martha said. "You know me. I'm easy-breezy. Remember our room at Madame Beringer's house in Paris back in 1969?'

Of course I remembered the unorthodox and not entirely comfortable set up *chez Beringer* off la Place de la Concorde where Martha and I had been roomies.

"Do you have heat?" Martha asked me. "Remember how cold it was in our bedroom at Madame B's?"

"Hah, Hah," I laughed. "I remember. No problem with cold here at Pech Menal right now. If anything, it's too hot."

"Yeah, I see," Martha said. "Are you still painting?"

"Yes, I am." I told her. "Are you still cycling? Do you still have those beautiful calf muscles I put in the portrait I painted of you in our Paris days?"

"I surely am and I surely do. In fact, after I visit with you for a couple of days, I was hoping you would drive me to Biarritz to meet up with a group who are bicycling around the Basque Country for a week. I'm taking a little vacation."

"Why, of course, I'll drive you there. That sounds great! I'd love to see Biarritz again."

Thirty years ago, Martha and I had spent six weeks of preparatory French immersion classes in Biarritz before our Junior Year in France program moved to Paris for the start of the academic year at the Sorbonne.

Martha said, "We're all set then. I'll give you the details of my arrival at Montauban train station as soon as I know them. I'll take the train. That way, it's easier to bring my bicycle. I have a fancy new model."

"This is so exciting! I can't wait to see you. I can show you all around. We'll really have time to catch up with one another."

Martha agreed. "Yes, and we can reminisce about old times," surprising me since she was not usually sentimental at all.

"Où sont les neiges d'antan?" She quoted the famous poet-

outlaw from the Middle Ages, Francois Villon. He had been at the Sorbonne in medieval times a couple of centuries before us, when it had just opened.

Wow! Martha remembered that line from literature class. It meant 'where are the snows of yesteryear?' In other words, where had all the time flown? It seemed like yesterday that we were young coeds disembarking from the ocean liner, France, at le Havre and heading down south to start our immersion program in the Atlantic seaside resort town of Biarritz. Biarritz was in the heart of the Basque country, near the Pyrénées mountains. I remembered it all so well.

We arrived in Biarritz by train and we college students from the Junior Year in France program settled into our respective lodgings where we would spend the six week preliminary session before the start of our academic year at the Sorbonne in Paris.

Martha and I were not boarding together. In fact, we weren't especially close at the beginning of the program. I was assigned to be a *pensionnaire* at Madame Salerni's house in Biarritz. Martha was rooming somewhere else.

My landlady was a childless, middle-aged widow of a doctor. Nancy, not Martha, was the roommate assigned by the Junior Year in France program to be with me. Madame Salerni had another boarder in our house too. His name was Monsieur Lieux, an elderly man who was quite untidy in appearance. His personal hygiene was bad. He made a mess in *le petit coin* so I always used the toilet in the room I shared with Nancy.

M. Lieux's political orientation was communist. It was shocking to me to meet an avowed communist sympathizer and party member. He had a subscription to the communist newspaper '*L'Humanité*' which he liked to read sitting in an armchair with his cat, *Mirette,* on his not too clean lap. *Mirette* means pretty eyes. *"Mirette, Mirette,"* he would croon.

Mme Salerni's political views were diametrically opposed to M. Lieux. She was a great admirer of Generalissimo Franco, the fascist dictator of Spain, which was just over the border from Biarritz. Another shock to my naïve American self.

I wouldn't have known all this except that every evening during the news hour on television, Mme Salerni and M. Lieux had verbal duels in which they heaped scorn on one another's point of view. And on one another. I didn't understand everything they said, but I got the basic idea.

Even in what seemed to me to be his decrepit state, M. Lieux liked to pass the time down at the town square looking at the girls' thighs, *leurs cuisses*. One day he suggested to our landlady that he take Nancy and me down to the casino with him. Mme Salerni's negative reaction was instantaneous and explosive:

"Ces demoiselles ne sortent qu'avec moi!" she announced in no uncertain terms. "These young ladies only go out with me!"

Wow! I had never been called a demoiselle before.

At *chez Mme Salerni*, lunch was the main meal of the day. Dinner, served at the usual French dinner hour of eight in the evening, consisted of a hot soup. It was hard to wait for dinner time, especially since there was no possibility of snacking between meals at Mme Salernis'.

The kitchen was most definitely off-limits at all times. Driven by an attack of the munchies, I did sneak in there once. I scored a wizened yellow apple. I was struck by the tiny size of her refrigerator. There was not much room in there. It was definitely not large enough to fit the bottles of the soft drink she bought for us. Not Coke®, but a carbonated beverage called *Pschitt,* which we drank lukewarm. I kid you not. The name was supposed to make you think of carbonated gas escaping. This soda was popular in France at that time.

Just like the tiny refrigerator, the wastebasket in our room was also undersized by my American standards. The day I arrived and unpacked, it immediately overflowed with papers and plastic wrappings cast off from my luggage. Mme Salerni was sitting by me on the edge of the bed, probably admiring the cornucopia of stuff emerging from my suitcases. She patted the back of my hair. *"Si lisse"* she said. I learned that it meant 'smooth'.

Madame Salerni was frugal. She liked to take her little car with meager horsepower, *une Citroën deux chevaux,* just across the border into Spain to do her shopping at less expensive Spanish prices. This is how I can attest that there is no comparison between the taste of a French *éclair*, and one made in Spain. As you already suspect, the French one costs a little more, but is much more delicious.

There was a fancy bakery on the main *place* in the center of Biarritz. It was called *'Dodin'*. Their window display was mouth-watering and jaw droppingly beautiful to look at.

In those days before I had learned about the taste delights of *gâteaux St. Honoré, les jésuites* and *la figue*," which comes covered with green marzipan, my favorite *pâtisserie* was the *Napoléon*. At least that was its name at home.

'O là là!' The layers of crispy *pâte feuilleté* pastry alternating with scrumptious *crème pâtissière* topped with the almost, but not quite too sweet icing in the signature bands of chocolate and vanilla stripes.

I waited in line at *'Dodin.'* There was always a line. When my turn came, I asked for *"un Napoléon, s'il vous plaît."*

"Ha, ha, ha," chuckled the serving girl from behind the high counter, barely able to disguise her hilarity. "Tee hee hee.

Napoléon, il est mort, Mademoiselle. He's dead," she told me when she had controlled herself a bit.

I blushed at my error and sputtered, "the, the, the one there," pointing to the pastry of my fondest desires lying in the glass case like a shiny jewel.

"Mademoiselle, the pastry you indicate is called a *mille feuilles*," another young clerk said haughtily.

"Oh, it's called a thousand leaves. I see. *Je voudrais un mille feuille, s'il vous plaît,"* I said, repeating like a puppet the words necessary to get me the treat.

If I was obsessed by a love of French *pâtisserie*, then Madame

Salerni, my landlady, was obsessed by fear of telephone bills. I don't know what had happened in prior years with previous *pensionnaires*, but she all but had the phone under lock down. The rare calls I received from my boyfriend, Alex, back in Chicago were strictly monitored for time restrictions. And I wasn't calling out. Alex was calling me!

Those long-distance trunk line calls sounded so weird. You could almost hear the sound travel along the bottom of the ocean through fathoms of water to your far away caller. But it was a connection to home along with the daily letters, or even twice daily on an exceptional day, since mail was delivered in the morning and again in the afternoon.

Bath time at Mme Salernis' was an event. You had to turn on the little heater in the bathroom and wait a while for the water in the tank to heat up. Once hot, you could fill up the bathtub with the steaming hot water. I was allowed a bath once a week and I appreciated every minute luxuriating during this special time. What a delicious feeling it was to be all scrubbed and clean. I emerged from the tub feeling newly born.

I liked Madame Salerni despite her penny-pinching ways. She had spunk. I think she liked me too. Nancy, my roommate, got fed up with the household and moved out. But I hung in there.

I came close to leaving over the fleas. I noticed little black things jumping around the bed. Then I discovered itchy red blotches on my body. I talked to Madame about it.

"Look at these," I said one evening as we were walking back together from the *place,* the main square. "I have red marks all over. And they itch! They itch terribly!"

I used the word *gratter,* which means to scratch. I had probably looked it up in the dictionary specially to talk to her about it.

"Not *gratter,"* she said. *"Gratter* is not polite. You should say *démanger* instead. You have a *démangeaison."*

I didn't get anywhere with her. I later went to the drugstore and got some powder to put in the bed to control *les puces,* FLEAS!

Madame Salerni could also be fun. I loved going on outings with her at the wheel of her little sardine can of a car with her *amie d'enfance* beside her in the passenger seat. My seat was always in the back of this childhood girlfriend.

We often went to San Sebastian, the summer capital of Mme's hero, Francisco Franco, Spain's iron fisted ruler. As we drove down the steep hill into the beautiful seaside city, the flag might be flying from the palace. This meant that President Franco was in residence which was quite exciting to Madame Salerni.

We would wander the old streets looking at the shop windows. The Spanish made beautiful leather goods then, as they do now. Madame treated us to lunch. She knew some good restaurants. I had *lotte à l'américaine,* monkfish in a tomato sauce. It was delicious. Monkfish is called the poor man's lobster. I was a little confused by *'l'armoricaine'* and *'l'américaine.'* I had tasted *'lotte à l'armoricaine'* on our crossing to France on the ocean liner. I knew *l'Armor* meant the coast of Brittany which was famous for its fish. Here in Spain though, they served it American style, i.e. with a red tomato sauce. It made the dish all the better as far as I was concerned.

Driving by the giant Atlantic beaches like the one at Hendaye, Mme would point out landmarks such as Charlemagne's tower. *How ancient! What history!*

In San Sebastian itself we visited the church where Louis XIV married the Infanta of Spain. As the royal newlyweds left the church in 1660, the door was walled up forever to commemorate their passage through it.

As we drove along, other drivers would pass us by since we were going much slower than the speed limit. The two ladies would curse out the other drivers gleefully shouting, *"Salamis! Saucissons!"* out the open windows. I guessed anything to do with the pig was highly insulting.

Madame Salerni took me under her wing, so to speak. Sometimes we had the treat of *pâté d'Armagnac* for lunch. I loved this *pâté* flavored with *Armagnac* brandy from the *Cognac* region of France not too far to the east of Biarritz.

I also accompanied her on evening strolls. One time we went to the big garden across the street from our house. In the cool of the evening, she unlocked the garden gate which I held open for us. Madame took some lettuce, *des salades*, from the shopping bag she carried.

Following the garden path with me close behind her, Madame called out in a high-pitched voice, "Fifi, Titi. Titi, Fifi!" Nothing happened. She called out again, "Fifi, Titi!"

I couldn't imagine who she was calling. There was no one there. There was just a well-tended lawn bordered by parterres. But then I saw them.

First one and then the other of two greenish brown tortoises lumbered out from the flower beds. The prehistoric looking creatures were sweet. They were a married couple. Fifi was the wife and Titi was her husband. They had come to get the lettuce we offered to them. Madame's neighbor had asked her to look after her pets while she was away.

For me it was a magical moment. A secret in a secret garden.

Our preparatory six week French workshop or *stage* in Biarritz passed by pleasantly. The classes at the château were generally not too difficult. There was one professor I was afraid of, M. Guerlain de Guer. He sat up high above us students on a dais behind a lectern. His *dictées* were difficult.

A *dictée* is a French language exercise in which you transcribe a passage that is read aloud to you. It could be a passage from literature or really anything at all. The challenge is to put the spoken words into writing using correct spelling and grammar.

For example, if you heard the teacher say the sounds 'pass ay,' for example, this could be spelled *passait*, as in he used to pass by or *passaient*, as in they used to pass by. Or maybe *passé*, as in he has passed by, past participle. Or she, *passée*. Or they, *passés*, masculine plural, or *passées*, feminine plural.

Maybe in this case 'pass ay' was a noun, not a verb, as in 'THE past,' *le passé*. Challenging. In fact, some *dictées* could be real *casse têtes*, brain breakers. But dictées were not impossible, if you knew how to decipher the clues from the reading. The context of the reading told you which spelling was correct. If you understood what was being read to you.

I tried to avoid M. Guerlain de Guer's gaze. I didn't want him to call on me. He had a sardonic wit. One of his signature expressions was *couleur cuisse de nymphe émue*, which meant color of the thigh of an aroused nymph. He managed to work this phrase into every class to the delight of the guys in our program.

Another feature of our time in Biarritz was the evening visits we made around the area to meet local dignitaries and to toast to Franco-American friendship. These were organized by a bear-sized, darling of a man, M. Hérisson Laroche, the guiding spirit and organizer of the Biarritz preparatory stay. We would go in the evening to one or another town hall close by and drink champagne with local dignitaries in honor of the Biarritz wartime airfield and the American pilots who had been stationed there.

For amusement, there was always the beach. Biarritz had been a famous beach resort since the turn of the century. Empress Eugénie had made it *de rigueur* for French aristocrats to visit when she built herself a palace right on the shoreline in the 1880's at the height of the *belle époque*. Her palace was now the most deluxe of all the luxury hotels dotting the beachfront. It attracted celebrities and movie stars like Frank Sinatra and Brigitte Bardot.

Although Napoléon III and the aristocratic Russian émigrés who once flocked to Biarritz were long gone, the beaches were still as alluring as ever. In a recent twist of fate, the waves of Biarritz and nearby Anglet were becoming a magnet for surfers. A nascent French surfing culture was springing up in imitation of California.

Our whole group of students loved going to the beach. I was

lucky because the main beach, *la grande plage,* was just down the hill from Mme Salernis' house. One day I spent at the beach stands out in my memory.

There were a group of us students, as usual. The beach was crowded with holidaymakers, as usual. It was hot on the sand. I went in for a dip. It was a beautiful summer day, not a cloud in the sky. The white lighthouse sparkled in the sun from high on its cliff in the distance. The famous Biarritz lighthouse was designed by Gustave Eiffel, the same engineer who built the eponymous tower in Paris for the International Exposition in 1900.

The wavelets danced merrily around me. The water was a deep sapphire blue. I felt myself carried out somewhat deeper in the ocean than I might have liked. No lifeguard made any motion toward me, however. I didn't panic. I was a good swimmer. I slowly and deliberately tried to swim and float my way back into shore. It was a long process, but I made a little more headway with each attempt, taking advantage of the lull between the waves.

When I successfully arrived back on the beach, I was tired. I got out of the water and went looking for my beach towel and clothes. I had left them near my friends from the Junior Year in France program. I searched around. They were gone, both my friends and my clothes!

The beach was deserted. No more vendors of treats shouting, *beignets d'abricot* doughnuts. No more families building sandcastles. No more wriggling figures trying to change from their bathing suits into their clothes under the cover of a personal towel tent with a tie at the neck.

Suddenly I noticed that the bright day had faded into evening more than anything else. *Could I have been in the water for such a long time? Was it possible that I had really been in danger out there in the ocean? Was it possible that nobody had missed me?*

Biarritz and the Bay of Biscay are famous for their strong currents. There is a legend about one of the beaches there called *'la Chambre d'Amour.'* It seems that two lovers sheltering on a nearby beach one evening were caught in the riptide and carried out to sea never to return.

I gave up the search for my affairs. I would have to find out who had my towel and clothes another day. I wondered why none of my friends had sounded an alarm for me. Perhaps they had searched around for me before giving up looking. (This is what had indeed happened. My friends couldn't find me so they took my clothes home to keep them safe.)

Perplexed, I started off home to my landlady's house. I was so embarrassed. In 1968, you did not parade about town in your bathing suit. Bathing attire was worn on the beach only. Having no choice, I crossed the boardwalk and hurried up the hill from the beach, hoping no one would notice me. I couldn't wait to dry off and get ready for the hot soup dinner waiting for me back at *chez Madame Salerni*. I shivered a little in the evening air and with the realization that I had had a close call. Protected by youthful invulnerability, I soon dismissed the whole episode from my mind.

For entertainment on the rare rainy afternoon in Biarritz, there was also a movie theater not far from my house. A bunch of us went to see '*Le Train Sifflera Trois Fois,*' an old American classic film which turned out to be '*High Noon*' in the French translation of the title.

At first, I didn't understand why the film was called, 'The Whistle Will Blow Three Times,' in French. After watching the movie again, I understood the logic of it. When the whistle blows, the decisive cinematic moment arrives when the heroine, played by Grace Kelly, must finally choose sides. She chooses to stay with Gary Cooper, of course.

The film was so old, it had long ago been dubbed into French. It was very funny hearing the French actor reading the part of

Gary Cooper. He rendered Coop's signature, laconic 'Yup' as a high pitched *'oui, oui, oui, oui.'*

The six week *stage* in Biarritz passed by quickly. It was almost time to head north to Paris and the academic year at la Sorbonne. The fall weather was getting colder. However, there was still no heat turned on at Mme Salernis' house. For heat, it was customary to wait until November 15, the proper date when the furnace could be turned on without guilt.

Learning that we still had plenty of time before the start of classes in Paris, I decided to use the two extra weeks to go home to visit my boyfriend, Alex, at school back in Chicago. Our daily letters back and forth had only deepened our commitment to one another. I had to see him! I couldn't wait. Time was playing into my hands. I was free until classes began at the Sorbonne in mid-November.

I had a bit of cash which my grandmother had given me as mad money. I went to the travel agency on the main square, *l'Agence Havas,* to see if I could afford this side trip home to see my honey. *L'Agence Havas* arranged the tickets. I would travel by overnight train from Biarritz to Paris. No *couchette,* that was over my budget. I would sit up all night. From Austerlitz station in Paris, I would find the Air France bus to Orly airport. From Orly, I would fly to Heathrow airport in London and catch the plane for Chicago where Alex would meet me.

To my surprise, Madame Salerni was one hundred percent behind my plan. She thought it was so romantic that I wanted to see 'my Johnny boy.' I think she was thinking of the war years. Probably World War One.

When the momentous day of my departure arrived, I was nervous. It was a big trip to undertake by myself at the tender age of nineteen. The world seemed bigger in those days. Biarritz was a little speck lost on the map and Chicago was very far away. "Al Capone, bang, bang," as the French said whenever Chicago was mentioned, making pretend pistols with their pointer finger and thumb.

The train departure was at *22h,*10 p.m. Traveling all night, the train arrived very early in the morning in Paris.

Madame accompanied me to the station, the two of us lugging my big suitcase between us. It was cool and misty. I must have been rather pale with excitement.

My landlady concluded wisely that I could use a dose of artificial courage, a pick-me-up.

"Let's stop in here and get you a *grog*," she told me, leading the way to the bar at the train station, *la buvette*. "I think you need a warm drink."

"What's a *grog*?" I asked her.

"You'll see, my dear. You'll like it."

It turned out to be what I would call a hot toddy, a mixture of very hot tea, lemon and sugar with a big dollop of whiskey. It was the most delectable drink I ever tasted up to that moment.

Leaving Madame Salerni standing on the platform, I got on the train and found my compartment and my seat. I was wearing my best traveling outfit, a dress with a very short tweed skirt and an off-white wool sleeveless mock turtle top. Over the dress, I had on the matching belted, brown leatherette coat buttoned up tight.

My compartment mates greeted me. They were three Basque men, typical *bérets* perched jauntily on their heads and all. We said our "*bonjours.*"

Biarritz was in the heart of the French Basque country. The Basques were an ancient people whose origin was mysterious. Their language was untraceable because it wasn't related to any other language group in the world. They had their own customs, such as *pelote* or *pelota* in northern Spain where there was also a big Basque population. *Pelote* is what we call jai alai, the fast-paced ballgame played against a wall with long basket-shaped scoops.

Basques were traditionally shepherds in the Pyrénées mountains where they were also mountain guides and smugglers. They were fiercely independent and were fighting both France and Spain to free the Basque people and create their own country. Recently, there had been armed insurrections and even murders in the name of their cause. You would see their rallying sign *'Euskadi'* painted on rocks and the sides of buildings. From most points of view, *ETA,* their organization, was considered a terrorist, separatist group.

The three Basques in my train compartment, however, would prove to be my faithful guardian angels during the long night train ride. But we were just introducing ourselves at this point.

"I see you're Basque," I said to the men.

"Yes, are you Basque?" said the most forward of the trio with a leer. *"Êtes-vous basque?"*

"In spirit," I replied without thinking. *"En esprit."*

"En esprit ou en espray?" he countered, and all three of them started laughing uproariously. "Are you Basque in spirit or some-where else on your body?"

I blushed. I had no idea what he meant exactly but it seemed to be something risqué, a Basque *double-entendre.*

As the train chugged slowly out of the station, I spied Mme Salerni out my window still waiting on the platform. I waved and caught her eye. Then she reached into her purse and took out a white lace handkerchief. She waved it at me just like in the old movies as the train picked up speed on its way north to Paris. Her figure retreated into the distance and disappeared from view.

A tear crept into my eye.

Our six week preparatory stay in Biarritz was over. The students from our Junior Year in France program headed from Biarritz to Paris and the start of the official school year 1968-69 at the Sorbonne. *La rentrée,* the new school year, was about to begin.

I had just returned from a quick visit back home to Chicago. In the short break between Biarritz and Paris, I had managed to squeeze in a quick trip to see my boyfriend, Alex, who was now my fiancé. He had proposed and I had accepted.

My engagement was so exciting! Alex had bought me an

engagement ring. We had broken the big news to our parents and friends. But I was still intent on spending my junior college year at the Sorbonne. Alex and I could be married when I returned.

My new Paris lodgings had an elegant interior. The owner, my new landlady, was Mme Longueville. Bridget, my new roommate from the college program, and I were seated next to her on low, velvet chairs with fringe. Marie-France, Mme Longueville's pretty sixteen year old daughter had already left for class at her *lycée* or highschool.

Our seats were flanked by mirrored *vitrines* or display cases full of oriental ceramics, objets d'art and a collection of Chinese jade snuff bottles. The apartment overlooked the treetops along the *avenue Niel* in the fancy 16th *arrondissement* of Paris, one of the bourgeois residential enclaves of the capital city. At this time in mid-November, the treetops were mostly bare of leaves.

My trunk had arrived before me and it sat open in front of us in the living room. Its black metal bulk looked out of place in the beautiful decor. I unfolded some clothes from the trunk. My mother and I had carefully selected a few special outfits for me to wear in Paris. There was a new white piqué shirt with a *jabot* tie like French nobles used to wear. It went under a long, red wool vest with gold buttons, a *redingote*, a sort of George Washington looking garment. There was a fuzzy red dyed rabbit coat with a lining printed with purple flowers. It was very 'Carnaby Street' for this was 1968 and swinging London fashion was all the rage, *dans le vent*.

My mind was not on the task of unpacking. It was a thousand miles away, back in Chicago with my fiancé. I couldn't stop fingering the diamond engagement ring on my finger. I loved showing it off.

"*Que c'est beau!*" Mme Longueville said, admiring the little diamond set on a plain yellow gold band.

"It's just like Barbra Streisand's in the movie, "Funny Girl," gushed Bridget, my new roomie.

If there was a resemblance, it was in miniature. My little

diamond was much smaller than the rock Omar Sharif bought for Barbra Streisand in the film. In fact, I would have preferred another style of ring altogether; a sapphire surrounded by diamonds. I thought it would look more European, but Alex had said that he wanted me to have a single diamond, an American style engagement ring. To Alex, a diamond solitaire was the signal which announced that the wearer was engaged, *affiancée*.

Madame Longueville politely inquired about Alex. I explained that he was in law school back in Chicago, '*L' École de Droit.*'

"Why isn't he in the army?" she wanted to know.

It was a fair question. The U.S. was embroiled in the Vietnam War. Most young men of Alex's age had been drafted. Madame had a special interest in Vietnam and southeast Asia where she had lived for many years before her husband's death. He had been an important colonial official overseeing the French-built railroad system in Hanoi and Saigon. In fact, her daughter, Marie-France, had been born in Hanoi.

"Well, you see, Madame," I explained, "Alex would have had a deferment because he is in law school, but he didn't need one because he was classified 4F by his draft board."

"*Et alors?*" Mme Longueville required further explanation.

"He has flat feet," I told her, slightly abashed. Alex did have very flat feet. They were almost deformed, a fact which somewhat embarrassed me. In my eyes, my fiancé was perfect in every way.

"Harumph," she sniffed. "The American army never marches anywhere. They drive!" she announced definitively.

Aha, I thought. *What about those GIs I saw on the TV news doing foot patrols, slogging through the high jungle grasses?*

There was no point correcting my new landlady. She was a tall, imposing woman with short, dark black hair. Her manner exuded authority. 'Ernestine,' her first name, led one to think that her parents might have preferred a boy.

Life at the apartment soon fell into a routine. Mme Longueville worked in advertising. She kept long hours at her agency, leaving early in the morning before I left for class. I would leave the apartment being careful to close and lock the door with my key. Marie-France, Mme Longueville's daughter had her own school schedule and Bridget, my roommate, also kept her own separate hours, depending on her class schedule.

Stepping into the dark hall at the top of the staircase each morning, I would press the *minuterie* or the button which turned on the lights in the hall just long enough for me to descend the staircase to the ground floor. If you were a slowpoke and you ran out of light in the middle of your descent, there was another thoughtfully placed *minuterie* button along the wall of the stair-well. You just had to learn where it was.

Passing the *loge* of the *concierge*, I gave a wave just in case she was peeking out the window of the little ground floor apartment where she kept a weather eye on everyone coming or going in and out of the building.

Most mornings I took the métro from the nearby stop at la Place Pereire to the *quartier latin* where my school was located in the traditional student area of Paris since the middle ages, the Latin Quarter. In medieval times, Latin was the 'lingua franca' of the international students gathered there around la Sorbonne, one of the first universities founded in Europe. *Le quartier latin* was still the artistic, bohemian heart of Paris. All the five American universities which had college credit programs in Paris shared space there at Reid Hall, near the métro stop, *Notre Dame des Champs*. The famous 'Académie Julian' where the budding impressionist painters had studied was just up the street. 'La Closerie des Lilas,' where a young Ernest Hemingway had nursed his glass of wine to save money, was around the corner.

The *Boul Mich,* le boulevard Saint Michel, traditional thor-oughfare of Parisian student life was there too, as well as the *grands cafés* of le boulevard Montparnasse where Diego Rivera and Picasso had rubbed elbows with Anaïs Nin, Modigliani and Kandinsky. Matisse, Josephine Baker, Scott Fitzgerald and Zelda, all had their favorite café terrace. Jean-Paul Sartre and Simone de Beauvoir once hung out there as well.

Le Jardin de Luxembourg was a short walk away for a relaxing stroll in the beautiful garden. It cost a few *centimes* to sit down by the pond there. The chairs were patrolled by a set of no nonsense female guardians.

On my way to school, I went down the steps into the mouth of the métro, my *ticket* in hand. The ticket takers on the métro platform controlled access to the *quai* where you caught the train. They made little holes in your ticket with their *poinçonneuse* hole punch. This showed that you had used your ticket and couldn't reuse it. Woe betide you if you tried to evade those dragon ladies and men!

There were plenty of unwashed bodies jammed into the métro car. Not everyone had such a lovely bathroom with its powder blue porcelain fixtures at home the way Bridget, my roommate, and I did.

I loved arriving at school in Reid Hall. I walked from the métro along the winding *rue Notre Dame des Champs*, taking my time like all school boys and girls, the proverbial *'chemin de l'écôlier.'* Reaching my destination, I ducked through the door on the *rue de Chevreuse* and passed under the shadowy, wooden covered entrance hall. I nodded towards the little sliding window, *le guichet*, on the left to be waved through by the concierge sitting there.

The school complex was an old-fashioned, rambling building built in a 'U' shape around a spacious courtyard, dotted with wrought iron lawn chairs. It had once been the hunting lodge of the Duc de Chevreuse in the 17th century when the Left Bank was still a woods and full of game to hunt. With its warren of rooms, sunny glass-paned passageways and crooked flights of stairs leading off in all directions, the building seemed to have grown like topsy.

This premises had been donated to Columbia University in 1913 by the Whitelaw Reids, an American ambassador to France and his wife. A fine portrait of Mrs. Reid surmounted the fireplace mantel in the most formal space in the building, an upstairs, wood paneled library. The library overlooked a big, double height space where the students from all the five American junior year programs in Paris would gather in small clusters of friends and acquaintances. I would sometimes run into my friend from my university back home, Martha, there, or in the dining room where the excellent restaurant was.

This dining room was presided over by a group of older women, dressed in black with white organdy aprons, the waitresses, *les serveuses*. When they asked you how you wanted your tea, "*au lait, au citron ou nature,*" you needed to answer quickly and correctly or risk a withering stare. And perhaps no tea service. Tea was the least expensive choice for a pick-me-up in the middle of the day: tea with milk, with lemon or black. It was like running a gauntlet to order tea there and good French practice as well. There was no deviation and be quick about it.

My French grammar classes were held at Reid Hall. Martha was in one of them. In theory, we were also to attend classes at the *Université de Paris* itself, me at the *Sorbonne,* Martha at *Sciences Po.* However the French educational system was so different from the American one that, in practice, I was never actually in class at the *Sorbonne.* "*Le professeur est souffrant,*" "The teacher is sick" would read the notice posted on the Sorbonne classroom door, the few times I tried going there before I gave up. I think Martha had better luck with her political science classes in their building in the *6e arrondissement* or out in Nanterre.

To get a diploma, the French students didn't have to attend class at all. There was no grade for class participation. They could study for a subject entirely on their own as long as they could get a hold of the reading list and pass the final exam. These old-fashioned, autocratic educational methods were part of the reason for the violent street demonstrations, *les manifs,* short for *les manifestations*, happening all around the student quarter in 1968. The students were protesting to reform and modernize this system, as well as France in general.

We didn't know it then, but the student protests of May '68 would shake French society to its very foundations.

The classes organized by my Junior Year in France program, on the other hand, were run according to American pedagogical standards, in other words, a real class was held at the scheduled place and time. This backup system permitted us American students to receive credit from our home universities or colleges.

The teacher at Reid Hall who was helping us unravel the mysteries of French grammar was a wonder. She could speak so fast, as it seemed to us students, that her nickname was 'Madame Motormouth.' Her lips, teeth and jaw were wonderfully elastic and mobile. The French sounds she emitted were so pure. The words were perfectly enunciated as they came at you at a rapid fire pace.

Not all of my classes were at Reid Hall. I took an art history class at the Louvre. No slideshows for us. Our small group was guided along the corridors of *la Grande Galerie* of the Louvre art museum by our lovely instructor to study the original artworks hanging on the walls.

We did a survey course of the periods of French painting. From imposing canvases by Poussin and le Brun, court painters to Louis XIV, to the charming nymphs and flowering bowers by Fragonard and Boucher preferred by Louis XV, his successor and grandson, we moved on to Jacques-Louis David and the classicists who painted the heroes and heroines of ancient Rome.

David also painted the giant canvas of *'le Sacre de Napoléon'* depicting Buonaparte, the soon to be emperor, taking the crown out of the Pope's hands and placing it on his own head as Joséphine, his wife, and the court looked on.

But first, we didn't neglect earlier French masters of the 16th and 17th centuries like Claude Lorrain and his paintings always lit by a glowing candle flame or the le Nain brothers and their sensitive portrayals of peasant life.

We were, of course, leading up through art history to the Impressionists by way of their precursors, the Romantic painters. There was Géricault who painted '*le Radeau de la Méduse*' with shipwrecked bodies strewn over the rudderless raft lost at sea. Not to forget the magnificent Delacroix. His canvas '*la Mort de Sardanapale*' showed more scantily clad bodies, concubines heaped around the sultan, splayed out on his luxurious bed along with his horse's dead body.

We studied Jean Dominique Ingrès, the antithesis to Delacroix's riot of color and movement, with his purity of line and invisible brushstrokes rendering the elegant necks and profiles of exquisite *odalisques* from the harems he visited or imagined.

Dark and exciting, Gustave Courbet painted the Spanish dancer, Lola Montez, and of course his scandalous canvas, 'The Origin of the World,' a woman's birth canal. The great Édouard Manet too, was influenced by Spanish art and was master of the color black.

The Barbizon School painters in contrast, made delicate renditions of the mossy rocks and tall leafy trees they sometimes painted in nature on their walks in the Barbizon Forest.

It was fantastic to stand in front of these masterpieces while gentle Madame Duval expatiated and elucidated. She had a slight limp and walked slowly with the aid of a medical appliance—a sort of crutch—which somehow accentuated her delicate beauty. We would have followed her anywhere.

And we did follow her on architectural tours of the Louvre palace itself. We felt protective of her as she led us through the Richelieu courtyard to the staircase built in the Renaissance by King Henri II whose coffered ceiling is embossed in marble with intertwining 'H's' for Henri and 'D's' for Diane de Poitiers, his mistress. Diane's namesake was Diana, Roman goddess of the moon and the *devise* of a crescent moon was also carved in the marble as a little clue as to the mistress' identity. Hint, hint. Wink, wink.

My roommate at Madame Longueville's, Bridget, had selected

a different course of study. She was taking a class in cinema. I often tagged along with her on her 'assignments'. We went to the Cinémathèque, a grand movie theater in the Art Deco Palais de Chaillot palace museum across the Seine from the Eiffel Tower. Comfortably ensconced in the balcony there, we saw classics like Sergei Eisenstein's *'Ivan le Terrible'*. Fur clad *boyars* crouched down through many low ceilinged archways as Ivan lorded it over his courtiers and vassals.

The Cinémathèque was the brainchild of Henri Langlois who was also behind *'les Cahiers du Cinéma'*, a French magazine that took movies much more seriously than was the norm in the U.S. The French actually considered the movies the seventh art form, *'le 7e art'*. Why, they even thought Jerry Lewis was a comedic genius in the tradition of Charlie Chaplin, not just Dean Martin's silly second banana. There were lots of teeny, hole in the wall movie houses scattered around the Left Bank of the river Seine where Bridget and I saw films like 'The Big Sleep,' with Humphrey Bogart and Lauren Bacall, an American classic, and *'Ordet,'* 'The Word,' a powerful Danish masterpiece.

Life back at the apartment *chez Madame Longueville* was somewhat strained. Madame's job at the advertising agency was demanding. She seemed under stress. It bothered me to discover that she had no bedroom of her own in the apartment. She slept on one of the elegant velvet *canapés* in the living room since Bridget and I occupied one available bedroom and Marie-France the other.

There was also tension between Marie-France and her mother. In typical teenage fashion, Marie-France was testing the limits. She wanted to go skiing during winter break with a boy called Bertrand.

I quote Madame Longueville:

"You are too young to go away to *les Alpes* with Bertrand, young lady! You are only 16 years old!"

Marie-France's response:

"I am not too young! I may be 16, but I am in my 17th year! I'm going and you can't stop me!"

The bedroom door slammed.

Madame Longueville must have wondered where they had gone, the good old days we saw on the screen in the eight millimeter home movies she sometimes showed us. In those grainy color films, adorable baby Marie-France was wheeled about in her pram by the *ayah*, her Vietnamese nanny. M. et Mme Longueville were shown on horseback galloping on handsome steeds through exotic landscapes, jumping over obstacles with grace and ease. Madame appeared to be quite an excellent horsewoman.

One Saturday, she invited me to come with her to her riding club in the Bois du Boulogne, a fancy section of the city with parks, elegant eateries and the race track where Degas had painted the horses. Bridget had weekend plans with her French boyfriend, a nice fellow who was doing a course to become a pastry chef. Marie-France was otherwise occupied as well.

I declined Madame's invitation to the club, preferring to stay in the apartment by myself to relax and watch TV. There were delicious leftovers in the refrigerator from a party given for Marie France's recent 16th birthday—a veal roast rolled around a delectable herb stuffing and some fancy leftover *pâtisseries*.

Bridget and I had been invited to the party. Several young people gathered in the Longueville's elegant living room. The atmosphere was decorous and formal. Although teenagers, the guests were dressed like adults and comported themselves as grown ups too. 45 rpm records played softly on a portable turntable. It seemed a pretty stilted affair to Bridget and me and we didn't stay long.

On the Saturday evening when I declined the horseback riding invitation, I was watching the little black and white television set tucked into a corner cabinet in the Longueville's living room. Simon and Garfunkel came on the screen and played their song, 'Homeward Bound.' They sang "*I'm homeward bound. Home, where my thoughts are 'scapin, home, where my love is waitin.'*" I felt homesick. I missed Alex. I had a bout of *le cafard*, the ubiquitous water bug whose name is slang for homesickness in French.

Later that evening *Canal 2*, the second of the two French TV channels, showed an old American movie about the Depression Era. In this classic film, called *Our Daily Bread*, by King Vidor, some down and out farmers from the Dust Bowl finally made it to California and started a farm. In the exciting climactic scene, water flowed into the irrigation ditches they had dug leading from the river into their newly planted fields. The harvest was assured! They did it!

In the film, 'Yacob' or 'Jacob,' a Swedish farmer talked about yoking his mule at the same time as he was making a little joke. The subtitles mixed up 'yoking' and 'joking ' since 'joking ' is pronounced 'yoking' with a Swedish accent. And I caught the discrepancy! I was making progress in French.

Was this fun? I asked myself doubtfully if I shouldn't have gone to *équitation* to ride horses with Madame Longueville instead. But she seemed under such stress.

I sensed that she was trying hard to provide her daughter with a suitable upbringing so that she could one day make an advantageous marriage. This was perhaps understandable, but it didn't leave room for much lighthearted fun around the apartment.

So when an opening occurred at my friend Martha's house, at the other end of the Champs Elysées near la Place de la Concorde, I decided to leave Mme Longueville's. I could become Martha's roommate at her landlady's house just off the famous landmark.

One Corner of la Place Nationale in Montauban

CHAPTER 14

More Memories of Paris and Moving in with a New Host Family

Over Christmas vacation, I moved out of Mme Longueville's apartment and into my new quarters on *la rue Saint Florentin*, just off la Place de la Concorde and its obelisk and fountains. I moved in with my friend, Martha. I knew Martha from before the junior year in France program because she and I attended the same university back in the United States. In fact, I had met Martha through my sophomore year college roommate. They grew up together in the New York suburbs.

The little pavilion where Martha's landlady lived was situated in a courtyard behind an enormous green painted door with a brass knocker. You actually entered the courtyard via a much more human scaled door cut into the Brobdingnagian one.

Le top du top Hotel Crillon and the American Embassy were right nearby on la Place de la Concorde. Traffic swirled around the obelisk which Napoléon had brought back from his conquest of Egypt. The *couturier* Jean Patou's boutique was down the block. I knew his signature perfume, 'Joy', was very expensive.

The neighborhood was less residential than my old one on the avenue Niel, but just as fancy in its way. Most importantly, *chez Mme Beringer* and her young son, Victor, they seemed to be having a lot more fun than back at Madame Longueville's apartment.

The decor inside the little pavilion which was my new home was unusual. Everything that wasn't covered in bamboo paneling was red tartan plaid. Lampshades were red. Or plaid. This gave a subdued light to the little bamboo clad rooms. There was an iron spiral staircase leading to the upper floor, *un escalier en colimaçon.* It indeed curved like a snail. You couldn't climb it very fast and you went down it slowly like a snail, if you didn't want to trip.

To access Martha's and my bedroom, you mounted the curving staircase and walked through a carpeted passage which was also the bathroom, complete with a big bathtub. There were doors at each end and a door which closed off our bedroom area. It was a slightly bohemian arrangement which didn't always guarantee complete privacy, but it worked. Madame Beringer's bedroom was further down the hall from the bathroom. At this point, you entered the main building to which our pavilion was an annex. That structure had more standardized apartments. I once peeked into Madame's bedroom. Her bed was covered with a luxurious chinchilla throw. It looked very elegant to me.

Émeraude Beringer, my newest landlady, was a good looking woman with her own tailored style. She had a steel gray coiffure highlighted by a pure white streak near one temple and an upright bearing. She was no longer young but she moved in a sprightly manner and was quick witted with a deep, ready laugh. She had few clothes, but those she did wear, were *tailleurs* suits from the couture houses. She was never without her matching necklace and bracelet made of heavy gold links.

Mme Beringer could whip up excellent meals in the tiny bamboo kitchen of our little pavilion in no time at all. Most of the main courses were based on rice. At her table, I discovered that rice desserts were quite delicious. She had raised her family in North Africa where her husband had been stationed with the Navy. She felt strongly that too much cleanliness was unconducive to good health. She was happy that her four children had all been able to build up immunities by running free and barefoot around the casbah.

Victor, her youngest son, 14 years old, was an appealing kid, the baby of the family, *le petit dernier*. He may not have been the most excellent student at his prestigious *lycée*, 'le Henri IV', but he surely had a winning personality and he was athletic. He and Martha batted a soccer ball around in the nearby Tuileries Gardens most evenings before dinner. Madame Beringer also had an older son, André, named after his father and, like his father, a Naval officer in Toulon. There were also two grown daughters, one newly married and the other an interior designer in Geneva. *More red plaid and bamboo like the décor of our pavilion?* I never learned.

There was space for me *chez Beringer* because one member of our junior year group had been sent back to his college in New York under a cloud. He was the son of the college president, in fact. The young man had stopped going to classes altogether to become a *clochard*.

The *clochards* were a Parisian tradition. A *clochard* was a kind of hobo cum poet, sleeping rough under the bridges of the Seine. They were 'drop outs,' perhaps alcoholics, perhaps formerly productive members of society—doctors, professors, philosophers, even former bankers—who chose to live on the fringes of society in a quest for the essence of humanity stripped of any of the extraneous trappings of bourgeois life. At least that was the romantic version.

While I wished the returnee well, I was happy to take his spot in the household. It was fun to live at Madame Beringer's and I enjoyed being closer to my friend, Martha. I was painting her portrait at Reid Hall where I had been allowed to set up an art studio in a vacant attic room, thanks to the good offices of M. Miller, the head of our junior year in France program. All of us students loved Bob Miller, his French wife and their adorable passel of bi-lingual kids.

I was a novice painter and although inspired by the setting of my Left Bank studio, in my first attempts to capture Martha's image, I cut off the top of her head. Her muscular calves turned out wonderful though. Martha loved cycling and had the legs to prove it. She was a good sport about my painting efforts and kept on posing for me.

I couldn't get over my good fortune to set up an easel with a view out of the window to a plaque which explained that the painter Othon Friez had lived and worked in the garret across the street. Friez was a founder of the *fauve* movement whose more renowned adherents were Derain, Vlaminck and Matisse. These so-called 'wild beasts' were the painters of imaginative, colorful canvases with red trees and yellow skies.Although laughed at in their day, these paintings were now among some of art history's most admired works.

Back at Mme Beringer's, the pavilion's heating system was not very functional that winter. I slept with my red rabbit coat on top of my blankets to keep warm. We all spent a good deal of time together at the dinner table where it was warmer. One evening, after declining another serving of *riz à l'Impératrice*, a delicious rice dessert, I said,

"*Je suis pleine,*" the literal translation of 'I'm full' in English.

There was a pregnant silence. Then Madame and Victor laughed heartily:

"Oh, Barbara, don't say that," said Madame. " It means that you are *enceinte*, pregnant."

Oops?! I quickly learned to say instead, "*J'en ai assez,*" I've had enough.

On another occasion, handsome Victor, our 'little brother,' tied a paisley ascot around his neck and these words came out of my mouth as if by magic:

"*On se croit chez Cardin.*"

For once, I struck just the right chord. I had even used the reflexive tense correctly. Victor and Madame loved imagining themselves dressed by Pierre Cardin. His spaceship ready clothes were all the rage for men and women at that moment in 1969.

At Spring Break, many of our friends from the junior year in France program went by train to the Soviet Union for ten days. It sounded like an adventure to see Soviet Russia first hand. As it turned out, it was a hard trip. Behind the Iron Curtain, *le rideau de fer,* in 1969, life was pretty grim. Our friends didn't see a green vegetable or a leaf of lettuce for the whole ten days.

Martha and I, on the other hand, were invited to Mme Beringer's summer house in the hills above Toulon in the south of France. We would be near Nice and the Côte d'Azur. We could go to '*le Carnival*' they had for Mardi Gras in Nice like the ones they have in New Orleans or Rio de Janiero. Victor, our 'little brother' also came along.

Even Madame Beringer's husband made an appearance. He was dashingly handsome in his naval uniform. He looked much younger than Madame.They lived separate lives; he in Toulon, headquarters of *la Marine,* the French Navy, she in Paris. They behaved very cordially with each other however.

The Beringer's summer house was low and compact with big windows overlooking *la rade de Toulon,* the great Mediterranean harbor. Victor, Martha and I enjoyed playing around on *mobylettes,* in the sandy driveway of the house. These motorized bicycles were very popular at the time. I tried to learn the trick of kickstarting the motor with my foot and turning the handle bars to get up a head of speed before losing my balance and falling over.

We three young people made an overnight trip to Nice for Mardi Gras. Unfortunately, the night of Carnival that year was a washout. It poured rain. The parade and its giant cartoon figure-heads were drenched.

Victor, Martha and I walked back to our little hotel along the dark and soggy *Promenade des Anglais,* the walkway which borders the beautiful *Baie des Anges,* Angel Bay, in Nice. Victor said:

"*Regardez les bateaux particuliers,*" gesturing towards the yachts moored out in the water. If only I were *un fils à papa*, he said with a sigh.

"What's *un fils à papa*?" I asked him.

"It means to be born with a silver spoon in your mouth," he explained to me, in other words, 'a Daddy's boy.'

He seemed so reflective. It occurred to me that he was growing up.

The next morning, in the wan February sunshine, we posed for a moment on the little lawn in front of the deserted Hotel Carlton, a fancy hotel, *un palace*. I sent Alex, my fiancé, a photo of me sitting at a wrought iron table there in my camel hair coat. I was thinking of him more and more longingly as the academic year went by.

Spring break over, Martha and I returned to the Beringer's house in Paris. March and April passed by. The letters Alex and I faithfully wrote to one another flew back and forth across the Atlantic even more frequently as the time for our reunion at the end of my Junior Year in France program grew closer.

Alex was coming to meet me in Paris in June. I was over the moon with excitement and anticipation. I had a box where I saved all of his *aérogrammes*, those crinkly onion skin papers which folded into their own envelope. I would read each new one avidly. I reread the old ones over and over as well. I rationed them out. I had calculated that I could reread three old ones each day before we would be together again. I doled them out like candy.

In the meantime, there were some interesting activities. Madame Beringer took us to the '*Comédie Française*,' the famous theater near le Louvre where prestigious actors performed the iconic works of the holy trinity of French classical drama, Racine, Corneille and Molière. We had studied their plays in class and it was exciting to see them performed on stage.

And what a stage! It was a beautiful theater. With excitement we heard the '*toc, toc, toc*' of the hammer which signaled that the curtain would go up. The actors declaimed the poetic verses about love, honor and duty. It was stirring and beautiful.

In the mornings as I left for school, street cleaners dressed in blue overalls used witch-like brooms to sweep the gutters they flushed with water every day. Manual workers all wore their distinctive blue coveralls while smartly dressed office workers hurried around and among them.

Slim men in European cut suits and ties and svelte, smartly dressed women with their hair piled in a French twist high on the back of their heads passed by me with a certain *hauteur*. They were proud, even perhaps stuck up. The French still felt culturally quite superior to other peoples, Americans especially. Americans were thought to be rather unsophisticated and childish. Money, after all, could not make up for centuries of *savoir-vivre* and *savoir-faire*. It was that French elegance in the smallest detail which I admired, even in the women's ability to artfully tie a designer silk scarf at their necks to accessorize their look.

Many people smoked the strong *'Gauloise'* cigarettes, although not in the street. American tobacco brands like Lucky Strike and Marlboro were very desirable but more expensive. Lots of people rolled their own cigarettes, sprinkling a little tobacco onto a cigarette paper square, carefully rolling up the little package and licking an edge with their tongue to seal it together.

You could make a phone call in the street by ducking into a bar or a cafe and buying *jetons,* special little disks you bought expressly for the phone. Phone calls could also be made at the post office, *la PTT*, which stood for Post, Telephone and Telegraph agency.

You gave the telephone number you wanted to the clerk at the window and sat down to wait for him or her to place your call. When she had your party on the line, she indicated the number of a *cabine* where you sat down to talk in privacy. Call finished, you stopped back at the window to pay the requested amount. This method was good for international calls as well.

In case of a call of nature while out and about, you could buy a coffee at a café and use their bathroom. It was usually a dank, grubby cubbyhole. The toilet was an old-fashioned tank mounted high up on the wall with a chain mechanism, a *'w.c.,'* short for water closet. For toilet paper there was cut up old newspaper or worse, a kind of toilet paper which was completely non-absorbent and resembled wax paper more than anything else.

Les pissoirs buildings were available for men to relieve themselves. There were also 'Turkish' toilets, which were just a hole in the floor and two slippery ceramic foot pads—one on each side of the hole. All in all, it was preferable to have excellent retentive powers.

People still talked in 'new' and 'old' francs, which could be confusing to me. The devaluation of the French currency from 1000 old francs to 100 new francs had taken place after the war. Old habits died hard though and many Frenchmen still added a couple of zeros onto prices when money was under discussion. *'Cent francs'* was really *'dix francs'* and conversely *'cent nouveaux francs'* was *'mille anciens francs.'*

There was a further devaluation of the franc against the dollar during my junior year in Paris. I thought this might work to my advantage buying some gifts for the folks back home. I went into a shop where I had identified some souvenirs I liked.

"Bonjour, Monsieur."

"Bonjour Mademoiselle, vous désirez ?"

There was no looking around. You came into a shop with a purpose or not at all. It was considered very rude not to acknowledge the proprietor with a hello. He or she would help you with your purchase. Self service did not exist.

"I like those model Eiffel towers, *monsieur*," I said. "I would like to buy some as gifts for my nieces back in the United States, but I think I will wait until tomorrow, after the devaluation."

I thought I was being so worldly wise and astute:

"After all, I'm American and they will cost me less tomorrow," said little Miss Smartypants.

"Ah," said *le patron,* the boutique owner, "but *Mademoiselle,* by tomorrow I will have raised the price."

In the end, I bought some silk scarves like those I admired on

Frenchwomen in the street to bring back home as gifts. I made a selection from designers like Jacques Fath and Nina Ricci and each scarf was wrapped in its own flat cardboard box. It was fascinating to watch the saleslady wrap each box with gift paper using only ribbon to tie the package together, no tape required at all.

The trick was to fold the gift wrap paper at one end and hold it together against your stomach while you folded the other end. Holding that end together, you carefully freed one hand to wrap the ribbon around the folded ends of your wrapping until you had tied it all together with a knot in the middle, finishing with a big bow.

Street demonstrations, *les manifs,* continued that spring in 1969. President de Gaulle had proposed sweeping reforms to decentralize the French government and reform the Senate. When he lost the referendum, he suddenly resigned. Georges Pompidou became the new head of state.

Madame Beringer thought that Pompidou was a *torcheur de boeufs*, a peasant, only good for cleaning up cattle dung. France was at a crossroads caught between the old guard's ways and the modern trends of a new era. There were violent clashes between students and the police. A new, more modern France was suffering birth pains.

My friend, Keith Van Dorn, from our program, got caught in the fray. He showed up at Reid Hall one day, his face bloodied. He wasn't badly hurt. In fact, he was rather proud of his battle wounds. Sitting together in the high ceilinged hall with other students, he showed off:

"Look at this," he said, taking a strip of photos out of his pocket. "I went right to a 'fotomat' booth to memorialize what happened. I can show these photos to my grandchildren to prove that I was here in Paris during the riots of May, 1968-1969."

Little did we American students know that we were living

through the tail end of an iconic period in French social history. The Paris student demonstrations of 1968-69 shook French society and its politicians to the core. The students were joined by the labor unions. All over France, people took to the streets in *manifs* demanding change to the status quo.

Not only demonstrations happened in May with the arrival of spring weather. The grass turned green and the buds on the trees opened. The flowers bloomed in the *Jardin de Luxembourg* and elsewhere. The plane trees with their peeling beige and brown bark and the chestnut trees leafed out again.

We students prepared for exams. Martha had her exams at *Sciences Po* and I had mine at another part of the Sorbonne. I had an oral exam at the *IPFE,* the *"Institut des Professeurs de francais a l'Étranger,"* to contend with. I had never taken an oral exam before. I would be asked to answer some questions in French in front of a panel of examiners to prove my ability to teach French language abroad. The idea of the oral exam made me nervous. I wasn't sure how to prepare for it. The rest of my finals didn't really concern me. I had successfully completed the coursework necessary to receive credit for the year's studies from my home university.

The time soon came for a round of farewells and our return passage to New York on the *SS France*. Before my voyage home on the ship, Alex was coming to get me at the end of the school year. We were headed for England for a pre-honeymoon trip to London, Wales and the Lake District. Then we were going back to the U.S. where Alex would graduate from law school, we would be married and live happily ever after.

I took the Air France bus out to Orly airport to meet him, so excited and happy that I thought I would burst. The Paris airshow was going on and the bus was crowded. I waited at the bottom of the escalator at Orly for Alex to descend and there he was, as handsome as ever!

Alex made an appointment at Reid Hall, the headquarters of my Junior Year in France program, to ask M. Miller, the head of the program, for permission to take me away from exams early. Monsieur 'Mee lair,' as he was called in French, was a very nice man, a young and dynamic professor and administrator. It was he who had given me permission to use the painting studio up in the attic of Reid Hall.

All of us students adored Mister Miller, Madame Miller and their four little Millers.

I can still picture my fiancé, handsome Alex, wearing his long, tan 'London Fog' trench coat, seated at the desk in M. Miller's office that May afternoon. It was as if Alex were asking my guardian for my hand in marriage. As M. Miller explained to us, he was not 'in loco parentis.'

"I have no authority to stop Barbara from leaving with you, young man. Good luck to the both of you!"

Before taking off for London, Alex and I spent a few days in Paris. We couldn't stay with my landlady, Mme Beringer. There wasn't room and it wouldn't have been seemly. I found a cheap hotel for us. It was truly awful. I should have checked out the room before reserving it.

Our hotel room was triangular in shape. The bed was at the point of the triangle. The mattress was completely worn out. The decor was depressing. The paint was dingy. The towels were paper thin. The management was surly.

Alex and I had a wonderful time. We were so in love!

At the conclusion of our pre-honeymoon idyll, I was taking the ocean liner, France, back to New York, but Alex was flying home. So before his departure, he gallantly accompanied me to Southampton, England, where many of my fellow students from the junior year program were embarking onto the ship for the homeward bound trip back to the U.S.

To my delight, we ran into my Paris roommate, Martha, by surprise at Stonehenge, which is not far from Southampton. We all clambered up and down the ancient Druid standing stones taking photos of one another.

"See you at my wedding," I reminded her. "Don't forget now. You're one of my bridesmaids."

"When am I going to get my own 'MRS' degree?" she lamented. "It has to happen before the end of senior year," she moaned in mock alarm.

"You'll manage it," I assured her.

Just like her determination to visit every Wimpy Burger hamburger franchise in Paris, once Martha set her mind on something, it was as good as accomplished.

After my solo voyage home on the ocean liner, we docked in New York harbor. There was no one there to meet me. I felt very grown up and a little bereft too. I remembered my leave-taking from the same pier ten months before as our excited group of American college students waved goodbye to friends and family standing on the pier.

The ship's whistle had blown deep, sonorous toots, just like in the movies, as we headed out to sea full of high hopes for our year to come in 'la vieille France,' the old country. Those deep sounds traveled right through you to the core.

Hemingway once said that Paris is a "moveable feast." If you are fortunate enough to have spent some of your youth there, the experience never leaves you wherever you go.

Paris was far from my thoughts when the great ship entered New York Harbor. Perhaps time would tell about Paris and Hemingway. In the hustle bustle of our arrival, I collected my luggage and hailed a taxi. The cabbie barreled along the FDR Drive to LaGuardia Airport, launching me into my future life as a married woman.

In Front of the Tourist Office in Montpezat de Quercy

CHAPTER 15

Back at Pech Menal After Martha's Visit

More than thirty years had elapsed since that taxicab ride in 1969 from the pier in New York harbor to LaGuardia Airport. Where had the time flown! *"Ou sont les neiges d'antan?"* to quote François Villon again.

I had married and become mother to two fine sons. My husband, Alex, and I had *fonder un foyer,* we had made a home for ourselves and our children in Manhattan and then in the New York suburbs in New Jersey.

Alex had a successful career as a corporate lawyer. I worked as a French translator and teacher, pursuing my painting as a hobby.

The children became young men.

I became a partner with my friend, Pepita, in her small group tour business. I designed and escorted tours to France, Romania and India. Alex took semi-retirement and we moved to Sarasota, Florida. We hoped we could make a new start there and repair our fraying marital relationship. It didn't work out. There was no 'rapprochement' between us. We got divorced.

Life now found me living at Pech Menal in little Cayrièch, France.

My old friend, Martha, who was coming to visit, knew all about my life history. She had been there 30 years ago when we were roommates at Madame Beringer's in Paris. She had been at my wedding to Alex in 1969. She knew my sons.

It was fun visiting with her and reliving old times. We could talk frankly with one another without the need to explain the backstory. We could compare notes. We could open our hearts to each other about the joys and sorrows we had experienced on the separate paths we had taken since our junior year in France. We knew each other too well to pull any punches. There was no need for false modesty, but no self-serving justifications were permitted either.

Martha and I spent a wonderful couple of days at Pech Menal and in the *Tarn-et-Garonne*. I showed her around my new house and my new area. While we filled one another in on our present activities, we remembered old times. Martha's visit did me good. It brought back old memories and created some new ones. Our time together was a pleasant distraction from my day to day life at Pech Menal, *le petit train train*. I got to put all my projects on hold for a short while.

At the end of Martha's stay with me, I drove her to Biarritz as we had arranged. She was to start her bicycle tour of the Basque country while I would return to Pech Menal.

The pretty, seaside resort of Biarritz had a special meaning for both of us. We knew Biarritz pretty well. We both spent six weeks there in 1968 during our 'French immersion' before the start of the junior year college program at the Sorbonne in Paris.

Arriving in town, we stopped in at the *Dodin* pastry shop on the main square for a pâtisserie. *Dodin* was still as busy with customers as we remembered, and the *pâtisseries* were still as beautiful and delicious.

The main square, *la grande place*, had been redone since our school days. It had been beautified and modernized with new stonework and new lighting. The beach in Biarritz was still the same however. Martha and I spent a moment watching the big breakers of the Bay of Biscay roll in from across the Atlantic to crash on the enormous sand crescent of *la grande plage*. Eiffel's lighthouse still overlooked the scene from its lofty position on the heights of a nearby cliff.

"Have a wonderful bike tour," I told Martha. "It was great to see you. Thanks for coming to see me and Pech Menal for a couple of days. It meant a lot to me."

Martha gave me a big parting hug. "Well, of course, Barbara, You're my old roomie. I needed to make sure you had a nice place in France. You're doing a great job on Pech Menal, by the way. It's a big project. Send me photos of your next improvements."

I returned Martha's hug and wished her *bonne route* and a good journey.

"Don't forget to take some photos of your *circuit* and don't try to pedal too fast up and down those hills. This is the Pyrénées mountains after all."

In reply, Martha pointed to her impressive calf muscles and then she was gone around the corner of the boardwalk to meet up with her fellow cyclists.

After she left, I spent an hour visiting the Biarritz aquarium. I remembered it fondly from 1968. It was right near the beach out on a little promontory. I loved its 1930s art deco charm. The fish looked so pretty in their pretend rocky alcoves studded with seashells.

Satisfied that it at least hadn't changed, I got into the Citroën and pointed the wheels of the car toward the autoroute and home in the *Tarn-et-Garonne.*

Summer was passing by and there was one big renovation project left to tackle at Pech Menal, the installation of a real kitchen inside the main house. The 'summer kitchen' in the old pigsty, *la porcherie*, was cute but inadequate.

The rate of exchange was in my favor, so I decided to go for it. Although the new currency, the euro, was introduced at par with the U.S. dollar, in the early 2000's, it fell to about fifteen percent of a dollar's value. This state of affairs made my purchases a bargain for the time being so I decided to take action on this big expenditure.

After making the rounds of different kitchen installers around Montauban, I chose *Entreprise Schmidt* since I liked their plan the best.

The new counters, refrigerator, sink, cooktop and oven were installed in a corner of the living room. The installer's name was M. Sbardellini. I liked the sibilant sound of 'Sbardellini' on my tongue and he seemed like a nice, quiet young man and serious. He worked alone without a helper, as was the norm in France. Almost no artisan could afford to hire a helper and pay into the tax system for them. In the end, I was very happy with the fit and finish of M. Sbardellini's handiwork. Now I just had to learn how to use all the bells and whistles of the new oven and the induction cooktop.

Energized by my success with the new kitchen installation and still exasperated by all the flies that constantly hovered around Pech Menal due to the herd of cows across the road, I consulted with some artisans about adding screens to my windows. To be sure, screens were not customary here. But I'd grown used to them back and home and wanted to install some to keep out the flies.

I bought a roll of very flexible screening material and found a carpenter to install an ingenious system of screens on the windows. His name was François Bellac. He was a tall, gangly fellow. He was recently divorced and seemed a little depressed. When I called him on the phone, I could hear his herd of cows mooing in the background. We both laughed at that.

He devised a system which allowed me to open the shutters through the screened windows. His screens prevented the flies from entering but allowed the cool breeze to waft in. *Quelle merveille!* It was marvelous!

You may ask, why not just leave the shutters open all the time? In France, this is unthinkable. '*Les volets*,' the shutters are not just for decoration. They are a very functional system for security purposes and to regulate the amount of heat you wish to keep from escaping outside from your heated house or conversely, to keep the cool air inside the house, if you wish to prevent it from warming in the heat of the bright sunlight. Summer and winter, *'les volets'* are very useful temperature regulators. Anytime, once closed and locked, they are a very effective barrier against intruders.

When I went to visit my favorite carpenter, Monsieur Bellac, at his house to pay him for his beautiful work, I noticed that his barn was made of a dun colored, muddy material that I had seen used in other constructions around the countryside. It looked to me as if this stuff was falling apart or was unfinished. I learned that contrary to my impression, this lumpy material was a prized building technique from olden times called *le torchis*.

Basically it was roughly fashioned adobe bricks which were excellent insulation, durable, inexpensive and easy to repair, if you knew the way to mix and dry the mud and straw together. French children sometimes had summer camp projects where they practiced making *le torchis*. No computers for them. *le torchis*. Typical —the country that had held on to the perfect croissant over the centuries, wasn't going to give up easily on *le torchis*.

It would seem that my giant barn at Pech Menal was once constructed mostly of *le torchis*. Unfortunately, this material, which was strong yet delicate, had collapsed during the renovations. Therefore my barn had been reconstructed using more modern and less old-timey methods, lending it a less charming aspect. It was impressive, but not particularly picturesque.

I worked on improving the immense barn and making it more to my taste. I had hanging lights installed in the giant bays to shine at night and illuminate the courtyard when I came home after dark. I started some wisteria vines growing up each of the supporting poles to soften the outline of the cavernous space. I hoped to keep the vines under control and prevent them from lifting up the red clay tiles and generally playing havoc with the roof. I made the barn more usable by spreading a load of gravel over the rough dirt floor which was a big improvement and easily accomplished.

My neighbors, the Belons, felt strongly that I should not leave my big property '*en friche*,' or permitted to go wild as M. de Paris had liked. They felt that left to return to nature, the high grass and brambles would shelter snakes and other pests. The wild look offended their sense of propriety so they recommended that I have the property tended to by M. Dupain, pronounced 'Dupaing,' like *twang*, in his very countrified accent. He had the necessary tractor attachment for turning over the soil of the field. It was called a *girobroyeur*, which means to turn and break up.

M. 'Dupaing' turned out to be an out of shape fellow in a wife beater tee shirt with a cigarette butt, a *mégot*, constantly held between his stained teeth. The first time he appeared at Pech Menal, he took me by surprise.

I was wearing only my bathing suit. It was a hot evening and I was out watering the bushes which composed the *haie*, as usual. I felt a bit overexposed but I brushed aside my discomfiture since it was too late to change clothes. We quickly negotiated a price for his taking care of the property.

"*Quand, comment et combien?*" I asked him in a few words, keeping it really simple. "When, how and how much?" I went right to the point.

M. 'Dupaing' appreciated my brevity. We quickly concluded an arrangement. Of course it was the Belons, my neighbors, who had steered him my way and told me how much to offer. Despite his very thick local accent and my American one, there was immediately a good feeling between us.

Unfortunately, when the high grass was cut down, it revealed a pile of unsightly cement poles in one corner of the property.

"What could those be?" I asked Clothilde.

"Those are a great find," she told me. "They are old telephone poles. You can have them cut up into fence posts and strung with fencing wire. Being cement, they'll last forever," she enthused.

Not my style of fencing, I thought to myself. *Long lasting perhaps, but ugly. Rather like a prison yard. I'd have to have the big poles hauled away somehow. Or maybe the grass could cover them up again.*

In another attempt to make Pech Menal more comfortable for me, I considered renovating the stable building which was next to the barn. It was long and low. From the courtyard, you saw only the double door entry disguising the great length of the structure which continued longitudinally out toward the field. After tossing around the idea with the Belons, I got Madame Biau from Montricoux to come over to give me an estimate on making the stables into living quarters. This would be a way to make an area for guests at Pech Menal, something I felt was lacking.

Madame Biau, pronounced Bee Oh, and her husband owned the firm which had built the beautiful mortise and tenon roofs and custom made doors at Pech Menal for M. de Paris.

A name like Bee Oh was funny to my ears since it meant Body Odor to me. But in France those two syllables had another connotation, 'bio', as in biological, meaning untreated with chemicals. Just as we say the fruits and vegetables are 'organic', they say "*bio*." Bee Oh.

Madame Biau was a petite, cute lady, pert in her pretty pants suit with a long braid down her back and bangs on her forehead. She climbed up with ease onto the stable roof to take the measurements with her little laser machine. As my British friend, Maggie, said admiringly, watching another darling French woman climb up on top of the fuel tanks at the gas station:

"Only in rural France do you see a sight like that!"

The Belons and I discussed the pros and cons of turning the stable into a guest house. I wanted to have guests visit me and the main house at Pech Menal didn't lend itself to having overnight visitors. It was spacious but there wasn't much privacy.

"What is that giant trough running the length of the building?" I asked them when we were inspecting the stable one day to bounce ideas off one another.

"That's it exactly," said Pierre Belon, the old *mangeoire,* the trough. It's a great feature and very desirable."

"I don't know," I said. "It seems to get in the way of any room plan we come up with."

There were windows all along the sides of the stable. They were small and set high up in the wall. There was not much natural light. You could open up the roof with skylights or *veluxes,* but this would no doubt add to the already considerable expense of renovations. You could make a big window at the end of the building toward the field and you would let in more light, but the view would remain rather unexciting—just grass.

I said, "It might be nice to put a donkey out there in the field. It could eat the grass and look adorable." The French love donkeys. Even so, the Belons looked skeptical.

We came away rather discouraged. At least I did. It wouldn't be easy to come up with a way forward to change the stable into a space for guests.

One part of the stable was occupied by the very large old cart which had been the principal means of transport in the olden days. It had a high seat and traces to harness the horses. The big wheels were still in place. I had seen others of its kind painted light blue, French blue, and decorated with flower pots in several front yards as I drove around. I asked Philippe, the man who was doing some painting for me, what I should do with the old cart. It was gray with age and covered with dust and spider webs.

"You can clean it up and paint it in your *heures perdues,*" he immediately answered.

Oh no! I thought to myself. *I must have something better to do in my spare time!* I didn't have the necessary commitment for that laborious project.

Likewise, I abandoned the idea of transforming the stable. It too, like the main house and the barn, was not so easily adaptable to my needs and desires.

As for the main house, the new kitchen had turned out great even though it took up a big part of the living room. As the

French say, it nibbled or *grignoté* quite a chunk out of it. The effect wasn't charming. The spaces were a bit awkward. The layout of the rooms wasn't conducive to a cozy feeling. The charm had been obliterated by M. de Paris' beautiful, but 'tabula rasa' renovations.

I felt that I had done as much as I could to make Pech Menal over. I was starting to question my need to own this impressive house which was much admired, but which didn't really speak to my soul aesthetically or meet my needs on a practical level.

Every time some well-intentioned person admired Pech Menal, I felt a little trapped. *Maybe I had been too influenced by my real estate agent's enthusiasm about the property? Maybe I was no longer quite the same person as I had been right after my divorce when I had purchased Pech Menal?*

Summer had drawn to a close. My thoughts were turning toward home back in the United States. The French summer season for village festivals, concerts and outdoor movie showings was ending. The Brits, Danes and Netherlanders were going home for the winter. The time had come for me to leave Pech Menal for a while and go back to my 'real' life in the U.S. I was looking forward to catching up with my American friends and most especially with my family. It would be great to spend some time in my home country where I understood every nuance of every conversation. I would be back in the land that I loved, my birthplace, *ma patrie*. I was a product of the U.S. just as much as the Quercy melons were a product of their *terroir*.

Before my departure, I hosted an *apéro* in the big barn, inviting all my new friends and acquaintances from St Antonin, Cayrièch and the surrounding area to an *apéro-dinatoire*. This is when you have so many appetizers that the guests can make a dinner out of them alone. In other words, a cocktail party. I put a big table with all the food at one end of the big space and the guests milled around the table. The turn out was good.

There was Mme Lemoine, the real estate agent and her lovely daughter, Émilie. Like mother, like daughter. My neighbors, the Belons, came, of course, and other members of the Cayrièch festival committee like Suzy and Patrick. Jerry, from the painting group came with his wife, the other Barbara. They brought their friends, the Anglo-American couple, their neighbors from Cazals. My house painter, Philippe, came with his mother, Geneviève. She helped me out with house cleaning. They brought Philippe's ex-wife and her teenage son with Philippe, Mathieu. The artist, Éric Maurel came with his girlfriend, Chantal, the watercolorist. His wife, Nicole, stayed home in Brousse-les-Antibels. Momo and his family sent their regrets.

The simple sandals I wore to the party were much admired. They were from *Macy's*, the house brand, 'Charter Club.' Just as I admired the French clothes, the French admired mine. We had champagne. One of the guests explained how to open the champagne bottles by a method called *sabrer*. This is when you use a saber to cut open the neck of the champagne bottle with one masterful stroke. *Quel panache!* What a stylish move! At my party, we just opened the bottles the old-fashioned way by popping the corks.

Sipping at my glass, I asked a friend from Caussade, Marie, if she would drop me off at Caussade train station the day of my upcoming departure and she agreed. My Citroën would be safely stowed under the bays of the barn at Pech Menal. The Belons were going to keep an eye on it for me during my absence.

From Caussade, I would go to Montauban to catch the night train to Paris. This time I had reserved a *couchette*, a leather covered plank, a sort of bunk bed, to stretch out on overnight while the train chugged its way to Austerlitz station in Paris.

On the appointed day, Marie took me to catch the last evening train from Caussade to Montauban. The French National Railroad, the '*SNCF*,' which stands for *société nationale des chemins de fer,* was always threatening to close down the little station in Caussade, but so far it had escaped the ax. I had signed a petition, along with many others, to help keep it open.

At the Caussade train station, Marie insisted upon waiting with me until the train for Montauban arrived *'en gare'* and stopped at the platform. We hugged and exchanged cheek kisses, *la bise,* on *'le quai.'*

"Au revoir, Barbara."

"Au revoir, Marie. Merci. See you next year."

When I arrived in Montauban at 7 p.m., I still had several hours to spend before my overnight train to Paris, which didn't leave until shortly before midnight. How to fill the intervening time?

Montauban was divided into two towns really–the old town center, high on a hill over the river Tarn, and the lower town, where the train station was located, called *'la ville Bourbon.'*

Did I ever mention that the famous painter, Jean Dominique Ingrès was born in Montauban? The museum in the upper part of town was named for him.

The train station was located a good piece away from the attractions of the Montauban town center. It would be a long walk to get there. I also had my suitcase with me to take into consideration. As usual, there were no taxis in rural France. Taxi service was expensive and by appointment. It was only used by people who had to go to the hospital or doctor's office. This was paid for by the French health service. The *Ville Bourbon* train station wasn't big enough to offer a bag check room, *une consigne.*

How to spend the evening waiting for the train? As I reviewed my possibilities, I regretted not having asked Marie to drive me all the way to Montauban late at night, just before my train's departure time. She would probably have done so, but I hated to put her out that way.

I looked around and wheeled my rollaboard right across the street to a restaurant called *'la Table d'Alain.'* This restaurant had an excellent reputation. My plan was to have a nice meal, slowly savoring each course and lingering over my coffee until it was time to return to the station for the night train.

Uh oh! Change of plans required. 'La Table d'Alain' was closed that evening. I had neglected to check their scheduled closing days.

A wicked little wind kicked up and was blowing fallen leaves around my shoes as I stood there on the sidewalk. The bright blue skies of summer in southwestern France had turned overcast in the fall. I needed to find somewhere pleasant indoors to spend my long wait time.

Reconnoitering, I saw a sign down a side street. It said '*Le Cheval Blanc*.' It advertised itself as a *RESTAURANT / BAR / CHAMBRES*.

Any port in a storm. I headed there and pulled my suitcase into the entry hall right behind me. The floor was covered by a thin, red, not too clean carpet, a *moquette*. The dining room beckoned off to the right through an archway. It was modest looking, but gave off a clean and comfortable air.

The hostess seated me at a table nicely covered by a white cloth to have an apéritif while I waited for the official dinner hour service to begin. The dining room slowly filled with other patrons as I sipped my glass of *Martini blanc* vermouth over ice with a twist of lemon peel. I pulled the novel I was reading out of my travel tote to help me pass the time.

When the clock struck eight, I ordered the *prix fixe* dinner menu along with a glass of red wine. I tried to pace myself by eating in a desultory manner, stretching out the time between bites. But the main dish was *blanquette de veau*, veal stew with mushrooms in a velvety sauce over rice. It was one of my favorites. All too soon, I had finished it and my *crème brûlée* for dessert as well. I ordered a coffee. It was only shortly after 9 p.m. and I still had more than two hours before my train.

I was just settling back into my book when a waiter appeared at my table.

"*Mademoiselle*," he said, "Sorry to interrupt you but I have a note for you. The man over there at the table by the window asked me to bring it over to you."

Quoi! What! I looked up from my book in surprise and my gaze followed the waiter's finger as he pointed out the dark haired man seated across the room near the window and the bar.

The stranger made eye contact with me for a moment. I bent my head down to read the note which said in French:

> *Chère Mademoiselle,*
> *Comme le nécessite l'usage, il ne peut être concevable de nous convier à boire un café à cette heure tardive. N'hésitez pas à me contacter demain en fin de matinée, cela sera un honneur pour moi.*
> *Claude Siteon*

As I started reading, I was in wonderment that this gambit which I had seen in movies was being played out on me. It was certainly flattering in a way. But then, what was there about my appearance or demeanor that made the man feel he could proposition me like this?

Was it possible that I was so alluring that he just couldn't help himself?

More likely, he thought I looked lonely and that I might be an easy pick up. *What a dragueur! A pick up artist!*

I was getting upset when I took some time to translate the note more carefully:

> *Dear Miss,*
> *As convention dictates, it is inconceivable that we should get together for a coffee at this tardy hour. Don't hesitate to contact me late tomorrow morning. It would be an honor.*

The note was signed, 'Claude Siteon.'

He had written the number of his *portable*, his cell phone, underneath his signature.

Wait a minute. This isn't what I expected. What delicate consideration! What gallantry! If this was his twist on a pick up line, it certainly worked on me. *How gentlemanly!*

Claude Siteon arose from his table and passed in front of me. We nodded at one another as he went by. He smiled as he inclined his body slightly towards me. He was a conventional looking man in a tweed sports coat. He was medium height with rather long hair carefully combed. Without a word, he went into the restaurant anteroom and up the stairs into the hotel section of the establishment.

Unbeknownst to Claude Siteon, I had a train to catch. Our meeting for a coffee was not destined to be. It was time to head back to the train station. After spending all this time waiting, I certainly had no excuse to be late. I paid the check, retraced my steps, and got myself settled in a plastic chair in the grimy, utilitarian waiting room at the train station. My suitcase was by my side.

Sitting there, I pondered my recent experience at the restaurant. My spirits were light. How nice that someone wanted to connect with me!

'Quel beau geste!' 'What a nice gesture! Stylish, just like a movie scene – a single scene from a never to be finished scenario.

I unfolded Claude's note and read it over again. Then I carefully tucked it into a compartment of my purse for safe keeping. I wasn't sure something like that would ever happen to me again. In fact, I could already hardly believe it had happened at all. I smiled to myself.

Maybe my luck with men was changing? Perhaps this frog would have been worth kissing?

Finally, the overnight train to Paris pulled into the station. I sleepily found the number of my *wagon* on the platform. I stowed my suitcase in the darkened compartment. The other passengers who had boarded earlier in Toulouse were trying to sleep. I gingerly climbed up into my top bunk *couchette* trying not to disturb the recumbent forms beneath me. I fell into a light sleep swaying to the rhythm of the *'Intercité* train as its wheels clacked along the track to Paris.

My journey home for the winter was underway.

The Medieval Carving Above the Door of
La Maison de l'Amour in Saint-Antonin-Noble-Val

CHAPTER 16

Barbara Meets Sam in Florida

When I returned in the spring to Cayrièch from Florida where I had spent the winter, there had been two developments. Firstly, during the winter, I met Sam at a mixer for singles.

Somehow it came up over cocktails that I had been on a trip to Romania for Pepitours one year when Pepita couldn't escort the tour group. As soon as I mentioned Romania, everyone at the mixer told me that I had to meet Sam since he was born and had lived in Romania, before becoming an American citizen. Everybody knew Sam, it seemed.

"Sam, Sam," they called him over. "Here's somebody you ought to meet," the singles said.

He and I hit it off immediately.

Sam was very unlike my ex-husband. He was a factory worker, not a corporate lawyer. In fact, he was an immigrant who had never finished high school. He spoke English with an accent and not always idiomatically. Alex, my ex-husband, came from a family of English professors. His father had won a Pulitzer prize for biography.

Alex had always to be in control whereas Sam didn't get upset when things went wrong. Sam was used to problems. His parents were Holocaust survivors. The family lived through most of the repressive Ceauşescu era in Romania. Sam's older brother was interned in a work camp building the railroad. The family was finally allowed to emigrate to Israel where they had to cobble together a new life with few resources.

The contrast between Alex and Sam put me in mind of the Serge Gainsbourg song, 'Émmanuelle.' The lyrics go, "Émmanuelle. Émmanuelle. Elle aime les intéllectuels et les manuels."

I had to laugh at the truth of it. I sure was attracted to both types of men.

As Sam and I drove around Sarasota during my winter at home, we would sometimes get lost. Instead of getting upset, we would laugh at our ineptitude. This was in the days before GPS. We were both newcomers to Sarasota and the streets were confusing. They were ramrod straight and went on forever. It was hard to tell if you were headed north or south unless you knew the order of the cross street names. *Was Orange Street south of Lime or north?* As for east and west, once you got out of sight of the ocean, i.e. the Gulf of Mexico, you lost your point of reference unless you had memorized the street names and their order in that direction. The ocean was on the west, since Sarasota is on the west coast of Florida, not east like the Atlantic, which added to our disorientation.

On one of our first dates, Sam and I went to the opera. Sam loved classical music and especially opera. For an uneducated person, he was quite a culture vulture. Sarasota had a nice opera house and another big music venue called the *Van Wezel*. It was designed by Stalin's daughter, Svetlana, who was married to an important acolyte of Frank Lloyd Wright at one time. The building was painted a shade of orchid. It was located right on Sarasota Bay and was easy to find.

Sam got us tickets for 'La Bohème' at the Van Wezel. We arrived early while the sky was still light over the giant parking lot.

We parked and headed into the theater. The performance was wonderful. The concert hall was crowded and including the intermission, we were inside for three and a half hours.

When Sam went to fetch us some glasses of wine at the first entr'acte, who should I spy at the bar but Alex, my ex-husband!

I was stricken with embarrassment. It was so silly of me, but I couldn't help my reaction. I wanted to hide under a cocktail table.

Alex was with a pretty brunette, dressed in a black sheath which revealed her nice figure. I was with Sam who I feared would reveal his lack of education if we met and talked with Alex. It was silly of me to feel intimidated by Alex.

Did I still care about his opinion?

I was with a cute guy who looked great in his dark suit and tie and who was politely fetching me a glass of champagne. *Even so....* I was still entrapped by my fear of what 'others' would think of me, what 'they' would think. *Who were those all powerful 'others' exactly? Why did I give them power over me?*

Perhaps it was time to free myself from these rigid concepts of what was right or wrong. My efforts to please these self-appointed monitors of my behavior were getting in the way of my happiness and self fulfillment. Or was it me, myself, who was putting limitations on my possibilities?

Could I make my own choices as best as I saw them and take responsibility for them? Perhaps not just yet, but the light might be dawning.

Sam brought the drinks back to where I was standing. "Let's move away," I said to him.

"Why, what's the hurry?" said Sam, taking a sip of wine.

"I just saw my ex-husband over there." I pointed to the left of the bar.

"Great," said Sam. "I'd like to meet him. Let's go over and say hello."

"Oh no, no," I told Sam. "I'm just not up to that right now. Let's get back to our seats. They're ringing the warning bell."

"As you wish," Sam said, perhaps sensing my reluctance to encounter Alex.

The opera ended. Poor Mimi! The curtain fell to thunderous applause. When we emerged into the dark parking lot with a throng of other people, neither one of us could locate Sam's car. We were nonplussed. It had to be there somewhere. As we wandered around, perplexed, I couldn't help hoping Alex wouldn't come upon us lost sheep. And luckily, he didn't.

Eventually we found Sam's Toyota parked in the spot where we had left it. Rather than wasting time on angry recriminations such as, "Why didn't you remember where we parked?" or "Why didn't YOU!?" we laughed about it.

Reclaiming our car, we set off for a jazz club up north on Tamiami Trail on the traditionally black side of town. They had a great saxophonist according to Sam. Sam played the sax, really badly, but with enthusiasm. We were going to go dancing.

What a change of pace for me! What a relief compared to Alex's rigidity. Sam was a breath of fresh air in my experience.

He was full of life. He had boundless energy. He worked two jobs. He tested hydraulic valves Monday to Friday and often on Saturdays, since there was a lot of overtime. Then very early on Sunday mornings, he worked putting together the Sunday edition of the Sarasota Herald Tribune, inserting the special sections into the main body of the paper.

Generally speaking, he got up at 5 am to go to work testing hydraulic valves. He got off of work at 4 pm and went to the gym. After his workout, it was back home to his little condo on a lake, or at least the little retaining pond which they call a lake in Florida. Maybe he'd make a stop at the grocery store before preparing dinner. He often had fish. The George Foreman grill was one of Sam's most important cooking tools.

There was always a big salad to make. Maybe an Israeli salad, because Sam had spent a few years in Israel between Romania and Canada before coming to the United States. He loved baguettes from Publix Supermarket which he served before dinner with a glass of wine. He used olive oil—extra virgin, please—and spices, including his beloved paprika, to prepare a dipping sauce for the baguette.

Paprika came from the town of Szeged in Hungary near Sam's hometown in Romania, Satu Mare. It was so close to the Hungarian border that Hungarian was Sam's first language. He also spoke Romanian, Hebrew and English, after his fashion. I was impressed that Sam was multilingual, but surprised that he could hardly write. He used block letters, not script. And he couldn't spell correctly at all. Just like royalty used to do, Sam made up his own spelling rules.

However, he loved setting a beautiful table and enjoying what the French call *la bonne chère*, good food, good wine and good company. Strains of classical music played in the background at dinner at his house.

Sam was careful about his diet. He cut out articles about healthy eating and pasted them in a notebook. He ate so much salad at work that his nickname was 'the rabbit.' He even ate the kale which decorated the platters of the catered parties the executives sometimes gave. This amazed the rest of the workforce who favored smoked red mullet and peach pie among other southern delicacies. There were so many dishes and desserts of so many nationalities shared at lunchtime at the plant, it's a wonder that some crumbs didn't occasionally fall into the hydraulic valves. In fact, I think they did!

Although he was disciplined about what he ate, Sam also loved splashing out from time to time. He would say with gusto, "tonight, we eat with the big spoon!" his dark brown eyes dancing in his tanned face.

I was having a ball with Sam. And he was a wonderful and indefatigable lover too. His 'hard one' never let him down. By 'hard one,' Sam meant 'hard on.' Several of Sam's American expressions were almost, but not quite idiomatically correct. I found his mistakes charming, not irritating. The way he got them wrong made the expressions new again for me.

Sam could not come to France for the summer with me. He had to work. And to be honest, I was still evaluating my feelings toward him.

I was very attracted to him on many levels. *Did I want to commit to limiting myself to a monogamous relationship with him?* The verdict was still out. Perhaps the summer months we spent apart would lend some insight. Just as in English, there are two corresponding French proverbs to describe the situation I found myself in:

'Out of sight, out of mind' and its opposite, 'absence makes the heart grow fonder.' In French, they say,'*Loin des yeux, loin du coeur*' and its opposite,'*l'absence rend le coeur plus tendre.*'

Which one would win out in this instance for me?

The second development of the spring was a sad one. I received a letter from my Parisian friend, who ran the '*chambre d'hôtes,*' Micheline Dubosc. Over the winter, her husband, Paul, had fallen ill and died. Micheline was bereft. She wrote that she had nursed him with all of her considerable determination. She had commuted back and forth to the distant hospital where he was treated, but to no avail. He languished and then expired.

I invited Micheline to come and visit me at Pech Menal right away when I returned there. I would be on my own. Sam would be back in Sarasota working. A visit would give Micheline a change of scene and her company would distract me from missing Sam.

I asked myself what there was about Micheline that led me to pursue a friendship with her. Of course, her beautiful Paris apartment was an inducement. As was her knowledge of the city and its attractions. Perhaps on an unconscious, more psychological level, she was a sort of mother figure. I liked seeking and receiving her validation and approval.

Micheline took me up on my invitation to come visit. She arrived at Montauban train station, late one May afternoon. She descended from a first class carriage. She knew all the ins and outs of getting a good deal from the *SNCF*, the French national railroad company, by reserving early and using her senior citizen card. We greeted one another with kisses on the cheek. Micheline launched right in:

"Barbara, I have made two restaurant reservations for us. I want to try the local specialities, especially *foie gras*."

"*D'accord*," I said agreeably. "Where are we going ?"

"Well, there are a few Michelin one star restaurants in your region. Not many, but even so, there is the '*Auberge du Chapeau*' in Caussade."

"Yes, of course, I know it. That's right nearby."

"And then we will go to Moissac, rather further afield to the '*Moulin du Tarn.*'

"And finally?" I asked.

"I have a few more under consideration," she informed me. "We'll decide *définitivement* later on."

Taking her little suitcase in hand, we got into my Citroën station wagon. On the drive back to Pech Menal from Montauban, Micheline seemed ill at ease.

"*Barbara! Tu coupes les virages. Ne coupe pas les virages! C'est dangereux.*"

It was true that I didn't always hug the right side of my lane on the curvy blacktop.

It was easier to drive more in the center of the road. There were so many curves and often so little traffic from the other direction that I was tempted to get lazy. "*Ne coupe pas les virages!*" became a theme of our drives together, me at the wheel, *le volant*, and Micheline intoning the warning now and then, "Keep to your side of the road!"

I admitted that my driving style was a bit erratic. I had made a lot of progress driving the manual transmission of the Citroën, but my stick shifting wasn't always as smooth as desirable.

Sometimes, I even forgot what gear I was in altogether. But I got where I needed to go. That was the main thing.

At Pech Menal, I made Micheline comfortable downstairs on the lower level where she would have easy access to the new 'indoor' bathroom. I could sleep on the sofa upstairs for a few nights. Like most of my French acquaintances, Micheline loved Pech Menal. She thought it was beautiful and impressive. M. de Paris' renovations were faultless and my improvements had made it quite livable.

She was less satisfied by our restaurant meals in the *Tarn* and the *Tarn-et-Garonne*. As we sat by the pretty swimming pool on the shady patio at *l'Auberge du Chapeau*, Micheline complained to me:

"I don't find the *foie gras* sufficiently buttery. Very ordinary." *Quelconque* was her verdict, although of course she was very polite and discreet about her feelings whispering to me under her breath. As for myself, the *foie gras* seemed quite fine enough. I was hardly a connoisseur. I thought the white pepper we sprinkled lightly on top enhanced the flavor, as Micheline said it would do.

Foie gras is the liver of a duck or goose fattened by force feeding, *le gavage*. It is a popular and well known delicacy. The southwest region of France where we were was particularly known for its production. It was sold whole and could be eaten sliced or prepared into a mousse or pâté. My friends, Jerry and the other Barbara, made it at home one time, buying a whole, raw, fattened liver and dressing and cooking it very slowly as directed by a neighbor. It was a time-consuming process but not really difficult.

French law stated that *"Foie gras* belonged to the protected cultural and gastronomic heritage of France." *Foie gras* production had become controversial in some places, like California, due to concerns that force feeding violated animal rights. France was the largest producer and consumer of *foie gras* although there were producers and markets worldwide. *Foie gras* and all the tasty duck by-products were very appreciated in the Midi-Pyrénées where they represented a thriving little industry. There were ducks farms and *foie gras* sellers along the sides of all the local roads.

The following day, Micheline and I drove to Moissac, about an hour away from Cayrièch, to the next restaurant on the schedule. It was in an old mill on the Tarn River. Although *Le Moulin du Tarn* was in a picturesque setting, the food was a real disappointment. Our meal was lackluster and the service was negligent.

Micheline said,"This is *inadmissible*. I'm not going to take this treatment lying down. I'll write to the Michelin people and register my disapproval as soon as I get home. They will want to know."

I had to agree with Micheline's negative assessment of our lunch, but her complaints were getting me down. I was starting to feel defensive on behalf of the restaurateurs of my region.

Hélas, Alas, gastronomically speaking, Micheline's visit was not a success. The last restaurant we tried was my suggestion. It had no Michelin star but I thought it was very good.

Micheline was unimpressed by this restaurant as well, but the other aspects of her stay with me had pleased her. It was nice to get out of Paris for a long weekend. The countryside was beautiful. We visited some of the highlights of the region—the ruined castle perched precariously above Penne, the attractions of well-preserved Saint Antonin with its renaissance mansions. She appreciated spending time with a younger friend. It made her feel vicariously younger.

From my side, it was nice to have company and to be treated to delicious meals, even if they had not been perfect. It was fun to show off Pech Menal to an appreciative audience although I felt less and less committed to it myself. It felt good helping to distract my friend from the shock of her husband's death. She occasionally seemed a little unsteady on her feet, but she used her cane to good effect. She was indomitable.

During one of our drives together, Micheline told me a shocking story about her life in the south of France before she and

Paul moved back to Paris. While she was living in her farmhouse in Provence, she was raped at knifepoint.

The *mas,* as they call a farmhouse in the *Midi*, was in rough mountainous terrain. The *Maures* mountains there, named for the Moors from North Africa in the Middle Ages, tumbled steeply into the sea near Nice. In the olden days, the marauding North African brigands arrived by sea to raid the inhabitants so the population preferred to live in the hills high above the beach. It was safer. Of course, these days it was reversed and it was the beachfront property which was the most desirable. However, the hills above the sea did not prove safe for Micheline.

"One sunny lunchtime," she recounted to me, "I was in my kitchen. I had a backsplash covered with those pretty provençal tiles from Salernes, a beautiful blue color. Next thing I knew, someone grabbed me from behind. He put a knife to my throat. I didn't even have time to scream. My assailant left as fast as he had appeared. He was never found."

This account left me speechless. Micheline, who was so beyond reproach, so dignified, so correct! If this could happen to Micheline, it could happen to anyone. I didn't ask her for more details. I felt that she had confided as much as she felt comfortable doing.

I took her story to heart, as a cautionary tale. I had never felt afraid living all alone in the countryside at Pech Menal, but one could never be too careful. I was also impressed by Micheline's resilience and her lack of self pity as she told the story. 'Life moves on,' seemed to be her attitude. I felt this way of thinking boded well for her eventual recovery from the loss of Paul and was a helpful attitude for everyone in general.

Micheline returned to Paris. She had a full calendar of clients at the *chambres d'hôte.*

Now that I was back in France at Pech Menal for my second summer, I had the pleasure of renewing contact with friends and places I knew and appreciated from last year. Pech Menal was much more comfortable this year with a real bathroom and kitchen. The house was properly furnished and equipped. The property had been cleaned up and looked well tended. There were some flowers on the hedge, *la haie*, on which I had lavished so much attention last year.

Even the weather was cooperating. Last summer's historic heat wave was over and the weather was more typically temperate. I was expecting some guests to visit; my sons, my friends, Margaret and Susan. Susan owned a house in Isle-sur-la-Sorgue in Provence. She and Margaret were going to drive over to see me.

I needed a spare bed at Pech Menal for my guests. Since I didn't have a separate guest bedroom, I had bought a convertible sofa bed from another era. It weighed a ton. I thought this sofa bed would come in handy for guests whether sitting or sleeping.

Once I put it in place, I realized that the upholstery was in very rough shape. It was torn and soiled in places. That was the trouble with a lot of the old upholstered pieces of furniture found at *brocantes*. Used furniture was less expensive to buy. It was very well built and had the cachet of a former era, but often needed redoing. Once you paid for reupholstery, any price advantage disappeared. However, you did get exactly the fabric covering you wanted.

This was another project to take care of. I would look into my options sometime in between painting workshops. I had signed up for Chantal's classes painting *en plein air* again this summer.

One day strolling around Saint Antonin after a painting session, I spied a little sign in a shop window which advertised an upholstery service. The window was mostly filled with an arrangement of lacy old tablecloths, filigree silver spoons, porcelain doll heads, and gewgaws of all sorts. It all had a very feminine air. The owner was also renting rooms, judging by another sign announcing *Chambres d'Hôtes*.' Bed and breakfast were available.

I went inside and talked to the owner whose name was Jacqueline. I explained about my sofa bed and told Jacqueline that its covering was old-fashioned in an unattractive way and that I wanted to change it to something more to my taste. Jacqueline was willing to take on the job. She said we must first find the appropriate fabric. She suggested we visit a store in Montauban.

One day soon afterwards, I found myself riding along in Jacqueline's car to the new shopping area on the outskirts of Montauban. As we passed around the many *rondpoints* on our way, we saw swimming pool stores with their empty, upended swimming pool shells, tractors, harvesters and other farm equipment stores, vineyards, farms offering *foie gras* and other duck specialties and many apple orchards with their trees covered with white netting. After thirty minutes or so, we arrived at the final rotary on the national road. We had saved a few euros by skipping the *autoroute* and taking the old national highway.

"Barbara,' Jacqueline announced, "we need to make a detour to the Ministry of Finance, '*le Trésor Publique*,' so that I can drop off my tax return. I'm late and I'm going to miss the final deadline if I don't get it in today."

"Sure, Jacqueline, do what you need to do. I'll wait."

By way of apology, Jacqueline explained her situation to me: She was a *pied noir*. Figuratively, she had one foot in North Africa and one in France. She was born in Algeria and had come to France as a girl, torn away from the country where her family had lived for generations when President De Gaulle had decided to cut Algeria loose from French domination in 1962. The *pieds noirs*, members of the French colonial ruling class, felt betrayed when Algeria became an independent country with a stroke of a pen. Jacqueline and her mother had come to France with nothing and had to start all over from scratch.

"I guess as a *pied noir* I feel a little ambivalent about paying my taxes, Barbara. Well, no use dwelling in the past," Jacqueline told me. "My taxes are paid now and we can get on with the business at hand of finding you fabric for your sofa bed."

Our destination turned out to be a combination art supply, craft and fabric store --a sort of French 'Hobby Lobby'. A salesman directed us to the fabric section. Pickings were pretty slim, I thought. I had been envisioning a thicker fabric for covering the sofa bed.

"Jacqueline, are you sure these fabrics aren't too thin for upholstery?"

"*Regardez, Barbara,*" Jacqueline said. "Isn't this shiny beige one nice? I think I could make it work out very well."

"Hmm," I said, assessing the possibilities. "It might work. Or this one, the blue. Could I look at them at home, back at Pech Menal?"

The salesman spoke up. "Oh, no, *mesdames.* We couldn't possibly let you take anything out of the store. You would have to buy a meter of whatever interests you."

Typical, I thought to myself. Marshall Field had made a fortune at his Chicago department store "giving the lady what she wants." His money making philosophy hadn't crossed the Atlantic even after a hundred years of business success.

After all the trouble Jacqueline and I had taken organizing this buying trip, I hated to return home empty handed. I felt downcast. To gain time thinking, I started to look around the store. It wasn't very large. Maybe I should buy a canvas or two or some paintbrushes as long as we were here, I considered. I headed for the art supply section of the store.

"Wait, *attendez, mademoiselle,*" the salesman said, following me down an aisle. "If there are a few fabrics which really interest you, I could bring them to your house. That way you could make a better decision."

"*Impeccable!*" I said, turning to face him. "That sounds great! Right, Jacqueline?"

"*Parfait,*" Jacqueline enthusiastically agreed. "*Très bonne idée.*"

I gave the salesman, whose name was Jean, the address of Pech Menal. Or rather I gave him directions on how to get there since the address was only Pech Menal, Cayrièch.

"Once you get to Cayrièch, look for the sign '*direction St. Georges.*' Take that road and make a left onto a dirt track when you see the garbage bins. Pech Menal is at the end of the road. There is a little sign saying *Pech Menal.*"

Jean wrote that down, along with my name and telephone number. He also made a note of the stock numbers of the three fabrics which were possibilities.

I took a better look at him. He seemed presentable enough. An ordinary guy. As the song goes: "*Je cherche un homme, un homme, un homme.*" Then Eartha Kitt continues crooning, "*Whether his name is Peter or Paul or Tom. An ordinary guy's alright with me.*"

On the appointed afternoon, Jean climbed the stone steps to the landing and knocked on the front door of Pech Menal. He carried the fabric samples under one arm.

Jacqueline had not been able to make the drive from Saint Antonin to Cayrièch to join me looking over the fabrics.

No matter. Jean and I quickly concluded that the champagne colored one with the little chevron pattern in the material would go with my eclectic assortment of *brocante* items, the big leather club chair and the new sofa purchased in Toulouse.

The new sofa reminded me of the one on the hit tv show, 'Mad About You.' The back and arms of the couch were boring beige but the cushions were green and brown checkerboard. This green pleased me because it matched the finish on my *Godin* wood stove over on the hearth.

Jean and I got to talking. We sat together on the edge of the sofa-bed. After all, it was already opened up. His was a common story. Unhappy marriage. Dead end job.

"You're so pretty," he told me. "You're foreign. That's so exciting. I love your cute English accented *français.*"

Pourquoi pas? I thought. *I can test out the sofa bed mattress.*

Jean undressed me and himself. As I lay back watching him remove his pants, he revealed a pair of underpants the likes of which I had never seen. His *slip* was positively psychedelic. The cheap looking nylon of his underpants was covered with yellow stripes and purple circles traversed all over with fuschia colored darts. I couldn't help myself. I burst out laughing. This put quite a damper on Jean's ardor.

"*Qu'est-ce qui ne va pas?*" he sputtered. "What's so funny?"

"*Je suis désolée,*" I said, genuinely sorry to have hurt his feelings by my fit of giggles. "I don't think this is a good idea, Jean. I don't like the idea that you're married. And I don't want to hurt my boyfriend back home, if he knew what I was doing."

I didn't know how to tell Jean that I just couldn't get by his underwear. It was a culture clash, or at any rate, a clash of colors. And the thought of Sam was in the back of my mind as well.

Jean went on his way, back out the old red door and down the long staircase. At least he had the fabric order to show for the afternoon. I closed up the sofa bed again, the old mechanism groaning and creaking as the bench seat went back into place.

What time was it? Four o'clock. Still too early to give Sam a 'buzz' back in Florida. It was only 10:30 a.m. there. He would be at work.

I made a mental note to call him later at around six p.m. his time. I really needed to talk with him even if I had to stay up until midnight to catch him at home.

Just like that, I knew that I really wanted to share the end of my summer in France with Sam. I was no longer indecisive. Sam did not fit the preconceived image I had in mind of my future partner, but he seemed perfect to me at that moment.

I called Sam long distance that evening. I wasted little time on the formalities:

"I think you should come and visit me in Cayrièch, Sam. How many vacation days have you accrued ?"

"I have a month coming to me. What's up? What's the hurry?"

"I'd really like to see you. I miss you. I feel as if I might be captured by one of the crazy people I meet here."

"A crazy *male* person?"

"Oh, Sam! Can you come? I'll pick you up in Toulouse at the airport."

"Well, I'll check into it," Sam ventured cautiously. "But if I come to France, we'll have to go to Paris. I'm not coming all that way without seeing Paris."

"OK. Sure," I said into the receiver. I was thinking to myself that it was unlikely that Sam would ever manage to make the necessary arrangements. It was easy enough to agree to tack a visit to Paris onto this imaginary get together.

Later that very night, much to my surprise, Sam called me back. It was very late my time but I didn't mind.

"Hi Barbara. I decided to give you a 'buzz' even though it's late where you are."

I didn't much like that 'buzz' expression of Sam's. But it was at least the correct usage.

"Hi, Sam. It's late here. What's going on?"

"Well, I made the plane reservations. Sarasota to Atlanta. Then Atlanta to Paris and onto Toulouse."

Well I'll be a monkey's uncle, I exulted. *He's gone and done it!*

"Sam, that's great news! When do you arrive? I need all the details. This is fantastic. I can't wait to see you." All my pent up longing burst out. All my hesitations and self protective justifications evaporated.

Time alternately dragged and flew by until the day of Sam's arrival. As I drove to Toulouse Blagnac airport to pick him up, I was so excited that my gear shifting was even more erratic than usual.

Waiting for his familiar figure to emerge from the double doors of the baggage and customs area, I was nervous.

How did I look? How would he look?

I studied each person who came out into the reception area, wheeling their rollaboards behind them.

No, not him. Too young. No, not that one, too old. There he is!
No, wrong one. That's not Sam.

And at last it really was him! Sam, trim as ever, his shirttail carefully tucked into his belt, with a big smile on his face revealing his crooked front teeth. He grabbed me in a big bear hug and I returned his embrace.

"Barbara, you look beautiful! I am so excited to be here."

"Oh, Sam, this is going to be wonderful. I have so much to show you. Are you tired from your trip? You look fresh as a daisy."

"And you are lovely as a rose."

I blushed. We were both so excited. It was as if the other arriving passengers and their reception committees ceased to exist. We were blocking their exit. We got out of the way and headed to the parking lot where my car was waiting.

Driving back from Toulouse Blagnac airport to Cayrièch, I felt a little shy. We had been apart for two months. If Sam was tired from his trip, you couldn't tell. We spent some time filling one another in, on the last 24 hours. Sam told me how the trip had gone for him and I told him how hard I had found it to sleep last night waiting for him.

Sam had a misadventure at Charles de Gaulle airport. He had misplaced his wallet. When he checked all the many pockets of his cargo pants, it was gone! Luckily he had found the customer service counter in time before his connecting flight and succeeded in getting it back. Some good Samaritan had turned it in! Everything was going our way.

As the Citroën rounded the last twists and turns to Cayrièch, over the little stone bridge, past the rows of poplar trees lining the banks of the little *Lère* river, skirting past the fenced in cattle grazing near the big *pigeonnier*, Sam was astounded.

"Barbara, he exclaimed, how did you ever find this place? This is the boondocks! It's you and 500 cows."

I laughed. "You've about summed it up alright, me and 500 cows."

Sam got out to open the gate to Pech Menal. We entered the courtyard and *nous voilà! Enfin.* There we were at last.

I had the pleasure of giving him a quick tour of Pech Menal before we toppled into bed and made love as naturally as if we'd never been separated and as passionately as if we'd been apart for a few months, which was indeed the case.

Caussade's Tolosaine-style Church Bell Tower

CHAPTER 17

Sam Auditions in the Tarn-et-Garonne

S am met my neighbors, the Belons, the next day. They clicked right away. Soon enough, Sam was borrowing Pierre's *tronçonneuse* to chainsaw down the scrubby plum trees near the well.

I introduced him to Mme Lemoine at the real estate office in Caussade. She took us to the café next door for a coffee and to talk. All of Sam's French reading paid off. He could communicate after a fashion. Most of all, his big toothy smile and irresistible good humor won people over.

It was the *Foire aux Vins* in Caussade at the *Intermarché* supermarket with special fall promotions on wine. Sam was in heaven deciding which wines to buy at the reduced prices. We went back to Pech Menal laden with our wine purchases and provisions from the Monday market in Caussade.

Over the coming days Sam made us lots of delicious meals in the little 'summer kitchen.' Soups and stews were his specialty. I made us a *lapin à la moutarde,* rabbit stew. It was so cozy sitting there in the 'summer kitchen' of an evening gazing out through the gingham curtains I had hung on the little windows as the sun set over the fields.

One balmy evening, we were outside at the plastic table in the courtyard preparing the apéritif. We had a jar of *foie gras* to put on toast points for a special treat. Sam wanted to have some *foie gras*. His mother, back in Romania, had force fed the geese and sold the livers for a handsome price. Sam told me proudly that her livers brought the highest price of anyone around their area.

"Do you know what we could get with the money from one of our fattened goose livers, Barbara? Guess!"

"Gee, I don't know, Sam. A handbag? A tea kettle?"

"No, not at all, silly. We could buy a new goose to start all over again."

"Wow!" I was completely out of my depth.

M. Delpech, the plumber, came out of the house where he had been doing a repair job for me. As he was preparing to get into his truck, Sam and I were struggling to open the *foie gras* jar.

"No, it's like this,' I told Sam, trying to wrest the jar away from him.

"No, I tried that, Barbara. This is impossible. Let's get a hammer," suggested Sam, not entirely in jest.

"M. Delpech, s'il vous plaît," I called out to the plumber. "We're stumped. Can you help us, please?"

"What's the problem here?" said Jean-Claude Delpech, walking over to see what was going on.

"We can't open the *bocal* of foie gras. We've tried everything we can think of but the lid won't budge."

M. Delpech laughed. *"O, là là. Quelle tragédie!* Give it here."

And with that, M. Delpech took the jar and pulled on the pink tongue sticking out of the side of the top. The lid opened like magic with a little whoosh and a pop. We all had a big laugh together. M. Delpech accepted a glass of champagne and we toasted our hero.

"Jean-Claude, if I may call you that," thinking to myself how hard it was to remember the Jean-Claudes from the Jean-Pierres and the Jean-Michels, "how's your family?"

"All very well, thank you. I have four children. Three daughters and finally, the youngest, a son, *un fiston." Fiston* was an affectionate word for *'fils,'* which means son. "My wife is a teacher in Caussade."

"How did you get into plumbing?" I asked.

"I could have gone to work at *Caussade Semences,* the big seed company. My father had a connection there. But I didn't want a desk job and I wanted to be on my own."

"You should come visit us someday in Florida," proposed Sam. "Bring the family."

For an instant, Jean-Claude Delpech seemed to seriously consider the invitation. Our good spirits were so infectious.

"Oh, we couldn't just *débarquer* like that, all six of us. I should be getting home now. They'll be expecting me."

"*Bonsoir, notre héro. Merci!* Have a good evening."

"*Bonsoir. Merci pour le champagne,*" he waved from the van as he drove out of the courtyard.

The days of Sam's visit were passing merrily by. We visited the Musée Ingrès in Montauban. Most of the famous paintings by the artist were in the Louvre in Paris. I had studied them there in my student days. But it was still an honor for Montauban that one of France's most famous painters was born there.

Before the Impressionists burst on the scene in the 1850's, the two giant figures of French salon painting were Eugène Delacroix and Jean Dominique Ingrès. Delacroix was famous for his romantic, over the top depictions of historical events. Ingrès paintings were often elegant portraits.

Ingrès was also a talented violinist. His violin was preserved at the museum in Montauban in a recreation of his studio with his actual easel and paintbox. Since he was a genius painter, his violin playing remained just a hobby. This gave rise to the French expression for a hobby, *un violon d'Ingrès.*

Sam and I toured all around. I wanted him to meet my friends from Cazals, Charles, the Englishman and his American wife, Eloise. They had us to dinner at their lovely house set in the big garden that Charles was always working to improve. Eloise was a great hostess. Charles could be rather stuffy like a gentleman in a British novel, but the evening went off well.

One of the other guests at dinner that night was a French woman we called Ginette 'de Régie.' Her real last name was Delpech which was a common one in the area. Ginette 'de Regie' was a tiny woman with dyed red hair and beautiful blue eyes which she emphasized with blue eyeshadow. I had met her several times at my friends' parties. Now in her late eighties, she must once have broken many hearts. She still had a boyfriend down the hill with whom she had an assignation once a week, walking carefully down the slope to meet him at his house in the village proper. Her sexual activity was common knowledge. Everybody knew she was going to meet her lover when she walked down the hill on Fridays, all dolled up. Good for her. *Tant mieux!*

Ginette was called 'de Régie' because she lived in a hamlet of ten houses called *Régie* in which she was the last inhabitant in any of the homes. Everyone else had died or moved away. The little town belonged entirely to Ginette by default. When she was gone, *Régie* would most probably cease to exist. As Louis XIV, the sun king said, *'Après moi, le déluge.'*

The hamlet of Régie was just up the road from Charles and Eloise's house. Ginette had become kind of a mother figure to Eloise whose own mother had died young. The old woman had a son but he lived his own life in Toulouse. She liked the role of marriage counselor, beauty consultant and Miss Lonelyhearts. She was full of hard headed advice on all subjects.

After dinner, she took me aside, "I approve. *J'approuve,*" she told me, gesturing toward Sam. "But watch out, don't gain any more weight, Barbara. You're still Ok, but no more."

Another highlight of our touring around Cayrièch was the Offenbach festival held in Bruniquel every summer. An amateur troupe had performed a different operetta up there each summer season for many years. Since Offenbach wrote over one hundred operettas, there were still plenty to choose from. We caught one of the last performances of *La Grande Duchesse de Gerolstein*, an *opera bouffe* full of comedy, satire and farce.

Parking the car down below Bruniquel, we climbed up the almost vertical streets of the perched village to the ruined castle courtyard where the troupe performed. Our seats had been arranged for us by my friend, Marie Angibaud, a boutique owner from Caussade.

I had bought many little things to set up housekeeping at Pech Menal from her cute shop, *Chez Amandine*, named after her daughter. We had really met when she and her husband had delivered the big leather club chair from the boutique's window to Pech Menal. I had fallen in love with that chair. It was so retro looking. It was the largest item in her boutique by far.

Marie, in high heels, and Raymond, in the smart suit he wore to his insurance agency, carried the chair up the big stone stairs and into the living room of Pech Menal by themselves. It was quite a feat. I was surprised that this was what they meant by delivery. I had been expecting delivery men. I was a little embarrassed and I fluttered around, trying to help them tote the chair.

Tragically, shortly after this, Raymond committed suicide, in despair over his gambling debts. He ended his life by jumping off the cliff called *le Roc d'Anglars* in Saint Antonin. 'The Rock of the English' was a local landmark, one of the highest points in the gorges of the Aveyron River valley. There was a little road up to the giant granite outcropping. It had been named during the Hundred Years War with England. I learned that this was not the first time that *le Roc d'Anglars* was used for this desperate purpose.

The Offenbach operetta was a far cry from such horrific occurrences. It was all fluff and silliness with catchy tunes and funny lyrics. A spirited *cancan* ended the show.

Afterwards the audience moved to long tables where dinner was served. It was local pork, *le porc de Calvignac*. Conviviality reigned. Sam and I were seated next to the cousins of the cousins of one of our neighbors from Cayrièch. And so it usually went.

Many people were interrelated in the area. Everybody was delighted to meet the Americans and they would report the occurrence back to their cousins. It made us feel special.

All was well and good. Sam's visit was going splendidly. We didn't have disagreements about expenses. Sam had devised an easy system for keeping accounts. We kept a running tab of his outlays and mine in separate columns. Each week we would add the totals in each column and we would settle up, if one owed the other.

We tried not to break the bank. Our biggest expense was the upcoming excursion to Paris which was slated to be the culmination of Sam's visit. We were planning and strategizing so as to make the most out of our days in the capital. Sam loved Chagall and opera. So it was a given that we must pay a visit to the Paris Opera house with its Chagall ceiling.

Before I recount our visit to Paris, I'd like to say a word about Sam. Sam was not your typical romantic hero, although he was handsome in a rough hewn way. When we first met, he lied to me saying that he was a hydraulic engineer. That was false. He tested hydraulic valves for a living. It was manual labor.

At the plant there was a lot of overtime which was theoretically optional. In reality, it was compulsory, if you wanted to keep your job. The European market for hydraulic valves was hot because of the rate of exchange. The dollar was low against most other currencies. Therefore you could buy an American made part for a relatively bargain price. This meant that the plant could hardly keep up with the demand for their product. It was odd to think that our lives in sunny little Sarasota were affected by global markets and the rate of exchange. However, all the overtime hours did cut into our ability to be together as much as we wanted.

When we were in Sarasota, we had a weekly ritual of meeting for a late afternoon movie at the Dollar Cinema whenever possible. Tickets cost a dollar per person. Often we were the only customers in the movie theater. I mean the ONLY ones. It was a private showing for us. We would snuggle together, high on one another's sheer presence.

We saw some really forgettable films, but no matter. After the show, we would go for an early dinner at the British pub restaurant in the same shopping center. How Sam loved French fries with pepper and smothered in ketchup! No salt for Sam. It wasn't healthy in his opinion, and Sam tried hard to eat healthy. The French fries were a special exception.

Sam's second job early Sunday mornings was also heavy work putting together the Sunday edition of the newspaper. Sam's attitude in general was the tougher the job, the better he liked it. The pay was literally pennies per hour, another questionable benefit. Yet, by dint of careful saving over the years, Sam had paid for his daughter's beautiful wedding in Philadelphia. Sam also loved getting a free Sunday paper at the end of his shift around 6 am. He relished the idea that he got the news before almost anybody else in Sarasota.

My boyfriend was a smart guy and had cultivated tastes, but he had very little formal education. He spoke several languages, but he never learned to spell at all correctly. A grocery list or a note from Sam was an original document, all his own and no one else's.

Sam read a lot, especially romance novels. Barbara Cartland was a favorite. He also enjoyed opera, classical music and theater. He especially loved the ballet because it was beautiful and also demanded physical prowess. He was impressed by the dancers' muscular dexterity. He liked best watching the ballerinas' bodies. I felt jealous as he admired the play of their muscles. I knew that I couldn't boast muscles like theirs.

Sam dressed well, although not expensively. His boyish physique permitted him to wear some of the latest trends. He liked cargo pants which were all the rage. For going to the chilly air conditioned movies after work, he had a hoodie jean jacket with pretend fleece. But he was not sloppy. He was dressed in an appropriately casual style for a painting job with his white painters' cap on backwards. He was suitably attired in a formal dark suit and tie for a fancy dinner or to go to the synagogue where we went on the Jewish high holidays.

How we laughed at the temple's fundraising letters Sam received in the mail! He was to choose whether he wished to donate to the building fund at the sapphire, ruby or diamond level. We were more interested in the free dessert and coffee which were available after the services.

For really cold weather, Sam had a broken-in, leather bomber jacket. It was the real McCoy from the Israeli air force and had a lot of cachet. It was a gift from his brother who was an Israeli Army colonel.

When he wasn't wearing his work shoes, Sam was often shod in mocassin style boat shoes with rawhide ties. His knots never came undone. Not his style. His striped tee shirts were usually carefully tucked into the waist of his belted khaki shorts.

Clean shaven, his short hair well-combed and graying at the temples, Sam most prominent feature was his easy smile. His big eyes were hazel under somewhat bushy brows. There was a gap between his front teeth which gave him a somewhat off-kilter appearance which I found endearing. His skin was smooth and brown. He had the kind of skin which tanned easily. He never got sunburned at the beach. He just turned a slight shade darker.

Born in Romania, he had emigrated to the United States after living for a time in Israel and in Canada. He had a funny accent and mixed up American expressions, a bit like Mrs. Malaprop in Charles Dickens.

He was a careful driver because we were past the age for hot rodding but also because he did not want the police to 'blow him in,' mixing together 'turn you in' and 'blow your cover' or 'blow you away'. It seemed that back in Romania, somebody might 'blow you in,' meaning that the police could turn up without warning and take you away never to be seen again.

Sam was a sexual tiger in the gentlest way. We made love every night. It relaxed him and helped him to fall asleep. I got so as I anticipated the pleasure it gave me every evening.

I would say, "Sam, it's so late. We don't have time. You have to be up in a few hours to go to work."

"You worry too much, Barbara," Sam told me with a smile I could see in the dim light of the bedroom of his little condo. "Repeat after me," he would coach me, "Fuck It! Fuucck It!"

I knew what Sam meant. When I got worried about details or things outside of my control, Sam would have me practice saying after him —"Fuucck It!" It was a good strategy and seemed to work calming me down and putting things in perspective. *Je m'en fous* and the slightly more polite, *je m'en fiche,* worked quite well in French too.

What a character Sam was! Or several characters. He wasn't just named 'Sam.' He was 'Gula' in Hungarian, his first language, pronounced 'Yula.' He was 'Schmuel' in Hebrew and 'Sam' in English.

He had lots of stories about growing up in a small town in Romania. He idolized his father and mother who had both passed away. Sam's father supplemented his income by repairing shoes. He specialized in 'ladies' shoes, Sam would say with a gleam in his eye. Like father, like son, since Sam also rather specialized in 'ladies.' I eventually found out that Sam had been married and divorced three times. He admitted readily to his first two marriages, but I only found out about the third one many years later. At least he was serially faithful and not a cheater like Luc.

For the shoe-making business, Sam's father had stacks of beautiful leather cow hides in the attic of their house. There were several Singer sewing machines to stitch the hides together into shoes. These all disappeared in the war. In his youth, Sam would help his father harness the horse cart which took the shoes to the weekend market. Full time, Sam's father worked in a factory in Sanislow, the watermelon capital of Romania, Sam explained to me. Sam's father had a gentile friend who had helped him get the factory job. Sam's father then helped a lot of his neighbors in Satu Mare, the town where the family lived, become employed at the same factory.

Sam's father was a tall, handsome man with a dark complexion. He was a good dancer. All the ladies liked to dance with him. Sam's mother was a petite blonde with freckles. She never stopped working all day long, taking care of household chores. She grew vegetables and fruit, canned food, cleaned the house, made goose down pillows and comforters and looked after the children. Yet she still found the energy to read big heavy books at night before falling asleep. Sam revered his parents, an attitude that I didn't encounter often. It impressed me.

Sam didn't know how his father had gotten through the war years. Perhaps he escaped the concentration camps by being so useful to the soldiers, of which army was unknown. He became a barber and jack of even more trades than before the war.

Sam's mother was in Auschwitz. She was examined by Dr. Mengele as a candidate for one of his monstrous experiments. Luckily, she was rejected because "she was perfect," Sam would say with tears in his eyes and his voice gravelly with emotion.

One of the guards had a soft spot for Sam's pretty blonde mother. He sometimes allowed her to dig up leftover roots in a field near the camp while he serenaded her with Romanian love songs. She would share out these vegetable leavings with Sam's aunts back in the barracks. Perhaps it made the difference between life and death for them because they survived.

At the end of the war, Sam's parents were eventually reunited. Several years passed before Sam's mother was physically and psychologically recovered to the point where the children were conceived.

Sam had an older brother who was an excellent student and the most able of all the village boys at whatever he did. He won a prize in the machine shop, as well as prizes in academic subjects.

Sam, on the other hand, was the class cut up. He was known to climb up on the window ledge and moon the whole class, and the rabbi too, at the *cheder*, or religious school where he went.

However, he did like the French teacher, who was a pretty, young woman. In that class, he made an effort to please. He learned to recite, "*La plume de ma tante est sur le bureau de mon oncle.*" This immortal sentence about the aunt's pen being on the uncle's desk is famous among French students of all nationalities.

Sam also had a baby sister he adored. He was in charge of watching over her in the crib at night. They both slept near the kitchen stove where it was the warmest in the house.

Sam was responsible for the family cat. Each night he would send the cat out onto the roof to go to work catching mice. "OK, cat," he would say, "get out there and go to work." The cat's name was 'Cat.' There were no cutesy pet names for that feline.

It took years before the family was allowed to leave Romania in the 1960's since most Jews were not allowed to get exit visas. Sam's father hoped to come to America but the U.S. immigration quotas had changed by the time Sam's family was released. They were accepted in Israel instead.

Once arrived in Israel, Sam worked on a kibbutz where he learned Hebrew. He was a valued worker with his boundless energy and practical good sense.

He envied the American kids he saw who were spending a summer on the kibbutz. From his point of view, they loafed around all day in their rooms, smoking marijuana.

Sam was working on the conveyor belt where the glass jars were filled up with olives when he saw that someone further up the line had caused a jam. The cut-ups laughed gaily as the jars of olives smashed onto the tile floor one after another. Sam jumped up and pressed the emergency stop switch. His quick thinking and decisive action saved a lot of the kibbutz olive production. He may have been a desirable future kibbutznik, but Sam wasn't interested in the communal lifestyle. He wanted to 'fulfill his father's dream' and come to America.

But first there was the obligatory detour for new arrivals into the Israeli army. Basic training was tough. In one exercise, Sam and the other enlisted men were dropped off somewhere in the desert to spend the night. They were supposed to find their way back to base the next day without a compass. Sam never had a great sense of direction, as I knew well from driving around Sarasota with him, but his tentmate was even more hopeless. He was an overweight, out of shape Moroccan Jew who was traumatized to the point of paralysis by their predicament.

As Sam trudged along, unsure of which way to go, the guy was lagging behind, crying like a baby. At one point, he just gave up in despair. He sat down in the sand. He just couldn't or wouldn't move his bulk another inch.

Sam picked him up and loaded him onto his back. He kept on walking, carrying his heavy burden. He tried to orient himself by what he remembered from the position of the stars. It must have worked because they both made it back into base camp as required.

Sam's older brother had a different experience in the Israeli army. He quickly rose through the ranks, probably in the intelligence service. It was all very hush, hush. The brother eventually became a lieutenant colonel with many hundreds of men and women under his command. All this responsibility took its toll however. He couldn't pick out new underwear without Sam's advice.

Sam left his family in Israel and went to Canada. He had a few relatives in Toronto. One of them tried to do him a favor by helping him to marry into a prosperous family. The cousin's friend had a thriving grocery business and an unmarried daughter. The friend liked Sam a lot. He asked Sam to marry his daughter and take over the store. He felt that Sam would be just the man to stand honorably by his daughter and take over stewardship of the business.

But Sam, regretfully declined. "I just don't love your daughter, sir," he explained.

Sam's further romantic history was complicated. Once he got

to the United States, he did get married. He made an awful mistake in his choice of partner. His wife was originally from Romania too. She was totally under the control of her over-bearing parents, especially her father. This unscrupulous man made the newlyweds' life hell. Sam's father-in-law cooked up ways to torture the young couple. He threw their new mattress out the window of the couple's tenement apartment in South Philly. He inveigled Sam into a failing grocery store business so that he could steal the slim profits for himself.

Sam's wife and their infant daughter were virtually captives in their own home. The in-laws' cruel and unusual behavior would be unbelievable, if it weren't true. Sam's poor, young wife was so needy. Sam must have been drawn to the role of savior like a moth to a flame.

By the time Sam extricated himself from the situation by divorcing his wife, he was working in a delicatessen in downtown Philly where his good humor, hard working habits and genuine appreciation of food made him a valued employee. No education was required which was important because Sam had none. He never went to school beyond the fourth grade.

Looking for more opportunities outside of Philadelphia, he took a truck driving course, but as hard as he tried, he just couldn't get the knack of how to back up the big rigs. After a while, he landed a factory job in Delavan, New York, near Buffalo. He remarried, a teacher this time, and they had a daughter together. He and his second wife succeeded in raising his girls from both mothers to be confident, independent young women. But Sam's second marriage did not succeed in the long run.

Divorced yet again, Sam moved to Florida where he estab-lished himself with a house and a job. That is about where I came into the picture. We met and talked and talked. We played golf together, both pretty badly. We went to the beach near my house and collected shells. We went out to dinner and to the movies. Sam was always on time, always a gentleman. He helped me out by painting my garage floor. We took a few excursions up north of us in Florida to Lake Dora and Micanopy. We drove down south in his car to the Corkscrew Swamp and Naples. We gave a Christmas party for friends where the main course, a Christmas goose, came out so poorly that we ordered in Chinese food for everybody.

The winter months passed swiftly by as we pursued our courtship. And now, here we were together in France about to fulfill Sam's long-time wish to visit the French capital city.

Some Rooftops of Montpezat Looking Toward Brousse

CHAPTER 18

Paris à la Sam

And so on to Paris we went. Our trip started out in an ordinary enough way—we took the daytime train from Caussade to Montauban and then Cahors, Brive-la-Gaillarde, Limoges and Orléans, on our way to the capital.

We relaxed in our seats and stored up our energy to expend in a burst during the long weekend ahead. We were intent on seeing as many of the famous sights as possible, but Sam had a slightly different slant on our tour program. As I've already mentioned, he had to see the Chagall ceiling at the Palais Garnier Opera House. Furthermore, he wanted to visit la Grande Synagogue de Paris and the traditional Jewish section of the city in the Marais. This sounded interesting to me too.

The five hour train journey passed by quickly enough. In the morning, to wake ourselves up, we bought coffees from the catering cart which was rolled down the center aisle of our carriage. At lunchtime we munched on delicious, long baguette sandwiches which we had thought to purchase in advance at the boulangerie in Caussade before entraining. I did crossword puzzles and Sam worked at his word finders. We laughed and chatted, exchanging puzzles from time to time. I found his word finders to be very easy. I was working on the N.Y. Times Sunday crossword which I had saved for the trip from the weekend edition of the International Herald Tribune.

I was stumped by one little corner. I had thought about the clue from every angle, but I couldn't find a word that fit in. It was frustrating and I was about to give up. Sam, despite his not always correct English vocabulary, took a look at the problem and had an off the wall idea about it.

Eureka! His point of view unlocked something in my brain which led to the solution. We laughed ourselves silly at this unexpected turn of events.

I sure did love that guy!

We arrived at the Gare d'Austerlitz, the Paris train hub for travel to and from the southwest of France. We made our way to *le Colbert*, a little hotel I knew from my days touring with Pepitours. It had a wonderful location on la rue Saint Dominique, one of the longest and oldest streets in Paris. *Le Colbert* was less of a hotel and more of a restaurant with some rooms above on the top floors. There was a discreet side door from the street to the hotel section of the restaurant which opened if you knew the code.

"This is cool," Sam said when they buzzed us into the lovely, carpeted reception area.

Some of the staff recognized me from my prior stays when I was there with Pepitours and Luc which gave an added piquancy to my being there with Sam who was, of course, unaware of this aspect.

We hit the ground running after lunch. *Le Colbert* was near le Musée Rodin and its lovely grounds surrounding le Palais Biron. We spent the best part of a beautiful afternoon there. We admired Rodin's monumental sculpture of the disgraced Burghers of Calais, chained together in stone for eternity, and his sculpture of the famous author, Balzac, enveloped in his voluminous dressing gown. We contemplated Rodin's well-known bronze of 'The Thinker,' his chin resting on his hand.

When we saw the smaller, more romantic works in the room

devoted to Camille Claudel, Rodin's protégée, we were entranced. We both preferred her less monumental, but no less powerful bronzes and marble pieces. She was a famous artist in her own right. No easy feat, given Rodin's overarching shadow.

Camille Claudel's story is so sad. She was Rodin's muse, mistress, student and artistic rival. Their relationship was tempestuous as she established and proved herself to the artistic establishment as an equal to the great man. Her affluent and intellectual family disapproved heartily of her artistic accomplishments.

When Rodin died in 1917, Camille became depressed and refused to leave her studio. Her mother and brother took this opportunity to have her interned in an insane asylum.

Was she psychologically disturbed? Did she sign the papers which committed her? Despite several recommendations from the asylum doctors that Camille be reintegrated into society, her family, apart from her father, paid the doctors no heed. When he died, her fate was sealed. Her mother never mentioned her name again. Her famous playwright brother, Paul Claudel, nominated many times for the Nobel Prize for Literature for his heavily Catholic-oriented works like 'L'Annonce Faîte à Marie,' hardly visited her.

Camille Claudel died in 1943. She was interned for the last 30 years of her long life. At his death, her brother directed that her bones be scattered in a pauper's communal grave not far from his own tomb in the family's marble mausoleum.

Sam and I were lost in thought for a moment ruminating about Camille Claudel's tragic end.

He said, "Gosh, she had no luck, that Camille Claudel! She got crushed between two gigantic male artistic egos, the sculptor Rodin and her playwright brother. Although come to think of it, I never heard of Paul, the brother. Camille is still celebrated for her artistic genius so perhaps she got the last laugh after all."

I said to Sam, "I remember now. There was a film about her life. Did you see it? Isabelle Adjani played Camille Claudel. I think she won an award for it.

"Oh yes, that rings a bell, now that you mention it, Barbara. I think she might have got the Oscar for best actress."

"No, she lost out to Jessica Tandy in 'Driving Miss Daisy.' I remember that because I was disappointed," I said.

Sam read to me from the placard on the museum wall: *Isabelle Adjani, a beautiful French actress from the 1980's, portrayed Camille Claudel on film and won a César in 1988 for her performance.*

After a refreshing cup of tea and a pâtisserie in the museum garden, we crossed la Place des Invalides to see Napoléon's tomb. We stared down at the oxblood colored, granite cenotaph which contained the 'little corporal's' remains. Here lay the dust and bones of the *le petit caporal* who had conquered France and then brought all of Europe to its knees. 'Sic transit gloria mundi.'

"This is getting creepy," said Sam after a bit. "Let's get out of here."

And we hurried out of l'École Militaire towards the grandiose bridge of Tsar Alexandre III, gilded and adorned with its gorgeous art nouveau street lamps. Now that made for a change of scene! *Glorious,* we thought to ourselves. Breathtaking!

We walked on the bridge over the Seine past the statue of Winston Churchill towards the Champs Élysées. We were heading for l'Arc de Triomphe, Napoléon's triumphal commemoration of his many battlefield victories in the style of the ancient Roman emperors he admired when he was the 'scourge of Europe.' We could see the roofs of *le Petit Palais* and *le Grand Palais,* museums which look like botanical conservatories on either side of le Rond Point of les Champs Élysées in the distance. We could take the *métro* up to l'Étoile from the Franklin Roosevelt stop.

"Sam," I said, "I'm getting tired."

"You're right, *ma chérie.* I'm tired too. We've done a lot. Let's head back to *le Colbert* for an *apéritif.*

"Yes." I seconded that motion. "A little rest and brush up before dinner would suit me. I need a break."

Sam said gaily, "*D'accord,* my dear. Enough sightseeing for now. As they say, *'demain* is another day.' And so is tomorrow, ha, ha."

But after dinner, we couldn't sit still. We were irresistibly drawn to the Eiffel Tower whose lights we could see blinking in the distance from the rue St. Dominique. So as I had done many times with the Pepitours tourists, Sam and I strolled from *le Colbert* to the base of the tower in le Champ de Mars. We waited in line to take the elevators to the top and gaze at the 360 degree bird's eye view of Paris spread out at our feet. In French, it was called *la vue à vol d'oiseau.*

On our way down the tower in the elevator cab, I had a sudden flashback. Back in 1969 when my fiance, Alex, came to meet me at the end of my junior year in France, we had visited the Eiffel Tower. The lines were a lot shorter then, but the tickets to ride up were over our student budget. We decided to walk up the tower as far as we could. We were young and energetic.

"Sam, I want to tell you about the time I peed here in the Eiffel Tower stairwell."

"What? You made pee pee on the Eiffel Tower? How did such a thing come about?"

"Well, Alex and I were walking up the stairs since the elevator entry cost too much. It was dark and cold in the staircase. We were pretty much the only climbers. I had to pee very badly and there were no facilities around at all. I had no choice but to pee in a dark corner of the stairwell as fast as I could. Alex was the lookout. Luckily I was wearing a skirt. No toilet paper of course."

Sam laughed. "You and your uncontrollable urges, Barbara. You've left your indelible mark right here somewhere like a lioness."

'Sam," I tried to explain, "I couldn't help myself. It's kind of a disgusting story. I shouldn't have told you."

"Not at all," replied Sam, sniffing. "It's kinda, um, pungent. I think it's very sexy," he ended with a pretend leer.

For Sam, I could do no wrong.

From the Eiffel Tower, Sam and I walked to the nearby *Pont de l'Alma* to catch a *bateau mouche* on the Seine River. These tour boats with 'fly eyes,' so named for their many observation windows, ply the Seine continually.

We clambered on board and found seats along with many other tourists and visiting school groups. As usual, it was magic passing under the famous bridges over the Seine. We glided by Notre Dame cathedral, la Conciergerie, le Louvre and the historic buildings lining the banks of the river. Then, at midnight, arriving back at the Pont de l'Alma, the Eiffel Tower was set ablaze with glittering strobe lights which showcased its shimmering outline against the black velvet of the sky.

Magnifique! What a beautiful ending to the first day of our Paris trip.

"Tomorrow, we'll find the synagogue," I said.

"And don't forget that we have to arrange opera tickets for one of our evenings," Sam reminded me.

By this time, our footsteps had carried us back to *le Colbert* and we were buzzed in. We found our room and fell sleepily into bed, windows closed, curtains drawn and shutters, *les volets*, shut tight against the night.

Sam wanted to see the main synagogue of Paris, *la Grande Synagogue de Paris*. The next morning, we set off for *la rue de la Victoire* near the opera house Garnier with high hopes, but the street was blocked off. Access was *interdit*. We were forbidden to get anywhere near the impressive building. Sam tried to intercede with the guards, but without success. Perhaps this wasn't so surprising given the bombing in 1980 and the other anti-semitic attacks which still occurred sporadically in Paris and in France more widely. We had been naive to think we could just waltz in. Sam was disappointed.

Not giving up, I remembered a smaller, more humble synagogue near la Trinité Métro stop which I had often passed by during my student days. Was it still there? Sam was enthusiastic about trying to visit the temple in that neighborhood. We hopped on the métro and found the synagogue without trouble. There was even a Sabbath service taking place. *En l'occurrence,* as they say, meaning 'as it happened,' the synagogue turned out to look like any other orthodox temple back home. Sam was disappointed again.

But not for long. We headed for the Marais district, reputed to be the traditional Jewish quarter of the city. The Marais had a long history. It was originally a marshy area near a former branch of the Seine. This well watered ground was good for the vegetable gardens whose produce had once supplied the city. In the 17th and 18th centuries, the Marais became home to the mansions and palaces of the nobility. King Henri IV built la Place Royale, now called la Place des Vosges, there in the early 1600's. Louis XIII's equestrian statue, erected by le Cardinal Richelieu, presided over the center of the square until the French Revolution. The so-called pavilions of the king and queen were there, although no royalty ever lived on the square. It was a suitable urban background for the French aristocracy and nobility when they were in town.

In the 18th century, fashions changed and most of the nobility moved to the Faubourg St. Germain. In the 19th century, Baron Haussmann carved out the new *grands boulevards* around la Place de l'Étoile. The rich and titled classes moved west, erecting and adorning new mansions more in keeping with the style of the times. The old palaces of the Marais lost their glory and then fell into rack and ruin. Down at the heel and neglected, the district was settled into by Jews and other poor immigrants. It became a slum.

Most recently, in another about-face of the winds of fashion, the charms of the Marais were being re-discovered. The magnificent 17th century palaces and their decor were being refurbished. The tide of redevelopment started by the Pompidou Museum of Modern Art and the Picasso Museum, implanted in the district in the 1960's, was sweeping over the area. The old streets were lined with too many boutiques to count. Upscale shoppers, young and chic, *le gratin*, the upper crust of the city, thronged the sidewalks of the old streets.

Sam and I looked around for *la rue des Rosiers*. This street was until recently chock-a-block with Jewish delicatessens and bakeries. Here, at Jo Goldenberg's Delicatessen, once a landmark for Jewish cooking in the city, there had been an explosion in 1980 which had killed eight people, all non-Jews. Many others were injured. The perpetrators were never identified. The Goldenberg sign was still there, but the premises were now a women's clothing store. We asked a passerby about it and were told that the deli had gone out of business just recently. The new owners had kept the sign on the awning as a remembrance. The area had evolved. Hardly any traces of the former Jewish neighborhood remained.

"Well, so much for that idea," said Sam. "What's the new plan, my dear?"

I was a bit at a loss. We sat down for lunch in la Place des Vosges to consider our options and admire the architectural purity of Henri IV's square. Victor Hugo's house was right over there. Le Musée Pompidou wasn't far away, but we couldn't go in. They were between exhibitions. We could go and enjoy the scene in front of the museum on the Beaubourg plaza with all the jugglers and balloon sellers, but we didn't want to just mill around with other sightseers like ourselves.

"The Marais certainly is a beautiful and historic area," Sam told me between bites of lunch.

"You know, Sam," I said, reading from the guidebook, "La Place des Vosges used to be called la Place Royale."

"So why is it called 'des Vosges' now? I thought the Vosges were some mountains near Germany."

"Michelin says that Napoléon renamed this square after *les Vosges* because they were the first province to pay their taxes to his new government."

"Aha," said Sam. "Money talked, then as now. You know, I'd like to learn some more about Paris history, Barbara. Any thoughts of where to go?"

"Mmm," I considered. "There's le Musée Carnavalet, the museum of the city of Paris, which isn't far away. It's a beautiful mansion. It belonged to Mme de Sévigné, the noblewoman who wrote the letters about her life at the court of Versailles during the Sun King's reign. I've been there several times.

But let's try *les Archives*. I've never been there. It's also a 17th century palace. It houses the Paris Archives and it's also got a museum according to the guidebook."

The Archives was an inspired choice. We both loved seeing the objects on display which the guidebook said were changed from time to time. The lights were dim. We felt far away from the bustle of the streets outside. We concentrated on the old documents, deeds and maps. We peered at the original Paris city charter. There were some exhibits devoted to Dr. Guillotin, the inventor of the guillotine. He hoped to create a more merciful, humane way to punish evildoers.

On the other hand, we read about the grisly punishment meted out to Damiens, the would-be assassin of King Louis XV in 1757. Damien's body was ripped asunder by four horses pulling in different directions, a medieval torture called drawing and quartering resurrected for the almost regicide by the city authorities. The very dagger which Damiens plunged into the king's chest was preserved and on display. It was long and pointed. It certainly looked lethal.

Louis XV was not the first French king to be attacked. We read about the successful assassination of King Henri IV earlier in French history in 1610 by François Ravaillac, a Catholic fanatic. King Henry was a famously tolerant king. France thrived under his reign and his acceptance of Protestants. Henry himself was born a Protestant, but he famously converted in order to be crowned king. He is reputed to have said, "*Paris vaut une messe,*" in other words, "It's worth saying mass one time in order to become king of France."

"Wow! What a pragmatist that Henri was! I never knew about this stuff," Sam said. "It's fascinating."

"Me neither," I joined in. "What's around the corner of this room? I've never been to the Archives before."

It was fun to find a new Paris landmark to visit. The city was so overlaid with history, art and architecture that a person could always find a new favorite. It was an equal pleasure to re-visit sights in Paris which I knew and loved. I learned something each time. It was fun seeing some of my favorite places through Sam's eyes. Touring the city with him made the experience fresh. And then it should also be said that the city of Paris didn't rest on its laurels. The city government was always renovating and updating its rich patrimony. Even the old sights seemed new because they were freshly beautified and redone.

As we wandered around the Archives building, we somehow ended up in an annex up the stairs from the garden courtyard with its classical pyramids of boxwood trees.

To our delight, we then found ourselves in a suite of exquisite rooms, their 17th and 18th century interiors intact. The light of huge shimmering crystal chandeliers played on the delicate plaster moldings decorating the pastel colored walls. The intricate parquet floors creaked slightly as we walked around in a state of suspended animation. Mirrors reflected our rapt faces back to ourselves. We felt as if we had entered a magic lantern and had gone back centuries in a time tunnel.

When we came out, Sam asked me, "Did you know we would have this surprise at the end of the museum? This visit was fantastic! Thank you."

"Sam, I had no idea. Isn't it fun when you just happen upon something wonderful like those rooms? I'm so glad we stumbled upon them together."

"It is wonderful. I hope we can have many more adventures together, not just on this trip, but in the future."

I was thinking to myself that the idea of taking on my future life's adventures with Sam by my side sounded like a fine prospect.

In the coming days in Paris, we walked our feet off. Even athletic Sam, who loved to walk, was put to the test. There wasn't much we missed of the main sights. We went from the Arc de Triomphe to the Musée d'Orsay. We oohed and aahed over the Impressionist paintings and had lunch behind the big clock installed for the convenience of travelers when the museum was a train station. We crossed the Pont des Arts to the Louvre and on to the Tuileries Gardens near the Place de la Concorde.

Sam found a charm on the sidewalk in front of the gates to the *Jeu de Paume* museum. The *Jeu de Paume* was a royal tennis court in the 18th century. Now it housed art exhibitions.

We thought the charm was gold. It was in the form of a horse shoe. Sam tested it with his teeth. We looked around for someone who might have dropped it. So many people passed us by in those few minutes that there seemed to be nothing to do but put it back on the pavement. Instead Sam gave it to me as a souvenir.

One day, we walked up to Montmartre from the Place de Clichy, no easy feat, or feet. Excuse the pun, please. Pun is *un calembour* in French, or easier, *un jeu de mots*. Famished, we fell into a cafe we found along the route for lunch. The artists were doing tourist caricatures in the Place du Tertre. The view over Paris from beneath Sacré-Coeur church was stupendous, *époustouflant!* We passed la Place Pigalle which reminded me of another old story from my student days that I wanted to share with Sam.

During my junior year in Paris, I had gone to the Place Pigalle only once. It had an unsavory reputation.

I had a prescription from the American Hospital in Neuilly, a fancy Paris suburb. The hospital was reputed to be excellent. After all, it was American. The prescription was for a diaphragm. To my surprise, the doctor had given me an address on the Place Pigalle where I was actually to pick up the contraceptive device. On the lookout for prostitutes and pimps in this disreputable neighborhood, I went down some basement stairs to collect the 'Dutch cap.' I paid the money and came home on the métro to the Place de la Concorde with the diaphragm in a brown paper bag.

When I told my landlady, Mme Beringer, about my errand, she was aghast.

"You could have been abducted by white slavers, my dear! *Mon Dieu*! What were you thinking of?"

"What *were* you thinking of?" asked Sam.

"I was thinking that I didn't want to get pregnant on my pre-honeymoon trip to England with Alex," I answered. "I didn't know how dangerous my errand was. I still think Mme Beringer was exaggerating. Although I did sometimes read about white slavery in *France Soir* newspaper."

"Well, all's well that ends well," said Sam.

"Yes, it ended well," I agreed. "I didn't get pregnant. But I learned later on from my gynecologist in the U.S. that the diaphragm they prescribed for me at Neuilly was completely ineffective! It didn't really fit me."

We laughed. France was a very Catholic country in those years. Things had really changed! The beautiful churches were still there. It was just the congregations which had gone missing.

We had a nice dinner with Micheline Dubosc at a restaurant she suggested. I wanted to introduce my good friend and bed and breakfast hostess to Sam. She immediately took to him. I was almost a little jealous. For dessert, we had a wonderful rendition of *profiteroles*.

This very common dessert is always good but can rise to gastronomic heights if the *pâte à choux* or pastry shells, which hold the vanilla ice cream, are tender yet crispy. The chocolate sauce which is poured on top is very important too. It must be excellent. That evening, the profiteroles were memorably good, we all agreed.

After escorting Micheline back to her apartment building on the avenue de Belleville, we walked by a restaurant called *Le Cholent*.

"Here's a Romanian restaurant," said Sam. "They've got 'cholent.'"

"What's that?" I asked him.

"It's a Romanian stew, usually a brisket of beef. It's cooked slowly in an oven, over very low heat. This reminds me of a story I'd like to tell you, Barbara."

Oh, good, I thought. Sam had the funniest stories about his life growing up in Satu Mare, a little village in Romania. He recounted the events as we walked along the rue St. Dominique back towards *Le Colbert*.

"When I was about ten years old back in Satu Mare, it was my job to watch over the oven where all the Jewish families cooked their cholent. Each housewife prepared her dish of stew. All the 'cholents' were to cook slowly in the community oven while the families were praying in the synagogue during the Sabbath."

"So you were a responsible lad even back then and already a cook!" I joked.

"Yes, that's right. But wait and hear what happened. You know that Jews aren't allowed to turn on an oven during the Sabbath."

"Yes, I heard that. No telephones or cars or any machines or appliances."

"Uh huh. So 'cholent' is perfect because you can leave it to cook on its own in a hot oven with the heat turned off for 24 hours. When the Sabbath is over, you open the door and you've got a ready cooked meal."

Sam continued: "But this one Saturday, I was loading the 'cholent' dishes into the oven with the long paddle and a cat jumped up and destabilized everything. The ladies' 'cholents' overturned. They got disarranged. I had to reassemble them as best I could."

"Oh no! What happened?"

"They didn't notice," Sam said with a satisfied smirk. "I was so relieved. I guess one 'cholent' looks a lot like another after so long in the oven. I got away with it. It was a close call though."

"Tsk, tsk, Sam," I said. "Maybe you'll make a 'cholent' for me someday."

"Anything for you, my darling," Sam said gallantly.

As an opera buff and great admirer of Marc Chagall, Sam absolutely didn't want to miss the Paris opera house, le Palais Garnier, with its Chagall ceiling. We were watching our budget, but I had read that we might be able to get discounted opera tickets at the box office in the afternoon before a performance. We went to the Boulevard Haussmann next morning and we scored two seats in a box close to the stage for that very night, our last night in Paris.

To celebrate, we went back to our cozy room at *Le Colbert* overlooking the busy rue Saint Dominique with its chic clothing shops and food emporia. The restaurant, 'Le Violon d'Ingrès,' was just down the street. I smiled as I remembered seeing Ingrès' violin preserved in the museum exhibit in Montauban. Great painter that he was, he was also a good violinist.

Sam and I closed the heavy drapes against the bustle of the thoroughfare and had a fabulous lovemaking session as the late afternoon slid into evening. After our dalliance and a little nap, we got up and dressed in what passed for our nicest clothes. Sam, dapper as usual, put on a tie and his blue blazer. I donned my favorite outfit of the moment. Chantal, the artist Maurel's girl-friend back in St. Antonin, had the very same linen dress with an asymmetrical hem, so I felt that I looked very French indeed. Around the neck, I wore the necklace of iridescent abalone shells that I had bought one time at the Musée Guimet gift shop. *Très chic.*

But first, dinner which was wonderful and *arrosé du vin*. I mean we drank a lot of wine. We weren't eating Romanian at *Le Cholent*. Too far away. We couldn't afford 'Le Violon d'Ingrès down the street. It had one Michelin star. If that restaurant was the chef's hobby, I wondered what his real talent was.

We were dining at *le Colbert*, the restaurant downstairs in our hotel. *Le Colbert* restaurant was a noisy place with booths separated by etched glass panels and brass railings. The white tablecloths and black jacket clad waiters made you feel welcome and also special. It was an easygoing place with a touch of class, a real old-fashioned brasserie. Nothing terribly fancy, just good food, good quality, and good service. The old standby French dishes were prepared flawlessly.

"Barbara," Sam asked, as the plates were cleared, "what time is the opera? We don't want to be late."

"Oh, we have plenty of time," I smiled at him across the table. "What shall we have for dessert? More *profiteroles?*"

After dinner, we were a little tipsy. I had trouble finding the métro entrance at *Latour-Maubourg* which was the best stop to get from *Le Colbert* to la Place de l'Opéra. We lost some time while I oriented myself after a false start.

For the second time that day, we arrived at le Palais Garnier. This very elaborate, baroque building from the Belle Époque used to be the only opera in Paris. Today there is a second, modern opera building on the Place de la Bastille.

Wow! We're in luck. There was no one in line to enter!

Our tickets were taken and we were directed up the stairs to the boxes.

"Oh, Sam, wait. Let's take a photo of us with these beautiful pink marble pillars. And look at the elaborate wrought ironwork on the stairs!"

"Pose over there, Barbara. That's it. Next to those elegant windows. They're over the top! I'll try to get the crystal chandeliers in the photo too."

"Ooh! Do you see that mirrored wall, Sam, with all the gilding?"

"Yes, I love it!" Sam said. "This is really beautiful! This decoration is from my favorite era."

We were having a ball admiring the fabulous decor and snapping photos of one another when it occurred to us both simultaneously—*where were all the people?* Some ushers were sitting on a bench in the corridor watching us dispassionately.

"*Où est tout le monde?*" I said to them. "Where is everyone?"

They pointed to the door in the wall beside them.

Sam waggled a finger at me, "We're late! Everyone else is already seated inside the theater!"

Ouf. I was very embarrassed! I had made a mistake about the curtain time. *Quelle honte! What a disgrace!*

Presenting our *billets* to the usher nearest by, we were shown into our loge. The box was already occupied by another couple. We took our seats behind them, mightily excusing ourselves for the interruption.

"Not at all! *Pas du tout!*" They didn't turn a hair.

We relaxed into our plush red velvet chairs. The music caught us up in its spell. The magnificent ceiling didn't disappoint. Chagall's colorful, dreamlike fantasy of people and animals flew around and around the crystal chandeliers. There were beautiful voices wafting up from the stage. The costumes and the set were beautiful as well. The name of the opera was *Les Indes Galantes*. It took place in America, an America as conceived in the seventeenth century at the court of Louis XIV by the court composer, Lully.

When a triad of real horses galloped onto the stage, we were transfixed. How grand!

After the performance ended, and our seat mates left, we stayed a while alone, canoodling on the velvet banquette at the back of the box.

"Oh, Sam," I breathed into his ear. "Kiss me again. I feel like a character in a *fin de siècle* novel. It's your favorite era, the turn of the century."

"Our night at the Paris opera," he whispered, nuzzling my neck. "We almost missed it, you naughty girl!"

"True," I giggled. "I can be so careless sometimes. I should have paid more attention to the time. But what great photos we took of us all by ourselves cavorting around the beautiful Paris Opera house!"

"Yeah," repeated Sam. "It was our night at the opera alright."

We headed back to the hotel. We were on our way back to the Midi-Pyrénées the next day.

Some Fifteenth Century House Façades in Montpezat

CHAPTER 19

Sam and Barbara's Move

S am and I returned from our Paris trip. It had been a huge success. During our time together in France, we had grown closer as a couple. I could see that Sam would be a great life companion. We had a lot of common interests, shared values and points of view. He had grown up in Europe and he loved being in France. He was good at picking up the language. He had learned the knack from his peregrinations from country to country. He fit in well. He wasn't interested in Monday night football or hanging out with the guys. His physique was more European-style. He was trim and athletic. He liked to hike, a very popular pastime in the Midi-Pyrénées. He enjoyed driving and drove a stick shift with ease. Although he had no special training in carpentry or plumbing, he was handy and industrious. He loved putting things in order and fix-up projects. He was hardly a *prince charming*—little money and less prospects—but he was fun. He didn't take himself too seriously and he was open to adventure. Most of all, Sam was crazy about me. He put me up on a pedestal and I rather liked it up there.

However we could both see that if we were going to be a couple, we would be spending a good part of each year in Florida, at least until Sam's retirement. Therefore we wouldn't need such a big property as Pech Menal for the few months per year that we would live in France.

This realization had big implications. Did I want to sell Pech Menal? Could I sell it? Where would we go? Was there a smaller French house with less upkeep which would appeal to us? I had put so much money and effort into making Pech Menal a home for me. Although I realized that in some ways it would never be the charming, old-fashioned place I had once envisioned, it was impressive. Perhaps I could downsize and at the same time reap a profit on all the improvements I had made to the house and property.

While we were mulling over these weighty questions, Éric Maurel, the famous local artist came over to Pech Menal for a visit with his girlfriend, Chantal. They were curious to see where I had hung the painting which Sam and I had bought from him after a lot of deliberation over which one to choose.

It was a big landscape painting. It was not painted in our area, *le Quercy blanc*. Instead Maurel had painted it on a visit to the neighboring Aude *département* where Carcassonne was situated, more to the south and east of the *Tarn-et-Garonne*. It was an area which was once overlooked but now attracted a lot of tourism. The beige earth tone colors with reflections of turquoise and orange in the painting were more typical of the drier conditions in that region. There was a ruined building in the background of our painting, outlined against the desertic, ochre cliffs. It didn't resemble the pigeon cotes or red tile roof houses which nestled in the rolling, fruit tree covered hills around Cayrièch. Sam and I both liked the freedom of Maurel's brushwork.The painting seemed dreamlike and set one's mind to wandering.

Before we went into Pech Menal to show them the painting in situ, we gave Éric and Chantal a tour of Pech Menal, the house and property. We began with the huge stable building and the giant open sided barn facing the olive tree in the courtyard. Clothilde had predicted the early demise of the olive tree, but so far it looked fine. The two artists admired the plantings of lavender along the house and the hedge of many varieties of flowering shrubs which was slowly growing in along the fence thanks to my faithful watering.

Our next stop was the summer kitchen with its giant stone bread oven. Its interior was always blissfully cool. Whereas before it had been dusty and mournful, the new tile floor now gleamed and the pizza oven hearth was freshly swept. Our guests seemed to like the red checked curtains now decorating the little windows. Ducking out of there, we climbed the monumental limestone staircase on the side of the house to the little covered landing which looked out over the fields towards the gorges of the Aveyron River just beyond the hills to where our guests lived in Brousses-les-Antibels.

Throwing open the gorgeous oak Dutch double doors, installed by M. de Paris, we entered the outside bathroom just across the landing from the main house. I had installed a triangular bathtub and decorated the walls with the pretty blue and white tiles I had found at a *brocante* sale. I was pleased at their reaction to my tall *bonnetière* or *homme debout,* which just fit under the high ceiling.

I was excited to showcase the main part of the house starting with the rustic wood front door with the old iron locking mechanism that led into the double height great room with its impressive, exposed post and beam ceiling.

It was in this room that Sam and I had hung Maurel's painting just beside the sofa. The four of us pondered its exact placement, considering various options. We agreed that it looked splendid in its present position against the sandy color of the walls, not paint but a special, traditional, hand-applied wall treatment which was granular to the touch and would last forever. This artisanal plaster was very durable but did disgorge a gritty residue until it would finally set completely many years from now.

From the sofa, we crossed the room just a few steps to the stone slab sink which I used as a bar. It still emptied out into the dirt behind the house, but water was supplied from the tap. No need for a bucket of water to rinse it out anymore. The French doors next to the sink opened out onto a view of the well and the newly mown field. I had found a little balustrade to fence off the bottom portion so no one could fall out. It wasn't wrought iron but *fonte*, cast iron. It was still a nice touch as a *garde-fou*, or madman guardrail.

We had planted a birch tree near the well. Sam had chopped down the former scraggly plum trees which had grown into the stones of the coping. We had considered planting a palm tree there instead. Palms grow in the south of France and in the north too, especially in Normandy where the nearby passage of the Gulf Stream keeps the climate temperate. But we finally decided we had enough palm trees back in Florida and so we chose the birch, *un bouleau.*

Éric and Chantal liked the elegant shape of *le petit Godin* wood stove. They admired the beautiful woodwork of the window frames with the ingenious screen system devised by M. Bellac.

At the end of our tour, our guests joined us at the dining table. Sam prepared a little *apéro* in the brand spanking (or 'spink-ing,' as Sam pronounced it) new kitchen, which now took up a corner of the living and dining area. I had just learned how to use the induction heat cooktop for which he and I had bought special pots and pans from the north of Italy where they do a lot of metal manufacture.

"*Santé!*" we cheered, raising our glasses. "A toast to our good health."

In between sips of *kir*, Chantal inquired about our weekend in Paris. She was eager to hear Sam's impressions. We passed a pleasant hour or so together with Éric sharing details of their upcoming painting excursion, scheduled for early fall.

Before showing our guests out, Sam and I showcased Pech Menal's newly renovated lower level. Descending the curving staircase, we began with our big bedroom, followed by a viewing of the sitting room and toilet and shower I had installed along with a washing machine too, thanks to M. Delpech, the plumber.

We retraced our steps back out to the courtyard through the little door secreted under the giant stone entry stairs.

"This area might make a great wine cellar," Éric pointed out. The white limestone building blocks of the house, cleaned and regrouted *à l'ancienne,* glowed in the gentle sunshine as we stood in the courtyard by their car and said our goodbyes.

It was at this moment that Éric, who was not one to hold his tongue, chose to render his opinion.

"*Barbara, cette maison est mal foutue.* Your house is beautiful, but the layout is fucked up. It just doesn't flow."

I laughed ruefully. "Éric, you're right," I said. I took no offense at his frankness. He'd said out loud what I had been thinking for quite awhile. My many improvements had made the house more liveable and more handsome. Yet something was lacking. I agreed with him. The house didn't flow. It wasn't charming.

Perhaps his opinion made it easier for me to put Pech Menal on the market. After discussing it with Sam, I agreed to list it with Mme Lemoine's real estate agency, *Quercy Immobilier.* Despite my hard work and the expense of getting the house and property into good shape, I had to admit that it just didn't suit my lifestyle and more importantly, my future plans for a life shared with Sam. I no longer needed to shield myself behind the walls and hedge of this big property. I wanted to be free to see what might be around the corner of the next few years with Sam. Who knew what adventures we might get up to together? House renovation didn't interest me the way it had before.

Our enjoyment together was now the priority. We didn't need the responsibility for such a big house. We wanted to travel more during our summer vacations in France. And lucky for us, the French real estate market was booming. Many British people were buying properties in France where prices were much less expensive than for comparable country properties in England.

In France, there were no leasehold requirements, unlike

England where buyers were sometimes just leaseholders until their lease time expired. A fifty or one hundred year lease seemed like a very long time, but it was a disincentive to some buyers.

Much to my surprise, Pech Menal was snapped up by a young English couple almost too quickly. Sometimes properties stayed on the market for years so I was prepared for a long siege and a long goodbye to Pech Menal. But things didn't work out that way.

Our buyers loved the idea of being out in the French country-side. They intended to hitch the hanging coach lights I had installed in the barn at great trouble and expense much higher to make room underneath to park their giant caravan, *le camping car*. They could also store their extensive collection of CD's in the stone bread oven. *What! Quelle idée!* Their ideas were anathema to me, but to each his own. They made me an offer I couldn't refuse. The place was theirs now.

Mme Lemoine and her real estate agency had found an adorable medieval townhouse for Sam and me in Montpezat de Quercy, the town with the splendid church tapestries. The new house was just the kind of ancient, higgledy piggledy affair I had originally been looking for. It had no big property to care for. Instead, there was a tiny walled courtyard off the dining room in back of the house.

The home was much older than Pech Menal. It had been built in the 15th century at the same time as most of the village. Montpezat was one of the most picturesque villages around the area. Sam and I would be living right in the center of town just through the ancient stone gate and right off the main square with its arcades and half timbered facades.

It was the end of one era and the start of another. But first we had to move.

Sam and I were moving. Pech Menal was sold. It was a *fait accompli*. I had purchased a medieval town house eleven kilometers away in the stunningly beautiful village of Montpezat de Quercy.

There was only one snag: Sam's vacation time from his job was up. He had to return to Florida and go back to work. Somehow he would try to arrange a leave of absence and come back to France in a month's time to help me on the moving day.

I was sad to see him off for Florida at Blagnac airport in Toulouse. We consoled one another that we wouldn't be apart for long. In the same airport hall where we had greeted each other so joyfully four short weeks ago, we now pulled long faces as we parted at the entrance to the security line. I waved at Sam's retreating form. Sam blew me a kiss. He disappeared down the corridor.

It was hard to confront making all the preliminary preparations for the move by myself. However, I had acted independently before and I could do it again. Keeping Sam and my goal in the forefront of my mind—moving together to the new little house in Montpezat de Quercy—I got to work organizing how to make it happen.

First, I needed to find a moving company to transport my furniture and household goods from Pech Menal to the new village. I decided to give *Déménagements Séguy* a call. I often passed by their big storage warehouse and ad for moving services on my way to and from Montauban. I called their telephone number and the phone was answered with a musical jingle. A recorded voice asked me to hold the line. *"Ne quittez pas, s'il vous plaît."* I dutifully held on while a tinny soundtrack took over playing "It's a Small, Small World."

"Nah, nah, nah, nah—Nah, nah, nah, nah, nah. Nah, nah, nah, nah, nah—-Nah, nah, nah, nah. It's a small, small world." And so on, ad nauseam.

The music went on for what seemed like forever. I was almost hypnotized by the repetitive little tune and my head was spinning when a person finally came on the line. "*Déménagements Séguy,*" the lady said. I explained my need for a moving company and the woman from '*Séguy*' said that M. Seguy himself would come out to Pech Menal to look over the job and give me an estimate. "That sounded great," I told her.

M. Séguy arrived for our meeting right on schedule. He was a short, powerful-looking man in an ugly shirt with a brisk, no-nonsense manner. He looked over my furniture. I explained to him that I would pack the clothes and smaller items myself. He said that he could provide me with some boxes, if I needed. I should come by the warehouse.

Oh no! I hadn't thought about boxes. The reality of how much trouble it was to move set in at that moment.

M. Séguy left me a piece of paper with his estimate and the proposed moving date in a month's time. He told me to sign and return it, if I accepted his bid.

I called Sam in Florida later that evening. He had big news. His company had given him the green light to take a leave of absence. He would be able to help me in person on the moving day! Fantastic!

"I'm making progress too, Sam," I said into the phone. "Today I got an estimate from 'Séguy' movers in Montauban. They seem okay."

"Yes," Sam agreed, listening to me recount M. Séguy's visit. "But maybe you should interview somebody else. Just for comparison's sake."

"I suppose you're right, but I'm not sure who to call. 'Séguy' is the only one I know of. I guess I'll look in the phone book, *Le Bottin.*

"Good idea," Sam opined. "Not too long now and I'll be there to help you. And other things, more fun things we can do together, you sweetie pie."

"Oh, Sam, I miss you. You don't often call me a 'sweetie pie.' That's really high praise indeed."

"You are my sweetie pie, sweetie pie. Want to try some phone sex?"

"Oh, Sam, you know I'm terrible at that. Just wait until you get here, I'll make it up to you, I promise."

"I'll take you up on that promise and raise you one. I'm counting the days."

"Me too. Twenty-eight and counting. Love you."

"Love you. Take care of yourself."

"Call me tomorrow."

"I'll give you a buzz."

I still had a month to get organized before the move. I thought of another moving company which I had seen advertised on a billboard as I was driving around. This one was called 'Martinez.' I gave them a call and arranged for them to come and estimate.

In the meantime, my friend from Paris, Micheline Dubosc, came for a short, valedictory visit to Pech Menal. Micheline hated to see Pech Menal be sold and hoped that I had made a wise decision. I drove her over to Montpezat so that she could see the new house we had bought from the outside. She agreed that the town was very beautiful and she was interested to note that my new house was next to a fancy *chambre d'hôtes, les Trois Terrasses,* which she said she would like to visit when she came to visit Sam and me in our new place.

Micheline was still staying with me when M. Martinez came to Cayrièch to look over the moving job. Martinez Movers, *Déménagements Martinez,* was located in Moissac, a little city with world famous, Romanesque church carvings about 50 kilometers from Pech Menal. On her last visit, Micheline and I had gone to a restaurant in Moissac which we had found wanting. She had even complained to the Michelin Guide people about our bad experience there, but she hadn't heard back yet.

Moissac was very far away from Cayrièch by the standards of the *Cayrièchois*. And even far from Montauban by the lights of the *Montalbanais*. This is partly explained by the fact that although Moissac is in the same *département* as Cayrièch, the *Tarn-et-Garonne*, it is in a different grape growing region. Around Moissac they have the *chasselas* grape variety which is famous in its own right. They have their own *Appellation d' Origine Contrôlée, 'le Buzet,'* different from the *'Côteaux du Quercy'* appellation around Cayrièch or the *Fronton* appellation wines from near Montauban.

M. Martinez, the mover from Moissac, was quite different in appearance from M. Séguy. The moving man from Moissac was a handsome, blond man wearing a houndstooth sports coat. He was well-spoken and polite. While M. Séguy looked like one of his moving men or a bartender or bouncer, M. Martinez was more like the *PDG, Président et Directeur Général,* or CEO of a big corporation. I was impressed.

My friend, Micheline, grilled him on the details of his company's practices. She even persuaded him to reduce his estimate. I was won over. Micheline had not met M. Séguy, but she endorsed the man from Moissac, *le moissagais.*

In France the inhabitants of each city and town, male and female, have a name. Micheline was a *parisienne* and her self-effacing husband, Paul, who died, had been a *parisien*. People from Bordeaux were called *bordelais* and *bordelaises*. Those who lived in Biarritz, for example, were *biarrots* and *biarrotes*. And so on and so forth, sort of like Chicagoans or New Yorkers, but with a masculine and feminine form required. In my new town, Montpezat de Quercy, men were *montpezaltais*. Women and girls were *monpezaltaises*. Hopefully I could avoid saying that tongue twister very often.

My houseguest, Micheline, went back to Paris. I signed the contract with Martinez Movers and sent in my deposit. As time went on, I wanted to ensure that M. Séguy understood that I had hired a different moving company. I had never followed up his bid by returning his paperwork. However, my neighbors, Pierre and

Clothilde, told me that 'Séguy' moved everyone in the area. Clothilde was skeptical of a mover from Moissac.

"Barbara," she said to me, "you are taking a risk. 'Seguy' moves everyone around here. How do you know that the other movers will even show up?"

With Clothilde's warning words about using a mover from outside of the area ringing in my ears, I told her firmly that Martinez Movers seemed very professional and I wasn't worried. However, to make sure there could be no misunderstanding with 'Séguy Moving Company', I made several attempts to contact them.

"Nah, nah, nah, nah—Nah, nah, nah, nah, nah. Nah, nah, nah, nah, nah—Nah, nah, nah, nah nah. It's a small, small world."

I tried reaching them on the telephone without success. Their little ditty played over and over in my head. I was about to give up when, after many phone calls, I hit paydirt and the secretary answered. I explained to her that I had not returned their signed estimate because I had selected another mover. She acknowledged my communication and I felt virtuous for having dotted all the 'i's'and crossed all the 'tees.'

The days sped by. I had some time to reflect while I was alone at Pech Menal getting ready to move. Many people did not understand why I was giving up a big property to which I had made so many improvements to move to a smaller, more ordinary house in the center of a congested town.

Their opinions gave me pause for thought of course. However, I realized that I had grown more confident in my own mind since my divorce. I was less swayed by what others thought I should do and more in tune with my own instincts for what would give me happiness and satisfaction. Come to think of it, linking up with Sam was another of my independent-minded decisions since he was not a conventional partner in the eyes of my upper middle class world.

I had found a new willingness to accept the consequences of

my choices and the internal resources to make adjustments as unforeseen circumstances required.

It seemed the only constant in life was change. To quote King Henri II, *"Il n'y a qu'une chose qui est sûre, femme varie."* "There is only one sure thing, women change their minds." As Hillary Clinton said, "Every moment wasted looking back keeps us from moving forward." To quote Marie Curie, "Have no fear of perfection. You'll never reach it." I mentally patted myself on the back. I had learned to *assumer*, in other words, to accept my own individuality and take responsibility for it.

While I was doing this deep thinking, I was sorting, wrapping and packing my belongings. I notified the *mairie* in Montpezat of our move-in date. The town hall had arranged to close the narrow street at our new address so the movers and their truck would not impede traffic for that afternoon.

I went through my possessions and winnowed out some which were no longer useful. I gifted some items of furniture from Pech Menal which wouldn't fit in the new house to friends. The Montpezat town house had four floors, but they were all long and narrow. Some things from my old life were just too big to fit in comfortably. The very modern style, faux suede sofa went to Pierre and Clothilde's son and his wife. They had always admired it. Suzy and Patrick, the dancing couple from down the road in Cayriech, took the enormously heavy oak farm table on which I had cracked my shins many a time when it was serving as an oversized coffee table.

Instead of a two hectare property, the new town house possessed only a small outdoor space so Geneviève, my cleaning lady, took the big garden table set while I kept two of the chairs for my tiny, new courtyard. She also got the reupholstered sofa bed which wouldn't fit up the stairs of the new house.

I regretted leaving behind the old threshing stone which I had used as a small table in Pech Menal's garden. M. Dupain had unearthed it in the field when he had cleared up the brambles with *le girobroyeur*. But it was just too bulky and heavy for the new courtyard which was only as big as a minute. It was better suited to stay where it was.

I was keeping the old wooden yoke from the barn though. It had once held the oxen in place as they ploughed the field. People sometimes hung the old yokes up as decorations and it would be a memory for me of my days at the farmhouse. I was also taking a stone fossil of a fern I found at Pech Menal. It fascinated me and it took up no space at all to speak of.

Sam arrived back in France on schedule and as promised. We had our usual joyful reunion *arrosé de champagne* with *foie gras* on toast points. We had also had several reunion *apéro* evenings over at the Belons. They were sorry to see us go and even a little miffed by our desertion, but they were basically supportive of our decision.

The big 'M' day arrived, 'M' for moving. The Normandy invasion (I am not exactly comparing our moving day to Operation Overlord, but...) is called 'D' day for 'day.' In French, it is *J* day for *jour*. For Sam and me, this move was a big deal. It was one thing to buy the first house in France, but now a second one! And the actual moving process itself was stressful. We didn't want to break anything, or forget anything. We hoped the movers could wrestle the furniture up the narrow staircase into place in the new house without too much trouble.

I had carefully mapped out the new positions of the furniture. Sam and I had minutely measured the clearance in the stairwell of our new digs. We had our fingers crossed that everything would fit through the tight space up to the higher floors. Fortunately some of the big pieces of furniture like my giant *garderobe* from the 1940's and the tall bonnetière were broken down into pieces by the movers. They could be reassembled once upstairs in place on the *1er or 2ème étage,* meaning the second or third floors. As for the *3ème étage*, or fourth floor, there was a bathtub up there, under a little window in the roof. I had purchased the twin beds already up there from the former owner.

I planned to use the space as a combination guest room and painting studio.

We were excited and a bit apprehensive as we went to bed on 'M' day, minus one. The weather forecast, *la météo,* for the next day was ideal, clear and dry. The movers from Moissac were scheduled to come at 10 a.m. After a restless night, early in the morning we were blissfully asleep in the bedroom on the lower level of Pech Menal when our slumber was interrupted by an insistent, not unfamiliar noise:

"Nah, nah, nah, nah–Nah, nah, nah, nah nah. It's a small, small world."

The annoying tune was wafting down the lane, growing louder and louder. Sam and I jumped out of bed and ran into the courtyard. We saw a big moving truck inching onto our road from the corner at the garbage cans. It lumbered along playing the smarmy, catchy jingle as it approached. Marked on the side of the truck in big letters was: *SÉGUY, LES GENTLEMEN DU DÉMÉNAGEMENT.* The letters swayed back and forth and up and down as the truck jounced along the rutted road.

Turning laboriously into our courtyard, expertly missing the gatepost, the truck stopped, air brakes hissing. In front of our wondering eyes, four 'gentlemen of moving' dressed in matching green bermuda shorts and white knee socks jumped down from the cab of the truck. Their white polo shirts proclaimed 'Séguy' in green print letters. They were quite a vision at 7:30 a.m. For a moment, I was dumbstruck. When I regained my voice, I said, *"Messieurs,* I am surprised to see you. You're not supposed to be here. I hired another company to move me. I never signed with M. Séguy."

Surprised, but not unduly distressed, the head gentleman of moving and his crew had a short confabulation. Then they piled back into the moving van and slowly and tunefully retraced their route down the lane to the main road and out of sight.

Sam and I looked at one another wide-eyed. I said, "I don't know what to make of that."

"Me neither," Sam concurred. "Let's have some breakfast. And some coffee. Everything is always better after coffee."

Later that morning, Sam and I spotted Clothilde across the fence in her vegetable garden, *le potager*.

"Clothilde, do you know what happened? 'Séguy Movers' was here. They came for nothing."

"I know,' she responded. "First of all, I heard their theme song early this morning. Then I just got back from the market in Caussade and I saw them sitting in their outfits at a table at the café having a coffee.

I hope you know what you're doing, Barbara. M. Séguy moves everybody. What will you do if your other movers don't show up?"

Sam and I said nothing. Clothilde's question hung ominously in the air.

At ten o'clock, we breathed a sigh of relief when we spied a ramshackle, white, unmarked truck turn off onto our little track. By this time, we could tell by the sheer sound of the wheels whether a vehicle was coming down our road or continuing on by on the main drag towards St. Georges and onwards. It was amazing how you learned to interpret the slightest noise when it was basically quiet all around, all the time. The movers from Moissac had arrived! We breathed a sigh of relief.

'Martinez Moving' was as good as its word. They were a crew of just two guys. One was tall and wiry, 'the brains' and the other was shorter and overweight, 'the brawn.' In their stained, tattered work clothes, they were certainly not as spiffy looking as the men from 'Séguy'. However we learned as the day wore on that they were wonderful workers, indefatigable problem solvers and careful too.

It didn't take more than two hours to empty out Pech Menal. It looked so desolate to me without my furnishings. How quickly it had all been spirited away! The battered white truck was loaded and the moving men drove off to Montpezat where they would take a break for lunch and wait for us at the house to begin the reinstallation process.

Sam checked one last time that Pech Menal was entirely empty. Our neighbors, the Belons, had come over to see us off on our way to Montpezat. Sam and I stood by our Citroën station wagon waiting as Clothilde made some adjustments to our arrangement of the delicate items in the cargo section of the station wagon. Clothilde was an excellent packer and we all stayed out of her way as she arranged the breakables to her satisfaction. Her husband, Pierre, was standing next to me as we let his capable wife take over:

"I hope those chimes in Montpezat don't bother you, Barbara," he told me feelingly. "I could never put up with them, I'll tell you."

At first I wasn't sure what Pierre meant. Then I realized that he was referring to the church bells which chimed the hours in Montpezat. In fact, there was a special long set of bells which rang from the church belfry at seven in the morning and at seven in the evening like the angelus of olden times.

"Well," I said to Pierre, " I'll let you know, We won't be very far apart. It's only, what, twelve kilometers away? That's barely seven and half miles."

Pierre nodded. Clothilde had joined us, packing accomplished. Wiping her brow, she spoke, "I really don't understand why you're going. You and Sam fit in very well in Cayrièch. You were *bien intégrés*."

What could we say? It had all been explained before.

We hugged and kissed cheeks all around trying to keep our emotions in check. "*Au revoir, Barbara. Au revoir, Sam. Bon déménagement! Bonne Installation!*" They wished us happy moving.

"*Merci, Pierre, merci Clothilde!* We'll have you over soon to *pendre la crémaillère.* We'll have a housewarming party." And we really could hang an adjustable iron hook to suspend the soup pot over the fire in the massive old fireplace of the medieval house at our new address which is what *'pendre la crémaillère '* literally meant.

I climbed into the passenger seat of the Citroën and Sam took the wheel. I got a tissue out of my purse but no tears came. I blew my nose anyway, just for good measure. The moving men were probably already waiting patiently for us in front of the new house.

A new chapter was beginning for me. After all my adventures at Pech Menal, *les hauts et les bas*, the highs and the lows, it was bittersweet to leave the old farmhouse behind, let alone the world's best neighbors, the Belons. But these feelings were overshadowed by my excitement and anticipation.

Sam looked over at me searchingly to make sure that I was alright. "*Roule, ma poule*?" he asked me, smiling broadly. This was one of our new French expressions. Literally, it meant "Shall we drive on, my hen?" In other words, 'shall we get going, honey?' Pedal to the metal?

I answered him gaily, sweeping aside any misgivings.

"*Oui*, let's roll, I mean *roule!*" I said decisively.

And off we drove out of the gate, our tires crunching a little on the dirt road. We were finally on our way to our new French house in our new French town assured of more adventures and challenges to come. Sam and I would experience them together.

I glanced backwards and saw the Belons standing there. As I watched, Pierre turned to close and latch the gate. He took a moment to straighten the little wood plaque where *'Pech Menal'* was written in wood-burned letters, letters indelibly etched on my heart.

LA FIN—THE END—OR IS IT?

Medieval Gate of la rue de la République in Montpezat

Epilogue

Barbara and Sam arrived later that day at their new house in Montpezat. They moved in and started to meet their neighbors and other townspeople. Some people they met were part-time, summer residents of the village like themselves. Some were Parisian transplants. Some were from families who had lived in the village for many generations.

Before long, it was time for Sam to return to Sarasota and his job. Barbara accompanied him back to Florida for the winter. The years went by. Each summer, they returned to their townhouse in Montpezat and became more and more involved in the life of their new village. Naturally, their attachment to Cayrièch and their adventures at Pech Menal receded into the background with the passage of time.

Through one of their new friends in town, they were drawn into the saga of the mysterious disappearance of a precious artwork which the artist, Sonia Delaunay, created after the war to decorate Montpezat's notable church, the pride of the village.

A following summer found them tracking down the connection between a valuable N'Kisi Kongo African tribal sculpture stolen from an exhibition at their local bistro to a fabulous oil deposit in the Niger River Delta.

While still enjoying the laid back French lifestyle of apéro hours and outdoor village festivals, and while continuing to take excursions to points of interest all around France, Barbara and Sam combined their art historical inclinations with their investigative instincts.

You can read about this new direction their curiosity and persistence took them in the *Vanished!* series of books available on Amazon and at Barnes & Noble.

Please look for *Vanished! A Valuable African Statue Stolen in Southwest France.*

Sam and Barbara's adventures will soon be featured in yet a further book, *Vanished! A Modern Masterpiece Missing from a Medieval French Village.*

Glossary

Chapter 1

Page 5.   *Orange*, one of the biggest French telephone service providers.

   Alain Delon (born 1935), a famous French award winning movie actor, member of the Légion d'Honneur, a screen sex symbol from the 1960's to the '80's.

Page 7.   *Vézelay*, a church which is a significant example of Romanesque architecture transitioning to the Gothic style.

Page 8.   *Auberge*, an inn.

   Albi, the mid-size city two hours north of Toulouse where Toulouse-Lautrec was born.

Page 9.   *À tout à l'heure*, See you soon.

Page 10.   *L'addition*, the bill.

Chapter 2

Page 14.   *Perrier citron*, sparkling water with lemon.

   Quel plaisir, What a pleasure!

   Coup, a blow, strike, slap, punch.

   Quercy, the old name of a province in the southwest of France which is now part of the modern Midi-Pyrénées department which is part of the new Occitanie region.

Page 15.   *Plombier/électricien*, a plumber and electrician.

   L'entreprise, a company.

Page 17.   *Eh bien*, well, so.

Page 18.   *Au revoir*, good-bye.

   Canicule, a heat wave from the Latin for the dog days of summer.

   Tarn-et-Garonne, a French département or geographic administrative division in the southwest of France whose administrative center is the city of Montauban, an hour north of Toulouse.

Page 19.   *Débordé*, literally overflowing, busy.

   N'est-ce pas, right? Isn't that so? Presumes a 'yes' answer.

   Étage, a floor, as in the 2nd floor.

   Rez de chaussée, literally level with the street.

Page 20.   *Castiné*, a pounded smooth ground treatment.

   Baguette, literally a stick, wand, a long, thin crusty loaf of French bread.

   Putain, literally a prostitute, a swear word meaning shit or fuck.

   Et comment! And how!

Page 21.   *Blasé*, unemotional, unimpressed.

Chapter 3

Page 23.   *M*, the abbreviation for Monsieur, like Mr. In English.

Page 24.   *Brocante*, used furniture, household items and decorative objects.

   Quonset hut, a hastily built wartime metal construction with a curved roof which was supposed to be temporary but often remained in use.

Page 25.   *Un homme debout*, literally a man standing upright.

Autoroute, expressway.

La rocade, ring road around a city.

Page 26. *Un break*, a station wagon.

la patronne, the woman owner.

Aubergine, eggplant.

D'un certain âge, middle aged or older.

Ce n'est pas normal, It's not normal.

Page 27. *Centre commercial*, a shopping center.

Page 28. *Exceptionnel*, an exception to the rule.

Contretemps, an upset.

Place de la Concorde, a beautiful and famous square in Paris at the opposite end of the
   Champs-Élysées from the Arch of Triumph. During the French Revolution the square was
   the location of one of the guillotines.There is now an Egyptian obelisk brought to France
   by Napoleon and installed in 1836 at the center of the square's two fountains.

Hôtel Ritz, a famous, historic luxury hotel in Paris.

Place Vendôme, a famous Paris octagonal square around a column commemorating
   Napoleon's victory at Austerlitz. The square is lined with high end jewelry stores and the
   Hotel Ritz.

Rue Saint Honoré, a street on Paris' Right Bank which is lined with fancy shops along some
   parts of its long length.

Page 29. *Belles chaussettes*, beautiful socks.

Voulez-vous prendre un verre avec moi, Mademoiselle? Won't you have a drink with me,
   Miss?

Je suis fiancée, I'm engaged to be married.

Page 30. *Abordable*, affordable.

N'est-ce pas, Mademoiselle? Don't you agree, Miss? Presumes an affirmative answer.

Quel pervert! What a pervert!

Page 31. *Déguelasse*, disgusting.

Tant pis, too bad.

Objet d'art, a work of art.

Chapter 4

Page 33. *Les Salers*, a cattle breed from le Cantal, a plateau area north of Villefranche de Rouergue in
   south central France.

Terroir, an origin, provenance, literally territory..

Midi-Pyrénées, a former geographic and administrative region of southwest France around
   Toulouse made up of several former old French provinces like Gascony, Languedoc and
   Quercy. Now part of the Occitania region.

Page 34. *Potager*, a vegetable garden.

Valide, in good health.

Page 35. *Lotissement*, a new housing development.

Apéritif, Apéro, a cocktail, a drink before a meal.

La fête du village, a street party, a village party.

Heures, hours.

Les Belon, the Belons, no 's' on a family's name in French.

Kir, a before dinner drink of wine mixed with some black currant liqueur.

Godin, a brand of wood stove available in traditional shapes.

Page 36.   *La Sorbonne*, the historic University of Paris or one of its successor institutions. The name of a building in the Latin Quarter of Paris which from 1253 onwards housed one of the first universities in the Western world.

Paquebôt, an ocean liner.

Je m'appelle, My name is.

Fräulein, Miss in German.

Mädchen, girl in German.

Page 37.   *S'il vous plaît*, please.

Santé, a toast to your good health.

À vos amours, a toast to your loves (romantic loves, not family).

Page 38.   *'Instamatic'*, a popular brand of inexpensive, automatic, point-and-shoot camera that used easy-to-load film cartridges. It was made by Kodak in the 1960's.

Page 39.   *Get sorted*, a British expression for to figure things out, to take care of things.

Page 40.   *Salvador Dali* (1904-1989), a Spanish surrealist artist known for his attention getting personal style as well as his art.

Beluga caviar, the finest caviar from the Caspian Sea.

Chapter 5

Page 44.   *Secteur*, sector.

Raison d'être, a reason for living.

Fête, a party.

Franc, the French currency before the introduction of the euro between 1999 and 2002. At that time there were about 7 French francs to one US dollar. The euro was launched at a worth of $1.17 against the dollar but then its value fell in the early 2000's to about 85 cents per dollar yielding a benefit of about 15% to dollar holders. Since that time, the euro's value has never fallen below the US dollar in value.

Pâté, a chopped liver or other meat preparation bound together by fat.

Charcuterie, cold cuts, usually sausages.

Cornichon, a miniature pickle.

Page 45.   *20h*, 8 p.m, The French use military time to indicate the afternoon and evening hours after 12 noon on schedules and printed material. So 8 p.m. is 'huit heures du soir' in conversation but 20h, vingt heures in print to avoid confusion.

Traiteur, a caterer.

Paëlla géante, a giant paella, a Spanish rice and meat dish.

Paille, straw or a straw.

Page 46.	*Garagiste*, a garage mechanic or garage owner.
	Sieste, a nap.
	Comité des Fêtes, a festival committee.
Page 47.	*Appellation*, a name, for wine a legally defined and protected geographical indication used to identify a wine like 'Appellation d'Origine Protégée.'
	Société du Tastevin, a medieval brotherhood of wine connoisseurs founded in Burgundy to appraise and describe the characteristics of fine wine.
	Tombola, a raffle.
Page 48.	*Le cafard*, homesickness.

Chapter 6

Page 51.	*"Jean de la Florette"*, an award winning film starring some of France's greatest actors, a 1986 period drama based on a novel by Marcel Pagnol (1885-1974) who was a great French novelist, playwright and filmmaker.
Page 52.	*Jean Giono*, a prolific French writer (1895-1970) whose works of fiction were mostly set in Provence.
	Charmilles, a bower of trees.
	La météo, the weather report.
	La douce France, sweet, mild France and its temperate climate.
Page 53.	*Louis XV d'époque*, authentic furniture from the reign of King Louis the fifteenth whose time period was 1715-1784, not a reproduction or lookalike.
Page 55.	*La Guyane française*, French Guiana.
	Enchanté(é), Nice to meet you.
	Soigné, well-groomed, elegant.
Page 57.	*Black Penitents*, one of the medieval religious confraternities practicing mortification of the flesh through fasting and wearing hair shirts as penance for sins.
Page 58.	*Armoire*, a storage piece of furniture with two doors to use as a closet.
Page 59.	*Les Couleurs du Mexique*, The Colors of Mexico.
	Gare de Montpezat, Montpezat train station.
	Le Petit Bal Perdu, the secret dance floor lost in the fields.
Page 61.	*Enchiladas suizas*, enchiladas with creamy Mexican salsa verde sauce.
	Gare Saint Lazare, an important Paris train station.
	France Telecom, the French National Telephone Company.
Page 62.	*Ooh là, ma chérie!*, Ah hah, honey!
	Ouf, quel embarras! Whew, how embarrassing, how awkward!

Chapter 7

Page 65.	*Arrondissement*, one of twenty administrative divisions of the city of Paris.
Page 66.	*C'est inadmissible*, It's not allowed, out of the question.
	En France, In France.
	En suite, attached room.

Radio-France, the French National Public Radio.

Page 67.   *Musée*, a museum.

Page 68.   *Le dernier cri*, the last word, the latest. Literally the last shout.

'*La Semaine de Paris*', the 'This Week in Paris' publication.

Les Champs Élysées, literally the Elysian Fields from mythology. A beautiful and grand main avenue on the Right Bank in Paris which runs from the Arc de Triomphe in the center of l'Étoile square to the Place de la Concorde.

Page 69.   *À la française*, French style, in the French manner.

Métro stop Franklin Roosevelt, the Paris subway stop named in honor of the United States president during WWII. There is also an Avenue and Place President Wilson in Paris, honoring the American president and founder of the United Nations.

Le Rond Point, the round square midway along the Champs-Élysées.

Pierre de taille, cut, dressed stone.

Bonsoir, good evening.

Je m'appelle, my name is.

Enchanté(é), happy to meet you, delighted.

Et moi, me too.

Avec plaisir, with pleasure.

Hôtel de Ville, the Paris City Hall. Other city halls are called 'la mairie.'

Les allées, long narrow walkways, driveways.

Page 70.   *Édith Piaf* (1915-1963), a French singer known for cabaret songs, widely regarded as France's greatest popular singer and one of the most celebrated performers of the 20th century. Small in stature, she was known as 'the little sparrow.' Her signature song was 'La Vie en Rose,' Life in Pink.

Simone Signoret (1921-1985), an award winning French actress who also won an Academy Award, married to Yves Montand.

Dutch treat, the custom of each paying their own way on a date.

Le cancan, the cancan, a Belle Époque dance which showed a scandalous amount of leg for the time, a specialty of the Moulin Rouge nightclub in Montmartre.

Le Moulin Rouge, the landmark Red Windmill cabaret and nightclub.

Le Lido de Paris, a nightclub known for beautiful, scantily clad female performers.

Parisien(ne), a native of Paris.

Chapter 8

Page 76.   *Et voilà*, And there it is!

Page 77.   *Poitou-Charente*, an administrative region on the southwest coast of France now part of the Nouvelle-Aquitaine region.

Alsace, a cultural region in eastern France bordering Germany which blends French and German influences and whose capital city is Strasbourg.

Page 78.   *L'hôtelier*, a hotel owner.

Le Lys Bleu, the Blue Lily.

Moissac, a town in the southwest of France known for its abbey church whose portal is considered one of the masterpieces of Romanesque sculpture.

Conques, a commune in the Aveyron area of southwest France known for its abbey church which was a stop for pilgrims on their way to Santiago de Compostela in what is now Spain.

Page 79.   *Impasse*, dead end.

La Maison des Consuls, the medieval city councilors' house.

Notre Dame de Paris, the medieval Catholic cathedral of Paris built on an island in the Seine River in the center of the city. It was considered one of the finest examples of French Gothic architecture. It was partially destroyed by a fire in 2019 and is expected to reopen after restoration in 2024.

Emile Zola, (1840-1902) a famous French novelist and playwright, proponent of the literary school of naturalism who wrote "Nana" and "Germinal." He helped to exonerate Alfred Dreyfus.

Alexandre Dumas, (1802-1870) a famous French novelist and playwright who wrote the "Count of Monte Cristo" and "The Three Musketeers.

Montpellier, the third largest French city in the south of France after Nice and Marseille.

Page 80.   *À tes ordres, commandante*, Yes, sir, commander.

Gouverneur, governor, a device to control speed and mileage.

Kilometers, a metric unit of length equal to 0.62 miles.

Le disc, a record, a recording device for the gouverneur.

Page 81.   *En brosse*, a man's hair style, parted and combed over to one side of the head.

Ils n'ont pas terminé leurs nuits, They didn't get enough sleep.

Bahia, Brazil, a northeastern state in Brazil, epicenter of Afro-Brazilian culture. Its capital city, Salvador, was Brazil's first capital city.

Rio de Janeiro, the second most populous city in Brazil after São Paulo and the sixth most populous city in the Americas.

Jean Racine, (1639-1699) a French dramatist, one of the three great playwrights of 17th century France along with *Pierre Corneille* (1605-1684) and Jean-Baptiste Poquelin known as *Molière* (1622-1673). Molière is widely regarded as one of the great writers in French language and world literature. He wrote comedies and farces while Corneille and Racine wrote tragedies.

Page 82.   *La belle France*, beautiful France.

Bois de Boulogne, a large public park in the west of Paris with a racetrack and fancy eateries.

Palais de Chaillot, a landmark art deco construction housing museums facing the Eiffel Tower from a hill across the Seine River.

Grande dame parisienne, an elegant, older Parisian woman.

Page 83   *Colbert* (1619-1683) an able finance minister to Louis XIV.

La France profonde, deep France, France off the beaten track.

Pourboire, a tip. Literally so one can have a drink.

Page 84. *Au revoir*, bye, bye.

Chapter 9

Page 87. *Le Limousin*, a sparsely populated historical region in south central France.

Page 89. *Insolite*, unusual.

Page 90. *Amour-propre*, vanity, self-regard.

Grande finale, a grand finale, end, culmination.

Barbizon Forest, a forest in Fontainebleau, France, southeast of Paris, where many
    pre-Impresssionist painters found inspiration.

Château de Fontainebleau, a very large palace of the French monarchs.

Page 91. *Pâtisseries*, pastries, desserts.

Page 92. *Asana*, a yoga pose.

Page 95. *Basilique*, basilica, a church with royal, commemorative associations.

Dordogne, a large, rural department in southwest France.

River Lot, a tributary of the Garonne River, which flows west through Quercy.

Page 96. *Force de frappe*, the French nuclear deterrence force.

Djibouti, a former French colony in the Horn of Africa on the Red Sea.

Page 97. *W.c.*, a water closet, a toilet, used as well as the word 'toilettes.'

Chartres Cathedral, a late 12th century cathedral which marks the high point of French
    Gothic art. It is southwest of Paris.

Page 99. *Notre pauvre Émeraude*, our poor, dear Esmeralda.

Une américaine, an American girl or woman.

Évidemment, evidently, obviously.

Page 100. *Km*, short for kilometer, one kilometer is about ⅝ of a mile. 130 kilometers is about 80 mph.

Page 102. *Marais*, a swamp.

Poitevin, in or of the province of Poitou, near the city of Poitiers in mid-Atlantic France.

Page 103. *Caravelle*, a small, fast sailing ship used from the 15th to 17th centuries.

Chapter 10

Page 108. *Chapeau*, a hat.

Bas, low, down.

La Belle Époque, the prosperous era of the 1880's and 1890's.

Page 109. *Bastide*, a medieval town plan with criss-cross streets to repel invaders.

Page 111. *Parthenay*, a mid-size town in Poitou-Charentes, mid-Atlantic France.

Page 112. *Lot département*, an administrative district of France around the Lot River north of the
    Tarn-et-Garonne department, now part of the Nouvelle-Aquitaine region.

Page 113. *Le lit*, the bed.

Page 114. *Mon Dieu*, my God, *Bon sang*, my God, *Merde*, shit, *Putain de merde*, fuck, *Zut alors*, damn,
    O la vache, darn, *Bordel*, damn, *Bordel de merde*, shit. All common swear words. *Bordel*
    literally means bordello or figuratively, a mess.

Beurk, Ugh, Yuck.

Page 115. *Qu'est-ce que c'est que ça?* What is that?

Ça ne risque rien, no danger, it's nothing.

Page 116. *Dérangeant*, deregulating, upsetting.

Nappe phréatique, a water table.

Les sauterelles, crickets.

Page 117. *Salle*, a theater, auditorium, room.

Page 118. *Jean de la Fontaine*, a 17th century French poet famous for his moralistic Fables like the grasshopper and the ant. The grasshopper who played all summer had nothing to eat when winter arrives, not even a piece of fly or worm whereas the industrious ant who worked all summer has plenty to eat.

Bonne Nuit, good night.

Dors bien, sleep well.

Page 119. *Endormie*, asleep.

Page 120. *La Maison de l'Amour*, the House of Love.

Louis Philippe (1773-1850), ruler of France from 1830 to 1848, the next to last monarch of France.

Art Déco, a decorative art period in the 1940's and '50's known for streamlined, modern design.

Buffet, a big serving and storage piece of furniture for dishes.

Page 121. *Bibelot*, a small, often precious, decorative object.

Page 122. *Grotte de Lascaux*, a cave in Dordogne known as the Sistine Chapel of prehistoric cave art. It was discovered by chance in 1940 by four teenagers.

Olivier, an olive tree.

Page 123. *Les commerces*, the shops.

Bon appétit, Enjoy your meal. Literally good appetite.

Page 124. *Sang-froid*, literally cold blood, composure.

Pieter Bruegel (died 1569), a Dutch artist famous for his detailed paintings of country scenes and peasant life.

The Book of Hours of the Duc de Berry, 'Les Très Riches Heures du Duc de Berry,' an illustrated, medieval 15th century prayer book owned by the Duke of Berry, whose dukedom was in the center of France.

La vieille France, the old, traditional France with its layers of history and its worldly experience of human frailty and bad behavior which contributes to an attitude of having seen it all.

Chapter 11

Page 127. *Stagiaires*, workshop participants, apprentices.

La causse, a small limestone plateau common in south central France.

25 km, about 15 miles.

Page 128. *Le grand maître*, the master.

Page 129. *Le Quercy blanc*, the part of the old province of Quercy in southwest France which has whitish soil due to the heavy concentration of limestone in the region.

Un beau geste, a nice gesture, a classy move.

Je ne sais quoi, hard to explain, an air of some indefinable quality.

Amour, a nice person, love.

La vieille Europe, the old continent with its hide-bound, worldly-wise and traditional ways.

Page 130.   *L'atelier*, the workshop, the studio.

Sotto voce, under the breath, in a whisper.

Ménage à trois, a marriage of three people rather than a couple.

Sauvage, literally wild, untamed, shy, keeping to oneself.

Page 131.   *L'Aude*, a French département southwest of the Tarn-et-Garonne around Carcassonne now part of the Occitania region.

Quercynois, from or of the historic region of Quercy.

Page 132.   *Airbus Industries*, a designer and manufacturer of commercial aircraft, a multinational aerospace corporation. Since 2019, the leading world manufacturer of airplanes and helicopters.

Laissez-faire, live and let live, hands off.

Atelier chez Maurel, the painting studio at the Maurel's house.

Corniche, a steep mountainside.

Page 133.   *Voilà enfin arrivé*, there you are, arrived at your destination.

Page 134.   *Histoire*, a story, love story, tale, history.

C'est la vie, that's life.

L'homme ou la femme de leur vie, a soulmate, a perfect partner.

Une quinzaine de jours, literally 15 days, the way to say two weeks in French.

Page 135.   *Merde*, shit.

Boulangerie, a bakery.

Le pain industriel, the mass-produced, chain store packaged kind of bread.

Page 137.   *Cotisations*, payments, required, scheduled contributions.

Page 138.   *On se téléphone*, Let's call one another.

Chapter 12

Page 142.   *Ma belle*, my lovely friend, my good friend.

Solitude à deux, together yet alone, each in their own space.

Page 143.   *5 km*, 3 miles.

Page 145.   *Je ne sais quoi*, unquantifiable quality, can't put your finger on.

Chapter 13

Page 148.   *Chez Beringer*, at the Beringer's house.

Le Pays Basque, the Basque Country, the southwest part of France in the foothills and mountains of the Pyrénées near the Bay of Biscay, home to the Basque people, their language, culture and traditions.

Biarritz, a turn of the century seaside resort on the Atlantic coast of France just north of

Spain.

Page 149.   *"Où sont les neiges d'antan?"*, a quote from a poem by French medieval poet/outlaw, François Villon (1431-1463). Literally it means 'where are the snows of yesteryear?" Figuratively, it means where has the time gone, where is my youth? How quickly and imperceptibly things change and disappear like melting snow.

Pensionnaire, a boarder.

Le petit coin, the toilet room.

'L'Humanité', 'Humankind', is the name of a newspaper formerly the mouthpiece of the French Communist Party.

Page 150.   *Chez Madame Salerni*, at madame Salerni's house.

Page 151.   *Si lisse*, so smooth.

Amie d'enfance, a friend since childhood.

Une Citroën deux chevaux, the least expensive and smallest car made by French car manufacturer Citroën, now discontinued. It looked a bit like a Volkswagen Beetle and was utilitarian and low-powered. It has become a cult classic.

Éclair, a long pastry shell filled with custard and covered with chocolate or coffee icing, lightning bolt.

Place, a square as in main square.

Pâté feuilleté, puff pastry.

Crème pâtissière, pastry cream or custard.

Gâteau Saint Honoré, a confection of cream puffs topped with sweetened whipped cream before being drizzled with spun caramel.

Les Jésuites, triangular shaped French pastries filled with almond paste. The name comes from the shape of a Jesuit priest's former hat.

La figue, a fig shaped pastry featuring a cream puff shell and almond paste covered with light green marzipan.

"Je voudrais un mille feuille, s'il vous plaît.", I would like a napoleon, please."

Page 153.   *San Sebastián*, a Spanish city and Atlantic seaside resort with wide beaches near the French border.

Hendaye, a small Spanish seaside city with a huge beach north of San Sébastien (French spelling).

Salamis, saucissons, salamis and sausages. Parts of a pig, 'cochon.' Calling someone a pig in French used to be very insulting before the use of other stronger swear words became more widespread.

Page 154.   *Parterres*, French formal style garden with geometric shaped flower beds.

Page 155.   *De rigueur*, necessary, obligatory.

Napoléon III (Charles-Louis Napoléon Bonaparte 1808-1873) was the first president of France from 1848-1852 and the last monarch of France as Emperor of the French from 1852 until he was deposed in 1870. He was nephew of Napoleon I and cousin of Napoleon II.

Émigré, an emigrant, a person who leaves his own country to settle in another country. In this context, the word refers to the Russian aristocracy who fled Russia after the revolution starting in 1917.

Page 156.   *Gustave Eiffel* (1832-1923) was a French civil engineer who is best known for the world famous Eiffel Tower designed for the 1889 Universal Exposition in Paris and his contribution to the Statue of Liberty in New York harbor.

Beignets d'abricot, apricot jam filled doughnuts which were typically sold on the beach in France.

La chambre d'amour, the bedroom of love.

Page 157.   *Chez Madame Salerni*, at Mrs. Salerni's house.

Oui, oui, oui, yes, yes, yes.

Page 158.   *Stage*, a workshop, preparatory session.

La Sorbonne, the historic University of Paris or one of its successor institutions. The name of a building in the Latin Quarter of Paris which from 1253 onwards housed one of the first universities in the Western world.

L'Agence Havas, a well-known French travel agency, originally the world's first news agency created in 1835. Havas is now the world's largest global communication group.

Couchette, a vinyl covered, upholstered plank bunk bed for sleeping on a French overnight train.

Johnny Boy, a nickname for WWI American soldiers after 'Johnny Doughboy,' a popular song of that period. The name was replaced in WWII by 'G.I.'

Al Capone (1899-1947), a famous Chicago gangster during Prohibition who controlled the mob in that city. He is sometimes known as 'Scarface'.

Page 159.   *Béret*, a soft, round, flat-crowned hat usually of wool felt.

Bonjour, hello in French.

Page 160.   *Euskadi*, Basque language for the autonomous Basque Country.

ETA, an acronym for the armed Basque nationalist and separatist organization in the Basque Country between 1959 and 2018.

Risqué, naughty in a sexual way.

Double-entendre, a pun, a phrase with two meanings.

Page 161.   *Piqué*, a special honeycomb weaving style of cotton like a polo shirt.

Jabot, a pleated frill of cloth or lace attached down the center front of a shirt, worn especially by men in the 18th century.

Redingote, a frock coat, a full-skirted, double-breasted, short-waisted outer garment adapted from the English for riding coat.

Dans le vent, in style, trendy, literally in the wind.

Que c'est beau! How beautiful!

Page 162.   *Et alors?* And so, what then?

Omar Sharif (1932-2015), a famous Egyptian actor known for his award-winning appearances in American, British and French films.

Barbra Streisand (born 1942), is a famous American award-winning singer, actress, and film producer and director. She won the Academy Award for Best Actress in the film "Funny Girl."

Page 163.　　*Loge*, a small compartment, booth.

Concierge, (especially in France) caretaker of an apartment complex or small hotel, typically one living on the premises.

Lingua franca, common language.

Les grands cafés, the famous trendy and chic Paris cafés on the main boulevards where artists, intellectuals and society people traditionally socialized.

Diego Rivera (1886-1957), a prominent Mexican muralist painter. His third wife was fellow Mexican artist, Frida Kahlo (1907-1954).

Pablo Picasso (1881-1973), a renowned Spanish artist who spent most of his life in France. One of the most influential artists of the 20th century for co-founding Cubism, collage and a wide variety of artistic styles.

Anaïs Nin (1903-1977), a French born American novelist and writer of erotica. A friend and lover of writer, Henry Miller (1891-1980).

Amadeo Modigliani (1884-1920), an Italian painter who worked in France known for portraits and nudes in an elongated style. A rival of Picasso's.

Vassily Kandinsky (1866-1944), a Russian painter generally credited as one of the pioneers of abstract art. He became a French citizen in 1939. .

Henri Matisse (1869-1954), a French visual artist known for his use of color and original use of line. Along with Picasso, he is generally credited with significant developments in painting and sculpture throughout the opening decades of the 20th century.

Josephine Baker (1906-1975), a black American-born French dancer and singer who took France by storm in the 1920's with her beauty and vitality.

F. Scott Fitzgerald (1896-1940), an American novelist and short story writer who is now regarded as one of the greatest American writers of the 20th century. Author of "The Great Gatsby" and "Tender is the Night."

Zelda Fitzgerald (1900-1948), an American socialite, wife of F. Scott Fitzgerald whose mental health deteriorated while traveling and living abroad with him.

Page 164.　　*Centimes*, the French denomination of cents before the introduction of the euro, one-hundredth of a franc.

Jean-Paul Sartre (1905-1980), a French existentialist philosopher, novelist, and political activist, a leading figure in 20th-century philosophy and Marxism.

Simone de Beauvoir (1908-1986), a French existentialist philosopher like her partner, JP Sartre. She had an important influence on feminist theory through her writings such as "The Second Sex."

Ticket, a ticket pronounced tee-kay.

Quai, a train platform.

Chemin de l'écolier, the roundabout way often taken by a child on the way to school.

Rue, a street.

Le métro, short for le Métropolitain, the Paris subway system, part of the RATP, the rapid transit system around the Paris metropolitan area which began operation in 1900 and has greatly expanded over time.

Le Jardin de Luxembourg, a beautiful public garden begun in 1612 on the Left Bank of Paris which surrounds the Luxembourg Palace, once a royal residence.

Sciences Po, abbreviation for Sciences Politiques, the Paris institute of Political Studies which is part of the Sorbonne.

Page 165. *Nanterre*, a suburb of Paris.

Page 166. *Le Louvre*, the French national art museum in Paris which holds some of the most well-known works of Western art like the Mona Lisa and the Venus de Milo. The museum is housed in the Louvre Palace originally built in the 12th to 13th centuries and converted into the primary residence of the French kings in 1546.

La Grande Galerie of the Louvre, a wing of the museum which houses its largest and longest room, one of the museum's iconic spaces.

Sacre, a religious ceremony marking the crowning of a king.

Page 167. *Le Radeau de la Méduse*, an oil painting by French Romantic painter, Théodore Géricault (1791-1824) which depicts the shipwreck in 1816 of the French ship, 'la Méduse' off the coast of Africa. People were set adrift on a raft. Most died in the days before their rescue. The painting is an icon of French Romanticism.

La Mort de Sardanapale, The Death of Sardanapalus is an oil painting by Eugène Delacroix (1798-1863), the famous French Romantic painter. The painting from 1827 is based on a Greek tale of a King of Assyria which inspired a Lord Byron play, a Berlioz cantata and a Liszt opera as well as this painting.

Odalisque, a painting of a harem concubine, typical of the Orientalism artistic movement in France and England at the end of the 19th century.

Page 167. *Richelieu*, Cardinal Richelieu (1585-1642) was a powerful and influential French statesman, Catholic prelate and patron of the arts. He was chief minister to King Louis XIII whom he helped to consolidate royal power.

Renaissance, a period in history and a cultural movement marking the transition from the Middle Ages to modernity covering the 15th and 16th centuries.

Devise, a slogan, motto, emblem.

Page 168. *Boyar*, a member of the old aristocracy in Russia, ranking below a prince.

'Les Cahiers du Cinéma', a prestigious and influential French film magazine founded in 1951.

Charlie Chaplin (1889-1977), an English comic actor and filmmaker who became a worldwide icon through his screen persona, *The Little Tramp*. He is very beloved in France.

Dean Martin (1817-1995), an American singer, actor and comedian who became one of the most popular entertainers of the mid-20th century. Known as the 'King of Cool,' he began his career as straight man for comedian Jerry Lewis.

Jerry Lewis (1926-2017), an American comedian, filmmaker, actor and humanitarian whose career lasted eight decades starting in 1949 when he appeared in 16 musical comedy films with Dean Martin as his partner.

Chez, at the house of.

Canapé, a sofa or by extension the base for an appetizer.

Les Alpes, the Alps.

Page 170.   *King Vidor* (1894-1982), an award-winning American film director and screenwriter whose career spanned the silent and sound eras. He was considered an auteur and an 'actors' director'.

    Équitation, horseback riding.

    Champs-Élysées, a beautiful and grand main avenue in Paris.

    Place de la Concorde, an architecturally magnificent square at the opposite end of the Champs-Élysées from the Arch of Triumph. There is now an Egyptian obelisk installed in 1836 at the center of its two fountains. During the French Revolution the square was the location of one of the guillotines.

Chapter 14

Page 173.   *Le top du top*, the best, top of the heap.

    Hotel Crillon, a Paris luxury hotel on the Place de la Concorde housed in a former 18th-century palace.

    Couturier, a designer and seller of fashionable, expensive, custom-made clothes.

Page 174.   *Un escalier en colimaçon*, a spiral staircase.

    Brobdingnagian, enormous, huge from Jonathan Swift's "Gulliver's Travels."

    Tailleur, a woman's tailor-made suit.

Page 175.   *Le petit dernier*, the last born, the youngest child.

    Lycée, a high school.

    Tuileries gardens, the public gardens of the Louvre Palace which extend from the now-destroyed Tuileries Palace to the Place de la Concorde.

Page 176.   *Left Bank*, 'la rive gauche,' the side of the Seine River in Paris which was traditionally more arty and intellectual than the Right Bank of the river which was traditionally more upper-middle class and more commercial.

    Riz à l'Impératrice, an elaborate molded version of rice pudding in French cuisine.

    André Derain (1880-1954), a French artist, founder with Matisse of Fauvism.

    Maurice de Vlaminck (1876-1958), a French painter and principal figure of the Fauve movement.

    Reflexive tense, a grammatical tense which refers back to oneself, as in 'Je m'appelle,' French for my name is, literally I call myself.

Page 177.   *Toulon*, a deep Mediterranean harbor near Marseille which is the headquarters of the French navy.

    Nice, a large city on the Mediterranean Sea near Cannes and Marseille.

    La Côte d'Azur, literally the azure coastline, the Mediterranean coast of southeastern France which includes many glamorous beach resorts like St. Tropez. It is sometimes called the Riviera in English.

    La Promenade des Anglais, a famous beachside walkway in Nice which was first popularized by English tourists in the second half of the 18th century.

    Regardez les bateaux particuliers, Look at the yachts.

Page 178.   *Hotel Carlton*, a famous luxury hotel built in 1911 in Cannes on 'la Croisette,' the main seaside boulevard. It is associated with the Cannes Film Festival.

Aérogramme, an onion skin paper, self-sealing, airmail letter which cost less overseas postage because of its lighter weight.

La Comédie Française, the famous French classical theater building and company of performers. It is the French national theater and the world's longest-established national theater founded in 1680.

Racine, Corneille and Molière, the three great classical 17th century French dramatists whose works are still performed at the Comédie Française National Theater in Paris. The first two wrote tragedies. Molière's satiric comedies "Tartuffe" and "The Imaginary Invalid," "Le Malade Imaginaire," are famous worldwide.

Toc, toc, toc, knock, knock, knock, the sound which traditionally indicates that the play is about to begin in classical French theater.

Page 179.   *Hauteur*, dignity, pride.

Savoir-vivre, the art of living well.

Savoir-faire, know how.

Gauloise, a French brand of strong, unfiltered cigarettes.

Cabine, a telephone booth or dressing room.

Page 180.   *Pissoir*, a men's toilet building in the street.

Vous désirez?, What would you like? May I help you?

Cent francs, 100 francs, *dix francs*, ten francs.

Cent nouveaux francs, 100 new francs.

Mille anciens francs, 1000 old francs.

Monsieur, sir, mister.

Mademoiselle, miss.

Page 181.   *Georges Pompidou*, a politician and man of letters who was President of France from 1969 to his death in 1974. He was prime minister of France under Charles de Gaulle. He initiated and inaugurated the Centre national d'art et de culture Georges-Pompidou in Paris which is also known as the Musée Beaubourg.

Fotomat, a booth where you sat for an inexpensive strip of photos which were taken, developed, printed and delivered in minutes.

Jacques Fath (1912-1954), one of the three French fashion designers considered to have had the most influence on postwar high fashion along with Christian Dior and Pierre Balmain.

Nina Ricci (1883-1970), an influential Italian born French fashion designer. Her perfume is the well-known 'l'Air du Temps.'

Page 182.   *Institut des Professeurs de français a l'Étranger*, a part of the Sorbonne to train French teachers living abroad.

Wimpy Burger, a fast food chain of hamburgers founded in the U.S.

Wales, a country in the west of England which is part of the United Kingdom. Its capital is Cardiff.

Lake District, a mountainous region and national park in northwest England famous for its association with the Romantic poets.

Page 183.   *London Fog,* a well-made, moderate priced brand of raincoat.

In loco parentis, Latin for a legal concept which means having parental responsibility for a minor child.

Stonehenge, a famous, prehistoric circular group of huge standing stones in the southeast of England.

Druid, a member of a high ranking priestly class in ancient Celtic cultures who may have constructed the standing stone circles.

Page 184.   *Ernest Hemingway* (1899-1961), an American novelist who had a strong influence on 20th century fiction. Winner of the 1954 Nobel Prize for Literature. He lived and worked in Paris for part of his life. He wrote 'For Whom the Bell Tolls' and 'The Sun Also Rises.'

Chapter 15

Page 187.   *"Où sont les neiges d'antan,"* a famous line from medieval French poet-outlaw François Villon which means where has the time flown, melted away like the snowfalls of long ago.

Fonder un foyer, French for to start a family, establish a hearth.

Rapprochement, an understanding, getting closer.

Page 188.   *Le petit train train,* the business of everyday life, the routine.

Page 189.   *Bonne route,* drive carefully, have a good trip. Happy Motoring!

Page 190.   *Induction,* a type of cooking which uses direct electrical induction heating of cooking vessels rather than radiation, convection or thermal conduction. An induction cooktop generally has a flat, heat-proof glass-ceramic surface.

Page 191.   *Quelle merveille!* Marvelous! What a marvel.

Page 196.   *Ma patrie,* my homeland, land of my birth.

Page 197.   *Austerlitz Station,* the Paris train station named after one of Napoleon's victories which is the train hub for the southwest of France.

La ville Bourbon, the train station area of Montauban named in honor of Henri IV, the first king of Bourbon lineage who was the one who founded this district.

Page 198.   *La Table d'Alain,* literally Alan's table.

Le Cheval Blanc, literally the white horse.

Restaurant/Bar/Chambres, restaurant, bar, hotel rooms.

Prix fixe, a set price menu including several courses.

Page 201.   *Wagon,* a train car.

Intercité, a French rail brand-name used for non-high speed trains traveling on the classic rail network in France.

Chapter 16

Page 204.   *Serge Gainsbourg* (1928-1991), a French singer-songwriter, one of the most important

and influential figures in French pop music who was often scandalous and
controversial.

"Elle aime les intellectuels et les manuels.", She loves both intellectuals and manual
workers. A lyric from one of Serge Gainsbourg's songs.

Poor Mimi!, a lead role in Puccini's opera 'La Bohème' about struggling young artists in
the Paris of 1840. Her death scene and aria are famous.

Ceauşescu (1918-1989), a Romanian politician widely classified as a dictator until his
overthrow and execution as part of anti-communist uprisings in Eastern Europe
in 1989.

Page 206.   *George Foreman* (born 1949), An American former pro boxer and world heavyweight
champion. As an entrepreneur, he is known for the George Foreman grill, a small
electric kitchen appliance and a big seller.

Israeli salad, a bounteous salad of chopped tomato, onion, cucumber and other fresh
vegetables.

Publix Supermarket, a successful supermarket chain in Florida.

Page 208.   *"Loin des yeux, loin du cœur,"* literally far from the eyes, far from the heart. Out of sight,
out of mind.

"L'absence rend le cœur plus tendre.", literally absence makes the heart more tender,
grow fonder.

Page 209   *Auberge du Chapeau,* The Hat Inn.

Moulin du Tarn, The Mill on the Tarn River.

Définitivement, finally.

Michelin, a French tire manufacturer which founded a guidebook in 1900 to rate
restaurants and hotels in an effort to encourage drivers to take to the road.

Couper les virages, literally to cut the corner turns, ie, to take the turns of the road too
sharply without staying in your lane.

Page 210.   *Tarn, Tarn-et-Garonne,* two adjacent French departments, administrative divisions,
named for their main rivers, both now part of the Occitania region.

Quelconque, ordinary. So-so.

Midi-Pyrénées, an administrative region of southwest France around Toulouse made up
of several former old French provinces like Gascony, Languedoc and Quercy.
Now part of the Occitania region.

Page 211.   *Inadmissible,* not permitted.

Penne, a medieval town in southwestern France in the Tarn department with a
picturesque ruined castle isolated on a rocky outcropping dominating the town.

Page 212.   *Les Maures,* a mountain range in the southeast of France behind the Mediterranean.

Salernes, a town in Provence in the southeast of France where ceramic tile has been
manufactured since Roman times.

Page 213.   *Isle-sur-la-Sorgue,* an ancient provençal town in the southeast of France with a thriving
antiques market.

Provence, a name for the geographical and historical former Roman province of

southeast France on the Mediterranean Sea and in the mountains and hills
behind Marseille. It has a mild climate and its traditional cuisine is based on olive
oil and influenced by nearby Italy.

En plein air, out of doors.

Page 214.   *Président de Gaulle* (1890-1970), a French army officer and statesman who led the
Free French Forces against Nazi Germany and chaired the provisional
government of the French Republic from 1944-1946. He was elected president of
France in 1958 and held that office until his resignation in 1969.

Pieds-noirs, literally black feet, Algeria-born Frenchmen.

Rond-point, a rotary intersection.

Page 215.   *Regardez,* Look.

Mesdames, Ladies.

Marshall Field (1834-1906), a pioneering retail magnate who founded an upscale
department store named for himself in Chicago in 1852. It stayed in business
until 2006 and was renowned for its level of customer service. Its flagship
building on Michigan Avenue is a National Landmark.

Parfait, perfect.

Très bonne idée, Very good idea.

Page 216.   *Direction St. Georges,* on a signpost, this way to Saint Georges.

Je cherche un homme, I'm looking for a man.

Eartha Kitt (1927-2008), an American singer and actress known for her distinctive
singing style. She played Catwoman in the 'Batman' television series.

"Mad About You", an American television sitcom starring Helen Hunt and Paul Reiser. It
aired from 1992 to 1999 winning many Golden Globes and Emmy Awards.

Godin, a well known brand of traditionally designed wood stoves.

Français, French.

Pourquoi pas? Why not?

Slip, men's briefs.

Qu'est-ce qui ne va pas? What's wrong? What's the matter?

Je suis désolé(e), I'm sorry.

Page 218.   *Toulouse,* the fourth largest city in France located in the Occitania region of southwest
France. The metropolitan area has one and half million inhabitants and is
growing fast. It is the center of the European aerospace industry. Originally a
Roman city, it has a university founded in 1229 and there is a very large student
population,140,000 strong. The city's unique architecture of pink bricks has given
it the nickname, 'La ville rose,' the pink city.

Chapter 17

Page 223   *Foire,* a fair, festival.

Foire aux Vins, a wine promotion sales event.

Intermarché, a big French supermarket chain.

Moutarde, mustard.

Tronçonneuse, a chain saw.

Page 224.   *Foie gras*, a very rich tasting delicacy of fattened duck or goose liver.

Bocal, a glass jar for preserving food.

Musée Ingres, an art museum in Montauban named for French painter
Jean-August-Dominique Ingres (1780-1867) and now also for French sculptor
Antoine Bourdelle (1861-1929). Both very famous artists were born in
Montauban.

Un violon d'Ingres, a hobby in French, literally Ingres' violin.

Quelle tragédie!, What a tragedy!

Page 225.   *Fils*, son.

Semences, seeds.

Débarquer, to disembark.

Héro, hero.

Merci pour le champagne, thanks for the champagne.

Page 226.   *Tant mieux*, all the better.

De Régie, from Régie, of Régie.

Louis XIV (1638-1715), also known as the sun king, the longest reigning French monarch
or any sovereign. He beautified and expanded the palace of Versailles. During
his reign France was the leading European power, militarily and culturally.

Après moi, le déluge, After me, it all falls to pieces, it's the end, the flood which destroys
everything. Supposedly, a quote from Louis XIV.

Jacques Offenbach (1819-1880), a famous French 19th century composer of light operas.

Page 227.   *Bruniquel*, a picturesque, perched village in southwestern France with a ruined castle
where an important Paleolithic site was discovered.

Duchesse, a duchess.

Opera bouffe, a comic, farcical opera.

Page 228.   *Marc Chagall* (1887-1985), a famous 20th century painter who lived in France. An early
modernist, his paintings are colorful, dreamlike, interpretations of his life
influenced by his native Belarusian town, Vitebsk.

Page 231.   *Je m'en fiche*, I don't give a damn.

Je m'en fous, I don't give a fuck.

Page 233.   *Kibbutz*, a communal farm and community.

Kibbutznik, a person who lives on a kibbutz.

Page 236.   *Lake Dora*, a city in central Florida known for its antique shops and annual festivals.

Micanopy, a charming, small town in Florida near Gainesville.

Corkscrew Swamp, a 13,000 acre nature preserve in Southwest Florida.

Naples, a sophisticated resort city on the Gulf of Mexico in southwest Florida.

Chapter 18

Page 240.   *Auguste Rodin* (1840-1917), a French sculptor generally considered to be the founder of
modern sculpture.

The Burghers of Calais, Rodin's best known public monument sculpture which
commemorates the heroism of the six leading citizens of the French city of Calais
who sacrificed themselves to the English in order to save their city at the start of
the Hundred Years' War (1337-1453).

Honoré de Balzac (1799-1850), a French novelist and playwright whose magnum opus
was 'La Comédie Humaine.' He is regarded as one of the founders of realism in
European literature. He was usually hard up and wrote prodigiously to make
money. A big bear of a man, and unkempt, he was known for wearing a robe
when he was writing at home.

Page 241   *"L'Annonce Faîte à Marie,"* "The Announcement Made to Mary," the Annunciation.

Place des Invalides, a famous landmark square in Paris in front of the Invalides Church
and near the French Military Academy museum.

Page 242.   *'Sic transit gloria mundi'*, a Latin quote meaning that worldly glory doesn't last.

Le petit caporal, the little corporal, a nickname for the young Napoleon.

L'École Militaire, a complex of majestic buildings in Paris housing the French national
military academy, a museum and Napoleon's tomb.

L'Arc de Triomphe, a triumphal arch erected between 1806 and 1836 at the head of the
Champs-Élysées in Paris by Napoleon to commemorate his military victories in
imitation of the Roman custom. It is at the center of la Place de l'Étoile, the
star-shaped grid of Parisian avenues which run off from it in different directions.
The eternal flame which honors all France's war dead burns underneath it.

Champs Élysées, a beautiful and grand main avenue in Paris which runs from
underneath the Arc de Triomphe.

Le Rond Point, a round square midway along the Champs-Élysée.

Ma chérie, my dear.

D'accord, okay

Page 243.   *Demain*, tomorrow.

Le Champ de Mars, the park around the foot of the Eiffel Tower, literally the field of the
Roman god, Mars.

Page 244.   *La Trinité*, a Paris métro stop named for the nearby Second Empire style church of the
Sainted Trinity in the ninth arrondissement of the city.

Pont de l'Alma, a bridge across the Seine in Paris named for one of Napoleon's victories.

Seine, the river which flows through Paris.

La Conciergerie, a medieval turreted construction on the Seine which was used as a
prison. Marie Antoinette was held there before her execution.

Magnifique, magnificent.

Page 244.   *Interdit*, forbidden.

Page 245.   *Faubourg*, a neighborhood, an area of Paris.

Page 246.   *Le gratin*, the cheesy crust on top of a baked dish.

La rue des Rosiers, Rose Bush street.

Victor Hugo (1802-1885), a famous French 19th century author, poet and playwright. He
wrote 'The Hunchback of Notre Dame.'

La Place Royale, the Royal Square, now the Place des Vosges.

Page 247.   *La Marquise de Sévigné* (1626-1696), a French noblewoman who wrote famous letters to her daughter about her life at Versailles and life at the court of Louis XIV.

Page 249.   *Le Pont des Arts*, a famous pedestrian bridge over the Seine River in Paris between the French Institute, the French Academy of Arts and Letters and the Louvre Palace.

Jeu de Paume, a classical building, now a museum which housed the courts for a 17th-century form of tennis or handball. Literally palm game.

Montmartre, a large hill in Paris' 18th arrondissement known for its artistic history and as a nightclub district.

Place de Clichy, a busy crossroads square at the base of Montmartre.

Place du Tertre, a square near the summit of Montmartre where street artists sell their wares to tourists.

Sacré-Cœur, a white domed basilica consecrated in 1919 which is at the top of Montmartre overlooking Paris.

Place Pigalle, a public square near Sacré-Cœur which has a raunchy reputation due to its many sex shops, theaters and adult shows.

Page 250.   *Mon Dieu*, my God.

France-Soir, a somewhat sensational newspaper like the NY Post.

Page 252.   *Baron Haussmann* (1809-1891), a 19th century official city planner under Napoleon III who modernized Paris by cutting wide boulevards through the medieval maze of streets. He is largely responsible for the street plan and look of Paris today.

Musée Guimet, the Paris museum of Asian art.

Arrosé, watered.

Page 253.   *Latour Maubourg*, a Paris subway stop near Les Invalides named for a nineteenth-century French Cavalry commander.

Place de la Bastille, a city square where the Bastille prison once stood until torn down in 1790 during the French Revolution.

Page 254.   *Ouf*, whew.

Billets, tickets or bank notes in French.

'*Les Indes Galantes*,' The Gallant Indies, Gallantries in the West Indies which was the 17th century New World, i.e. America.

Chapter 19

Page 259.   *Aveyron River*, a long tributary of the Tarn River which runs through Saint Antonin and further north of Cayrièch in the Aveyron department of France.

Page 261.   *À l'ancienne*, as it was done the old time way, the traditional method or treatment, usually more time consuming and longer lasting.

Cette maison, this house.

Immobilier, real estate.

Page 262.   *Quelle idée!* What an idea!

Page 263.   *Fait accompli*, a done deal.

Déménagement, house moving.

Ne quittez pas, s'il vous plaît, Please hold on, don't hang up.

Page 265.   *Les Trois Terrasses*, The Three Terraces.

50 km, 50 kilometers or 30 miles.

Page 266.   *Cayriechois*, a person who lives in Cayrièch, France.

Montalbanais, a person who lives in Montauban, France.

Page 268.   *"Il n'y a qu'une chose qui est sûre; femme varie."* "There is only one sure thing, women
change their minds."

Page 269.   *Arrosé de champagne*, literally poured over with champagne.

Jour 'J', D day.

Garde-robe, wardrobe closet.

Page 270.   *Les Gentlemen du Déménagement*, The Gentlemen Movers.

Messieurs, Sirs, gentlemen.

Page 271.   *Saint Georges*, a hamlet near Cayrièch.

Page 272.   *The angelus*, a prayer said at 6 am, noon, and 6 pm in olden times.

Kilometer, about 0.62 miles.

Bien intégrés, fit in well, accepted

Bon déménagement! Happy Moving Out Day!

Bonne Installation! Happy Moving In Day!

Merci, thank you.

Acknowledgments

I'd like to thank Lisa Pulitzer, an accomplished writer and author, leader of my writing group, for her encouragement and support. She championed this work from its gestation to its present form. I would also like to thank my first readers, my neighbor and friend, Nadine Helstroffer and my travel companion (China and French Polynesia) and friend, Susan King for their generous advice.

Most of all, I owe an inestimable debt of gratitude to my partner, Nathan Kujawski, whose belief in me and in this project never wavered and without whose patience and good humor this book would not have been possible.

Thanks are also due to all the wonderful and generous-spirited people I met over the years in France, many of whom became my good friends.

About the Author

Roberta Samuels earned degrees in French and Art History from Northwestern University and the University of Paris at the Sorbonne. *French Lessons, One Woman's Tale of Sex, Wine and House Renovation* and her art history mystery book series, *Vanished!* evolved from her passion for French culture, beautiful objets d'art and exotic travel. The starting point for the books is based on her experience living in an 18th century farmhouse and then in a medieval townhouse in a French village. She worked as a French teacher, translator, tour escort and art gallery owner, showing her own artwork among others. She speaks French fluently. She lives in New York City and Montpezat de Quercy, France with her partner.

www.ingramcontent.com/pod-product-compliance
Lightning Source LLC
Chambersburg PA
CBHW050024120726
47903CB00006B/1896